SKATE OR DIE

The Douglas is after me, I've called for help—and the black tank has come. . . . The tank is reaching my level. The avenue is nearly deserted now, the survivors fled, nothing but corpses. An odd silence settles down.

He comes through the smoke, grim. His hands are red with blood. *This will be over fast, one way or another*. . . . He stands below me, regal, erect, ignoring the approaching tank.

"I am a hunter, Lynx, not a butcher! I meant only to kill you, kill my target. Not this. . . ."

I laugh, then. "Remorse, hunter? Guilt? From you?"

He smiles, thinly. "I don't know if I should kill you now, Lynx. One more death, lost in the masses. It would lose its special quality, wouldn't you say?"

"Fuck off. . . let's finish this!"

I roll and jump up, running toward the tank. Its guns fall silent as I reach it. I look up at the overhead holo and see the distorted Douglas, right behind me, reaching out for my neck. . . .

I duck low to the left and roll, my arms over my head. *Now!*

BAD VOLTAGE

A Fantasy in 4/4

Jonathan Littell

A SIGNET BOOK

NEW AMERICAN LIBRARY

A DIVISION OF PENGUIN BOOKS USA INC.

PUBLISHER'S NOTE

This book is a work of fiction. Names, characters, places, and incidents either are the product of the author's imagination or are used fictitiously, and any resemblance to actual persons, living or dead, events, or locales is entirely coincidental.

Copyright © 1989 by Jonathan Littell

SIGNET, SIGNET CLASSIC, MENTOR, ONYX, PLUME, MERIDIAN and NAL BOOKS are published by New American Library, a division of Penguin Books USA Inc., 1633 Broadway, New York, New York 10019

First Printing, June, 1989

1 2 3 4 5 6 7 8 9

PRINTED IN THE UNITED STATES OF AMERICA

For Jesse

". . . but when bad voltage gets in your blood
my moon has a face to tame
your tides
sleep a little
let the water boil
at dawn the residue
will settle
you can walk the windless beach alone
to gather the pieces"

—Ethan Dunn
Bad Trip

"*Impolitesse du public: durant tes plus périlleux mouvements,
il fermera les yeux. Il ferme les yeux quand pour l'éblouir
tu frôles la mort.*"

—Jean Genet
Le Funambule

"*C'est le Diable qui tient les fils qui nous remuent!
Aux objets repugnants nous trouvons des appas;
Chaque jour vers l'Enfer nous descendons d'un pas,
Sans horreur, à travers des ténèbres qui puent.*

*Ainsi qu'un débauché pauvre qui baise et mange
Le sein martyrisé d'une antique catin.
Nous volons au passage un plaisir clandestin
Que nous pressons bien fort comme une vieille orange.*

*Serré, fourmillant, comme un million d'helminthes,
Dans nos cerveaux ribote un peuple de Démons,
Et, quand nous respirons, la Mort dans nos poumons
Descend, fleuve invisible, avec de sourdes plaintes.*"

—Charles Baudelaire
Au Lecteur

MARA

REMEMBER: IF YOU'RE SQUEAMISH, DON'T KICK THE BEACH RUBBLE.

I had to laugh when I noticed that. Sappho. *Shit.* I nudged Olric. "Hey, spud." I pointed toward the wall across the street, the purple and red wildstyle scrawl over crumbling mortar and faded stone bricks. "Check it."

Olric snickered. "Think the Uptown boys know how to *read* that?"

"Fuck, no. Skagheads don't have a fuckin *clue.*"

The high-speed escalator over to the left spat out an off-balance figure into the cool white cone of the streetlight's halogen. Kurt. "Yo, my brother!" I called out. "Eyes slideways."

Kurt turned and walked toward us under the dead neon Metro sign. "Cool runnings, spuds. What's happening in the Downside lines tonight?"

We dapped, hands flowing through the jive, exchanging the ritual All Clear signs. Olric answered him.

"JCH, Ctulhu, and the others are already at the Beach. We're having a war at the FFI around midnight."

"Rammin." Kurt grinned. "Got ammo for sale?"

"Ctulhu does. Five Euros a ten-pack, 200 Old if you're using paper. M-80s and Clusters, too."

"Slicin. Let's step."

"Solid, spud. We're still waiting for Toxic." Olric waved at the concrete. "Squat."

"Check."

Kurt dropped his pack on a parked skimmer and slumped against the wall of the station, next to me. He was wearing the obligatory Downside mud-crusted nylon-and-leather jungle boots, and a surplus United European

3

States flightsuit. My flightsuit was Chzecosov—I'd scored it in Berlin—and had STALIN stenciled in Cyrillic on the back, above a red star. Really ticks off the fuckin Mirrorfaces. Those boys don't like the Chzecosovs, UES party line and "ideological reconciliation" be fucked.

Kurt pulled out a crumpled pack of Gauloises and offered me one. I took two and passed one to Olric. We each lit our own.

We smoked for a while without talking. I watched some bloods as they walked by, jet-black exchange students from the West African Tribes' Federation studying at the old Cité Universitaire, the international campus that sprawled along Paris's southern rim. One of them looked straight at me for a beat, deadfish Dust stare. *Motherfucker'll be on the Street within the year. When the junk line sucks up his gov funds . . . Hope he knows the slice&dice, knows it but good.*

Olric and I were still pretty red from the bowl of Turkish we'd smoked. My unshaven chin itched. I keyed my armdeck and turned up the dub that was beating through my implants. It echoed through my skull, hardbeat bass and madness. Iron Bar Dub, check it.

I stared at the stone buildings of Cité U. The American House squatted in darkness, gutted by a terrorist bombing three weeks ago. Eighty-nine students had died. The Little Big Horn, a splinter group off the Alliance of the Nations, had claimed responsibility. The next day U.S. President Eastwood ordered a Cheyenne reservation village evacuated and razed in retaliation. I'd caught a lost shard of memory for an instant watching the newscast, my Cheyenne mother's thin smile, and I'd thought, *cowboy motherfucker . . .*

I looked up. All I could see of Paris was the dull orange glow of the night sky, the bulging dome of dancing photons, bright as a cloudy day.

We sat.

Kurt was the first to break the trance. He waved toward Cité U, the glowing tip of his cigarette leaving trails in the air.

"I hear the Belt is going to build a House here," he said.

The Belt . . . Kirishto, if only I could score the credit for a one-way! To climb the well . . . Out of the shit, the mud, the sisterfuckin Street . . .

I turned down the dub before I spoke, letting it fade into the backbrain. Subliminal riddim pulsing down the reggae wire deep into the blood and bone; bad music (LKJ had once called it), bad music soundcheckin down your spinal column, bad music tearin up your flesh. I rarely shut it down entirely. It's part of me, just like my blood, my bones, my silicon implants.

"Who? Cérès?"

"No, not Cérès, blankbrain." He grinned again, his angelic grin. "The Free Islands."

"Raas claat . . . Can they?"

"Unconfirmed. I got it from a gadjo jockey, oldman name of Case. He pulled a hardcore zap job, intercepted a data squirt on the Net. The detail's on the market, if you're interested."

"They got a treaty," said Olric. He ran his hands through his wirespiked black shag, scratching. "With Brussels."

"What?" Kurt, clueless.

"The Free Islands. A treaty. Signed it three years ago, in '30, with the UES politicos. Cultural exchanges, diplomatic recognition, the works. Uptown, the Zaibatsus, they can't do jackshit about it, and Ogoun knows the Suits *tried*. Same for the Americans and the Chzecosovs. The Chinese love it, of course."

"I remember that," I said. "Why did the fuckin UES sign it?"

"Usual Babylon reasons. To piss off Uptown, and the Powers. Political maneuvering, strategies."

"The enemy of my enemy is my friend." I smiled.

"Read that, my brother."

"Politricks," said Kurt. "It's all bullshit anyways." Kurt hates politics as much as Olric loves them. I'm apathetic, as long as they don't affect my drug supplies, like the Wipe did.

"Take a reality check, wildboy," Olric sneered. "Babylon is the *real world*, dig? You think the Street is outside Control? You think that what goes on in the Islands, or Stateside, doesn't affect your blackbiz? You think the

5

shitstem just squats there like a poisoned toad and *exists*, that nothing really changes? Bull*shit*!"

"Chill, my brother." Kurt raised his hands, defensive. "I just don't give a fuck, is all."

"Maybe you sh—"

"Eyes slideways, spuds," I said softly. "Mirrorfaces, ten o'clock."

We sat in silence while the three Mirrorfaces strutted by, encased in black Kelvar body armor and insectile helmets, MAS flechette SMGs at port. I stared at the distorted reflection of the three of us sitting in their mirrored visors. *Just like in a funhouse . . .* CRS, Companies Republicaines de Sécurité. They were probably nice kids back when they lived in the province, but being in the Big City with a badge, a gun, and no restraints does strange things to people. Like turn them into sociopathic beasts. The Faces greased more streetdrek than the streetdrek themselves these days. All it cost them was a week suspension, with the salary covered by their squad buddies. Picture it: Honey, moans the bored copwife, I wanna vacation . . . Not to worry, dear, next shift I'll bag me a few of those little punk shits and we're off to Normandy.

These three must have been in a real good mood cause they totally ignored us. We watched them enter the Metro station, a slow pan; Kurt spat viciously as the clear acrylic door hissed shut behind them.

His tone matched the sound of the hydraulics as he spoke:

"There is your precious reality, Olric. The Beasts, and us." Bitter. "That's all."

The spitting escalator saved us from further argument as it expelled Toxic from the depths of the station. Salutations and dapping, Toxic constantly pushing his antique wireframe prescriptions up his thin nose. We shouldered our packs and started walking up the street. Looking very casual—I hoped. Eyes flicking leftside-rightside. SOP, no problem.

We reached the grate and stopped. I ran a thorough scan and jived the All Clear. We dropped our packs. Olric bent down, pulled the grate up and over, and wordlessly slithered down into the darkness. Kurt and Toxic followed him.

I said, "One," and dropped the first pack into the hole; then Two, Three, Four. A final scope, then down. I stopped five rungs from the bottom and pulled the grate shut, the familiar scraping followed by the final clang of rusted iron on concrete. This was an old maintenance entrance, long disused.

I could still see the orange glow of the sky through the grate as I jumped down the rest of the way. The others were already gearing up at the end of the small landing. I walked over and opened my pack, extracting the mess of plastic and tubes and metal as Olric held up a penlight. The harsh light from the argon bulb threw stark, cutout shadows on the wall, making me squint.

Our equipment was antique, some of it going all the way back to the early '90s. Affectation, the mark of the true cataphile. Only tourists wore modern spelunking equipment: polystyrene plastic and halogen lights running off lithium batteries.

Our helmets, now . . . Old construction helmets, spray-painted and graffitied. We mounted a beam electrical lamp and a small gas nozzle on the front of each one. The nozzle is connected by a long tube to a belt gas generator, a fifty-year-old miner's contraption which drips water onto carbide to create acetylene. A Piezo lighter over the nozzle produces the sparks which ignite the gas. Chemical reaction, just check it, man.

We fiddled with faucets and whacked the generators against the walls until the acetylene lamps grudgingly flared into life. A whiff of acetylene filled the air, sharp characteristic tang, omnipresent Downside smell. The gas lamps behaved like bulbs, area lighting; walking the lines is a bitch if you can't see the ground and the sky simultaneously. We only use the electric beams for distance work, or for blinding people walking toward us.

We stood in the pool of dull yellow light while Olric went through his fiddling and whacking routine. I took point for the march, and Toxic took the rear. We went down a short flight of stairs, past where the mass of lead-wrapped vidphone cables grew out of the wall, to

7

the pit at the bottom. The cables flowed over the edge. I followed them.

The climb lasted a familiar eternity. Muddy rungs, packs catching against the cables, a thirty-meter chute mainlining us into the underside of the city, tunnels laid out like silvered circuitry under the streets.

I dropped the last meter and moved away a bit, out of the way. I wiped my hands on my flightsuit, scraping crusted mud off it as I pasted on a new layer. When my fingers were dry enough, I flicked the dull, burnished cover of my armdeck back, carballoy plates curvemolded like the chitinous armor of a beetle. My fingers flew over the keypad, cutting the dub and routing the audio to the miniature Sony speakers on my web belt. I keyed in the music, and the first operatic voices echoed through the tunnels as Olric thudded to the ground.

"Razor, spud," said Kurt. I'd picked some '90s German industrial music, the kinda heavybeat that paints silver-purple metal on your brain. Very German, very Berlin. I'd picked up a lot of music during the year I spent there.

Heute die welt
Heute die welt
Heute die welt

We headed west, down the concrete line, racks of vidphone cables stacked against the right wall. A PTT maintenance tunnel, boring, not yet the actual catacombs. We walked in silence to the beat of clanging steel pipes and single bass notes.

Four hundred meters later, we turned north, up a real line. Dug two thousand years ago and reconsolidated by the Inspection Générale des Carrières in the early 1800s; walls of limestone blocks, hand-carved for fuck's sake; muddy ground. The sky is low, so we walked with a perpetual, agonizing stoop. The smell, the catacomb smell that always Pavlovianly triggers memories and emotions, is dull, dank, moist; a clean earth smell, old and dead as the city itself.

The music echoed, muted auditory illusion of high volume. I sounded like I was wandering in a vast cathedral lined with felt.

A carved plaque on the wall, RUE NANSOUTY. The main

lines Downside are named after the street they more or less run under; a Downside map reads like a flawed copy of a street map.

Morgenn das sonnensystem
Morgenn das sonnensystem

Half a klik north. Nansouty becomes Avenue du Park Montsouris. Lots of graffiti, political or obscene, some small wildstyle murals. I noticed only one MADAME EURYDICE REVIENDRA DES ENFER, the slogan of the Artistes Terroristes, friends of mine. The acronym spelled MERDE. They'd lifted it from Cocteau, their patron saint. An old joke, a century old.

I ignored a few sidelines till we reached a particular west-running one. I stopped. So did the others, not that they had a choice.

"What says, spuds?" I asked. "Westways, short and dirty, or north?"

"I say north," said Toxic. "That vein into the Beach is a bitch."

"Fuck that," said Olric. "It's electric, man."

"Throw for it," I said.

Olric's scissors beat Toxic's paper; we turned west. A few minutes later, we reached the grid under the Réservoir de la Vanne. Concrete lines, series of right angles, the hard gray walls glistening with pearly secretions, tainted waters filtering down from the reservoir above. We went straight through, back into sandstone and mud. Then north, up the Rue de la Tombe-Issoire. Another half-klik, stooped in flickering light, and we reached the vein.

The veins, once called *chatière*, are the intestines of the Downside system. Some are very low, some a bit higher; some are short, some are long; some are sand, some are mud, some are stone. All of them, though, have this in common: you have to crawl through them.

Olric went first, pushing his pack in front of him. Toxic went next, muttering, cursing; then Kurt. I took the rear.

This vein is low, long, and sandy. I had zipped my flightsuit up and sealed the neck tabs, but it was useless: the sand still penetrated, itching, irritating. I dragged myself forward by my elbows, pushing my pack, whacking my helmet against the sky every half-meter. The music resonated louder than ever, echoing in my ears.

Heavybeat, heavy like stone and steel. Sound of machines, of work, presilicone, music for concrete barbarians.

Ewige schlangekraft
Ewige schlangekraft

I rolled out of the vein into one of the back rooms of the Beach, vast, labyrinthian complex of vaulted rooms with a thick layer of sand on the ground. Four breeds were sitting there, smoking a spliff around a sand table with a candle on it. Kurt had already disappeared into the Beach proper.

I dapped with the breeds. One of them, a sharp, skinny Eurasian woman, flashed the signal for black-market tech, on sale. I nodded, interested, and keyed down the music.

"DeVeres wetware logicals, commerical, IBM and Matsui-Mikoyan compatible. Sealed case of twenty, fifteen hundred Euros. What says?"

"Too much. One thou."

"Negative. Fourteen, min."

"Twelve and a customized Krytech trojan."

"Customized by who?"

"Billy Name."

She grinned. "I can run with that. Two of them. RAM, on needle."

"ROM, on CD."

"Three then. The money on crystal."

"On card."

"Acceptable."

"Done. Wherewhen?"

"Mamoun's, at the Forum. Tomorrow, 22:30?"

"Not Mamoun. They're kinked."

"No say?"

"Truth. 22:30 OK, though."

"McDonald's clear?"

"Yeah, far as I know. Some skins dusted their vidsystem last week."

"Isn't it fixed?"

I snorted. "Why bother? They know it'd get dusted again within the night."

"Check. I'll see you there, then."

"Salaam, chica."

"Salaam to you, breed. See you tomorrow."

I went on through to the main area, running the deal

on playback. It looked good. I could check the wetware on the spot, and I could download it for sure on Name for at least fifteen hundred, if I could ever find the fucker. The trojans would only cost me the price of the CD, cause they were a gift from Viper. *Looks like I'll score for three hundred Euros. Good biz, if it works out.*

The main room was *on*, like berserk, all the main spuds there. Flickering candlelight, pungent hashish smell, Rob and Dan's maddening conga polyrhythms. Primitive tribal scene, voodoo ritual or Niyabinghi feast. I cut the Industrial noise and started dapping.

Vulcain, JCH, Shadow the mapmaker, Richard, Brother John with his huge, knotted oak club, Pado, Maldoror, Sida on crutches, Coolbeat and five of his bloods from the Zone, Scalpel, paint-spattered and wired tight, MZ, Cochise . . . Like I said, all the main spuds. A couple of tourists huddled in the corner, nervous. Tourists, Uptown kids checking out the mythic Downside for slum kicks, maybe they got a map from a friend who has a friend. No one bothered them, no one talked to them. Tourists don't exist.

I dropped my pack, hung my helmet and generator from one of the rusted spikes that protruded out of the sky—relic of an older age, when the Beach was a mad scientist's lab—and sat down next to Olric. He handed me a brew, generic white can with the word BEER printed on it. I cracked it and drank.

I looked around. On the wall across from me, Scalpel's mural, a reproduction of Hokusai's "The Wave," two weeks old, already soiled. Toxic and Pado were heating a can of ravioli on a heatpad. Kurt was dragging Whizz off into a corner for yet another argument. Everything was hazy from the smoke, a foul, polluted compound of ganja and oily candles and cigarettes and acetylene. A rat scuttled out of a pile of garbage in the corner and ran across the room, dodged a tossed knife, and disappeared into the darkness. I laughed. *If you're squeamish, don't kick the Beach rubble.*

The flame on my helmet hissed and painted a black carbon spot on the sky right above it. Saxo wandered in, chipped, silver-plated tenor slung over his shoulder. He didn't even dap, just pulled up his horn, licked the reed, and joined the madjam.

I finished the brew and pulled out my butterfly knife, making faces at Scalpel. She winked while I flicked it open, teasing. Three chrome wings danced and glinted as I played with the knife, *snickt snickt.* Balisong game, flashy and deadly. I didn't get cut once.

I'd just completed a particularly tricky double *renversé* when Mara walked in, with Ctulhu, Kemar, and Patty. I flicked the knife shut and stood up as he came toward me, grinning, excited. He was wearing my black leather over a blue tank top, black battledress, and the ubiquitous jungle boots. We hugged, and I playfully licked his ear. He arched his back like a cat and kissed me, tongue darting. I ran my hand over the jutting angle of his hip and stared at him.

Mara, sometimes called the Dreamer. Tall as I am, though bonier. Blue hair cut in a spiked shag, blue lips, and white skin, bone white, stark in the black clothes, skin stretched over the sharp bones like pigskin on a drum. And those hard silver-gray eyes, congealed heroin eyes.

Mara was already shooting junk when I met him two years ago, though he wasn't hooked yet. I'd wandered up to him during a party in the Salle Z.

"How you doin', man?" I'd stuttered. "You look down, way down."

"Well . . ." His eyes wandered off, came back, focused. "I'm in kind of a metaphysical quandary."

"Oh," I'd remarked brightly. "I'm in a drunken stupor. Is that similar?"

We'd been sleeping together within the week. For some reason we never stopped.

Olric started trying to get people motivated. It took a half hour, which was above par. Ctulhu dished out ten-packs, clusters, and M-80s left and right. Mara and I had gone down earlier to Chinatown, near the Place d'Italie, so we were set. Eventually we headed north, up Tombe-Issoire.

I counted fifteen spuds. Ctulhu said six more waited at the FFI bunker. We walked single file, Mara in front of me and Scalpel behind. I keyed on some Dub, a different one this time, Brain Damage Dub. Mara liked this one, dug the riddim. I chuckled, remembering what he'd once called it, one night he was really fucked up: Drain Bramage Dub, check it . . .

Three hundred meters up, then west on Bezout. We took the Aqueduc-Arcueil diagonal, then west again on Dareau. Boring lines, all the same yellow limestone walls and occasional graffiti. EVIL EXISTS. SAVE AN INDIAN, NUKE EASTWOOD. GRAVITY SUCKS. WAR IS JUST MENSTRUATION ENVY (Viper, that one). THE SHADOW KNOWS. CUNNING LINGUISTS. SHOW ME A MOUSEHOLE AND I'LL FUCK THE WORLD. Another two hundred meters, then north on the Orléans mainline.

Avenue d'Orléans: vidphone cables filling half the line, and ten centimeters of water on the ground. Still the fastest way, though, and the sky is high and the jungle boots don't hold the water in.

There's a small blister at the Rue Denfer, where we turned. Four months ago the I.G.C. put a concrete plug in the line; a few nights later we dug a small vein through the sandstone blocks on the side and the soft humid sand behind them.

We rested a bit while Pado, who was leading, went through the vein. When my turn came, I wriggled through, dropped to the ground on the other side, and waited for Mara. Scalpel, who had gone right before me, was already ten meters ahead, heading for the FFI.

Mara's bag popped out, followed by his head. I kissed his razor lips before playfully grabbing his arms and yanking him forward, pulling him half out of the vein. He cursed and slid out all the way, throwing a snake strike at my eyes. I parried his blow and sent a crescent kick arching over his head. He caught my foot and twisted, sending me sideways to the ground. I thudded, rolled, and came up laughing. I slid my arm around his back in a studied angle of bone over rib cage before picking up my pack and starting to jog. He caught up, and, two right turns and one open grate later, we reached the FFI.

A short flight of filthy stairs led to the entrance. We

stepped over the two massive, rusted cable spools that blocked it and penetrated the bunker. I reached up over my forehead and flicked on the electric, playing the beam over the walls of an endless concrete line. Mara thumbed on a flash behind me. Down the line, dark, open entryways stood out as our intertwining beams flitted over them.

We walked down the line, vaguely glancing at the multilayered tapestry of fresh and worn graffiti that covered the walls. Only one stood out, a giant black anarchist A on a white background, with the words FREE BELT bombed in red across it.

The FFI was old, filthy. Built in the 1930s as an air-raid shelter, it had been used during World War II as the HQ of the Forces Françaises Indépendantes, the Resistance that arose a few weeks before the liberation of Paris. Abandoned after the war, it was rediscovered in the '70s by the first cataphiles, who immediately proceeded to turn it into a graffiti-covered and garbage-strewn mess. There were even holes in certain walls, testimony of various failed attempts at enlarging the small rooms on either sides of the lines. The bunker was laid out as a standard grid, but the warrens of rooms and the connections between them could get very confusing.

We found the spuds that had already arrived in one of the larger rooms in the back. They sat against the walls, small in the dull glow of the acetylenes. Mara and I grabbed a corner near Scalpel and dropped.

Scalpel is young, maybe fifteen, and paints murals and runs with the Livewires and was once my lover for eight months. Now she's hitched with Viper, my bloodsister. Her hair and skin are bleached white and her irises are red, Madrid albino style. A long scar runs along her rounded jaw. I'd once asked her why she didn't have it erased and she'd said, in her enigmatic tone, "It reminds me not to make mistakes."

Mara was already fumbling through his pockets for the drugs. I found the pressure spike I'd brought. I carefully filled it, .5 ccs of the Crank, and offered it to Mara.

"You got junk in you?"

"No." He grinned. "I planned for this, ate some inhibitors to keep the monkey off before coming down. Go for it."

I tied him up and shot it directly through his skin. I filled it again and offered it to Scalpel. She refused.

"I brought two rockets. I'll do them right before the war. Thanks anyway."

I decided that I needed a bigger dose and added another .25 ccs to the spike. Mara was already twitching next to me. I handed him the spike, pulled back my sleeve, and rolled back the flap of skin over the nylon polyethylene duct in my vein. I bent my arm, sending blood squirting out the duct, took the spike from Mara, and slipped it up into the vein. I triggered it, watched some more blood bubble up, and pulled it out. I just had the time to put it away and wipe the blood off my arm before the Crank hit me.

Crystals of ice grew and shot up my arm, up my neck, into my head, filling it. Tendrils wrapped themselves down my spine, around my nerves, strings of nylon, flaring and firing chaotically. My dick was so hard it hurt.

I cut the dub, crouched, and jumped up. Orgasm of strained muscles, erotic tension of movement. Mara rolled forward behind me and followed me up.

"Shadowhands?" It wasn't a question. "Yes," I answered. "I'll lead."

We started the dance. Hands up, palms three centimeters away from each other. I moved my hands, anywhere, and Mara had to follow.

We warmed up slowly. Mara's hands moved with mine, a fraction of a second behind at first, then simultaneous as he got in sync with my flow. ESP, subliminal cues, the Crank opens you to it. After a while I started moving my whole body. His hands never left mine.

"Switch," I said. He took the lead.

It took me longer to get in sync, but once I was there I couldn't lose it. He tried everything, feints, dodges, shifts. Nothing worked. Our palms were glued together with three centimeters of air between them.

We rode the rush for long minutes like that, freestyle, gliding all over the room. Our eyes were locked, immo-

bile. It's called Shadowhands, smooth and beautiful, Crank-
fueled and electric.

We stopped simultaneously as the last of the contin-
gent entered. We saluted and dropped back into our
corner, sweaty and breathless.

The gamewar got organized very rapidly. I took my
pair of thick construction gloves out of my pack, then
stashed the pack in a corner with the others. I gave Mara
the right-hand glove and kept the left. All around us the
others were doing the same, checking ammo and lighters,
pulling on gloves. Ctulhu yelled at everyone to ziplip and
quickly divided us into two teams. He passed out scraps
of red fabric to my team, which we tied around our arms.
Not that it would make much difference; in five minutes
we'd be lucky to see anything, much less a small armband.

Everyone was ready. Scalpel, Kemar, and Kurt hastily
pulled out their inhalers and fired rockets up their noses.
Ctulhu gave the signal, and we fanned out through the
bunker. I headed for the far corner, for the old communications room, Mara and Scalpel right behind me. The
Crank coursed through my veins, past the rush now but
still flying.

I don't know who initiated hostilities. I heard the hiss-
ing shriek of a bottle rocket somewhere over to the right,
cries of surprise and delight, a loud bang. Within seconds
five more had been launched, a staccato of explosions,
yells.

We reached the south edge without seeing anyone. I
peeked around the corner and scanned the empty line. I
jived all clear and moved, cautious, ready, adrenaline
rush intensifying the high.

We'd moved five meters down the line when Olric,
Ctulhu, and Shadow popped out of a doorway twenty
meters away and fired three rockets simultaneously. Lines
of fire left their hands, careening off the walls, howling
and shrieking. Smoke filled the line as Scalpel and Mara
ducked for cover; I just stood there, gambling that I'd
measured the range accurately.

I had. The three rockets exploded two meters in front
of me, concussive noise and blinding flash. I blinked and
ran forward, a rocket already in my gloved hand and my
Zippo ready in the other, my nerves singing a soprano

song of amphetamines and fear. As soon as I was within range, I dropped to my knees and touched the Zippo to the wick. I could barely see the enemy through the smoke, three hazy shapes. The wick sizzled and flame washed over my glove, barely heating my hand. I yelled "Mara!" as I grabbed a huge M-80 firecracker as long as a beer can though a bit thinner, lit it, and tossed it after the rocket. The rocket explosion seemed small next to the M-80, the concussion making me wince even from where I was. I grinned as I heard cries down the line.

I jumped up as Mara and Scalpel joined me and did a small war dance, yelling "Motherfuckers *die!*" Then two M-80s came arcing out of the smoke and we scrambled for cover before they went off—

—Double-barreled shock wave, leaving me stunned for seconds. A voice echoing down the line, gloating—"You nuked, Lynx! You're gonna die!"—followed by three more screaming rockets. We ran for a nearby doorway and rolled over each other getting in, our helmets falling off, and acetylene flame narrowly missing me.

We slumped against the wall, panting, and retrieved our helmets by pulling in the gas tube. The room—it was the old commo room, rusted lockers and cables against the opposite wall—was still fairly smoke-free. We looked at each other, two white faces and one brown, streaked with sweat and gunpowder, and burst out laughing, manic joy of drugs and excitement.

"Gamewar be cool, brothers!" shrieked Scalpel.

"Yeah," moaned Mara, "no one gets wasted."

A minute later Scalpel jived, Ready? I nodded, pumping my fist once, elbow by the ribs, the Livewire salute. She returned it, grinning. I took a cluster out from the bellows pocket on my left and lit it. I counted off with my fingers, One, Two, Three, and tossed it out into the line. We huddled against the wall while it went off, strings of firecrackers exploding like machine-gun fire, clearing the line for us.

As soon as it stopped, we dove out the door, firing off two more rockets into the smoke for good measure. We ran up the north line, firing more rockets ahead of us blindly. By now the bunker was completely smoky; everyone blind, the war degenerating into a free-for-all. We ran through the maze in random patterns, tossing M-80s and firing rockets at the slightest hint of noise or light. At one point we reached an intersection and a rocket shot out of a side line, bouncing off my chest and exploding a meter away. I hit the ground, heart pumping madly, and fired off two rockets in retaliation before leaping up and running on, giggling maniacally. Later on I lost both Mara and Scalpel, vanished in the smoke behind me. The rest of the war was a haze of noise and light, dashing madly through the fog, wired and crazy.

I threw my last M-80 at some dark shape that popped out of the haze and then tried to find the back room. I blundered blindly through the maze for a while, dodging two more rockets, before stumbling across a landmark I recognized. I winged it from there, collapsing exhausted into the more or less smoke-free room a few minutes later. By general consensus, the back room was off-limits. Since the smoke didn't move much, little of it got into the room.

Mara was already there, along with a few others. I grinned at Kurt and sat down. The Crank had worn off awhile back, unnoticed in the whirlwind of running and shooting and dodging. The lack hit me hard now, my systems crashing with painful rapidity. I went zombie for a while, fatigue numbing my muscles, unable even to light a cigarette or pull off my glove. A glance to my left showed me that Mara was equally catatonic.

We vegged in silence for half an hour, distant explosions cutting through the cotton in my head, the dub I'd keyed in just before crashing massaging my head in time with my alpha waves. People staggered in alone or in small groups as their ammo ran out. Eventually Kemar came in, the last one. Twenty-one exhausted and drenched spuds lined the walls. Slowly we came alive, rolling spliffs and passing them around, cracking open cans of beer and bottles of cheap wine, heating cans of deliciously bad couscous and cassoulet.

The party livened up as we got stoned and drunk. We traded stories of the war, boasting of our exploits, laughing at misfortunes. Pado and Whizz had caught some nasty burns, so Ctulhu gave them some burn cream. No one else was seriously hurt. I wolfed down a can of cassoulet, occasionally feeding Mara a spoonful, laughing and smoking. Toxic and Scalpel went off to find a wall to paint. Mara got into a discussion with Kemar and Cochise about Brettman's new film, *Blue Burn*. Then Olric came over and showed me a map he'd just obtained, of the westernmost sector of the catacombs. It had the location of the old Ponts et Chaussées antiatomic blunker on it. I goggled. We'd heard rumors about it for years, but never found it.

"You see, you follow the vidphone cables up Brune here, to where it becomes Lefebvre. The Bunker is right here."

"Razor, man. But won't it be sealed?"

"Yeah. But I figure it's old concrete. We find a spot next to one of the armored doors and drill."

"Sounds def smooth. You got a drill?"

"There's a construction site near my pad. They got this G.E. hypersonic vibro, it'll cut through that wall like butter."

"Sweet. Where do they store it?"

"They lock it in one of the prefabs. The alarm is simple, the lock primitive. Toxic can cut it, no problem."

"*Destroy*. When do you want to do it?"

"I figure we do the G.E. Sunday night, cause the Beasts will be slow from the weekend, and then the bunker next Friday."

"*Nyet, nyet*. I got the Champs Elysées run that night, with the Livewires. Besides, weekend night is no cool, too crowded. Want to do this discreet, keep the data sealed, till we open it to the public and score."

"Public . . ." He laughed. "Heavy status among the spuds, eh? I like it. How about Wednesday?"

"Yeah. Who do we bring?"

"You, me, Toxic, cause we need him for the drill, Ctulhu for more muscle."

"Not Ctulhu. He'll talk. How about Scalpel? She'll keep ziplip, and she'll cream over the clean walls."

"OK. You want to bring Mara?"

"I don't know if he'll be into it. If he is, def."

"Check. So that's either four or five spuds, good number. Let's do it."

"Wednesday. We meet at 20:00 by Cité U, go Downside through the Petite Ceinture. Check?"

"Yeah. What do yo think we'll find there?"

We speculated for a while on the possible contents of the mystery bunker. "Probably nothing we can sell, but we'll score some radical relics." We gloated at the idea of opening the bunker to the cataphile masses, the score of the year, status like a half-K of H or C. If it came off, it would be the biggest cataphile coup since Hadés—drunk, on four bottles of wine—cut straight through a two-meter concrete plug at the entrance of the Salle Z with a miner's pickax, *manually* for fuck's sake. Rad. *Balls* rad.

The ganja, the wine, and the food slowly ran out. Around 4:45 we decided to step, to make the first Metro. The I.G.C. cocksuckers had sealed the manhole right next to the FFI with thermoplast, so we had to foot it all the way back to Cité U. Olric, Kurt, and I cleaned up the litter, dumping the filled garbage bag down a deep pit in the old kitchen. We sealed our packs, banged our acetylenes to life, and started wandering through the still smoky maze, looking for the exit. I stopped by the room where Scalpel and Toxic were resting, a small, bright, psychedelic mural finished, and told them to call me around 18:30, re: a radical downside deal. "And ziplip, bigtime, you copy?"

The walk back was more or less uneventful. For variety's sake, we headed west, down the Boulevard Saint-Jacques, then south on Rue Saint-Jacques. West again on Emile Dubois, southwest on Dareau, south on Broussais, the lines like the dub, unchanging but with a *beat*, a riddim. Then by the Salle de Peinture, where we briefly admired Scalpel's latest mural, a full-scale reproduction of *Guernica*. Broussais angled a bit, the sky getting low, and then we cut straight south, joining Montsouris at the central pillar. From there we marched through the maze behind Montsouris, Ctulhu in the lead, mapless, unerring. We reached the Salle aux Chaises, a small room with a dozen rusted iron park chairs in it. As I passed by it, I noticed a flash of white; darting in, I saw a new flier on the wall, still wet with glue, glistening. I read it and burst out laughing. Scalpel peeked in, curiosity on her face. I

21

carefully peeled off the flier and showed it to her. It read:

CTULHU!

WE'RE LOOKING FOR YOU!

GUESS WHO?

Beneath that was the copy of a receipt from the Coq de Bruyère hunting store, on the Avenue des Ternes in the 17éme, for a 9mm. HW1G pistol and a hundred rounds. It was made out to a Mr. P.J., the full name blacked out, but the initials enough anyway. Pado and JCH again. *Iesu Kirishto . . .*

Ctulhu will freak!

This was the funniest flier I'd seen in ages. Scalpel was laughing, too, the laughter contagious as the flier got pasted around. We calmed down a bit as it headed up the line, waiting for it to reach Ctulhu, waiting for the inevitable with huge grins plastered on our grimy faces.

"*Motherfucking junkie wordshitters! Where is the meatpuppet who . . .*"

Pado and JCH, a few meters behind in the line, traded high fives, in stitches. Tears of laughter left streaks on Pado's mud- and powder-covered face. JCH just rolled against the wall, convulsive. It took three spuds and a well-placed Amobarbital derm to keep Ctulhu from tearing into them with his machete.

It took awhile for everyone to calm down, myself included. We eventually got moving again, Kurt helping a zonked Ctulhu along. Three minutes later we reached the exit shaft, straight through the maze. A few spuds were already climbing the ladder when I got there. I waited in the small area under it, sharing a Gauloise with Mara, waiting for my turn. Jokes and comments on the flier flew back and forth, Pado and JCH proud and glowing at the score. I gave Pado a smile and a "well-done" jive when he looked my way.

My turn came. I waved Mara ahead of me and hitched my pack. As soon as I got enough clearance I started climbing.

A thirty-meter shaft, straight up. Mud on the ladder, slippery and dangerous. Mud showering down, too, from Mara's feet, making it impossible to look up, to judge the distance left. Endless climb in the gloom, scraping noises and a pulsing dub.

Topside, an eternity later. I hoisted myself up through the hole, squinting at the bright light, acetylene still burning, useless now. Mara was already walking down the platform, Pado already climbing out behind me.

The shaft opened in the middle of the B2-North platform of the Cité U Metro station. Pretty fuckin stupid for twenty-one cataphiles to hit topside in the open like that, even if the Faces never patrol the Metro this early, but hey, what the fuck. On the opposite platform, two RATP workers in blue coveralls who didn't even lift an eyebrow at the sight of two dozen filthy streetdrek with strange helmets climbing out of a hole in the ground at 05:30, too bored or too fucked-up to care. I headed down the platform toward the others, a loud clank echoing behind me as Kemar and Cochise, the last ones out, jacked the eighty-kilo manhole cover shut.

"Fuck, I'm beat," I said to no one in particular as I dropped to the ground next to Mara. Scalpel was tracing a quick sketch in marker on the clear acrylic anti-suicide wall at the edge of the platform. I checked my armdeck: five minutes till the first train. I unclipped the generator from my belt, cracked it and unscrewed it, and started dumping hot, damp blue powder onto the platform. Water and carbide stones equals acetylene gas and hot, damp blue powder; gotta dump it now, and all the spuds are doing it too. A sharp whiff of stale acetylene, a line of blue mounds on the platform. I sifted through mine, the powder mixing with the mud on my hands, looking for uncycled carbide stones. I found a few, as usual, and tossed them back into the generator for the next time. The blue powder on my hands I added to the mud on my flightsuit. The train glided silently into the station. Two sets of doors hissed open, in the acrylic wall and the train. We moved into the train, a pack of carnivores after the hunt, tall and filthy and silent and proud; bright helmets slung over our shoulders by the gas tubes, packs on our backs, mud on our legs and hands and faces. I pulled off my *hachimaki* and shook my head as I entered the train, dreads and braids free at last of the cotton band. Beads and old Chinese copper coins clattered as I flashed my mane. A few low-level Suits and old ladies heading for work sat up straight and defensive as we sprawled across the soft seats, mud stains on the Textaline vinyl, a conquering army in occupied land. Rowdy and boisterous, clowning and dapping as the stations rolled by and a few spuds got off. The sheep getting off, too, most of them fleeing for a more secure car. The skagheads should know that no streetdrek would pull a slice&dice right after a Downside run, no class at all, no style.

Luxembourg. Mara and I got off, last daps and rendez-vous exchanged. Home now, some oj first and then a shower and then oblivion.

I woke up around 15:00. Mara was still sleeping, his arm and leg hooked through mine, bone-white skin across brown, the rigid angles of eroticism. I disentangled myself gently. Mara too comatose to even moan, and slid off the futon and the riser. I padded softly into the kitchen area, naked, and opened the fridge. I took out the plastic container of oj and frowned at the remaining inch. I drained it, tossed the empty container out the small window into the dumpster below, and padded on to the bathroom.

Not only did I feel like shit, I looked like it. My hair was a tangled mess of dreads and braids, my face was even thinner than usual, and I was carrying some heavy bags under my eyes. I took a piss and then filled the sink with cold water; I dunked my head and shook it, water flying around the bathroom. I toweled the mess, the coins in my braids clicking together, then just hacked at it with my fingers for a while. Dreadlocks look cool, but they're a *bitch*. At least the long braid at the base of my neck (the one with the Cheyenne beads my mom gave me a long time ago) was intact. So fuck it.

I dabbed some silicon oil on the jack behind my ear, left the bathroom, and started digging through the pile of clean clothes at the foot of the bed. I'd torn down the flimsy closet a year ago to expand my work space, so we just left all our clothes in a heap after we washed them. Our mud-stained Downside rags were puddled in a corner, waiting for the next run.

I finally snagged a pair of French cotton fatigues and a black Mute Pain T with slit sides and put them on. My ribs jutted out the sides of the slit T as I bunched it up over my shoulders, an angular rack exposed to the air or a reaching hand. I picked up my armdeck from the desk and snapped it shut around my left wrist. I flicked it open and killed the dub, which I'd left on for the sleep, just as Mara started to stir. I bent down and kissed the triangular slab of his cheek before picking up my jewelry and putting it on: leather neck thongs with crystals and beads of turquoise and a wolf claw and a tuft of small feathers and a miniature oak lynx which Mara had carved for me; bracelets of rawhide strips and hammered copper; a couple of stud earings, one an ebony and ivory yin-yang, the other an opaline triangle set in silver. I put these last two in my left ear, above the thick silver loop that never came out.

Dressed at last, and Mara waking up. I kissed him again and ran my fingers over his smooth, drawn skin. He groaned, and I playfully tousled his blue hair before going to the kitchen and thumbing the little Toshiba coffee machine on for him. Mara staggered up and started looking for his Syrettes while I picked up a half-empty bottle of cheap red from the counter and nursed it on the way to my work space.

I took a last pull before running my fingers over the deck, activating the whole rig. First the small, smooth, black Ashanti console with color-coded membranes, one of the best decks to come out of the new Africa, my only new deck. The rest of my tech was shit, second-hand, beat-up, obsolete dreck, but it worked: Yamaha HC-23 integral Hands and a JL-17 digital sampler library; Sony multitrack holoproj; McDonnell-Douglas 3Space Tracker, an old, stolen military job. LEDs flickered as I fished a DAF chip out of a plastic case, slotted it, and called up the program. The deck's prompts floated in front of me, ghostly green holographic letters dancing and flickering.

I skanked to a slow, silent beat as the Ashanti ran the program, interfacing with the rest of the rig. I turned around and keyed the Sony, calling up the holo map of the Champs Elysées. It grew slowly, tendrils of colored light meshing together, forming sidewalks, trees, obstacles, building facades.

Everything looked ready. I picked up the co-axial cable beside the deck and rammed it into the jack behind my ear. Strings of numerals appeared over parts of the holo in contrasting colors, fed simultaneously into my optic and auditory centers via the jack; each string represented a given set of pitches, amplitude, and timbre. I could now "hear" each part of the still unfinished soundscape as well as "see" it, the data processed multi-sensorially. In stereo, so to speak.

Soundscaping is the new style, high-tech music with a kink that'll put the console DJs out of biz when it finally hits the Street (though in fact the Bloodman and Big D. are already doing soundscapes, and the others are moving in fast). I just got into it myself, fresh off from the hardbeat consoles, after Mara showed me a piece he found in some spec tech journal. His full-time trip is books—*real* books, by old writers. There hasn't been a real writer since 2010, he says, at least not published ones, not that I'd know, or care; but when he gets bored with that sometimes he likes to skim the tech sheets.

I couldn't read most of the article, not having the tech lingo necessary, but still figured out what kind of tech I needed and what to do. It took me two months to steal all the tech, and of course by then it was obsolete, though you get used to that on the Street. No one can keep up, not even the big-money big boys.

Turns out soundscaping's pretty old, actually; the idea goes way back to the 1980s. The idea is basically to build 3D soundscapes with *music*. The scape interacts audially with the listener, same way a holo landscape interacts visually. The DJman creates the soundscape as a fixed set of data, laying down melodies and instrumentation over a 3D space, using a tracker which follows the movements of the hands to input the special position of the sounds into the deck, and a combination of keyboard or a set of Hands and a digital sampler library to beat out the music itself. I'd found the best way was to create a visual holo of the space you wanted and then to mold the soundscape itself over it, laying down the percussion and bass hardbeats first, then the strips of melody.

The way it worked in the tech sheet—it's written for Uptown *musicians*, not for the Street—you sit at home with a pair of earphones or implants slaved into a deck and a joystick; you use the joystick to pilot yourself through the soundscape, hearing whatever sound you go zooming through or next to. Examples they had were hills of string drones, the pitches rising as you climb the hill; canyons of wild guitar solos, with walls of horns, the speed of the solo matching the speed of your "flight"; bubbles of flute pitches, enclosing you and then getting smaller, the pitches dancing wildly as they get closer and closer, and other shit like that.

The scape I was working on was a hardcore Street special. I got the idea from my other main line of action, streetstyle skating with the Livewires.

The scape is a musical map of the Champs Elysées, for the Livewire run down the Champs next weekend. I had scored a perfect scale holo map of the Champs and was painting the soundscape over it: strips of melody over the various sidewalks and surfaces, columns of instrumental drones over the obstacles, hardbeats following the lines of trees and dropping at each side street. When we did the run, I'd have gravfield motion sensors taped to my skimboots, and the music would be synched in realtime to the terrain I'd be skating over. Razor*blood* scape, real hardcore.

I got to work. Shaping the melodies with the Hands, skanking in place to the beat the entire time whether the beat was on or not; picking the instruments and timbres from the library, laying them over the holo with the tracker, and finally downloading the whole mess into the DAF chip. Hardfast work, fingers like lightning over the controls, *electric*, better'n most drugs. I could hear the numbers inside my head as I painted them over the holo, testing, checking, modifying. I got lost in the scape, brainwalk, the rest of the world blindspotted . . .

The alarm I'd set in the Ashanti pinged three hours later, pulling me back into spacetime reality. I finished off the string I was working on and started shutting down the rig. I was exhausted, and my back ached. I stretched while the deck saved my work and ejected the DAF. I stored it, killed the power, and hit the kitchen for some eats. The apartment was empty, Mara gone. I thumbed my library on and called up an old Joy Division album, *Still*, Mara's favorite. Iceclean sound beat out of the four Bose speakers the corners, real beauties I'd lifted three years ago out of a big-money Uptown pad with a real softcore security system. I was quite the thief in my youth, hard-jiving streetdrek, you know. Right now the samarium cobalt drivers made me *feel* the rhythms, the snare thumping my heart, the bass singing through my ribs and pelvis bones, vibrating them . . .

I rolled myself a butcher spliff, Jamaican lambsbread with a bit of Moroccan black hash mixed in; a cone two centimeters in diameter at the tip with a rolled piece of cardboard for a filter. I kicked back on the hammock and swayed blissfully for a few seconds before lighting it. I inhaled deeply, smoke crisping my lungs, familiar pungent smell filling the room. I was high as an eagle before the third toke. I needed to be clearheaded for the deal at the Forum, so I put it out after taking another hit. I lay there, stoned, blissed-out, merging with the drum and bass rhythmlines . . . I slid into them, hung suspended between them, between the beats, moving with them . . . Forward, but unmoving . . . Forward stillness, yeah.

I emerged from the trance a timeless time later, still high, feeling good but a bit slow. I climbed out of the hammock and unhooked it, freeing up a large, empty space on the hardwood floor. I started running my favorite form, Lao Chu Chu'an, the Animal Form. Praying Mantis into Double-Clawed Eagle into Ape Offering Wine into Whip into Cranes' Wings into White Snake . . . Streching my body, clearing my mind, focusing . . .

I stopped after the tenth run-through, wired and concentrated now. I pulled off my sweaty T and fatigues and took a quick shower; first scalding, massaging the muscles, then ice-cold, shocking me into full alertness.

I was getting dressed again when the vidphone pinged. I whistled, A440 gliding up to high C, and the handset shot over, breaking and hovering right next to my ear. I buttoned up my fatigues while I answered, running the phone on audio only.

"Lynx?" Toxic's voice.

"This is Lynx's answering program. I'm afraid Lynx is out right now, but if you'd care to leave a message at the sound of the beep . . . Beep!"

"Uh, Lynx, this is Toxic, you told me to call you, I'll be down at—"

"Hey, Toxic," I cut in, "*qué pasa*, my man?"

"Lynx?" Confused as hell. I love that. "That you?"

"No, I'm just a very smart program that Lynx has set up."

"What the fuck . . ."

I played him sucker for a few more seconds before taking pity on him and calling off the game.

"Man, you had me fuckin soft there. You shouldn't pull that shit."

"Ah, just a lark, my man, practice for the biz, ya no see it?"

"Yeah, yeah." Toxic was not convinced, but decided to forget about it. "So what's the deal, what's happening?"

"Olric's got this hardcore scene, man, he found the Ponts & Chaussées bunker—"

"You're shittin' me, man, I don't like it—"

"No, man, it's the truth, hard truth. Olric, he's *crucial*, man, def razor."

"Truth?"

"No lie, man, Street honor."

"You're ain't got honor, Lynx. No streetdrek got honor."

"Like fuck—"

"About the bunker, Lynx, cut the shit."

I ran the data by him briefly.

"So Olric needs you to cut the prefab, score the drill—"

"Check, man, can do. I'll buzz him."

"Razor. See you Wednesday, or before that."

"Salaam Aleikum."

"Salaam."

I cut the connection and whistled the handset back to the master wallset. I found another clean T I liked, deVeres corporate logo over the breast, appropriate for the biz I was running tonight. I picked up the wine bottle by the rig on my way to the wallset and sipped it while I punched in Viper's code.

Scalpel answered the phone naked, her upper body distorted in the old cracked blue screen of my wallset. She smiled "Lynx! Hold on." She moved off-screen. I waited a few seconds, and she reappeared wearing a torn

Naked Pagans T. Her left nipple jutted out of one of the holes.

"That's not much better." I grinned.

She glanced down, noticed the protruding nipple, and shrugged.

"Fuck it. You've seen worse. What's up? Wanna talk to the Vipe?"

"Neg, neg. Your sweet eyes . . ."

I ran the deal by her. She was pleased.

"Razor, man! Virgin walls Downside, what a trip! I'm there, man, gotta go score some bombs now, gonna get a rainbow, man, colors, radical!"

"Slicin. Cité U?"

"20:00, Wednesday, check. Hey listen, why don't we just turn the whole place into a club-slash-art gallery? I'll do the deco with Whizz and, oh, Bando maybe—no, he's a dick—Kemar then, we charge and party, make some bread, whaddaya say?"

"Could be razor. Better run it by Olric, though. It's his data, all the way—"

"Will do. See ya Wednesday, babe. Better bring some old suit, cause I'm gonna paint paint paint . . ."

"Salaam, Scalpel. Love."

"Love ya babe." She grin-frowned. "You're sure you don't want to sleep with me again? We could work something out with Mara, fix him up with Vipe, a group grope maybe . . ."

I smiled, teeth showing. "Maybe someday. We'll see."

"We'll see, we'll see," mimicking my tone, "always we'll see." Raised eyebrows. "See my nipple?"

I laughed. "You're too much for me, babe. Besides, Viper would be pissed at me."

"Forget her, she's a cunt, never talks to me, never gives me flowers—"

"Not even desert lilies?"

"Yeah, well," she snorted, suddenly serious. "Ah, fuck. She does too many drugs, Lynx, she's gonna get fucked soon."

"More than me?"

"Oh yeah."

"Well, shit." I was truly impressed. "If that's her riddim, though, that's cold."

"Till she goes frit and comes at me with a meat cleaver—"

"—And you break both her arms and one leg—"

"—And toss her into a dumpster. Right. Well, shit, a girl's gotta protect herself."

"Check."

"Besides, I wouldn't do that to Viper. I like her."

I couldn't resist the tease. "More than me?"

She looked pissed. "Fuck you, Lynx."

"Hey, you set yourself up for that one."

"Well . . . No more nipples for you, you bastard!" She pulled the T over it. The other one popped out. I laughed.

"Fuck, fuck, *fuck*! You scumbag! Fuck off!"

"Awright awright," I gasped. "Enough."

"Fuck you!"

"Temper, temper. . ." I calmed down a bit. Scalpel *always* does this to me. *If it wasn't for Mara . . .*

I decided to say that out loud. "If it wasn't for Mara, love . . ."

That calmed her down a bit. It was all a tease anyway, an old game. The trick was to find the right line.

"Oh, darling Lynx, beloved mine—theatrics now—if it wasn't for Viper . . ."

I exploded again. She grinned.

"Score!" Her finger darted through the air, tracing two lines: II.

"Bullshit!" I licked my fingers and mimed wiping a blackboard. "That's only one."

The LCD in the wallset read 19:13 when we finally ended the rap. I kissed her nipple through the screen, static sparks stinging my lips, and cut the connection. I finished off the wine bottle and dunked it out the kitchen window, a ten-meter shot, perfect aim. I heard it shatter in the dumpster below.

Must've hit the edge.

I suddenly felt a vague impulse to scan the news before heading out. I pulled the Libération newsscreen out of the drawer, unrolled it, and pushed it up against the wall. It stuck there and shimmered into life.

I punched in the code for Short Cycle while the Libé

computer-animated logo did its thing. An LED pinged in acknowledgment and the cycle started.

The image of Natalie Clairemont, the caster—actually a computer construct—was slightly flawed. Thin lines danced across and through her elegant *gaijin*-bourgeois face. Her bright red electronic lipstick glistened moistly, an advertising exec's warped idea of sensuous. I adjusted the reception and the lines cleared up.

I'd chosen the female model when I subscribed on a least of two evils basis. The male construct looked like a real asshole, the epitome of old stuck-up French snobby bourgeoisie. Surprising, coming from Libé; I expected that from the Figaro, but not Libération. So much for marketing.

Natalie talked in a quiet, persuasive voice. Computer graphics or taped footage occasionally unfolded out of the corner of the screen, covering her face, and lingered while her voice-over continued its narration before refolding, origami-like, into the corner.

"The Chzecosoviet embassy in Lima, Peru, was bombed today. The casualty total so far stands at seventeen; more are missing. The Shining Path guerilla, active in Peru for the past sixty years, claimed responsibility for the attack, citing Chzecosoviet arms sales to the Peruvian government as the cause for the bombing. The Shining Path insurgent army now holds the northern third of Peru, with the help of U.S. millitary aid and advisers.

"Security in Paris was tightened today in expectation of U.S. President Eastwood's state visit next week. Terrorist threats were cited by the spokesman of the C.R.S. as the reason for the increased C.R.S. deployment throughout the entire city, and especially around the Elysée palace and the Avenue des Champs-Elysées. News agencies in the United States received a videotaped message from the leader of the Little Big Horn, a Native American terrorist group, vowing to assassinate President Eastwood. The president responded to the threat in a press conference today, declaring in a firm voice quote Make my day unquote."

I put the news on hold at that one, pissed. Tightened security around the Champs . . . Shit. That would make

Friday's run much more risky, trigger-happy Mirrorfaces everywhere and on edge.

Ah well, it'd be chickenshit to call it off. We'll just have to watch our asses a bit more carefully. Skate or die . . .

I retriggered the cycle.

"Officials of the International Organization of Medicine announced today that they have successfully cured the last known AIDS case on the African continent. AIDS, the great plague of the late twentieth century, has now been reduced to a medical rarity.

"Now for some local news: Two narcotics officers were shot and killed today near the Centre Pompidou. The murderer, a Caucasian male, has so far eluded the police. C.R.S. officials predict a rapid arrest."

The sagging red face of an aging Beast blossomed onscreen. CMDT. BRETON, CRS pulsed in holographic green across the bottom of the screen. "We'll get the little rat," snarled the captain. "He can't go far."

Natalie reappeared, still smiling. "That was commandant Breton of the C.R.S., in a press conference earlier this afternoon.

"Also in Paris. The leader of a Paris youth gang, the A.C.A.F., was arrested early this morning in a joint operation involving the C.R.S. and the Ministry of the Interior's security troups. Three soldiers and five gang members were killed in the shootout which occurred when the government troups surrounded the gang's hide-out, an abandoned warehouse near La Defense. Police believe that two gang members escaped by way of underground tunnels."

Downside . . . Shit. I cut the news cycle angrily. *Fuckin Beasts, can't fuckin leave us alone, gotta dust us and tilt us.* I didn't know the A.C.A.F., but chances were that it was just some dirt-ass streetdrek gang that got on the bad side of some Mirrorface with buddies in the Ministry. *Fuck them, fuck them all!* I ripped the screen off the wall, rolled it, shoved it in the drawer, and went to search for my skimboots.

I finally found them under an old towel and sat down to strap them on, pulling Velcro tabs tight and shut. Billy Name had made these for me; Billy Name, genius of the juryrig, my only oldtime friend still alive, except for

Viper. Name had salvaged two miniaturized Anubis directional gravfield units from a Maui jetboard and mounted them on the back of a pair of leather gloveboots, recalibrating them for the difference in weight distribution. They worked beautifully, behaving just like roller skates, but allowing much higher speeds; Viper had once clocked me at sixty-k.p.h. on the Saint-Michel hill, no speed wobbles, clean run. Their only drawback was the GF units' unfortunate tendency to short out once in a while, causing some pretty butcher slams, real bloody. Name had added a reactivating circuit, so that at least I didn't have to walk home when it happened, but that didn't help much. At least it didn't happen too often, and the idea that the GFs could cut out while I played tag with a fifteen-ton bus did add some spice to the whole trip.

Name had gone on to make skimboots for all the Livewires, and they had gotten so popular in Paris that Tao Ltd. had recently marketed a commercial version. I'd tried them, and prefered Name's by far; the corporate techs just didn't have his touch, the Street wizard touch.

I sealed the last tab and ran a mental checklist of essentials: wallet, weaponry (balisong, cobra, a switch Velcroed to the leg, and the seven-millimeter-thick razorsteel Gerber blade up my back), credit card, Zippo, cigarettes, shades, keys, some cash . . . I dug briefly through my electronics box, and came up with a pair of tester prongs for the wetware. I also snagged three copies of Name's trojan from the pile of CDs. I slipped on my leather, distributed items through the various pockets, and pulled on my fingerless cotton gloves. I set the alarm on the way out, LEDs on the motion sensors blinking softly, and killed the lights. I closed the door, reflexively patted my pocket for my keys, and headed for the stairs.

I paused at the top and activated the music. Mute Pain blasted inside my head, raw and crude and driving, perfect skating music. I checked that the way was clear and without further pussyfooting ripped down the short flight. Halfway down, I jumped up and out, reaching down and slapping the GF units on in midair. My favorite stunt. I pulled a perfect landing, knees bent and arms out, and shot through the doorway and over the sidewalk and onto the street, jerking hard left to avoid an incoming car. Brakes screeched, the shocked driver screamed insults; I ignored him as I tore downhill, toward Saint-Michel, lost in the unholy geometries of the run.

I pumped my legs a few times, out and then cross over, my feet feeling the texture of the concrete like hands caressing a lover's skin. I shot out of the small street and swerved right in a controlled skid onto the Saint-Michel sidewalk, terrified pedestrians scattering like pigeons. I jetted down the hill, dodging peds left-right, the boulevard one giant slalom with moving obstacles. I wrenched myself sideways to avoid a three-year-old clutching his mother's hand, hardtorque; leapt over a construction trench, knees folded in high, over the workers' heads; whipped by two Mirrorfaces too surprised to even shoot me. Mayhem and chaos, the Livewire voodoo; down the boulevard at the speed of light, hanging jaws and heart attacks in my wake. The High, the Kick. When I first met Scalpel she asked me why. I went off into a demented fastmouth C rap.

"Trouble is our central kick, lover, you copy? We do our Livewire voodoo, flat out down the boulevards, with all the skimmers around us, and that's the trip, you see, the Livewire weird. I mean, the *danger* is the Kick. You move fast, faster than the hardbeat itself . . . And the adrenaline rush, man, it cuts any drug I ever tried, even White Dust, and Kirishto knows I was into that shit. And the thing is, the closer you come to getting dusted, the heavier the trip, the wilder you feel. You get amped, man, fuckin *amped!* And when that gravity sucks you down into the cement and you fuckin *slam* . . . When you get blood, get hurt, that's like a fuckin explosion, you barely feel it, you're just up and *moving.* Raging and dancing, fuckin hardcore! That's the trip, lover, the voodoo. Skate or die. No bullshit, just you moving and everything else trying to dust you, grease you flat and bloody."

Scalpel asked me to teach her, and was hooked within two weeks. Same for Mara, a year later. Skate or die.

I cut across the boulevard in front of Gibert, perfect trajectory angling through the traffic pattern, my hands slapping the hood of a gray BMW before I used a bump in the concrete as a springboard and flew ten meters in the air, dreadlocks flashing. I landed low on the other sidewalk and used the momentum to cut hard right in a crossover, dodging a cluster of smooth and soft Uptown kids all decked out for their Saturday night revels and debaucheries.

I made it across Saint-Germain as the light turned green, in that fraction of a second between the down-pressed foot on the accelerator and the forward leap of the skimmer, traffic behemoth futilely snapping its jaws shut behind me. Riding the Edge, the unit of time solid like a hardbody . . .

I saw Kemar ahead, in front of Boulimier's, and came in low on his right, slapping his leg without stopping. I banked right off the sidewalk, onto the bus lane, and flipped around, skating backward while I jived at him. I flipped around again and narrowly dodged a honking bus that appeared out of nowhere, zipping in crisscross in the small space between the bus and the skimmer traffic.

Bright light as I came out of the tree cover, by the Fontaine Saint-Michel. I pulled out my shades and slipped them on as I boogied through the intersection, skipping and hot-stepping around the waves of skimmers. I picked up some speed on the Pont Saint-Michel, my legs pumping hard, and jetted across the Ile Saint-Louis with a quick, obscene gesture to the Beasts in front of the Palais de Justice. I laughed at the rage in their faces. They wanted to dust me so bad, but orders are orders . . .

Across the Pont au Change and through the Chatelet traffic. I stopped briefly by the fountain there to drink and dap with some bloods I knew, and then decided to cut through the Metro.

Into the station, Chatelet-Les Halles, a labyrinthian hydra that sprawls over a square kilometer. I bounced down the entrance stairs, a small jolt at each step, and leapt smoothly over the turnstile without slowing. Then hard left, down some more stairs, and hard right, into the thin passageway next to the endless slidewalk.

Frightened peds looked up as I howled "Heads *up!*" and flattened themselves against the walls as I tore by. The corridor took forever, too many peds to *really* cut loose, the peds on the slidewalks staring safely.

Out finally and into a short, wide corridor. I skittered left-right, dodging and toying, past the booths of candy-selling Hindu refugees.

A Mirrorface, his back to me, starting to turn as he heard the peds' cries. I slapped his burpgun out of the way before I even impacted on his invisible eyes and was over and down the stairs by the time he brought it back to bear.

Fuckers have bead mikes. There'll be more waiting. I ripped through the small nexus and cut left and flew down the steps to the Great Tunnel, catching a glance of running Faces in my peripheral vision.

The Great Tunnel connects the Chatelet part of the station to the huge Les Halles underground hall. There are three slidewalks, side by side, sloping down at a steep angle for fifteen meters before flattening out. All three of them were crammed tight with the rush-hour mob.

Fuck. Don't think, just do it! I bounced off a shocked Suit and threw myself headfirst onto the waist-high, polished metal divider that separated the slidewalks. I slid, tucked, rolled, twisted, and came up on my feet, shooting onto the flat part before I'd even gotten a grip on my balance. The momentum carried me for thirty meters, half the divider, and then I started pumping in crisscross, barely slowing. *Trouble . . . Legba, I love it!*

I gave the invisible watchers behind the surveillance vidcams the finger as I shot under the rows of electronic eyes. I arced off the end of the divider onto the thin, corrugated rubber matting that coated the floor of the hall and cut left—

"Mirrorface in front of me, burpgun leveled *No!!!*

I rammed straight into him, arms up in front of my face. He flew backward and I stepped on him and kicked his gun away and then—

Over the turnstiles, clenched into a tight ball, into the main area of the huge hall.

I used the crowd for cover, staying low, skating fast. A Face saw me, tried to shoot, but I dropped my weight and cut sharp around a Suit and behind a support pillar. Ten more meters and I shot through the Plexiglas doors, into the Forum.

Safe. *They're not dumb enough to follow me into here.*

The Forum des Halles, Streetdrek Central. Three levels underground, slummers' delight, if he survived; a riot of skinheads, rastas, jockeys, iceboys, verminhead slice& dicers, other spuds. Once a fashionable mall, most of the stores closed now; a shooting range, too, Mirrorfaces the target of choice, Uppers and Suits next on line. Streetdrek are safe, long as they don't cross the line. The Forum is a black-market warehouse and drug emporium, a squatter hotel where a multiplex of stolen items are sold or traded openly. Home Sweet Home.

I danced through the crowd in the main hall, spiked hair and torn clothes and baroque body jobs, a silent symphony of black and bright colors, Mute Pain in my head the only sound in the world. I slidestopped in front of the long steps where Mara sat with Olric and dropped next to him. I nuzzled his neck, still breathing hard, kissing and licking and biting, deaf to his greetings. Eventually I reached down and cut the gravfields. I waited for the end of the song before cutting the music.

"Yo, Olric, Mara, just pulled a hardcore run through the station, dig it."

"Razor, my brother," said Olric. "Faces get pissed?"

"Faces tried to dust me, yeah! I cut down between the slidewalks and nailed one of the fuckers, sent him flying, then made it out through the hall."

"Smooth." Olric paused a beat. "Heard about Kurt yet?"

"No. News?"

"Yeah. He was running some biz up by Beaubourg this morning. Seems some bag-o-wire set him up, his contacts turned out to be narcs. Loco fucker wasted them both, blew them away when they tried to tilt him."

"Fuck . . . Kurt? No fuckin way, man, no fuckin way."

"Solid, my brother, truth."

"Yeah, yeah, I know, shit, read it in the news earlier, didn't know it was Kurt. Fucker nuked but good this time. Shit . . ."

"Yeah, it's soft, my brother, not too cool. He's wet, real wet."

"Where's he now?"

"He's hot-stepping south, for the Gibraltar Free Zone. Might make it, too. He hung for a time Downside, got

Toxic and me to score him a skimmer in Vanves, then crossed the line on the RER. He's on the autobahn now, looks like he's clear. Got Billy Name to cover the Beasts through the Net. He says they're lost, totally clueless."

"Shit. Who's the bag-o-wire?"

"Dunno. We'll find him, though, shiv him good."

"Slice him and *dice* him, man." Mara spoke for the first time, violent, a snarl on his face, unusually tense. "Kurt was a good friend, man. I say we find the little shit who blew him and drape his intestines over Beaubourg."

"Check," said Olric. "We'll make it good, gruesome warning, spike his carcass on top, blood on the escalators—"

"Yeah . . . Make it bloody, real pretty, give the Faces the Fear."

Don't fuck with the streetdrek, spud, or it's Game Over for you . . .

We spent the next couple of hours rapping and smoking on the stairs, depressed. Friends and contacts sat and left; we traded gossip, talked about Kurt, about biz too. Slow night, the spuds angry and moody, violence in the air. A fight broke out, some blood jumping a prettyboy tourist and mashing his face against a wall, then tossing him through a plate-glass window while the prettyboy's squeeze shrieked for Mirrorfaces that wouldn't come. Blood on the rubber carpeting, the girl finally taking the hint and running. Later two spuds picked up the prettyboy, dumped him on the up escalator, the one that still worked: instant garbage disposal. I watched and smoked, thinking of Kurt.

22:30. Time. I told Mara and Olric that I'd be back and skated to McDonald's, around the central pit and then down one level. This McDonald's is a real slime pit, one of the few fast foods still open in the Forum. The mirrors are grimy and useless, the fake brass peeling off the nickel alloy railings, the cracked plastic tables stained with decades' worth of encrusted ketchup and soy and grease and salt and soda. I spotted the breed in back and picked up a small fries before threading my way through the crowd toward her booth, casually casing the tables near her.

The scan came up clear. I sat down in the booth of scratched, pale, varnished wood. The woman spoke first.

"Cool runnings, breed. You're on time."

She had a gadj with her, a sallow, greasy type with asymmetrical darkers and pizza stains on his fancy suit. I dapped with her and the gadjo muscle—name of Karl—and ate a few fries before she spoke again.

"You have the money—and the trojans?"

"You have the goods?"

She drew a rectangular blue plastic case from under her seat and placed it gently on the table, facing me. I examined the deVeres logo embossed on the case. It looked authentic.

I looked up at the breed. "I'm gonna open this here."

"That smooth?"

I shrugged. "I don't feel like hustling for a dark corner. Besides, the only spuds here who'd even try to fuck with me are the verminheads, and I can handle those fuckers without even catching a sweat."

She nodded. "Open it."

I thumbed the lock and popped the cover. Inside, four rows of insulated glass vials, carefully packed in bonded urethane foam. I pulled one out at random and held it to the light. The chip glittered, polarized mirror coating playing tricks with the light.

I looked at the woman before opening it. "Where'd you score these?"

"No can say, brother."

"Yes can say. I'm handling hot wetware, I wanna know the source. Copy?"

"Well . . ."

Pizza Suit cut in angrily. "She doesn't want to tell you, breed, dig?" He looked like he was about to cry behind his darkers.

Not muscle at all, no cool. More like her squeeze.

The woman waved absently. "Karl, it's OK. Solid." To me: "Friend of mine works there, he pegs stuff, fudges the inventory. Check?"

"Check." Pizza Suit was obviously the "friend."

Fuckin amateures . . . Dumb fuckin hustle, no way deVeres won't click to it. Oh well . . . SEP . . .

Someone Else's Problem. As long as I moved the wet

fast, the Beasts couldn't do shit, even if these softbodies fingered me.

I popped the vial I was holding. Escaping freon stung my fingers, frozen bite of superconductor cold. I lay the sheet of soft black acrylic I'd brought on the table and gently dropped the logical on it. I pulled the leads from my pocket and painstakingly tabbed them to the chip. *Should've brought a fuckin magnifier.* I plugged the business end of the leads into the jack in my armdeck and keyed the tester program. My fingers danced as I ran the functions, testing the logical, searching for bugs. The LCD flickered, strings of numerals flowing by, all green. I finally thumbed a membrane on the deck and untabbed the leads. I used the padded tweezers in my wallet to drop the chip back into the vial. I replaced the vial in the case, a small freon blister at the bottom automatically refreezing it.

"Satisfied?" snarled Pizza Suit. His aggressive tone utterly failed to cover his nervousness.

"No," I said. I picked another vial out of the case and spent another five minutes testing it. Pizza Suit sweating, the breed calm and distant.

I jived a reflexive All Clear at the breed when I finished. She smiled faintly. I noticed her huge pupils then, black holes in her orbs. *Dusted out of her mind, she is. Bad way to run biz.*

"The money," she said.

I handed her the CDs first. Pizza Suit snatched them out of her hand and glared suspiciously.

"What are these?" he asked.

I refrained from laughing out loud. The breed calmly reached over and pulled them out of his hand, slipping them into an inner pocket. "Something extra, Karl, a bonus. Not to worry, you'll get your share."

He looked crestfallen. I started feeling sorry for him. She was obviously playing him for a skin, hustling him with handouts and sex in exchange of his pirated tech. *And when he finally gets tilted he'll take the rap, cover her, and she'll walk.*

SEP.

"Your card," I said. She handed it to me and I slotted mine in, tapping out my authorization code and the amount. She checked the readout and put her card away, satisfied. She stood up.

I decided to do Pizza Suit a favor before leaving. I looked at the woman, smiling, and said "Breed. Tell your friend he's burned, bad. I caught two tracer circuits in the logical, slaved to the deVeres mainframe. They must have triggered when I opened the case. By now they know it's missing, soon they'll figure out who-and-how." Pizza Suit jerked up, shocked, darkers masking his eyes. The woman looked pissed and stalked away without talking. Pizza Suit looked at me and then shuffled after her. *Ah, the male libido* . . .

The bit about the tracer was bullshit, of course. I would have walked the instant I'd caught one. But it might make Pizza Suit think twice about what he was getting into. I'm just a skin for sob cases.

The rest of the night ran standard. Mara, Olric, and I got dusted and spent four hours hanging out before heading home and crashing. I made love with Mara before sleeping, sex with the bite of the Dust tail end. The next day I woke up at four, worked a bit on the scape, and put the word out that I had ware for Billy Name. I went through the usual bullshit; Leave-a-message-he'll-call-you-back, before cutting a friendly deal, 1,600 ESUs, real smooth. He sent a runner to pick up the wet, one of his thirteen-year-old little mutant fuckers, horror-movie zombie face, putrid, decomposing silicon flesh-substitute stretched over cartilage implants. Would-be Artiste Terroriste, running errands for the Man, aping a look the real ATs didn't need.

Sunday night we hit the Icehouse for an Alien Heat gig, me and Mara and Halflife and Jester, roaring drunk, the whole night on booze only. In smooth as butter, a phone call two hours before and a fast drek line put us on the VIP list. We cut through the crowd of faceless Uptown sheep, ignoring envious stares, up the stairs, and past the bouncer with a whispered name. Security was tight, rumor of an appearance, old Lydon himself maybe.

I'd never been in the Icehouse. Inside the doors, red velvet and people in black. We glided through the crowd, into the noise, the sound.

Shit bopper music, of course. We wandered through the side rooms and entered the Line.

The Line, long and high, a seething maelstrom of flashing lights and frenzied bodies. Milling sheep pressed up against the railing surrounding the dance floor. Through—

I smiled when I saw the dancer on the pedestal. He ruled above the crowd, sharp and slick in his starched white shirt and soft red vest, mime cool. Cuff links and bow tie too, and a black felt bowler topping it all off. Smooth . . .

We reached the back, a dark, hollow, calm spot. Thick steel I-beams rose through the hardwood floor, reaching up to the curved ceiling. Beautiful glass chandeliers hung from horizontal girders. Candles were scattered across the antique wood tables. I dropped into a large antique velvet chair and stared down the tunnel.

The raised wood floor stopped abruptly, cut off at a waist-high barrier flanked by two fake marble statues bathed in ghastly green light. The Line stretched on beyond it, long and somber, an old, abandoned Metro tunnel, thin platforms along the sides and two tracks separated by a row of rusted I-beams. Sharp white lasers and strobes cut through the darkness.

I looked up. Pipes, large and thin. Electrical apparatus on the brick walls.

Amazing . . . They must've hired some hotshit *designers. It looks like a holofilm director's wet dream fantasy of the ideal club. Bet the owners are Lebanese.*

I went over to the green and red marble bar and ordered a Kahlua & Bailey. I picked at the oddly lit dried flowers set in a large pot at the corner of the bar while the bartender mixed my drink. Mara and Viper and Scalpel had vanished, melted into the crowd. I wandered around, sipping my drink. The side wall was lined with small rooms, remodeled subway alcoves, each one with a different artsy decor. Halflife and Jester were in the third one, screwing on a foam couch in the soft blue neon light. I moved on without disturbing them.

I walked back to the large rooms at the entrance, feeling high and wired. *Where's the gig?* Sweat-soaked dancers stood with bowed heads in front of giant fans, cooling off in a position of prayer. I watched a beautiful girl, a blood with gleaming black skin, as she twisted and snaked on the floor, stripped to the waist, picking up empty glasses from under the furniture, bottles, syringes, inhalers . . . She moved like a professional dancer hardmuscled in her black tights, glistening with sweat. I felt my cock stir, aroused, lust for the hardbody.

Where's Mara when I really need him?

Then I noticed a group of people furtively slipping down dark stairs. *What the fuck* . . . I slipped down after them.

I descended into coldbeat music, nothing like the shit upstairs. We went through an open door into a roped-off alcove in the corner of a large, vaulted cave. I looked around. The lighting was a lot dimmer than upstairs. Sweaty bodies danced and twisted beyond the ropes. As for the people I was with . . .

They looked like classic poseurs, all in black with bouffant hairdos and curlicued face paint. *Who the fuck are they? Where are we?* I leaned against the wall, confused, lost. Then I saw the Man and everything clicked into place.

Johnny fucking Lydon. *Well shit* . . . Slim and unobtrusive in an old gray suit, his red shag as explosive as ever, a raucous grin on his face as he hugged a slim young woman. She had a model's face and body, an expensive job. As for him . . .

He looked about forty, though he had to be over seventy. Shiseido, I decided, only the Ginza for that kind of job. Four vidcams on remote floated over his head, filming him, the crowd, everything.

Then the bouncer noticed me, a fat bald faggot in a cherry red jumpsuit. "You with the band?" he growled.

I'm in a fucking VIP lounge or something. Holy shit . . .

I shifted into blandmode. "No. I'm with the press. I'm waiting for an interview with Mr. Lydon."

"You have a press card?"

"Mr. Lydon's press attaché has it. Security, you know . . ."

"Yeah." He nodded. "You'll have to wait a bit. Mr. Lydon's busy."

"That's fine."

Lydon had dropped into a couch in the corner. I found a chair and sat down. The flitting poseurs and muscle boys settled slowly, drifting into couches like falling leaves.

The crowd beyond the rope had noticed Lydon and started screaming and waving, pushing up against the ropes. The bouncers forced them back. Lydon waved, and the bouncers pulled back, opening the ropes. The crowd surged in, a pack of wolves, begging for autographs. One kid had Lydon sign his birth certificate, another one his draft card.

I waited calmly while Lydon suffered. The price of fame . . . Finally Lydon waved again and the bouncers shoved the crowd back. They had to get brutal with some of the more rabid fans, but eventually they cleared a decent-sized area and put up the velvet ropes.

Two strutting waitresses breezed in past the bouncers, carrying champagne bottles and a tray of glasses. One of the poseurs popped the first bottle, giggling madly, spraying foam all over his neighbors. Lydon accepted a glass without a word.

Motherfucker must be so bored . . .

I poured myself a glass and decided to cut out. *Fuck this scene. Lydon looks brain dead, and his people never had a brain to start with.* I snagged an unopened bottle and held it low as I slipped past the bouncers. Out into the crowd—

I caught a flash of blue and white and cut for it. Mara, leaning against a squat redbrick column, looking around. I held up the bottle victoriously as I kissed him.

"Compliments of Mr. Lydon," I yelled above the music. "Want some?"

He smiled. "Later."

I licked his ear and put on an arch, arrogant face.

"You see me over with Lydon?" I teased.

He waved dismissively. "Fuckin poseur."

I laughed, dropping the face. "Him or me?"

He didn't answer, just smiled.

"What is this place?" I asked with a wave of the arm.

"Downstairs. Sort of a separate club, for those too cool to hang upstairs with the sheep."

I grinned. "Uptown sheep up top, poseurs down here. Which is worst?"

"The music's better down here."

"Truth. Where's the gig?"

"Next room over, through there."

"Razor. Let me open this and we'll step."

Champagne bottles have a fault line build in around the neck, right below the top rim. I peeled off the aluminum and located the line.

"Mara, snag some glasses, will you?"

I pulled out my Gerber and held it in an ax grip while I gripped the bottle by the lower neck. Mara returned, holding two glasses.

"Ready?" He nodded.

I pointed the bottle in the general direction of Lydon's corner and chopped down hard on the fault line. The bottle bucked in my hand, spurting foam, the top of the neck gone, any stray glass shards blown away by the sudden explosive release of compressed glass. Mara held out the glasses as the pale liquid bubbled out, spilling everywhere.

I set the bottle on a ledge, giggling, wiped the Gerber on my sleeve, and slipped it back into its sheath. Mara held out a glass. "You nailed that bald bouncer," he said with a grin.

"Good." I drained the glass and tossed it over my shoulder. "Let's step." I grabbed the bottle and headed toward the side room.

I looked around as we threaded our way through the packed crowd. The whole cave was littered with artifacts, thick carpets, huge vases, large, ugly oil nudes on the walls, antique furniture, candles, verdigris copper lanterns.

I noticed a cute piece lounging on one of the couches. Ragged streetdrek clothes, rough shag cut. Her chest trapped my eyes. Her shirt was partially unbuttoned, exposing a brightly colored scorpion tattoed on the upper slope of her right breast. *Sexy* . . .

She stood up without noticing me. Her shirt was torn in back, the angled flap revealing a tan, slim, tight-muscled back. *Real sexy.* I ran my hand over Mara's back, feeling the muscle line, looking at the girl. Mara turned around, followed my gaze, arched his eyebrows.

47

"Cute," he said. He looked down at my crotch, noticed my hard-on. "Can I have some?" I kissed him as we staggered on.

We stopped two pillars over to examine a strange, clannish scene in a small, raised alcove. Three people lounged on a velvet couch behind an oval table covered with flickering candles. A tattoed leather spud sat on the left, and a fat woman in white face powder on the right. The creature in the middle was an improbably tall transvestite with a black turban, a huge, bulging alloy bracelet on one arm, and a tattoo of a burning head on the other. They were lording it high, holding court, real imposing.

"I know him," giggled Mara, pointing at the transvestite. "He used to be a skinhead. Now he's a seer."

"And a drag queen to boot."

"Weird. Give me some more champagne."

"No lie." I poured him some more and took a swig from the bottle. The cut neck felt pleasantly sharp against my lips.

"A lot of skins are turning into drag queens these days. That or Hare Krishnas."

I laughed. "Tough shit. Let's step, the gig's gonna start."

"Wait. Listen."

The drag queen was chattering to the fat woman. ". . . So this white boy here asks me why everyone's in black, is it a funeral? he goes. So I say, listen, white boy, if you can't put up with it, you can get your ass over to the Pyramid!"

Mara and I burst out laughing simultaneously. The drag queen shot us a furious look as we cut through the low opening, into the Pit.

Alien Heat was already on stage, tuning up. I yelled out, "Yo *Alice!*" She looked up from her bass and flashed a quick jive, What is this fuckin place? I shrugged and moved up front. Mara right behind me. Halflife and Jester were already up at the edge of the stage. I passed the bottle around. Jester handed me an inhaler and I fired up a rocket as the band kicked in, playing through the burner, fast and sharp and *butcher*.

We did more rockets and drank and thrashed, mad orgy of ritualized violence in the pit, slamming and shaking hard. The band raged badbeat, Alice's elongated fingers dancing over the bass strings, her purple filigree tattoo looking like a lace glove. After the gig I went back upstairs with Mara, and we slipped under the barrier at the end of the dance floor, into the unspoiled tunnel. We walked down the platform alongside the tracks, toward the darkness. The light show was dead, except for one running strobe down the middle. I saw ghost dances on the walls, on the edge of my peripheral vision, darting flickers like a good acid hallucination.

We went on for a while, picking our way over debris and stray equipment, past the end of the strobe, into the dark.

I closed my eyes and waited a bit. After a few minutes I opened them slowly, vision adjusted. We started walking again without glancing back. Finally we reached the giant mosquito netting that stretched over the end of the tunnel. We looked back.

The club sat a half-klik away, gleaming, a jewel of multicolored light squatting in the darkness. The giant chandelier dominated the view, reflecting red and poison green. I could make out hazy shadows, people standing against the barrier.

We sat and stared for a time, in silence. Eventually Mara touched me, and I leaned over and kissed him. We rolled back onto the grimy cement, ignoring the dirt, groping under shirts and into pants. He pulled my cock out, and I leaned back against the wall as his mouth slid down my chest.

At some point I passed out.

I crawled back to consciousness some time late Monday afternoon. I rolled sluggishly off the futon and stood up—too fast. I fell back on the futon, waking Mara, my head narrowly missing the wall. Eventually I staggered back up and headed for my drug kit. *Iesu Kirishto . . . I hate hangovers.* I fumbled through the box, looking for stims, finally coming up with two dexedrine halfderms. I pressed one against my wrist, just enough to cut through the fog without getting me wired, and brought the other one over to Mara.

Viper came over an hour later. Viper, my oldest friend,

partner in crime and madness since age six, moving with me from preteen slice&dicing to White Dust to computer raiding to, finally, the dumbest madness of all, the Livewires. We'd started on jetboards, just the two of us, playing chickietag with buses and skimmers and Mirrorfaces. When jetboards became too hip, banalized by Uptown surf punks, we turned to the skimboots, Name's creation. We raised hell through the city streets, drawing in other wildstyle spuds and finally forming the Livewires; stenciling colors on jackets and bombing them on city walls, let all the spuds know, Livewires too cool, too crazy . . .

Mara and I got dressed and we headed out toward the small streets between Saint-Germain and the Seine. For Friday's run I bought some Shiseido non-smear facepaint in a small cosmetics boutique run by a pretty young Burmese boy.

Finally we reached Max's, a small, dingy Armurerie nestled between a glossy hairdresser and an old residential building, genuine wood storefront, the plate-glass window filled with shotguns and burpguns and knives and other assorted ordnance. We went in, a bell tinkling as I pushed the door open. Max emerged from the back, a round, puckish man, unusually jovial for a weaponsmith.

"Hello, Lynx." He beamed. "What can I do for you?"

"Oh, nothing much, just dropping in. What's up?"

"I just got in some new balisongs, real beauties, you should look at them."

"Can do. Any new toys?"

He grinned. "One or two. Why don't you come over here?"

I left Viper and Mara drooling over some modified NATO assault rifles—unfortunately, Max could only sell guns to people with permits, meaning in effect only Uppers or Beasts—and followed him through the bead curtain. The back of the shop was badly lit, even more cluttered than the front, tools and parts and boxes littering the shelves. Max dug through an unstable stack of boxes, dropping two, finally found the right one. He handed it to me and sat down contentedly while I opened it.

The box was small, maybe ten centimeters to a side, covered with Japanese characters. A Fury. Inside was a small, square leather sheath wrapped in gauze paper. I snapped it open and pulled out the knife.

It was a miniature curveblade with two knuckleholes instead of a hilt, a seamless piece of vacuumground steel. I slipped it over two finges. It fit perfectly, the blade curving out toward my thumb. I tested the blade against the back of my hand and drew blood.

"Nasty, Max, razor nasty. I like it. How much?"

"Cheap. Fifty."

"I'll take it." I handed him my card while I slipped the sheath over my belt. It nestled comfortably next to my zipper, under my T-shirt. Drawing it was awkward, too slow. But once out . . . It was perfect for nonlethal dirtyfights, small and neat and impossible to drop.

I walked back out after looking at a few balisongs I couldn't really afford. We thanked Max and left, Viper casting looks of regret on a slick black full-auto H&K. Nice firepower, I decided, but a bit bulky for the Street. No discretion.

The week that followed was slow, practically dull. Olric and Toxic had nearly gotten tilted Sunday night trying to peg the G.E. drill; they'd escaped via Downside but lost the drill, so that we had to call off the bunker run till they could try again. I destroyed two plastic mannequins stolen from a department store practicing with my cobra—a wrist-snapping, retractable steel club—and finished the scape on Thursday. Mara went to work on a new sculpture, refusing to show it to me, even after he finished it. "After the run," he said. No news of Kurt, or the bag-o-wire for that matter. No one I knew got dusted. Scalpel broke a leg skating, trying to dodge a skimmer by jumping a meter-high barrier, and stomped around for three days in her plasticast bitching about having to miss the run. Security tightened up around the Champs.

Friday night now. 23:30. Time for the run.

We assembled at McDonald's, wired and tense, commando unit gearing up for a raid. Totally into the Livewire weird now, the voodoo mystique. I saw Olric in a corner of the McDonald's and ignored him, just another pedestrian. I wore my ritual warpaint, traditional Cheyenne markings on my face.

Jester and Bozo were already there when Mara and I arrived. Jester—thin, spunky, blond Jester—was skatedancing in front of McDonald's to the beat of some silent music, firedance melody piped in through his implants. Bozo leaned his two-meter bulk against the wall, red Mohawk brushing the ceiling, a grin like a jagged slash cutting through his beard. Ice arrived next, frog-leaping over a surprised skinhead before pulling a front flip and stopping, unholy glee on her face and speed twitches in her muscles. Then came Takuan, his hair pulled up in a traditional Samurai topknot, with Halflife and Molly and Rake. Viper arrived last, with the Rat, a slim, knife-edge beauty next to a juggernaut cannonball. The Rat dropped the duffel bag he was carrying while I embraced Viper.

Eleven Livewires in front of McDonald's Friday night before midnight, a real circus, raising hell and what a show. Scalpel of course didn't show, viz. the broken leg. Viper finally got everyone smoothed out and we moved into one of the small side tunnels, empty except for a few junkies on the nod, to discuss tactics and game plan.

We huddled around Viper as she gave us the brief.

"Y'all heard about the security lockup," said Viper, "on account of Eastwood. Looks real nasty, Mirrorfaces

52

in threes every block with burpguns, some even have lethal ordnance, trigger-happy motherfuckers too.

"So this how I figure it. We do the run. Get amped and wired, destroy on the Champs. Show the Uptown sheep some real class, real loco style."

"Hardcore, man," drawled the Rat. "Livewire madness, fuckin hardcore."

"As for the Faces . . . I scored some flak jackets off Name, Swedish Teflon threads, jackets and pants and hoods. That should cover us good as far as the needles go, so burpguns no problem. As for the live shit . . . Just stick to the crowds and you'll be cool. Use the Suits for cover. Faces won't dare blow away their paychecks."

Snickers as Viper continued. "We start at the top and do the run spread out on both sides, full speed. Cover your asses, head for the Metro at the bottom, and cut your GFs cause the Faces will be looking for skaters. We meet at Trocadéro, on the upper plaza. Questions?"

"What do we do with the flak threads?" asked Halflife.

"The threads roll up real tight, so strip 'em and shove 'em in a pocket as soon as you get a chance, no problem. That all?" She pumped her fist. "Let's do it. Time to strut our stuff."

"Skate or *die*," I added, lips peeled back over my teeth, a feral grin.

Viper dumped the contents of the duffel bag out and started passing them out. Smooth Teflon jackets and leggings, acrylic-spattered and spray-painted and stenciled for decoration and disguise, tight straps around the legs looking really razor. We pulled and strapped them on, in silence, like medieval warriors, our suits of armor.

We took off in formation, Viper at point, the rest of us clustered behind, exuding the eerie menace of total silence. The crowd parted in front of us, even slasher streetdrek moving back. Halflife rattled off strings of sixteenth notes on the walls with her drumsticks, sharp, fast clacks of wood on tile and glass.

We entered the Metro at the huge Les Halles hall. We picked up speed to jump the turnstiles, Ice and Jester doing handstand flips; shocked face of the controller in his booth registering briefly in peripheral as I leapt, knees tucked up and arms thrown out. We slowed down inside the hall, taking it easy near the Mirrorface patrols, saving the trouble for later. A harried RATP controller started babbling at us as we skated by him, "Regulations forbid—" only to stand open-mouthed in shock as Bozo snarled at him.

We skated to the other end of the hall, cutting through a sea of turning faces, and jumped the second set of turnstiles, into the Tunnel. The three slidewalks were mobbed, Uptown glitterkids out scamming the club scene, Suits coming home from their mistresses, streetdrek hustling for drugs and kicks. We picked up speed, pumping hard, silently separating into two rows. One after the other, we jumped up onto the metal dividers. We sped down them in two long files, oblivious to the banks of vidcams, and only jumped down onto the slidewalks when we reached the thirty-five-degree up ramps, too steep to skate.

Inside Chatelet, up an escalator, then out onto the Metro platform, direction Porte de Neuilly.

I sat down while the others clowned or danced around, running a last check on the soundscape. I'd downloaded it into my armdeck and key it to two GF motion sensors taped to my boots. The melody sections would be run individually off each sensor, providing two separate melodic patterns, while the hardbeats and the bass riddims would remain unified, area effects. The program was set up to start the scape at a specific point, a meter to the left of the Metro exit near the Arc de Triomphe. I tested the implant connection, making sure it was correctly rigged for directional displacement; this allowed the scape to remain fixed with respect to the implants, so it wouldn't rotate if I turned my head. I ran through the alphanumerics, checking section emplacements. All systems came up clear.

The Metro floated silently into the station with a rush of displaced air. We got on, the packed crowd somehow finding space for us, maximum power trip and already the preliminary adrenaline tang of fear, heart pumping out a 4/4 bass-drum beat, ice sensation in the bowels, silvernet tingling through the nerve paths. Stations flitted by, islands of light in the long, dark tunnel, the train sprewing out passengers and ingesting new ones at each stop.

We reached Charles de Gaulle-Étoile and poured out, instinctively converging together like oil particles in a glass of water. We pulled a hard, fast run through the corridors, dodging frightened peds, triggering the first adrenaline rush. My stomach tightened, caught in the grip of a familiar claw, fear rush racing down neural pathways toward leaden muscles, caressing them, tetanizing them . . . Speed itch building up, demanding, pushing . . .

We emerged from the Metro at the top of the Champs Elysées, on the left side. The avenue stretched down before us, Paris's main spinal stem; a wide gash between the buildings, filled with people and skimmers, light and movement. A few of the spuds fired rockets up their noses; I ignored a proffered derm, preferring the purity of the adrenaline high, the clean run. We all gripped hands, snarling "Skate or die," then six of them crossed the avenue, to run the other side. I pumped my fist at them, blowing a kiss to Mara as he looked back over the traffic.

We fanned out across the wide sidewalk, a few peds looking puzzled and reflexively nervous at the mere sight of streetdrek wildstyle. I took my place a meter from the Metro exit and activated the soundscape. A few notes echoed as I skipped in place, all hopped up, wired, ready to run.

I was run leader for this side, Viper for the other. I searched for her across the avenue, found her, locked eyes. We raised our arms and counted off together: One. Two. Three . . .

"*Do it!*" I yelled, as I catapulted myself forward, feet scrambling madly for acceleration, jumbled notes from the scape before I settled into the groove.

I jumped off the edge of the first sidewalk, feet together, guitar pitches rising with my leap, following me and pushing me. I landed on the driving bassbeat, no percussion yet, feet skimming over cobblestones. Muscles taught and singing, *gotta move gotta run faster faster* . . . I jumped entirely over the next sidewalk, a small island, guitar solo parabola, landing on bassbeat again, pulsing as I pumped, high-note guitar runs following the crossovers.

Halflife cut in front of me as I hit the next stretch of sidewalk, yelling "You're bogging, dude! Move!" This was a hard stretch, very thin, running alongside the tunnel entrance that channeled traffic off to the Porte Maillot. I followed Halflife down the strip, slaloming around trees, each one a snare-drum roll thundering as I cut around it; the tunnel a horn section, motif repeating on my left every ten meters.

I glanced left and saw that Bozo and the Rat had risked the thin pedestrian sidewalk on the other side of the tunnel. They streaked through the panicked crowd, howling crazed war cries, peds scattering and diving into café tables.

I started concentrating on my own survival as I reached the tunnel entrance, blocking out everything but the immediate environment. I saw my first Mirrorfaces as I cut across the traffic. A skimmer slewed out of control and plowed into another one, setting off a chain reaction of torn metal and shattered Plexiglas across the avenue.

An alto sax solo cut in over the hardbeat as I hit the sidewalk low, a spidery spray of burpgun needles fanning over my head, a few slivers spattering harmlessly on my hood. A glitterboy next to me dropped, caught in the fire, out for eight hours. I zigzagged hard down the parking strip that stretched along the whole avenue between the street and the sidewalk, the horn solo pulling fast runs up and down as I cut left-right. The lines of trees on either side beat out additional percussions, each tree a conga accent, keeping time . . .

Two hundred meters flashed by like that, sax solo and percussions dropping at every side street, leaving me suspended in bass; my heart pumping madly, *gotta move gotta move* . . . My ego vanished along with the shocked or terrified ped faces as I became immersed in a world of motion and insane geometry, aware of nothing except the obstacles in front of me and the feel of the ground under my feet and the music inside my head . . . Vectors of silvered movement, angles of electric attack . . .

. . . .
. . . .

Mirrorface in front of me, hasn't even fired yet. I bend low, dropping my center of gravity, cutting hard right and shooting around him. I see him frantically thumbing his throat mike before he vanishes, melting into the irrelevant world.

A skimmer now, slim Porsche, braking madly in the side street, too late to avoid it. I feel my leg muscles tensing as I fold tight and jump, using every iota of skill and momentum I have to clear the hood; an animal roar of triumph escapes my lips as I shoot past the windshield, crucified on a cross of Speed, mad bass notes running impossibly high and holding for an infinite second at the apex of the jump before falling . . .

I nearly slam on landing but stay up, cutting around two startled pleasureboys, howling uncontrollably now as I rip down the strip. I start crisscrossing, sax melodies interweaving and intertwining, maddening, the hardbeat pushing me on, on . . . I am totally gone now, beyond pleasure or the rush, movement and geometries my only reality. Crazed demon on the loose, mayhem and chaos the trip, Speed the Word. . . . .

Reality hit me in the face with the serene confidence of a brick wall staring at an incoming Ferrari. I felt a huge jolt in my left foot and went flying, gravity sucking me down, concrete rushing up toward my face, howling hysterically before

IMPACT

Gray haze, faint salty taste in my mouth, scape gone haywire, distant voices and laughter—

"Oh wow, wipeout!"

Giggles—

Knife edge of the pain cutting through the haze, knee and hip and shoulder, the animal cry of injured meat—

The laughter was mine, I realized, but not the voice—

I licked the blood on my lips and looked up.

A young girl, Uptown gadja, expensive clothes. *Very cute.* Then I chuckle, amazed, *The cock thinks first, then the brain cuts in.*

She bent down and gently touched me. "Are you okay?" I staggered up then, and she guided me and leaned me against a parked car.

I scanned the crowd that clustered behind her, nervous and excited. Glitterboys and glamourgirls, supermarket beauty and fashion magazine clothes. I looked back at the girl in front of me and was stunned by the contrast. She had incredible style, poise; her face was the work of a true artist, small, calculated imperfections setting off elegant, thin lines. Nothing like the media-derived face-of-the-week of the others.

Then I saw the muscle, a large, conservatively dressed man, lineshaved head, closing in on us, snarling. He reached out to pull the girl back, "Miss Angélique, I think—" but she waved him back, curt gesture of a person used to power. He backed off and stood with his hand twitching toward his armpit.

The girl looked at me. "Are you all right?"

"I think so . . ." I tried to wipe the blood off my mouth, smearing it some more. I flexed my shoulder, my leg, feeling out the pain—

—And realized as I was doing so that I hadn't hit a pothole at all. The fuckin GF unit on my left boot had shorted out, dead, overload.

"Fuck!" I spat out, exasperated.

"What?" Concern on her pretty face.

"Nothing . . . Fuckin skate shorted out. Hate it when that happens." I bent down and thumbed the restart circuit on the back of my boot, feeling the adrenaline starting to pump up again, ripping through the haze and numbing the pain.

Suddenly the girl grabbed my head between her hands and kissed me, hard. Her tongue darted in my bruised mouth for long seconds. At first I stood frozen, totally caught by surprise; after a beat I warmed up, returning the kiss. Someone in her entourage tittered.

She finally pulled back, smiling, and I saw the backs of three Mirrorfaces, galloping down the strip, waving burp-guns.

"Why?" I asked.

"Cause you're cute." Pert little smile, a moue.

I rekeyed the scape and started to slide away, my body insistent, singing its adrenaline song, *gotta move gotta move* . . .

"Look, love to stay and chat, but I gotta run, gotta move . . ."

"Where can I find you?" she called out as I passed the bald muscle and the entourage.

"Forum," I yelled, and I was off, back in the flow, the groove. Legs pumping, the high, the madness taking over, possessing me. I was howling again as I shot by the three Faces, their needles spattering on my back like raindrops. Alto sax at full throttle, insistent, blooddriving hardbeat, musical peaks driving my every dodge and swerve . . .

The ultimate marriage of geometry and meat; trajectories and music, angles and muscular response, more precise than a deck, flawless. Speed and music, wildcore; an unholy interface of music and body, the dance creating the music, the music driving the dance; high-speed symphony, wild, berserk . . .

My frontal lobes slowly regained control as I sped around the Rond-Point. A Mirrorface leveled a gun at me as I shot toward him, a MAS 9mm. assault rifle. I went in low, under the gun, keeping a group of peds behind me to make him hold his fire, and saw myself leaping at me in his visor as I body-checked him, sending him flying. I snatched the MAS out of the air as I crossed the street in front of the Drugstore Publicis and fired wildly in the air, peds ducking and scattering. The soundscape was dead now; I had crossed over the edge, no longer on the Champs. I fired a burst through the plate window of the drugstore, high so as not to hit anyone, diners screaming and falling under a rain of bullets and broken glass.

The streets around the Parc Marigny were crawling with Faces. I realized I'd never make it past them on skates, not enough peds to provide cover, and this close to the Elysée Palace they'd all be using live ammo. I looked around as I drove into a clump of bushes; no one was looking my way, the peds and diners across the street still screaming, a squad of Faces running toward the drugstore.

I tore off the flak suit, rolled it into a ball, and frantically dug a hole in the dirt, using the MAS as a shovel. As soon as it was deep enough, I dumped both the suit and the MAS in it, shoveling dirt back over them with my hands. I cut the glide units and crawled through the bushes; I peered out carefully, scanning the empty street corner, before slipping out and dusting myself off. I was wearing black battledress and a purple T-shirt, not quite triff enough for this neighborhood but at least clean enough to not be conspicuous. I hoped that anyone seeing me would mistake the warpaint for some new Uptown fad, the latest in chic. Only a Mirrorface would be that dumb, of course, but they were the only ones that mattered anyway.

I had exited the park on the far side, by the rue Gabriel. I turned left on Matignon, heading back toward the drugstore and the chaos. I melted into the panicked crowd as Faces ran back and forth. Ashen-faced peds, some crying, some in shock. Publicis was a mess, the whole front-plate window gone, glass fragments everywhere, overturned tables, some blood and vomit. *Hardcore.* An ambulance was parked in front, lights flashing, the medicals in back dressing cuts. It looked like no one was seriously hurt. *Good. Maiming civilians isn't part of the trip.*

I walked up to the ambulance and had a medical look at my face. I had split my lip in the slam, and my chin and lips were still covered with smeared blood. He hastily cleaned my face with alcohol, wiping the warpaint at the same time, and dabbed some gel on my lip. I thanked him and walked away.

I stopped at the edge of the Rond-Point and looked around. I could see pools of disturbances in the crowd across the circle and up the Champs, characteristic telltale of Livewire mayhem. Faces were running around like ants on a destroyed anthill, aimless and manic, shouting confusing orders at each other, useless. A whole squad stomped by, in full Kelvar body armor, heading up the Champs. I couldn't see any other Livewires, so I assumed they had all melted into the woodwork like me, heading up Avenue Montaigne or Franklin-Roosevelt toward the river.

I walked back up the Champs a bit, toward the Franklin-Roosevelt Metro station. Peds were scurrying and yammering, shocked and confused and disturbed, aware of some major disturbance but unsure of its nature.

I descended into the cool Metro station and jumped a turnstile, ignored by the controller in the booth. I walked down the steps to the platform feeling five meters tall, an elemental God, calm and unaffected by all the chaos and confusion I'd sown. I basked in the high on the platform, heartbeat slow and steady but the muscles still jumpy and leaden, still singing. I rode the train to Trocadéro like that, detached, flying, inhuman.

I realized something was wrong as soon as I saw the other Livewires on the Trocadéro. They all stood there, frozen, depressed, deadened. An icy claw squeezed my guts as I walked toward them, a different claw this time, a different fear, sharper and much more painful. I scanned the group frantically for blue hair, seeing only Bozo's red and Halflife's green. Each step came separately, like the frames of an old filmstrip lying in the dust.

Viper came toward me and hugged me, tears on her face, saying nothing, words unnecessary.

"How?" I asked, still not reacting, in shock I suppose.

"It was a Mirrorface, man," she sobbed. "Shot him in the face, needle must have gotten under his hood. He fell forward, into the street, a bus rammed him. I put a knife in the Face, but it was too late, oh man, I'm so sorry . . ."

I held her tight while she cried. I looked at the other Livewires, saw the grief on their faces. They must have wondered why mine was frozen, no emotion either inside or out yet; but none of them said anything, none of them moved. Halflife's eyes cried at me as I let go of Viper and walked away.

I locked the door to the pad, set up the answering program, got undressed, and took a shower. When I got out I pulled on a pair of rolled-up fatigues, still dripping wet. I clawed through my drug stash, came up with two derms of Blue Cloud and pressed them against my neck. They would take awhile to come on, so I also snagged a small ball of opium. I went to the kitchen and put a piece of the O in a spoon. I cooked it over a small Bunsen I kept for that purpose, melting it. I poured the goop into a small cup and cut it with hot water, thinning it out. Then I flicked open my butterfly knife, cut my left thumb, and dipped it into the solution, getting the O into my bloodstream as fast as possible. I barely felt the burn.

I felt the first mental tugs as I cleared away the center of the pad and programmed the music library, selecting the appropriate pieces. I was holding my grief in check the whole time, locking it in. I wanted everything to be right before I let it explode and possess me.

I sat in the middle of the empty floor, in a lotus, and waited. As the O hit me, I cued the music and gave myself over to the Demon.

My fucking fault
It was my fucking fault
Mara . . .
I should never have gotten you into this shit
My fucking fault. . . .

And the music started, Bach's Toccata in D Minor, and as the huge organ music swelled out of the Bose speakers, filling the room with sound, I went over the Edge I'd flirted with for so long. I dissolved into tears and agony, pain and grief, rolling on the floor, crying, hugging myself into a fetus; then rolling back, bursting into hysterical laughter; then into tears again. My face sopping wet, my muscles and fibers coursing with the grief. I screamed, ran, jumped. I danced, a different dance from the Livewire dance, the dance of Mara's death, giving myself wholly to the Demon that was just starting to haunt me; surrendering to the pain in hope of washing it out, exorcising it.

The piece ended, and the deck cut to Jimi Hendrix's "Voodoo Chile" (the long version), its guitar lines twisting through my brain, mapping the convoluted lobes, playing with my muscles, making love to me, manipulating my synapse/neuron/interface like a puppeteer.

I lit a cigarette as Bauhaus' "Bela Lugosi's Dead" came on, gothic masterpiece, death dirge for the old vampires; make way, old horrors, for the new generations. They're meaner and sharper and they got that Edge, so clean, so sharp, that razor's Edge. I lay on the floor, spread-eagled, the burning cigarette soon forgotten in my lips, calming down a bit, losing myself in the sad and melancholic chant.

And then came *The Requiem*, by Wolfie Amadeus. My mind exploded as the Cloud kicked in, lost and rushing through an infinite space of melting crystalline structures. Mental free-fall, thoughts slipping away like quicksilver. No reference point, no anchor, nothing for the thoughts to hold onto and grow off of. I was lost in the void, streaming out, and finally looping back to my only anchor—

MARA!!!

And the grief, the pain, the agony, indistinguishable from ecstasy in its infinite intensity. Mind flying in circles, shooting out and slowly looping back again, accelerating, as if pulled in by gravity, back to the Demon, back to Mara.

Dies Irae, dies illa,
solvet saeclum in favilla . . .

Neurals pathways warping, twisting. Bursting, writhing, screaming. Pain . . .

Mara . . .

Fireworks inside the eggshell skull, brain trying to burst out through neon-lit sutures. The rest of the body simple meat, flinging itself onto walls and floor, vainly trying to cope with the mental pyrotechnics.

Meat, blood, bones, wrapped around an awareness, a window through which *something*, sometimes called the soul, sometimes called Atman, sometimes called Ego, observes the world and reacts to it. This particular awareness calls itself Lynx (Me) and it cries for another awareness once called Mara (Not Me) for a closed window which opened on a universe that no longer exists since that which observed it is gone.

Lacrymosa dies illa
qua resurget ex favilla
judicandus homo reus . . .

My face was smeared with tears and blood, my body bruised and cut. My tendons were taut cables, and ripples of energy played through them. My hands were clenched open, and the muscles of my back chased each other under the skin.

The music ended, at last, and I screamed. My mind, still a chaotic storm of jangled neurons, actualized, and the transcendental grief became human, and therefore even worse. I screamed again, and ran toward the window, bursting through it, shattered glass and my hurt but unfeeling meat falling to the pavement fifteen meters below, bouncing off a parked car onto the concrete. I rolled into the gutter, filthy water and mud mixing with the blood, totally gone, totally lost, Demon's puppet.

MARA! MARA MARA MARA MARA MARAAAAAA!
AAAAAAAH!

oh mara friend/lover, dead mara friend/lover/dreamer you'll dream no longer. dead battered body in a cold morgue, brain flatlined and extinct, information and memory erased, emotions terminated, oh pale mara what is death to you . . .

my fucking fault. . . .

"Hey deuce, you okay? Hey? Well, maybe not . . ."

Sudden shock. My mind snapped toward the intrusion, the crazed dance of the Ego and the Demon abruptly interrupted. I looked up, and my uncomprehending eyes saw a young girl, a blood, with her hair shaved on one side and a stud in her nose.

"Hey, man, you need help. Looks like a pretty bum trip, no? Here man, let me help you."

She picked me up by the armpits, ignoring the mud and the blood soiling her clothes.

"Looks like you came out that window up there. 'S that home?"

I didn't answer. Blank. My body functioning, my eyes seeing, my ears hearing, but not understanding, not processing. Mental cruise control, brain on autopilot, only a faint whisper echoing through my skull . . .

My fault . . . ?

She dragged me to the wall near the door, and bent down over the magnetic lock. Scratching noises. The door clicked open. She picked me up again, her head under my armpit, and carried me inside, up the stairs. She stopped again by the door, did the lock—one-handed this time—and entered. She whistled and the main lights came up. She stopped in the middle, looked around, spotted the bathroom, and dragged me there. Inside, she turned on the shower—cold water only. She undressed me, like she would a child, tenderly. I stood there, swaying, unprotesting, mute. When she pushed me into the shower, though, I gasped, finally reacting to the freezing water. She washed me, efficiently, gently cleaning my cuts. I felt the first returning flicker of intelligence as I came out.

"Mara . . ." I moaned.

"Is that your name? I'm Domino."

"No . . ." I wrapped a towel around my waist and padded out, still dripping. "Mara's dead . . ."

She said nothing, understanding, and followed me out into the main area. I went over to the library and punched in Miles Davis's *Sketches of Spain*. I turned around and faced her as the first tentative notes of Miles's dry trumpet floated through the air, Spanish sadness and machismo.

"I'm Lynx. Thanks for bringing me back."

I woke up around noon the next day, my brain greasy and soggy like day-old scrambled eggs, my body frantically firing off pain signals to said brain. I sat up on the futon, and suddenly realized I had slept on the right side of the bed only; the left side was empty. Grief rose up my throat, a knotted ball, but somehow I was able to control it, to tuck it into a corner of my mind, to temporarily set it up like a display I could look at but not be hurt by—at least not too much.

Then I noticed the girl, stretched out on the old couch in the corner. She was wearing a red T and bright, multicolored boxers, the rest of her clothes bunched up on the floor. I got up, found a pair of leather pants, pulled them on, and limped over to where she slept—suddenly realizing exactly how much I'd messed up my leg. I looked down at the girl and realized she was probably all of fourteen, if not less. Judging by the state of her clothes, she was also poor, probably a squatter: streetdrek. *But not normal streetdrek.* Most spuds would have slit my throat and ransacked the pad instead of helping me.

I limped to the kitchen, wincing at each step, and started fixing breakfast. I was starved, so as the coffee machine dripped, I mixed some batter and started frying some *pain perdu*, French toast it's called Statesides. I had already made two when a voice at my side startled me:

"That coffee smells great, deuce. Is it ready?" Her accent was distinctly British.

"Uh, yeah, it is."

I found a not-too-dirty cup, rinsed it, and poured her some.

"Here."

She smiled.

"Thanks."

"Your name's Domino, right?"

"Yeah." She sipped the coffee. "And you're Lynx."

"Yeah. Let's have breakfast," I added, dumping two more of the French toasts out of the pan and turning it off.

"To get over a hardcore crash&burn," I said, emphasing my point by shaking my fork, "you can*not* beat French toast and coffee." The Naked Pagans' first album, *Trip Naked*, wailed and pounded in the main room, violent and depressing.

"I could see that, yeah." Domino, following my example, had drowned her French toast in ersatz maple syrup and was now frantically shoving the mess down her throat, trying to beat me to the last piece.

"Hey, hey, slow down, kid, you'll choke. I can make more if you want some."

"Yeah?" Suddenly her smile turned into a frown. "Hey, and stop calling me 'kid,' copy?"

"How old are you?"

"I'm thirteen, spud. So what?"

"I'm twenty. So I can call you 'kid.' Now ziplip and eat that shit."

We ate in silence for a while. Soon the pain started gnawing at my barriers, filtering through my thoughts. *Mara* . . . I stood up abruptly and went to fry more French toast.

Domino looked up when I slammed the hot pan on the table. She put down her fork and studied me.

"Are you okay?" she asked softly.

I fidgeted. "Yeah . . . No. I suppose not." I paced a bit. "Shit. I need a smoke."

I limped over to my worktable. My leg screamed at me angrily, *pain . . . It's only physical,* I yelled back silently, *only meat. Take it and shut up.* I rummaged around my desk and found what I was looking for: a small tin labeled TEA, a box of matches, and a long, beautifully carved pipe. I stomped back to the table and dropped into my chair.

"I tell you," I muttered as I opened the tin and smelled the contents moodily, "you just can't get any good hash since Afghanistan got the Big Wipe. This stuff is *shit.*"

I loaded the pipe and handed it to her.

"Here, get red."

"Radical pipe, man, where'd you get it?"

"It's an old opium pipe, from Thailand; it's about a hundred and fifty years old. My father sent it to me a few years ago."

"You got a father?"

"Yeah." I lit a match and held it to the bowl as she inhaled.

"You have to use matches for this, steels are no good. Like it?"

She nodded vigorously as she exhaled, a cloud of blue smoke filling the space between us. The unmistakable, pungent smell of the ganja permeated my nose. I took the pipe and sucked hard, dusting the bowl. I held the smoke in my lungs while I repacked the bowl and handed it over to her. I exhaled after half a minute, the familiar rush already grabbing my head. This shit was going to get me real strung-out, considering how I already felt, but the idea of being cold-sober terrified me. I wanted to stay fucked up for a while, only way I could deal. We smoked three more bowls before I put the pipe down and leaned back, stoned, the sharp pain receding to a dull ache.

I drummed on the table for a while, keeping time with the music. *Mara* . . .

I jumped up suddenly, rage welling up inside. I grabbed my chair by the backrest and smashed it against the floor, splintering it to pieces. I tossed the backrest toward the kitchen window. It landed in the sink with a crash of broken glass and plates. Domino watched me silently, her face serious, neutral.

"Fuck!"

I turned toward her with a sneer. "You wanna know what's really fucked? *I* taught him how to skate. I taught him to run with the fuckin Livewires. He spent two years trying to pull me *out* of the shit, and instead I pulled him down *into* it. And I fuckin got him killed!" I snorted. "Shit."

I threw myself against a wall and bounced off. "I fucking killed him! Everything I fucking touch turns to shit! *Fuck!!!*"

I stopped suddenly, the rage gone. I stalked over to the library and cut the music. When I turned back toward Domino my eyes felt wet. "Kid . . . Go away. I'm sorry . . . Come back some time, OK? I want to see you again. But not now."

Domino stood up, looking sad and wise. "It's smooth, man, I understand. Don't worry about me. I'll see you again." She walked over to the couch, picked up her remaining clothes, and shoved them into her bag. On her way out, she stopped next to me, and on tiptoes, kissed me on the cheek, wistfully.

"You take care of yourself, you read me?"

"Yeah, I will. I just need to be alone for a while. Stay alive, huh?"

"I will. Salaam."

She turned back for an instant as she passed through the door and looked at me. "Salaam, sad man," she whispered again, "I'll see you around." I barely heard her. And then she was gone, and I was alone again, with the Demon.

The next morning—or, more accurately, afternoon: hell. *Shouldn't have smoked that shit.* But I'd had to, only way to sleep, only way to get the grief and the Demon out of my head.

Sleep was heavy, dreamless, sweaty. Occasionally I reached out, pawed at the empty half of the futon, moaned. *Mara . . .*

Days go by, empty, numb, a blur.

Bits of memory, sticking out like jagged shoals . . .

Domino. I finally got off my ass and combed the Forum and found her. She was squatting on the fourth sublevel, sleeping on cardboard with a stolen cotton jacket for blanket and a small bag for a pillow. I invited her to move in to my pad, got her to accept by telling her I needed her, which wasn't really a lie. I rigged up a small room for her by hanging a blanket up around the hammock.

Domino, like a bright Mingus piece, lively and funky and wise. I'd never seen anyone, anyone Street at least, who behaved so playfully, so perpetually spunky, yet still exuded such an aura of *knowledge*. She wasn't just streetwise—all streetdrek are to an extent, or they don't live too long—she was *smart*. Evil old woman smart. Like the old blues goes: *Nobody knows what I know, they don't know, like I know* . . . Streetdrek by definition cultivate the Cool, the laid-back *look my brother no hands!* That, or the wired, frenetic pursuit of the Kick, the Trip, callous disregard for the meat and Mother Death; life in Edge City, some called it. Domino just got off on looking at things, on *seeing*.

One day I remembered how she'd gotten into my pad the night she found me in the gutter, and asked her where she'd learn to cut locks like that.

"In London, spud, from the best motherfucking lock picker in that fine city! Ghost, he was called. He was my mint—ment—?"

"Mentor?"

"Yeah, right, that's the word, mentor! I ran with Ghost for four years, he took care of me and taught me everything he bloody knew. Crud, I could of opened that door of yours with my feet, eyes closed."

"Bullshit."

"Bullshit my ass! I'll show you ratbait!"

"Awright, smooth, if you say so. So what happened to Ghost? Why are you here?"

"Well, we were doing this job, and the Ghost nailed these two sensors, but he missed a third and a laser fried him. I ran . . . and then I got some shit from a Paki gang he owed. So I split and hoboed it to here."

"Game Over, huh? I'm sorry."

"It's smooth, he had it coming, all the shit he pulled. I kinda miss the ugly bugger, though . . ."

We wander, we explore. I show her Paris, the Street, Downside. She tries to reinsert me into that illusion called life.

Pieces . . .

My rhythm: broken, gone, off-sync, off-beat. After a few days I tried to run the Street again; a quick hustle, biz as usual. I couldn't cut it. I'd lost the edge, the low. The spud I tried to set up a deal with could smell it; he backed out, no deal, can't trust a spud with no riddim and a Demon perched on his shoulder.

Shadows, too, haunting shades . . .

It took me a week to look at the piece Mara was working on before the run. When I finally decided to do it, I drank half a bottle of Mezcal and sat in front of the plain wood box for two hours without touching it. I finally reached out without thinking and flipped the cover back.

A rose. A black rose, with gleaming chrome dripping

from the thorns. I picked it up and examined it, pricking myself, a drop of blood staining one of the thorns. Un-identifiable materials, hard and light, maybe phrenolitic resin. The black petals, smooth as silk, with their labial curves; the long stem and the leaves, green; and the thorns, sharp and deadly, glittering chrome, technological monstrosities protruding from the flower. *Une Fleur du Mal.* The chrome a cancer, technological virus slowly corrupting the organic structure, growing.

I sat there for hours, staring at it, in silence, ignoring the blood dripping from my thumb. Finally I placed it on top of my library and walked out, into the night and the evil street, and watched people walking with jacks behind their ears and silicon in their heads and plastic in their chests and understood.

Fragments . . .

I took Domino to the Theatre de la Ville, to see a translated production of one of Dunn's early plays, *Black Snake Rising.* I went off on brainwalk, glazed, but she sat there, mesmerized, totally absorbed in the interplay of the characters, the identity ambiguities. Afterward she raved for two hours, about the acting, the script, the production. The next day she went out and stole a dozen plays and theoretical texts.

On my shoulder, a Demon, capering and gibbering and digging his claws into my flesh.

One night sticks out of the haze, the three weeks of dreams and fog.

I went out that night with Domino and Viper and Halflife and Scalpel—still on crutches—to Marley's Birth-day: an annual twelve-hour reggae memorial festival, at Bercy, all-night madness, ganja, and brain-mashing dub. They were all there, the skinny, wired DJs from Kingston, the ten-piece British bands with numbers tight as CD, the amped-up toasters with a head full of C and an endless flood of words. We danced for four hours, stoned out of our minds, next to dready rastas and sweaty streetdrek. Viper handed me a blue derm as I-King Jah came on. "Spin," she said. I shrugged, "What the fuck," and pressed it against my wrist.

I skanked, body's groove to the pulse of the riddim, and the Spin hit me like a psychedelic net of light, a quantum leap in perception. The input too strong, too fast, too loud. *Can't cope* . . . I decided to go ride the high outside, wait till it peaked before reentering. I frayed my way through the crowd, walls of sweaty black skin and dreadlocks and smooth muscles, made it to the exit, through the empty corridors, the whole stadium resonating around me to the wildbeat pulse, Viper catching up with me as I made it out—"Hey Lynx, you too high?" —out onto the concrete steps and the grass-covered artificial hill that ringed the stadium, the night, air, stars.

The blossoming paranoia attack evaporated as I sat with Viper on the steps and smoked a filterless Gitane. I put on my mirrorshades, retreating behind the mercury wall, hiding. The steps were crowded, though not nearly as much as the inside, and we sat and listened to the distant beat and smelled charcoaled shish kebob and ganja and scoped the crowd.

After a while a group of Rastas sat next to us. One of them, a young blood with a mane of dreads and a dozen bead necklaces, rolled a huge spliff, pungent indica, and passed it to us after sucking on it. We talked for a while, friendly vibes and the ganja intensifying the Spin high.

Suddenly Viper looked up and shouted, "Kari! Hey, Kari!" She turned to me and said, "Hey Lynx, wait here, will you? I'm gonna see that chica over there, she's a friend of mine."

"Yeah, no problem. I'll see ya."

Viper took off. I watched her leave and absently looked down at the step on which she'd been sitting and noticed that she'd forgotten her cigarettes. I grabbed the pack and shouted, "Yo, Viper! Your cigs!" But it was too late, she had vanished in the crowd.

I leaned back and glanced at the cigarettes I was holding. And saw a piece of bubblefoil protruding from the pack. I tugged at it and realized what it was.

"Shit! The Spin's in here!"

"You got some Spin?" said a voice behind me.

"Yeah, man, check it!" I said, thinking it was one of

the Rastas. Turning: "Must be fifty fucking hits!" and turned and saw:

Myself. My shades. Mirror within mirror.

Oh fuck. . . .!

The Mirrorface casually reached over, burpgun trained on my head, and plucked the pack out of my dead fingers. I felt the Claw grab my intestines and *squeeze.*

"What have we here?" I could tell from the Face's tone of voice that he was smiling. I started babbling, frantic, the fear paralyzing my neurons, "Hey, man, listen, it wasn't mine, I swear, it was some girl's, she left . . ." The Face snarled, "Come here, motherfucker!" and grabbed me and slammed me against a wall. I dimly noticed that the Rastas had vanished.

The Face patted me down and then started slapping cufftape onto my wrists. My mind was still stuck three reels back.

I can't believe I fucking told a Face I had some Spin! I can't fuckin believe it!

The Face took my arm and started dragging me toward an olive-drab armored Maria. I started babbling again. "Listen, man, I swear, it wasn't mine—"

"Don't tell me, punk," said the Face, nearly laughing. "Tell the judge when he nails you for five."

I can't fucking believe it! Tilted for shit that's not even mine! I'm fucked fucked fucked and it's not even mine.

Fear and loathing. Paranoia panic, and the Spin inside my head not helping much either. The Face opened the back of the Black Maria and tossed me in.

The inside stank of sweat and fear. I stumbled forward, my hands lashed behind my back, and fell on something soft.

"Cho, man, get the fuck off me!"

"Sorry, spud, chill."

I pulled myself up and slumped into a vacant place on the bench. The box was dark, a few slivers of light filtering through the airholes. I waited for what seemed like half an hour, half my mind flying and the other half scared shitless. Every so often the rear doors would open and another cursing body would fly in. When the holding

space was so full we could barely breathe, much less move, the wagon jerked forward and up and took off.
I can't fucking believe it . . .

The wagon stopped after an eternity of suspended movement. The rear hatch flew open and a voice yelled, "Out, assholes! Out!" All I could see was a nearby streetlight reflected in the Face's visor, and my mind latched onto it like a sick junkie to a scrap of paper that *may* contain a half-gram of the stuff. I only snapped out of the trance when a hand grabbed me roughly and pulled me out of the wagon, sending me sprawling on the concrete. I tasted blood in my mouth and started analyzing the taste. I was way beyond fear now, deep into the world of the drug.
Salty.
Return to reality, abrupt and painful. The Face pushed me through a door, into a world of bright light and noise and chaos. People were screaming all around me, and I had lost my shades at some point during the trip. A hand thrust me forward into the edge of a desk. I looked up into the eyes of a bored and irritated desk sergeant. The Face barked, "Name first name address!"
I mumbled, lost: "My shades, man, I need my—" and a gloved hand cuffed me across the head. I staggered and tripped over a chair. The hand caught me and threw me into the chair. It frisked me, came up with his wallet, and threw it to the desk sergeant.
"Here. Book him for dealing, Spin. Here's the evidence."
No! That's five fucking years!
I went through the booking procedures in a daze again. Fingerprints, holo, retinal prints. My only conscious thoughts were *Thank Ogoun I didn't bring my weapons tonight,* as they strip-searched me and tagged my belongings; and, over and over, like a scratched audio plate, *I can't fucking believe it . . .*
I suddenly realized someone was talking to me. I looked up, and saw a Mirrorface thrusting something at me. A Day-Glos orange something, psychedelic candy, fuckin wild.
I can't fucking believe this. I'm being tilted for possession and they give me psychedelic prison coveralls . . .
I stripped and put them on and let a Mirrorface lead

me into one of the holding tanks. Judging by the size, it
was probably designed to hold up to ten prisoners. There
were about sixty prisoners in it, I dimly realized, and the
other three tanks were just as crowded.

I shoved a bit at the crowd and finally managed to
secure a piece of wall, near the door, in the standing-
room-only cell. I looked out through the bars. I could see
the entire chaotic scene: Faces running around berserk,
the desk sergeant getting angrier and angrier as more and
more kids were dragged in, the terrified prisoners milling
around. I was so fucked up I only had to glance at a
person for my drug-fueled mental computer to give me a
complete rundown, subliminal clues coalescing into beautifully complete sterotypes.

*White skin dyed fancy hair clean hands purple nails triff
clothes.*

*Rich gadjo kid Neuilly sur Seine and slumming smoking
a joint near a Face gonna call his rich mommy and rich
daddy will call his friend in the Ministry and he'll be out
before the gig is over.*

*Oh fuck I can't believe this it wasn't mine five years
maybe seven and it wasn't even fucking mine . . .*

"Hey breed y'OK?"

"Five fucking years and it wasn't even mine . . ." I
realized I was mumbling out loud again. I turned and
started staring at my coveralls again, the fluorescent orange massaging my scrambled frontal lobes.

After a while the desk sergeant outside caught my
attention again. He was getting redder and angrier by the
second. A Mirrorface had dragged in five girls and was
standing there as the sergeant screamed at him.

"Fucking *roaches*! You assholes are dragging them in
for fucking *roaches*! Can you see how many fucking cases
I've got in those cells? Can you see? And you're dragging
them in for fucking *roaches*! Girls, too! I'm supposed to
put them in separate cells! Do you see any empty cells
here! Huh? Shit!"

He stopped screaming, and then turned toward the
first cell, mine. "Ah, fuck this!" He grabbed the cardkey
from the Face in charge of cells and opened the door. He
stood there, glaring, and then, pointing, yelled: "You!
You! You! You! Get the fuck out!"

Whaaat? Me?

"You, asshole! Out! Out!"

Nine of us made it out of the cell before the sergeant slammed the door shut again. Then he turned toward us. "Listen, punks! Arraignment is in two weeks, and you better be there or we'll fry your sorry asses! Now grab your clothes and get the fuck out of here! Now!"

I don't believe this this is just too *weird . . .*

A harried clerk gave me back my clothes and personal effects. I felt a crazed urge to ask the sergeant, *hey deuce, can I keep this orange suit here? It's just too cool.* Fortunately, enough basic-survival circuits were still functioning in my brain to squelch the thought and make me try to be as anonymous as possible.

"You!" Again, the claw, squeezing and twisting.

"Yes?"

"Here's your summons. You better be there kid, or—"

"Yes, sir, I will, sir, I promise, sir." *Like fuck I will.* The Beast knew as well as I did that the summons was going in the nearest waste bin. *So why the fuck are you letting me walk?*

My apartment was in my father's name—or in *one* of my father's names—and there was no other way they could track me down. But if I *ever* got tilted again . . .

Shit! I won't get a suntan for twenty *fucking years!*

I was still royally dazed and muddled when they kicked me out the doors. I stood in the street, still twisted.

Now what the fuck was that all about? What a weird fucking trip. I wonder? Nah . . .

These hallucinations are really getting out of hand. Should talk to Viper about it . . .

The next morning, burnt out. I rolled off the futon and mechanically brewed coffee, faint memories of a strange dream tugging at my consciousness. I saw the pink slip on the counter, and the chunk of memory bubbled up, bright and clear in my head like a flaring acetylene in a dark line.

Fuck.

So: I sit and stare at the black rose with the chromed thorns, and dream, dreams of blue hair, and speed, and death.

*   *   *

Three weeks. Dreams, shadows, pieces, fragments. A black rose with chromed thorns. Domino, a pixie. Dreams, and an empty bed. A Demon, too, relentless and nagging, clawing and dancing. Dreams, pieces of memory, like an ill-fitting jigsaw puzzle. A haze, a blur. Three weeks . . .

I sit and stare.

Mara . . .

Domino pulled me out.

She slipped in one night while I sat in front of the rose, brooding, lost. I felt her standing behind me even before she spoke.

"Lynx. Turn around."

She stood with her feet apart, wearing a dead serious, hard face. She slowly lifted her arm and held out her hand. Two green and black capsules lay in her open palm.

"Take one."

"What are they?"

"MDMA. Old psychoactives. You need a brain scrub, man, a good vacuuming to get all the shit and garbage out."

"I'm fine."

She exploded. "Like fuck you are! You're a fuckin braindead zombie, man, still stumbling around cause you're too dumb to figure out you're already dead! Eat one!"

I shrugged. "Okay." I picked one out of her hand and swallowed it. She grinned sharply. "Good." She ate the other one, her eyes never leaving mine.

"Now what?"

"Wait. It hits fast, twenty minutes tops. I'm going to take a shower."

I turned back to the rose as she walked away and picked it up delicately. I heard the shower go on. I sniffed the rose. It had no smell, which for some reason disturbed me. I put it down and leaned back.

I started feeling the first speed twitches as Domino came out of the shower. She pulled on a pair of black tights and a black tank top. She looked good, her body fully formed, lean and curved.

She tossed her head back and stretched. "I feel so *good*! I need music." She cartwheeled in slowmo over to the library and started punching.

The music came up loud, Gegensex, crystal-sharp hardbeat German dance music, all empty spaces and high pitches, the voice playing with and off the saxes. Domino ran forward and grabbed my hands, pulling me up.

"Come on! Let's dance."

I fell right into it, the speed in my blood synching with the hardbeat and pulling sensually on my muscles. We danced slowly and languorously, using our entire bodies, stretching the muscles, erotic pleasure . . .

We pressed against each other, back to back, hands reaching out and linking. We pulled each other's arms back and pressed our hips together, melting, tumbling.

Domino stopped when the music did and took my hand. She glanced at me, smiling, and pulled me toward the futon. I fell onto it and looked up as she peeled off her tank top and tights. She had a woman's body, wide hips and ripe, round breasts and a full bush between her thighs. She laughed, a crystalline tinkle meshing with the music. I felt wonderful, truly *happy* for the first time in years. She kneeled next to me and peeled off my pants, my hard-on lying on my tight belly like a steel bar. Her body slithered onto mine, over mine, along mine, water and music made flesh. A rush of erotic sensations, spreading through my body, running through my fibers, all in slow motion as if my neurons themselves had slowed down. I stretched ecstatically and hugged her, enveloping her, enfolding her, so small and smooth within the cage of my large, scarred body. I slid into her with a sigh, and she gasped, arching her back, and rolled over, pulling me on top of her without letting me out. I started pumping slowly, grinding myself into her.

Transformation, synergetic leap as the MDMA rolled in over the speed. I started pumping harder, violently. She grabbed hold of my arms, cabled trunks holding me off the bed, and opened up even farther, pushing up against me, helping me. She started coaxing me as I got more frantic, totally in the grip of the drug now, "Let go,

let go, come on, please let go, let go, please, let go . . ."
It turned into a litany, a soft chant in time with my
thrusts. I pushed, I rammed, and she sucked me in,
trying to pull me out of myself, to get me to—

Release. I exploded into her, in spasms, the nerve
pleasure of the orgasm washed out under the joy of
release. I fell back on the bed, gasping, blinking, heaving. Domino slid up next to me, curled up, her mouth
near my ear. I stared up at the ceiling, unseeing.

"Now just melt . . . Melt . . . Into the bed . . . That's
it . . . Melt . . ."

Slowly I relaxed, seeped into the bed, hypnotized,
muscles coming loose one after the other. I was totally *in*
my body, in the meat, animal consciousness, no conscious mind.

"Melt . . . Melt . . . Yes . . . Just melt . . . You don't
have to do anything, don't have to move, don't have to
think . . . Just melt . . . Breathe . . . Yes . . . Slow . . .
Calm . . . Melt . . ."

[ ]
Brainflex. My frontal lobes creaked into life, slowly at
first, like a rusty wheel being forced to spin, then faster. I
started to interface with the world again, put out tendrils,
reestablished lines of communication. I emerged out of
unconsciousness, into thought, data.

I sat up. Domino was still curled up, smiling beatifically.
I realized I was still under the drug, just over the rush,
into a slow flow now. Domino sat up and touched my
cheek.

"How do you feel?" Softly, softly . . .

"Great," I answered, and suddenly realized it was *true*.

"Talk to me," she said. "If you want to."

"I do." Everything was slow, dreamy. "Let me just get
some pants on. I feel like wearing pants."

"That's fine. There's plenty of time."

I stood up and pulled on my fatigues, rolling up the
legs to just under my knees. I smiled at Domino.

"Do you want some water? I'm thirsty."

"Yes."

I went over to the kitchen and poured two glasses of
water, letting the tap run a bit, waiting for cold water. I

carried the glasses back to the futon, turning on some music as I passed the library. I sat down in front of Domino and handed her a glass. She looked beautiful.

"Thank you," she said. We drank and put our glasses down. My jaw was clenched, teeth grinding involuntarily. I ignored it, characteristic speed side effect.

I started talking all of a sudden.

"I met Mara two years ago, at a party Downside. He was . . . different. I felt that immediately, as soon as I saw him. He wasn't like all the other spuds, racing after their dicks looking for the Kick. Shit, like me, for that matter. I was just another stonecrazed streetshit motherfucker, getting my rocks off on dancing with Mother Death.

"But Mara . . . He was a poet. I don't mean a writer poet, he didn't write much. Just a *poet* . . . An artist. It's sort of the wrong word, because these days art is just another biz, another hustle. Mara just did things for himself, or for his friends. He never sold anything; he just worked with all kinds of things, with beauty, expression. Like the rose, or like that, over there."

I got up and took the little Technics holoproj from the shelf. I brought it over to where we were sitting and triggered it. The holo shimmered into life, taking form.

An eye, a human eye, floating. White ball surrounded by trailing blood vessels and optic nerves.

"Look inside it," I said, "inside the pupil."
She looked in for a few seconds and then gasped.

"My face . . . It was there, and then it . . . melted. Even my skull, it turned to dust."

"I know. Keep on looking."

"Oh . . . The dust, it formed a flower . . . a rose."
She looked up. "It's beautiful," she whispered.

"Beautiful . . . yes. Poisoned, corrupt, tainted, but . . ." I stopped. "*La beauté dans le Mal . . .*" My voice trailed off into silence and memory. After a while I started speaking again.

"I don't really know why he liked me, at the beginning. Maybe cause I wasn't quite as mindless as the other spuds. And I liked him. Ah, shit . . ."

I wandered off, brainwalk again.

Domino touched my arm. "Look, you don't have to, if you don't want to."

"No. I *want* to talk . . . If you want to listen. I just don't know about what, really."

"Tell me about yourself."

"Myself?" I shrugged. "Why not? I mentioned my father to you, right?"

"Yes."

"My father was—still is, probably—a *gaijin* spy. He worked for the Americans, military intelligence, I think."

She grinned. "Isn't that sort of a contradiction in terms?"

"Yeah, I know, that's an old joke. Don't interrupt. Now, what was I saying . . . Oh, yeah, he was a spy. So one day he's in Paris and he meets this chica, a fullblood Cheyenne Indian whose parents had bagged the States in the 1990s cause of the Depression and shit. He fucked her. Then he fucked her over, cause a few weeks later he blew out of Paris and left her with only me—in her belly. No money, no address, nothing. A fake name . . .

"So I was born. And when I was four my mother got dusted in the Race Riots, the ones they built the Wall for, after. The Man stuck me in a fucking crèche, but I skipped out doublefast. At six I was out on the streets, squatting. That's when I met Viper. We slept together, for the warmth.

"I even ran with the Shiv Kids for a while, bunch of prepubescent psychopaths with a hard-on for anyone with hair between the legs." I snickered. "Nasty little fuckers. I bagged that fast cause I didn't dig that kind of shit. Most of them got dusted soon after, and the others probably greased themselves when they found out they were growing up.

"So I'm just hustling, eating when I can, more often frying my brains out on White Dust. The usual shit.

"Then my father showed up. Now, I was pretty pissed at the fucker, for ditching my mother and shit. So . . ." I shrugged. "I tried to have him shivved. Didn't work, though, he dusted two of the spuds I sent after him. I figured I'd be next, but . . . instead, he took off again, leaving me a deck, of all things. In one of the subfiles he left me a letter. He explained that he hadn't wanted to ditch my mother, but that he'd had to leave Paris doublequick when the shit went down between India and Pakistan. Remember, everyone thought then that the Chzechosovs and the Chinese would join the party, especially after some Hindu strays did the Wipe on Afghanistan, and then that'd be curtains for everybody. He didn't exactly *say* that he was MI in the letter, but it was pretty obvious. The bosses hit the panic button, and he had to go tear-assing all over the world, damage control for Uncle Sam and all that jazz.

"So a few years later, he finally makes it back to Paris. By this time Mom is meat and I'm gone. He didn't have any time, so he took off again. Finally, when I was fourteen, he was able to track me down—cause I got tilted by the Faces, actually, and he had tracers on to the Paris cop net, scanning the arrest files. And that was that. He wrote that he understood my initial reaction perfectly, he might've done the same, and he was sorry about my friends, but he couldn't control his reflexes fast enough to save the first two, the ones that he dusted. The others he left alive, by the way. So he wasn't pissed at me, and he'd even left me a present to try to make up for all the shit.

"Thing was, the sonovabith didn't even give me the present just like that. Instead he coded the data and hid it in the deck's hard disk. All I had to do was to learn how to punch deck, find the data, and break it, and I could collect.

"Sonovabitch was smart, you see. He saw that I was just a shit streetdrek, too dumb to live and too fast to die, and he figured that this way he'd make me learn *something* useful. Thing was, he wasn't smart enough."

"Why not?" he asked.

"I just hustled up some credit and got a tech to break it for me." I laughed. "Figured I fucked him good that time. Suppose I really fucked myself in the end, but hey, I was def stupid, so . . ."

"What was the present?"

"There were three, actually. One was the deck itself, that one over there, the Ashanti. The second was this pad. Permanent deed and utilities paid for twenty years—"

She raised an eyebrow. "You tried to dust this boy?

Shit, man, if I'd had a father like that I would *not* be hustling on these streets, let me tell you *that.*"

"Yeah, well, I figure he felt guilty and could afford it. Anyway, he gave me all this after I tried to waste him."

"So what was the third? A trip up the well or something?"

"No." I pointed at the heap of clothes next to the futon. "The armdeck."

"I don't get it. Why so special?"

"It's not *just* an armdeck. Friend of mine, name of Billy Name, an ordnance freak, told me it was a special model, developed and used by the American MI. That's why I think my father works for the U.S. Next to this baby the latest state-of-the-art Sony is kid stuff. This thing is a spy's all-purpose wet dream. Shit, it took me four years to learn how to use it properly. I don't even think I've figured everything out. The fucker forgot to enclose an instruction manual in the package."

"Maybe he couldn't get one. I mean, it must have been hard to score the deck itself. Tech like that is hard to come by."

"Yeah, you're probably right. Well . . ."

I leaned back and stared up absently.

"So what happened to you after he left? That was six years ago, right?"

"Yeah, it was. Well, for the next couple of years I just did my shit. I started getting smart around sixteen and kicked the Dust habit. Finally learned how to punch deck, too. Viper got me into it. Ha! We were gonna pull off this radical score through the Net. Break into the Beasts' central comp and wipe all the *casier judiciaires*, the criminal records and shit. Didn't work, but I learned how to punch, and I made a few scores after that.

"That was about when Viper and I started the Livewires. At the beginning, it was just a gag, you know, get some heavy status on the Street by showing how stone-crazy we could get for our kicks . . . and how good we were, too. But after a while it got real heavy; the more we did our shit, the more it became a Trip, the Livewire voodoo. It got real serious, skate or die, and all that.

"Mara wasn't even the first Livewire to get dusted. There were six before him—"

"Six?"

"Yeah, six of them. But it wasn't all that fucking important, you see, they were just these spuds, friends that got dusted doing their thing. It was part of the riddim, the riddim of the Street. You play, you die. That's where it's at, you know it. The Street's got a rhythm, a beat. You're just with it, and everything's cool, everything's in time.

"We weren't like those other chickenshit skaters at the Troca, Uptown surf assholes who painted "Skate or Die" or their jackets but didn't do jackshit except strut around on a marble plaza. We died for real.

"And then Mara got it too."

"I told you about Mara already. He was . . . like . . . translucent. We even used to call him Mara the Dreamer. He was into all this art stuff, went to museums all the time, read books, listened to music—I mean *real* music, not like the cyberpunk shit we get these days.

"After we started sleeping together, and he moved in, he kind of . . . pulled me in. Started to turn me on to all this stuff. See all those books over there? He bought them all, made me read them. He took me to the museums with him, to the underground theaters near Montparnasse. He just . . . started to show me all the beauty in life, stuff that wasn't the Kick or the Hustle but that was a trip anyway. He'd play me music, all kinds of music, everything from Mozart to jazz to the Eye to Alien Heat to the Sex Pistols . . . Joy Division, his favorite, so *intense* . . . And he'd stand there, and throughout the whole song he'd go frit giving me a running commentary of what I should be listening to, what was going on, what the musicians were *saying*. The bass solo here, down and down, the triplets on the piano there, soft, like a running bird but with the Power. The two-bar sustained note on the trumpet, and how the bass just rolled into it . . . Man, he was just so fucking enthusiastic, I mean, that's what he *dug*, what he breathed.

"And after a while I started getting into it, too. I started collecting old audio plates, records they were called, and building up a library in my deck. Stuff like the Velvet Underground, or Coleman Hawkins, or real old Japanese music, reed flutes and samisen. '90s digital symphonies, huge and infinite, written by one man but performed on banks of synths by a team of techs. Even stuff like Gegensex, the guys you put on.

"So Mara was laying all this stuff on me, and I was really digging it. And so after a year he got me into hardbeat. Just showed up one day with a console and some instruction software. I never found out where he got the credit for it. So he handed it to me and he said "Here. Do something. Make music." Ha. He never talked sideways with *anybody*. If he thought that you weren't doing shit he'd say so. Fuck Streetrules, Street politeness. So yeah, I became a console D.J. Lousy at the beginning, of course, till I got the hang of it. And then I got better, and now, you know, it's what I *do*. And I still wouldn't be doing shit if it wasn't for him.

"And then . . . Like I said. I taught him how to skate . . ."

I stopped talking and looked at her.

"Accept it," she said.

"What?"

"Accept it. Accept the pain, the guilt, and move on. You're stuck in a loop, and you're just eating yourself away. There's no confession no more, man, no absolution. Just get out of it. Go out again, get back in the world."

Silence. Then:

"I'll try."

ANGÉLIQUE

And then back to the world of the living, out of the shadows and the fragments of broken glass . . .

The Demon was still there, perched on my shoulder, but no longer harassing or clawing. He faded a bit, insubstantial ghost now, ethereal presence. I put the rose back into its wood box, strapped on my skimboots, and headed for the Street.

The first thing that hit me as I glided outside was the heat. It came down and closed around me like quicksand, suffocating me. I leaned against a broiling stone wall as my sweat glands turned into shower heads and drenched me. Eventually I stood up shaking off the sudden lethargy, and pushed off.

I skated to the Forum, flying fast and hard, but the edge was still gone, the Demon making me slow. I looked before crossing streets, no longer trusting my peripheral instincts, no longer reckless and wild. I absently gave the finger to some snarling driver, angry at still being close enough to hear him yell.

Entering the Forum was like plunging into a bath of mercury. It was even hotter than Topside, air conditioners stripped years ago by the streetdrek for spare parts. The crowd reinvigorated me, though. Colors, tensions, energy . . . I absorbed it as I walked down the dead escalator—GFs off—feeding, energizing. I dapped with some spuds I knew as I stalked the sublevels, reveling in the feel of the Street again.

I started hanging again, chilling out with Olric, getting red and listening to dub. One day we saw three skinheads slamming a cripple. We both stood up simultaneously, without a word, and tore into the skins. We beat the shit out of them, the old skills back like they were never gone. Afterward I held up one of the skins by the throat, against a wall, and fed him the line, "Ain't too cool to trash a crip, skin. Got no class, no style. Ya no see it?"

One day a few weeks later, wandering through the Forum . . .

I stopped at a newsstand, a recessed alcove tended by an old Arab, and examined the magazine rack. All the major papers had gone soft in he past ten years, running their issues online in the Net, but the smaller specialized sheets were still put out on glossy paper, pics and all. Dingy porno mags, pathetic streetdrek spreading their legs for a camera instead of a trick. Sports mags, null-grav fighters creaming each other up in the islands. Merc mags, for street razors and corporate mercs. My gaze lingered over those. When I was younger, I'd pulled slice jobs to buy these, and then spent hours huddled in a corner of the Forum, in the putrid light of the old neons, bypassing the articles and drooling for hours over the weapons and ordnance ads. I'd ordered a lot of stuff from those ads, over the years, knives and other fancy slicers. These days I preferred custom jobs, stuff from Max's, when I could afford it; and besides you couldn't order anything truly lethal from the mags. For the heavy ordnance, you had to have connections, good ones, especially these days with the Beasts cracking down on private firepower.

Bastards want to be the only ones with guns. They're scared shit.

Come to think of it, the Beasts *were* getting real paranoid these days, and not just about regular street activity; *that* was par. The scene at Marley's Birthday, for example, that'd been *truly* weird. No, this had a different smell to it, a smell as old as Paris itself.

Political.

Riots? I mulled that one for a bit. Not yet, not for a few more years. But the pressure was building up slowly, and there were few safety valves.

Fascist bastards can see it coming down the line. Five

years. They think they're gonna get their asses fried—and maybe they're right.

I smiled. I'd never really gotten into politics, but there was still time.

There's plenty of time—

Sounds of blood behind me suddenly, dreams of future revolutionary mayhem shattering like crystal and vanishing. A brief shriek, female, snarling grunts, the characteristic *snickt* of an opening switchblade. I turned around and saw three verminheads surrounding a girl, menacing, aroused. "Let's have some fun, sweetheart, no?" The girl looked street, too, at first, torn jeans, worn shirt, but I twigged to the details, fast. Makeup. Ironed shirt. Expensive laserpen haircut. Holes too neat, scissor-cut.

Uptown.

Fuck her. She comes here, decked like that, her tough shit.

She was on the ground now, the spud with the tattooed face catching her shirt, ripping. Cute little breasts, small, jutting, like oranges. She screamed, once, and suddenly looked at me, pleading.

Her face . . .

I recognized her, the memory like a glimpse of a few frames of old film on the cutting-room floor.

The girl . . . A voice above me on the Champs— "Are you okay?" An artist's face, a kiss while Mirrorfaces stomped by . . .

I ran forward, cobra snapping out, and clubbed the fist spud across the face before he even realized he was under attack. He dropped with a strangled cry, blood on the chrome stick, and I shifted into a wide bowed stance, ready for the spud with the knife.

A hand reached out from behind me and touched my shoulder while a gun snaked by my head. Long, black, deadly Mauser with a corrugated polysiloxane silencer. A muffled spit, and the spud with the tattoo dropped, a puppet with cut strings, neat little round hole between the eyes, not a lot of blood. The one with the knife tried to run; another spit, and he fell, sprawling meat on the Forum floor.

I stood there frozen while the verminheads died and then slowly turned, my head only, not moving the cobra.

He stood there, a thin smile on his narrow face, the gun still up though not pointing at me. I noticed the raincoat first, strangely enough, an expensive dark blue Burberry draped around him like a cape. A flash of memory, a line from an old song, "Never trust a man in a blue trenchcoat . . ." Then I saw the eye.

Red quartz lens, ridges of smooth Tombac; the curves of the inset flowing from the middle of his forehead, around the socket, tapering down the cheek. Baroque and decadant, an unnecessary extravagance, a piece of jewelry really, Berlin artistry.

He bent down without a word as I studied him, reached down with a gloved hand, and grabbed the spud I'd nailed by the hair. He pulled the head up, put the gun to the back of the neck, and shot him. He dropped the ruined head and smiled at me, the gun vanishing inside the folds of the Burberry.

I stood there the whole time, feeling like an idiot, my useless cobra in my hands. The girl was still curled on the floor, moaning. The man walked over to her, thin, pointed boots padding on the rubber floor coating, kneeled down, pulled her up. She had a bruise on her face and was still in shock, her eyes glassy; otherwise she looked fine.

He held her up by the shoulders gently, and then reached out and slapped her. "Mademoiselle de Seingalt?" She didn't react, so he slapped her again. I started to smile, getting the feel of his surrealistic scene.

She finally snapped out of it, eyes wide, "Leland . . .?"

He stood up, pulling her up with him. She wobbled a bit, but managed to stay up when he let go of her. I snapped my cobra shut and stowed it away.

"Miss de Seingalt, you know you shouldn't leave poor Lado like that. This area of Paris is not the safest place for a girl like you to visit alone—as you can see . . ."

That got a rise out of her. She stepped back and said, "Fuck off, Leland! I don't need your goddamn body-guards, or you! I was doing just fine . . ." She pointed at me. "He was about to save me, anyway!"

Leland turned, the thin smile again. "Ah yes. The gallant knight. Thank you, sir. It was very kind of you to step in as you did, even if it was . . . unnecessary. I'm sure some sort of appropriate monetary reward can be arranged."

You are a snake, my man, a fucking cobra. Wanna play games?

I returned his tight smile as I parodied his affected tone. "Ah, no thank you. Very kind of you to offer, but . . . a kiss from the lady will be enough."

He didn't answer. We stared at each other, his red lens seeming to strobe slowly, brighter. The girl suddenly stepped between us and glared up at him.

"That will be enough, Leland. You may leave us now. Thank you."

"I'm afraid I can't do that, Miss de Seingalt."

"Leland, it's an order. Leave. I can take care of myself, and I'm sure that this man here can defend my . . . virtue . . . as adequately as you can."

He stood in silence for a few seconds before answering.

"All right, if it's what you want." To me: "Young man, see that she doesn't come to harm. If anything happens, the consequences could be unpleasant." A bow, and then he was gone, the Burberry billowing around him.

I stared at the three corpses. The girl turned toward me and grinned. "Now, about that kiss . . ."

Later, at a café, Rue de Rivoli.

"So who the fuck are you?" A waiter glided up to the table, deposited our drinks on the clear glass table. I glanced at the printout. My beer cost more than four days' worth of food. Damn.

She lit a cigarette before answering, Benson & Hedges from a thin engraved silver case, the lighter a seamless Italian slab of steel.

"My name is Angélique. Angélique de Seingalt," she added as if that explained everything."

"That doesn't help me much." I smiled sarcastically. "I haven't consulted my Who's Who recently, I'm afraid. Besides," I added before she could say anything, "what the fuck were you doing in the Forum? That pet cobra of yours was right, you know. You're pretty dumb to strut around there decked like that. You got Uptown written all over you." ·

"I was looking for you." Totally deadpan.

Time for a change of subject. "Who is that guy, anyway? With the eye."

"His name is Leland. He works for me, takes care of my affairs, looks after me. My attorney, if you will."

"Nasty motherfucker. Didn't know that Uptown attorneys went around wasting people like that these days."

"His functions are a bit . . . broader than those of a simple lawyer. But he is far more than just a bodyguard, like Lado."

"That the bald muscle, the one on the Champs?"

"Yes."

I drank some of my beer, hoping she was planning to pay for it. I didn't have that kind of credit, not for a fuckin beer.

"So who are you?"

"My name is Angélique," she said with a smile, infuriating.

"I know that."

"My father invented the gravfield units. I own the Anubis Corporation."

My beer stopped in midair between the table and my mouth. I managed to regain control of my jaw before it dropped.

Man, when you step in it, you don't mess around.

Pierre-Henri de Seingalt, a theoretical physicist working at the CRNS, had cracked the problem of quantum gravity twenty-six years ago, in 2007. Instead of publishing a paper and getting a Nobel like he should have, he quietly resigned and started his own company, the Anubis Corporation. Using the family fortune, he hired a team of brilliant engineers and physicists to develop the practical applications of his discovery. Within three years he marketed the first glide unit and held every patent even remotely connected to the antigrav field. Within five years the Anubis Corporation was listed in Forbes' Top Ten Multinationals, and every vehicle and fancy furniture manufacturer in the world was going float. Glide units were cheap, small, and practical, though a tricky inverse-square problem made them highly impractical for anything larger than a truck (or a tank, as the

Pentagon discovered to its dismay when it was forced to scrap plans for floating battle fortresses).

Pierre-Henri turned financial control of his corporation over to a board of directors and retired at age thirty-two. He spent the next three years supervising the construction of a monument to his glory: the Anubis Pyramid, the only floating building in the world. The bulk of the pyramid contained the gravfield generators that held up both the pyramid itself and the tip, which floated above the truncated body and contained de Seingalt's private apartments. The whole thing looks exactly like the pyramid on the old U.S. one-dollar bills, especially at night with all the floodlights. Critics lambasted de Seingalt for wasting his money on a building the size of the Louvre with the living space of a large loft. Pierre-Henri laughed at them and retreated inside his creation, which floated randomly over various seas, usually in international waters.

Rumors of madness, decadence, and depravity drifted out of the pyramid over the next couple of years. Eventually the Corporation announced Pierre-Henri de Seingalt's death, along with his wife's. There were rumors of a double suicide, or of murder and *then* suicide. Ownership of the Corporation—it had remained private, rich enough to not have to issue stocks—passed on to de Seingalt's two children, a twin brother and sister, about fifteen at the time. The brother had died a year or so ago of an overdose. The sister was sitting across the table from me, casually sipping a rosé mixed with Perrier.

I willed my arm to move and drained my beer. She smiled again, Uptown cynical smile mixed with a curious innocence.

"By the way. What is *your* name?"

We had dinner at Enka's, an ultra-fashionable sushi restaurant in the 8ème, behind the Elysée. It was nestled in the basement of an old *hôtel particulier*, in a small, dark back street; faded white paint and a small, unnoticeable sign. For the cognoscenti only . . .

The headwaiter greeted her by name, of course, as we descended stone steps into the cool white light of circline fluos. Varnished black wood paneling, smooth oak floor, expensive prints on the white walls: a tasteful blend of corporate chic and traditional Japanese aesthetics, the favored blend of Uptown's jaded elite these days.

The waitress that guided us to a private tatami room in the back was obviously a *gaijin* under her white facepowder and her surgically sculpted epicanthic folds. She wore a red *atsuita* with an autumn field design, belted in the traditional manner with an embroidered obi.

She kneeled to slide the hand-painted paper screen open, and we removed our gloveboots before entering. Angélique was wearing a slinky backless Agnés B. dress, royal purple, cut very high over the hips. She'd bought it that afternoon in one of the dozen Champs Elysées boutiques we'd been in—boutiques that I'd previously only noticed, on crazed speed-fueled nights, as potential targets for a little bit of the old ultraviolence. Her streetdrek outfit had gone into the trash as we left the store, a small twinge in the back of my mind rapidly squelched as I remembered she'd paid for the beer.

We sat cross-legged on the tatami, separated by a smooth, long table of lacquered wood. The waitress brought us bitter green tea in antique *kensan temmoku* black stone tea bowls. We sipped it slowly, Angélique playfully toasting me, eyes glittering over the rim.

Dinner was served on a carved wooden boat, dozens of artistically sculpted nigiri and maki pieces. The sake was hot, expensive, and formally poured for us into the small porcelain taster's cups: bull's-eyes at the bottom of the cup to verify the quality of the sake: if the edges are sharp, it's good, if not . . .

The edges were sharp and the sake delicious, intoxicating, the tail glowing inside the throat for long seconds after drinking.

Intoxicating. A good word for Angélique, that, smooth pale brown mulatto skin, strong, sexy muscles alive beneath the skin. Hard and soft in all the right places, from what I could see, enough to replace the feel of Mara's body maybe . . . I hoped. I remembered the feel of her body against mine as she'd kissed me that night on the Champs when Mara died, and I had to shift my legs uncomfortably in the loose pants.

We ate and drank, exquisite food, our chopsticks hovering over the array of delicacies before dipping and then slowly rising, helpless prey caught in the wooden clamps, toward the other's mouth. We fed each other and got drunk, endless stream of sake, that wonderfully bright sake high.

We staggered out eventually, laughing and giggling, holding each other up. *The only way to leave a sushi restaurant . . .* I leaned against a wall to regain my balance and she slid up against me, hardsoft body molded against mine, expensive masculine perfume in my nose as she kissed me.

Later, at her place, a slick, black, high-tech penthouse apartment on Avenue Foch (on the good side, the one that got the sunlight). Glass and mirrors and stainless steel and vacuum-formed ABS and a huge, soft bed with silk sheets. A long night, her soft brown skin rubbing against mine, jutting nipples hard under my tongue as I nuzzled her perfect champagne-glass breasts; her raised mound cupped in my hand as I opened her and spread her liquids over her thighs. She rode me, a brown marble sculpture growing out of my hips as I lay crucified over the edge of the bed and sipped a sixty-year-old Bourgogne; her soft, birdlike cries melting into morning chirping as the sun slid over the balcony and the birds sang on Avenue Foch.

Breakfast in bed, strawberry crepes with whipped cream and Colombian coffee, served by Baldhead, who apparently doubled as a butler. I smiled at him as he placed the silver tray on the edge of the bed, and he in return opened his jacket slightly, purposely exposing a holstered automatic. Angélique sat there naked, oblivious to the exchange.

I got your number, spud. You're just paid meat. Leland, now . . .

We ate breakfast to Chopin's Nocturnes, then we made love again, long and slow on the sweaty sheets. Afterward she said, "I don't want you to ever leave me." I didn't answer, just bent over and kissed her nipple.

We spent the entire day in that bed, leaving it only for a shower or to go to the bathroom. Baldhead brought us meals. We drank expensive old wine and smoked smooth Lebanese hashish and talked and made love. I told her about the Street, about Mother Death and the Demon.

She traced my scars and pulled me down onto her, into her, banishing it again for a time.

She told me about her childhood, about being raised by nurses and lawyers, about Leland hovering over her since her father's death. She had barely known her parents, distant figures too absorbed in their frantic pursuit of the Kick to bother with children. She told me about her brother, too, her dead twin brother Xavier. "Once he tried to poke my eye out with a pencil. It left a small scar, see that brown spot under the iris, right *here*?" She kept on fingering the thick brass medallion around her neck as she described him. It hung between her breasts, the medallion, heavy and rough, with her brother's face chiseled on it in bas-relief. She never took it off, not even when we made love.

Day melted into night and we slept, satiated at last, exhausted. I dreamed of Mara and dead cities and woke up, caressed her sleeping form for a while. She moaned and curled up like a cat, but didn't wake up.

More days then, as I learned her body and the ways of Uptown . . . She took me out, to her clubs and her parties, Baldhead always in tow. I met her friends and their parents, the cream of the corporate aristocracy. The parents were lean and smart and hard, men and women like Leland, who as young wolves had worked hundred-hour cocaine-fueled weeks and climbed the corporate ladder over the smoldering, ulcerated husks of other, more unfortunate executives. The children, on the other hand, were nothing: vapid, mindless, empty eyes behind plastic faces, born aristocrats. They smiled and giggled and cooed around me, and treated me as fascinating but dangerous pet, as if Angélique had walked in with a tiger on a leash. Once in a while one of the women would step forward and run her hand down my face, and then flinch as I turned and snarled. The men would hang around in the background and sip their drinks and look threatened in their superbly cut clothes. I noticed bodyguards getting real edgy, and made a point of going out with all my weaponry, wearing my ragged streetdrek outfits, despite Angélique's halfhearted attempts to buy me "some decent clothes." I could tell by her face when I refused that she dug it, that it was the danger-and-madness-tinged aura that turned her on: loco streetdrek Attitude, wild and fast Livewire . . .

The Kick. Uptown had gone full circle there, to meet the Street. It had transcended the frenzied yuppie materialism of the '90s and the double-0s to achieve an exquisite and refined decadence, an orgiastic search for pleasure that equaled anything out on the Street. There was a difference, of course, and it was more than a matter of aesthetics: where the streetdrek chased the Kick by dancing with Mother Death, by putting their own asses on the line—and sometimes, like Mara, losing the game—the Uppers never really risked themselves. They went for expensive designer drugs and voyeurism, for dark clubs where the performers played out intricate and elaborate rituals of sex and pain and mutilation. They prefered murder to suicide, so to speak.

I only really understood the exact nature of Angélique's sudden passion for me when I looked at her face one night at the Rim, as she watched a knifeslim Thai woman slowly and excruciatingly flay her partner's back into a diamond pattern. Her eyes lit up like twin halogens, and her pink tongue darted out to lick her lips. I decided the blood on my face when I slammed at her feet that night must've been a kinghell turnon.

The Kick, God and Emperor. "If you're into this shit, then I gotta show you the Street, gotta show you some real kink, no lie. Gotta take you to Kurtz's Party."

Kurtz's Party. Some joker came up with the name a few years after it started, in honor of the mad colonel in *Apocalypse Now*. Can't say it isn't appropriate, either.

Kurtz's Party. Once a year, in July, at the height of the summer heat. Ten thousand streetdrek with a head full of acid or speed converge at sunset on the Père Lachaise cemetery; and there, among the ornate, baroque, and gothic nineteenth-century graves, proceed to go absolutely apeshit. Huge bonfires, groups of Niyabinghi drummers whipping everybody into a percussion trance-frenzy, dancing and sex and violence, drug-crazed spuds running amok among the graves and freaking out on the sculptures. The first time it happened, the Mirrorfaces tried to shut it down, and two hundred people got wasted, seventy of them Beasts. A couple of the streetdrek even went around cutting off mirror-helmeted heads with machetes and impaling them on the spikes of the grating that ringed the cemetery. Galerie des Glaces, the Hall of Mirrors . . . The year after, the Mirrorfaces just sealed off the whole area and waited for the thing to work itself out.

So I dressed Angélique in some of my clothes and messed up her hair and took her to Kurtz's Party. We ran around Downside first, to lose Baldhead, and then headed for the Père Lachaise.

Things were just starting up as we got there, around 22:30. We snuck by clumps of edgy Mirrorfaces and climbed over the old stone wall, the Mur des Fédérés, stacks of crates conveniently placed against it to form stairs. The heat was unbearable, and the bonfires made it worse, and combined with the relentless drumming it drove everybody nuts.

We shot up some crystal meth, sitting on Jim Morrison's grave, using antique manual syringes we'd found in the Puces. I did a desert lily, injecting half the dose and then pulling up the plunger, sucking up blood into the clear plastic spike and mixing it with the remaining meth in a beautiful red-white swirl before reinjecting the whole mess. It hit me fast, ice up my spine and fire down my nerves, flesh turning into clear glass and bones into chromed steel. After that I don't remember much.

I remember the drums and the dancing and the madness. I remember a news chopper hovering above us, bright halogen floodlight, filming the scene. I remember running among the graves, in the dark with Angélique, terrifying gargoyles and monolithic pyramids looming out of the night. I remember fucking Angélique on some cold marble grave, hard and fast and wild, nerve fire blazing through my groin and my brain, our bodies spasming uncontrollably as we came, explosion orgasm under the meth.

All in all, it was a great party. We got naked and daubed our bodies in paint and danced, mad, wild trance dance to the Niyabinghi polyrhythms, for timeless, drug-fueled hours. The party ended early, around four, when some asshole with a portable LAW missile decided the news chopper was pissing him off and took it down. Sudden fireball in the sky like fireworks, then it crashed, the blaze eclipsing the bonfires and casting twisted, psychotic shadows over the whole cemetery. That kind of brought most people down, and then some spuds to the north started getting into a heavy tussle with the Beasts, prompting a general exodus to the south. We ran in the streets, dodging harried Mirrorfaces, laughing, the noise of sustained gunfire and burning kerosene at our backs.

Uptown aesthetic: sharp and slick and black; mirrors and stainless steel and phrenolitic resin and polycarbonates. Smooth and cool, sometimes artificially rough, textured. Add to this, too, a touch of the ancient Japanese aesthetic, of paper walls and handmade stone artifacts, but just a touch, like a smooth, calculated ink brush stroke.

See the young Streetdrek amid the Uppers. Street-cool clashes with boardroom cool, hair-trigger reflexes and ingrained paranoia with studied politeness and corporate power. One night, at the Icehouse, an Uptown bitch with a face off an assembly-line surgery slab titters about my dreads, "Firecracker hairdo and do you think he knows what a comb is?" I snap back something about how many cheap sets of clothes she had to take off before she could afford to buy the ones she's wearing now. Her glitterboy gets pissed and tries to slap me, something about a "duel at dawn," and I reflexively break his wrist. A muscleboy tries to carve me up then, so I cave in his knee and crush his larynx, and then flashes go off in my face as he writhes on the floor amid shrieking dancers. Paparazzi. Angélique drags me out before I can waste them too, and we fuck madly in a back alley under a water drain, standing up against a wall. The next day I see a half-page spread in a gossip sheet, ANGÉLIQUE DE SEINGALT'S NEW BOYFRIEND WOUNDS TWO IN NIGHTCLUB BRAWL. *This is all seriously getting out of hand, too fast.*

* * *

It gets worse, too. We eat dinner in another sushi restaurant, and while we wait for the food in the tatami room, she lies down on the table, little cups and bowls of soya sauce spilling everywhere, and pulls my head between her thighs, for an appetizer. She comes while the waiter waits outside with the food, not in the least bit flustered. Later, she runs a tuna nigiri over her vulva, coating it in her juices, and plucks a stray hair off it before feeding it to me. Later that night at her apartment, she pulled out a small black box with two cables coming out of it and tried to plug one into my headjack.

I grabbed her hand and held it. "What is that?"

"Zanmai, Japanese sex toy. Puts me in your head and you in mine." She shivered. "Imagine screwing me and *being* me at the same time."

"Fuck that." I picked up the box and hurled it into a corner. "No fuckin way I wanna be in *your* head."

Of course it couldn't last. Kurtz's Party was the peak, and after that it was all downhill, into the kinky, plain sex no longer good enough to get her off. And then we went to Berlin.

Berlin . . . Evil old town, crawling with mean kicks. I stared out of the pyrex port of Angélique's Lear VTOL as it jetted toward a feather-soft landing on our host's private pad, saw the lights, the long strips of avenue, the blaze of private mansions, the gangs' torches lining the old Wall, itself a thin line dark as clotted blood. I noticed a strange tang in the air as I stepped off the plane, a whiff of putrefaction (or was it my imagination?), the disturbing smell floating through the rain. Ahead loomed the Baron's twisted, seashell-spiral concrete and polycarbon pile, a pseudo-organic castle of melted and congealed proto-plasm. Baldhead held an umbrella over our heads as we crossed the slick cement pad. Angélique huddled close to me, a rare display of tenderness. Leland walked next to us, his Burberry open, not seeming to notice the rain (Leland like the edge of a playing card held between two fingers).

The Baron met us at the door. My vague malaise zeroed instantly into the panic of hardwired inner alarm systems as our eyes met (his eyes pale blue *flat*—a lake's surface with nothing below—nothing showing—except the *idea* of nothing). Even Leland hadn't affected me that way. The Baron was short, stocky, and unattractive, a remarkable physique in an age of affordable beauty. Wisps of stringy brown hair surrounded his face, escaping the small topknot at the back of his head. He was wearing baggy white pants and shirt, and a casually rumpled pink sports jacket. A black cigarette holder holding an unlit cigarette bobbed up and down in front of his face. He raised a pointed eyebrow and smiled as we approached, and again I felt a tightening of the neck and lower back, streetdrek paranoia, feral fighting tension.

He embraced Angélique and then shook my hand as she introduced me, his palm clammy against mine. He also shook hands with Leland, greeting him warmly. Baldhead he ignored, rich man's blind spot for the hired help. *Of course, Leland is more than just hired help.* He ushered us in. I noticed Leland using a handkerchief to wipe suspended drops of rain off his inset as we walked down the hall.

The inside of the Baron's mansion looked like the work of a half-dozen interior decorators with radically conflicting aesthetics run amok. Baroque mixed with high-tech, classical rococo with Egyptian, streamlined synthetic with barbarian leather and brass, the flotsam of a thousand museums slapped together haphazardly.

Our coats vanished and drinks appeared in our hands. The Baron led us into the swimming-pool room. It was covered by a translucent Fuller half dome and lit by the dozen fires that burned on small buoys floating in the pool. The pool itself was dark, the water almost black. Guests of all ages lounged around it, and one very stoned skeletal man floated naked in the middle, staring into space in total immobility.

Things started to seem normal, by Uptown standards. I drank expensive Polish vodka and snorted expensive Peruvian cocaine while Angélique chatted with her friends. I lounged in a corner, an out-of-place wallflower. But something . . . I looked at my hands, felt the goose bumps. A Fear, a certain smell. Conversations were muted, unlike the chaotic babble of the Paris scene. No one stared or laughed at me. I had let Angélique dress me for this one; she'd come up with black tights and gloveboots, and an expensive gray oversized cotton shirt, buttoned in diagonal like a cossack shirt. But I still looked like a dressed-up streetdrek, my dreads and braids and coins and beads—pagan barbarian jewelry—clashing with the understated threads.

Angélique walked over to where I stood and took me by the hand. "Come. I want to introduce you to some people." I followed her through the crowd. A large, conservatively dressed Hindu stopped her as she passed by him. "Mademoiselle de Seingalt." He bowed slightly and smiled. "I knew your father. My name is Manamethe Pathrose—"

Angélique cut him off. "Oh yes, Mister Pathrose, so glad to meet you. I remember my father mentioning you. Now if you'll excuse me . . ."

She glided on, leaving him planted there, open-mouthed and frowning.

"Greasy Oxford pig," she muttered when we were out of sight. "Those shitheads think they're so smooth." She brightened. "This bastard saw the war coming, did you know? So he invested accordingly. I heard when the first reports of the Wipe came in, he threw a huge party. Half of London was there. It'd tripled his fortune."

She stopped in front of a tall, pale woman in her forties. "Leanda, darling, this is Lynx. Lynx, Leanda Issajenko." I reached out and shook her hand. Her hands were cold, and she held mine for long seconds, giving it a soft squeeze before releasing it. Her stare was coldly appraising. I held it, frozen, until she tossed her head and laughed lightly.

"Yes," she said to Angélique. "He looks strong." She turned back to me.

"So, Mr. Lynx, how are you enjoying this party?"

I mustered my best condescending smile. "I'm used to slightly . . . livelier scenes."

She laughed again. "Oh, I wouldn't worry. It'll pick up."

Angélique's eyes glimmered, suddenly interested. "Is the Baron preparing one of his . . . surprises?"

"Of course, my dear. Rumor even has it that it will outdo the last one."

"Mmmmh . . . I just can't wait. And here come Yusuf and Fikae," she added. I looked up and saw two elegant and haughty kids approaching us, drinks in hand. They were both very drunk, obviously drunk.

Leanda introduced them: Fikae Hadera, a young jet-black African whose father was an Ashanti S.A. VP, and Ya'qub ibn Yusuf, a Kuwaiti prince whose father paid him astronomical sums of money to live in Europe and stay out of his hair. Fikae I instantly pegged as a classic Uptown vacuumhead wastecase, but Yusuf was something else again, bright and sharp, the first Uptown kid

I'd met who had a *face*. He had boredom etched into his face, a lifetime of it, *lucid* boredom, and his eyes knew of fear. I mentioned that I did soundscapes and he started going off on the various DJs, even the tagspuds no one knew about. Soon, though, he wandered off into socio-psychology, discussing the Uptown/Street dichotomy.

A few people gathered in to listen as Yusuf launched into a manic lecture, waving his martini glass around wildly in time with his assertions, punctuating them. "You realize, of course, that we—that is, the disaffected corporate aristocracy—are the product of the same phenomena that created the streetdrek: technological innovation and corporate expansion." He stopped and drained his martini. "You see, when technology and automation finally got rid of most shit jobs, a lot of people were left out in the cold. So to keep them from thinking and agitating we gave them bread and circuses: the MAGI programs, the minimum annual guaranteed income, and continuous free TV, yes? And on top of this, the corporations took over virtually everything, restricting the options for the new generations, the kids. If you can make it through the gauntlet of *prépas*, or *hautes écoles*, or colleges in the U.S. no problem; you're guaranteed a cushy corporate job and a smooth, fancy, luxurious lifestyle. But if you can't . . ." A dramatic pause. "You're out on the street. Noncomformists have nowhere to go, especially since the corporations have taken total control of the art world, sealing off what was always the last outlet. Play the game by our rules, boy, or don't play at all, chuckle the fat bankers and C.O.s. So more and more kids start dropping out at younger and younger ages, hustling drugs or sex or shady tech deals, biz they call it, running on the Street.

"So the schism grew, see? And we Uppers went the other way, into luxury and decadence. Since most routine jobs were taken over by computers, those left became more and more brain-intensive, competitive, and high-pressure producing. The power-hungry corporate sharks—our parents—or at least yours—worked like dogs and had ulcers at twenty-three and so needed . . . how to put it . . . greater release valves, yes? Drugs weren't enough, too boring. So now we have this." He waved at the other guests, the dome. "We don't even have to do what our parents did to enjoy all this. We're born aristocrats, and by the time we're twenty we've seen everything there is to see and done everything there is to do and fucked everyone there is to fuck."

"So why don't you just walk out a window, Yusuf dear?" drawled Leanda.

"Because then, darling Leanda, I wouldn't get to watch you tear off your gown and beg Fikae here to fuck you when the Angel I poured into your glass starts to kick in."

I laughed then and traded eyebrows with Yusuf as Leanda went red in the face and stalked off calling for a medic. The boy had Street spirit, truth.

More of the same for a few hours, a confusing mixture of stimulants jumbling my brain and body. Finally a gong sounded and the crowd fell silent.

The Baron stood on a balcony, one hand in a pocket, and raised a champagne glass. "My dear guests," he called out. "As is my custom, I have prepared a very special surprise for you, a highlight to the evening, a trigger of sorts. If you would please move through the doorway down the end and surround the pit inside . . ."

It took a few minutes for everyone to drift over. The pit was wide and deep, a series of concentric steps surrounding a high, round table with a hole in the middle of it. A raised walkway joined the pit to a small curtained doorway. The room was covered in mirror panes, floor and walls and ceiling. The Baron stood a few steps down as extravagantly costumed servants led in the main attraction.

He was naked, a tall, tan, muscular streetdrek kid wired with a neural dociliator. The Baron waved for silence as the servants led him down into the pit. "What you are about to witness is a variation on an ancient Chinese custom. The Chinese used monkeys for this. However, I felt that it would take a man, not a monkey, to satisfy your jaded appetites. Watch."

One of the servants touched a switch and the table split in two, opening. There was a small hole in the ground under the hole in the table. The servants lowered the kid into the hole and closed the table around his neck.

Angélique clutched my arm as we watched. Unease crept into my drug-fogged brain as one of the servants produced a lasersaw and held it up with a flourish. I heard sharp inhalations around me, felt the anxiety, the excitement. The Baron raised his hand and held it up, drawing out the tension, holding it. Finally he grinned, a manic rictus, and chopped down—and did a dark light flicker behind the flat panes of his eyes?

The servant flicked on the lasersaw and started cutting off the top of the man's head. The fog in my brain vanished with the abruptness of a power failure.

Oh fuck . . .

Angélique's eyes did their halogen trick again, flaring open, glowing—brighter by an order of magnitude than that night at the club. Her hand gripped my arm convulsively. The Baron sipped his drink casually as the servant slowly worked his way around.

Angélique moaned as the top of the streetdrek's skull slowly came off, exposing his intact, palpitating brain. The man was dociliated and probably filled to the eyeballs with endorphin inhibitors, but I could see the naked terror in his eyes, piercing through the frozen mask like a bloodstained razor.

Fuck . . . Cannot deal.

Angélique was near orgasm, shivering with lust and anticipation. She ran her hand up my thigh and over my cock as the Baron stepped up to the table.

A servant handed him a long metal spoon. The Baron licked it once, smiled at his entranced guests, and dug in. Gently, delicately, a small piece of the forebrain only. "The idea is to do this slowly," he said, "so the subject stays alive as long as possible." The servant held out more spoons. "Would anyone care to try?" asked the Baron. A dozen guests stepped into the pit at once, on cue.

FUCKFUCKFUCKFUCKFUCKFUCKFUCKFUCK—

Something snapped. I hit Angélique, hard, and ran for the door. A servant tried to stop me and I kneed him in the groin and then in the face as he doubled over. I ran through the room with the pool, through vast halls full of mismatched artwork, lost in the maze. Eventually I found an exit and I was out on the grounds and into a parked skimmer. I hotwired it in no time flat and kicked it into gear, slewing over the front lawn. I didn't slow down for the front gates, thick iron bars and scroll-work. The skimmer rammed through them, screech of torn metal and bursting hinges, near whiplash in the safety web; and then out, into the streets and the night, the Demon on my shoulder gibbering and howling.

I ditched the skimmer ten block from the mansion and ran through the streets, crazed and aimless. Eventually I found a bar and I huddled in back, slamming down shots of cheap scotch.

"... ?"

I looked up at the girl talking to me, fast stream of German.

"*Nicht sprechen Deutch* . . ." I managed.

"Oh, French?" She was short, face powdered white with a black airbrushed bar across the eyes, teased blond hair: Berlin streetdrek.

"Yes."

"You okay? You look strange, no?"

"Problems, girl, got problems."

"You want a friend?"

"Yes," and all the longing and loneliness of twenty years in that word . . .

Her name was Liese. She was nice and warm and didn't eat people, and that was enough for me.

Leland was waiting for me, of course. A glint of red quartz and bluish Tombac in the dark, a thin smile, the hiss of a fletcher . . .

Shards, fragments . . . Liese, curled up, asleep in a small Berlin squatter's pad . . . A flight to Paris, lost in a haze of airplane booze and Seconal . . . Endless metro ride from Roissy to Luxembourg, stations flashing by, rumble of compressed air . . . A dark doorway, rue Cujas, home . . . Smiling Leland in his blue Burberry . . .

I woke up in Angélique's bed, naked, handcuffed, alone. I staggered up and started tearing through her drawers, looking for a paper clip or a piece of wire. The door opened as I was doing the dresser, clumsily tossing clothes all over the room. Baldhead walked in, and without a word picked me up, punched me in the stomach, and threw me on the bed. The aftereffects of the needle toxin hit me full force, and I doubled up and puked all over the expensive silk sheets, retching and heaving. I blacked out.

I woke up again on clean sheets. Smell of lemon aerosol in the air, masking the stench of vomit. Angélique was sitting cross-legged on the corner of the bed, watching me. She was wearing a long, smooth shift, open on the side and tabbed at the waist.

I looked up at her and jabbed my cuffed hands toward her. "Why?" I snarled.

"I knew you wouldn't come here otherwise. I'm sorry about Lado. He has been . . . disciplined."

"Fuck." My mouth felt as if a wad of cotton dipped in glue had been forced into it. I painfully pulled myself up so that I was kneeling in front of her. "Water . . ." The effort left me sagging.

She ran her hand lightly over my chest, brushing her nails over my nipples before sliding off the bed and disappearing into the bathroom. Sound of running water. She reappeared holding a tall glass full of water, still milky white from mineral deposits.

"Here." She reached out gently with her hand and pushed my chin up. With the other hand she held the glass to my lips. I drank greedily, convulsively, water spilling over my chin and chest. She put the glass down on the floor when I finished it and lifted a corner of the sheets to wipe off my chin.

"If I release you, will you attack me? We are alone here, you know." She seemed to relish the idea.

I didn't answer. She stared at me and then suddenly whistled, a high G sharp. The night table floated over to her side. She reached over to it and pulled the drawer open, her eyes never leaving mine. She took out a small key, an old-fashioned metal one. Then she climbed up onto the bed, kneeled opposite me, and unlocked the cuffs.

I rubbed my wrists, returning circulation making my hands tingle, and then flicked my hand out toward her neck, a sharp fake. She flinched but didn't move. I smiled and jumped off the bed.

"Where the fuck are my clothes?"

"Out in the corridor."

I left her kneeling on the bed and walked out. My clothes were there, neatly folded on a chair. They were the same clothes I'd worn to Berlin. I pulled on the tights and walked back into the room. She was still on the bed in the same position I'd left her in.

I kneeled on the bed, my back straight and my arms curved around to my knees, rigid formal Japanese pose; across from her, but farther back than I'd been.

"Why did you bring me here?" I asked her after a time. Instead of answering, she stood up and went over to her music deck. The first notes of the Nocturnes poured out of the speakers as she returned to the bed, rolling bass notes and then the high ones, intrusive, sad.

"You said you'd never leave me," she said at last in her small sad girl's voice.

"Like fuck I did!" I barked. "*You* told me never to leave you. You never assumed, of course, that I'd ever want otherwise, no? Uptown fantasyland, babe, if Miss Angélique wants it then it's just *there*, right? That's what you're used to. You got the credit, you got Anubis, and things just *happen*, right? And if things go wrong, then you got Leland, and he does his stuff and then everything's right again and clean and neat cause that's what he's paid for! Right?"

"Lynx, you're being unfair."

"Like fuck I am! That scene in Berlin, you know, that was fuckin *cracked*, I mean frit fuckin *insane*! And you were fuckin getting *off* on it! The way you're wired, you know, it may not be your fault, but you're one *twisted* bitch."

"Lynx. You're being so . . . sentimental. Silly. The man, he was only a brainwiped junkie, meat off the street, no more mind than an animal . . ."

"Oh, is *that* how you justify that kind of shit? I was wondering . . ."

"Don't give me that shit!" She looked pissed at last. Good. "*You* should talk about kink! You told me, about your life, about knifing people for a dinner, about running terror raids on the boulevards to get your kicks!"

"Sure, I've killed people. But only to survive, only when they tried to kill me. I've never killed anyone for credit. And I've never killed anybody to get a hard-on."

"Well fuck you, then." She smiled, a predator's grin. "I don't need to justify myself to you. Like you said: I got the credit. I got Leland. I can do whatever the fuck I want because who's going to stop me? Who's going to judge me?"

I stood up without a word and stalked out. She ran after me and grabbed my hand as I reached for my clothes. "Wait."

"What?"

"Lynx . . . Please. Don't leave. I'm sorry."

I snorted. "For what?"

"For everything. Please . . ."

I picked up the shirt and started to put it on.

"What do you want, Lynx? Please?"

"Nothing."

She slid out of her shift and stood there, naked except for the brass medallion. "Not even this?"

I laughed out loud. "I don't believe it. Fancy Miss Angélique, naked and begging to get fucked like a whore on Saint-Denis! If only the paparazzi were here."

She slapped me, hard. I stood there and realized that I was getting a hard-on.

Penis erectus non compos mentis. Old Latin joke, a stiff prick knows no conscience. *Fuck it.*

I picked her up by the waist and carried her flailing and cursing to the bed. I threw her on to it and pulled the tights off. She stopped cursing and grinned when she saw that.

"This what you want?" I pointed down at my erect prick.

"Yes."

I climbed onto the bed, faint twinge at the back of my skull, *don't do this.* I pushed her legs open and penetrated her, brutally, violently. I held her arms pinned down as I fucked her. She squirmed under me, pushing up against me. I pulled out of her at the last moment, and came over her belly, her face, the ultimate insult.

See how you *like being used, bitch.*

"That enough?" I stared down at her, panting.

"No." She rolled onto her stomach and pulled herself toward me. I just sat there, amazed, as she took my limp penis into her mouth, and started sucking, caressing, running her hand over my balls. When I was hard enough, she pushed me over onto my back and mounted me, impaling herself. She rode me for a long time, her back arched, my hands on her breasts and hips, small birdlike cries of pleasure. She came at last, inner muscles clenching, and then I came too, pleasure pooling at the base of my spine and then exploding up. A quelched *why?*

I pushed her off me and rolled over, limp, embracing the bed and the wet sheets.

Streetdrek paranoia, hardwired reflexes. I felt something behind me and whipped around, saw a thin stiletto plunging toward my chest, icepick grip and her face like stone. I blocked it easily and tore it out of her hands, slapping her across the face and sending her sprawling. I jumped on top of her and put the tip of the knife to her throat.

"Why? You bitch! Why?" I screamed.

She lay there, unresisting, dead. I pricked one of her nipples, eliciting a small cry of pain. I ran the blade over her other breast, not quite cutting.

"Why?"

She didn't answer. I slashed the breast, thin red line appearing along the smooth curve. Her nipples were erect, stiff.

"Why?"

"Because . . . you were going to leave me. I don't want you to leave me."

"Bitch!" I grabbed the medallion, the thick brass medallion with the bas-relief of her brother, and slashed, blade neatly parting the rawhide thong. "I'm keeping this as a souvenir," I snarled as I rolled off her and stood up.

///somewhere a ghost laughs ///

"No!" A reaction at last. "You can't!" I hit her hard in the jaw, and she fell back, her head slamming into the wall with a sharp *crack*. She lay curled up on the bed, sobbing, as I rammed my legs into the tights. She started screaming again as I headed for the door. "Motherfucker! You're *dead*! Leland will kill you and my dogs will piss on your corpse!" I slammed the door behind me. "You're meat!" I quickly pulled on the rest of my clothes and took off, medallion bouncing against my chest in the shirt's breast pocket as I ran. Out into the stifling heat, under the browning leaves of the trees of Avenue Foch . . . Out.

First thing I did, I hit a vidphone. I slammed the glass door shut behind me and then realized I had no card. I'd gone to Berlin with just my clothes and a credit spike, which I'd used to return to Paris.

Fuck.

I barged out of the booth and went up to a young Suit who was passing by, patent-leather briefcase under the arm.

"Excuse me, it's an emergency, could I borrow your card for a phone call?"

The Suit looked at me, a monolith of condescension, ice in his eyes, and barked, "Get a job!"

I stood there petrified for a beat, too stunned to move. The arrogance. I finally snapped out of it as he walked away. I ran after him, pulled him around, and hit him in the jaw. He staggered, and I grabbed him by the lapels and slammed him up against the vidphone booth.

"Give—me—your—fucking—card."

The Suit finally got the message and fumbled through his pocket, pulling out an expensive, stiff leather wallet, the kind pimps carry nylon imitations of. Plastic clattered on the concrete sidewalk as I grabbed the Telecom card and shoved him away.

"Get the *fuck* out of here, asshole!"

He stumbled, dropped his briefcase, picked it up again, and ran away. I ignored him as I rammed the card into the slot and dialed my number. I tapped nervously on the smooth steel panel of the vidphone as it rang. Once . . . Twice . . . The vidphone was a Stromberg-Carlson, a corner of my mind noted, made in the U.K. Three . . . Four . . . *Come on!* Five . . . *Come ON!*

Domino finally answered, rubbing her eyes and yawning as she peered sleepily into the cracked blue screen of my vidphone.

"Domino!"

"Hey Lynx. Long time no see, stranger."

"Domino. I don't have the time to explain now, OK? Just get the fuck out of the pad, *now*. Copy?"

"Whaaa—"

"There's a duffel bag behind the futon. Throw in as many of my clothes and yours into it as you can. Grab my weapons, my wallet, over by the music library, my skimboots, and get the fuck out. Go to the Luxembourg garden, and wait at the café Saint-Paul. I'll have Olric pick you up."

"But . . . but . . ." She was still half asleep and confused, but I didn't have the time to explain.

"I'm in trouble. Just do it. I'll find you, don't worry."

"Okay." She moved to cut the connection when I remembered the most important thing.

"Domino!"

Her hand stopped. "Yes?"

"You see a tall Suit, maybe in a blue raincoat, with a weird metal eye inset . . ."

"Yes?"

"Drop the bags and run like hell. The man is poison. See you."

I cut the connection and stepped out of the booth.

Time to get the fuck out of here. That Suit I ripped will have the Faces down on my ass in no time. I'll call Olric later.

I crossed the street and jogged up Foch, toward the Arc de Triomphe. I broke into a run when I reached the Metro, no need for discretion now. I galloped through the long tunnels, toward the station nexus at Wagram.

If only I had my fuckin skimboots.

I reached the Wagram entrance and paused by the bank of vidphones.

Fuck. I forgot the card!

I really didn't feel up to terrorizing another Suit, especially in the middle of a crowded station, so I waited, anxiously tapping my foot, till I spotted a suitably nice-looking young woman in the crowd. She looked like an art student, a large portfolio under her arm. *Good.*

I pasted on my nicest smile and stepped up in front of her.

"Excuse me, miss? I'm sorry, but I'm broke and I need a Telecom card for the phone, it's an emergency. Do you think—"

She returned the smile. "Sure, no problem. Here, can you hold this?" She gave me the portfolio and I held it while she dug through her purse.

"Here." I plucked the card out of her fingers and gave her back her portfolio, along with another smile, more genuine this time. "Thanks." I turned to the bank of vidphones.

The first one I picked was broken, no mike in the handset as I picked it up. "Fuck!" I dropped the handset and tried the next one. It worked.

I punched Olric's number and waited. He answered on the second ring.

"Yeah?"

"Olric . . . Need help, my man, got problems, big problems."

"What kind?"

"Heat on my ass, Uptown bitch wants my blood. I'll brief you later."

"Raas claat . . . What do you need?"

"I sent Domino to the Saint-Paul. Can you pick her up and meet me somewhere? I'll need a place, too, got to stay down for a while."

"Think it'll blow over?"

"Dunno. Where do we meet?"

"Mmmmh . . . Beaubourg. Lots of spuds there, no one will try to pull any shit."

"Check. See you, half hour, Beaubourg."

"Check. Luck, my man."

"Thanks. Salaam."

I hung up. The girl was standing there, an amused smile playing across her lips. I handed her the card with a bow and took off running without missing a beat. I headed for the turnstiles. No controllers. I jumped one and followed the signs to the Chateau de Vincennes line.

* * *

Beaubourg . . . Imagine a vast rectangle of a building flipped inside-out and planted on a small plaza in the middle of low, nineteenth-century stone buildings. Imagine the building painted in bright red and blue and white and green, the vents and funnels and tubes and ducts; with transparent plastic escalator tubes pinned to one side, and sheets of plate glass closing off the space between the monolithic steel pillars. Beaubourg, the Musée Pompidou . . .

The cobblestone plaza in front of the museum was as crowded as ever, lounging streetdrek and Japanese tourists with their machine-gun cameras, plus the usual assortment of fire-eaters and sword swallowers and tanned fakirs and bad magicians and even worse musicians. I went over and watched one of the magicians as I waited, amusing myself by following the little balls as he palmed them and hid them, then made them reappear in the pockets or noses of astonished salarymen. Then I felt a hand on my shoulder.

I nearly broke the arm as I whipped around, my left arm snapping up and down in a dragon claw. I froze when Olric's face registered.

"You shouldn't do that, man," he drawled. "If you fuck up your friends, who's left?"

"Sorry. I'm kinda edgy these days, gotta understand. You can't go around grabbing paranoid shoulders like that, you know?"

"Yeah. You okay?"

"Yeah, so far. You get Domino?"

"She's in the car. I passed by your place, gave it a scope. Looked all clear but—"

"Copy. Let's step."

Later, at Olric's. I'd changed into some real clothes, distributed my weapons around my body, put on my skimboots. Olric lounged on his bed, rolling a cigarette with Dutch tobacco and a few crumbs of hash.

"Ya gotta go Downside, man, hang there for a while. It's the only place the fuckers won't find you."

"Downside? Fuck that. It's cold, it's wet . . . Two, three nights, cool, but a couple of weeks? No fuckin way."

"Not the bunker, man." Olric grinned. "We did it, man, we opened the bunker."

"No shit . . . Truth?"

"Truth. Toxic and me, we did it a week ago, you were gone, so . . . It's beautiful, man, clean and dry and warm. The lights even work!"

"Fuckin hardcore. You score anything?"

"Yeah. See the phones?"

Shit. Must've been totally gone not to notice them. They were everywhere, large, chunky steel military telephones without vidscreens and with rotating dials. Olric had strung them around the room, wired them together, bolted a few to the walls.

"Do they work?"

"Yeah! I rigged an adapter, wired them into a patch box I also got there, and patched them into the system. It's fuckin razor, whenever anyone calls they all ring."

"Slicing."

I played with one for a bit. Domino sat cross-legged in a corner, silent, an enigmatic half smile on her face. Finally I turned to her.

"Hey, Domino. Wanna keep me company Downside for a stretch?"

Moving into the bunker was a bitch. The camping beds we'd bought at the Vieux Campeur didn't fit through the hole Olric and Toxic had made, so we had to go stomping through a muddy low-sky maze around Danzig, looking for the place Olric had stashed the G.E. drill. Then we spent an hour wrestling with the fuckin drill, widening the hole. We tossed the beds through when it was large enough, then the sleeping bags and the backpacks full of canned food and beer and a portable butane stove.

Finally I wiggled through the hole, feet first, feeling out for a foothold. Olric, who'd gone first, grabbed my swinging foot and placed it on a banister, and I slid out and jumped the remaining two meters. The hole was three meters up, right next to a pair of concrete-coated armored doors.

The bunker was huge, a high-ceilinged, L-shaped anti-atomic bunker built in the 1950s and closed down and sealed in 1978 for some arcane bureaucratic reason. It was pristine, as Downside bunkers go, virtually in the same shape as it had been fifty years ago when the Ponts et Chaussées workers poured the concrete over the two sets of armored steel doors.

We left our stuff by the hole as we explored the bunker, Olric proudly showing us the features. The lights worked, as he'd said, and we killed our acetylenes as the neons blinked into life. "You can't leave these on all the time," Olric explained, "cause someone upstairs might notice the added energy drain."

"What's upstairs?" Domino asked.

"The research laboratory of the Ponts et Chaussées ministry, 72, Boulevard Lefebvre. Come on, I'll show you."

We followed him as he pointed out various rooms filled with antique machinery dripping with grease. He stopped in front of one of them. Inside were four fixed bicycles that must have served to power the emergency generators.

"If you ever need any exercise . . ." He laughed.

The central shaft was huge, five meters in diameter and thirty meters high, the largest one I'd ever seen. Steel rungs ran up one side of it, and there were alcoves on the side of it every eight meters. I could see the night sky clearly through the grating on top.

"OK, you got to be real quiet here . . . See that grate? It's in the middle of the courtyard of the laboratory. And sound carries up these fuckers."

"Can I climb?"

"Sure. Have fun." He gave me an odd look. I shrugged and started to climb.

Ten meters up I understood the look. Every shaft I'd ever climbed had been real narrow, narrow enough to lean against the back wall if you got tired, narrow enough so that you couldn't really see down. This one was so wide it was like climbing a cliff. If I slipped . . .

Maximum street pizza, check it—

I forced myself to look up and continue the climb. At the top I wrapped my arm around a rung, heart pounding a fastbeat tattoo, not quite a vertigo attack but still . . .

I looked up, through the grating. I was stuck with a bad angle, so I could only see the top of the buildings. I hung there for a while and then climbed down, slowly and carefully. I stepped off the ladder at the first alcove and sat in it for a while, against the back wall, shaking. Finally I got my nerve up and finished the climb. I reached the bottom and stalked by an amused Olric, into the comforting safety of the bunker, the burrow.

Fuck . . .

Olric came after me, still smiling. "So?"

I took a deep breath before answering, and the capital F was in my voice. "That kind of Fear, my man, I can do without."

"Isn't it wild?"

"I dunno. I think that before I might of enjoyed it, you know, tripped on it and rode the high. But now . . ."

We stood in silence for a while. Finally I said, "I've changed, man. Since Mara got dusted . . . I just don't get off on this kind of shit anymore."

"So what *do* you get off on, Lynx?"

"I don't know, my friend. I just don't know."

The rest of the bunker ran pretty standard. Showers that didn't work, toilets that did. "Good," laughed Domino, when Olric flushed one as a demonstration. The only odd thing was the chairs, wood and metal school chairs strewn randomly through various rooms. We set up in one of the back rooms, the beds and the stove. I left the food in the backpacks, just in case we had to move fast.

I spent the next half hour kinking the bunker, motion sensors and IR detectors by the hole and in various rooms. Olric had told us that no one except him and Toxic knew about the bunker, so we'd be safe; I decided paranoia was even safer.

Of course, the alarms might not help much if Leland did try to pull a raid. I only had my cobra and a few knives, and Domino also only had shivs. If they came in after us, it'd be with fletchers or guns. Shivs wouldn't be much good.

Mmmmh . . . I'll have to go score some hardware soon. Cornelius maybe . . .

We settled in. Olric brought us candles, long, thick, milky-white tapers stolen from Notre-Dame, and we planted them in empty wine and whisky bottles and spread them around the rooms we were using. They flickered in the imaginary breeze and cast gothic gargoyle shadows on the walls.

Domino read, books she'd taken along with the rest of my stuff. I set up my two mini Sony speakers and my armdeck and listened to music, lying on my cot and smoking hand-rolled cigarettes from my supply of Drum. Angélique's brass medallion lay on my chest, heavy. I'd found it in my pocket when I'd changed at Olric's, and on a whim had strung it on a rawhide thong and hung it around my neck with my other trinkets.

The first night, bored, I programmed a simple holo light-show into my armdeck, keyed, and synched to the music. I spent the next few hours staring at the psychedelic patterns the deck projected in the air, swirling holos pulsing to the beat of the music.

I got bored of that pretty fast, too. I searched through Domino's stack of books for one I hadn't read. She looked up from her Müller play and smiled. "I got a new one, deuce, you might like it."

"Where is it?"

"In my bag, over there."

I dug through the bag and found the book. It was an old paperback, yellow and tattered and dog-eared, with a black-and-white picture of a beautiful young emaciated man on the cover. *The Basketball Diaries* by Jim Carroll.

"Is it any good?" I asked Domino.

"Dunno, man, read it and see."

I leafed through it, checked the copyright page. 1963. Well, shit . . .

I sat down against a concrete wall with a church candle and a bottle of cheap red and started reading. I was absorbed by the second page. Thirteen-year-old junkies and thieves, stealing and hustling and mainlining their way around New York, and kicking major butt in some ballgame called basketball between scores. It was fuckin *razor*, and I finished it in two hours. Unfortunately, that left me with nothing to do again, so I reread it and went to sleep.

*   *   *

Three days of that shit, and I went stir-crazy. I started skating around the bunker, seeing how fast I could cut the corners, or how high I could jump without hitting the ceiling, or how many chairs I could leap over without clipping the backrest. The painful answer to that last one, incidentally, was six. Lying on the ground with a scraped and bloody arm, sudden flashback to another night on the Champs, another scraped arm and a girl . . .

Fuck it . . . Time to move.

Olric wasn't due back for another twelve hours. I washed the blood off my arm at one of the sinks—they worked, fortunately, though the water wasn't drinkable—and changed my skimboots for my thick black leather biker boots. I slipped my combat blade up my back and put on my leather and went into the room where Domino, the Sphinx, was still reading. She looked up from her book as I walked in.

"Hey, kid, I'm going for a walk. Wanna come?"

"I don't think that's such a good idea, deuce."

"I'm staying Downside. I just wanna go run the lines, is all. Go to the Beach, all my friends'll be there, it'll be cool. Too crowded to pull any shit, we'll be safe."

"If you say so." She closed the book, stood up, and dusted off her butt. She grinned. "Come to think of it, deuce, I am going kinda apeshit here. Feels like a fuckin church with all the candles and shit. Let me get my boots."

I dug through my pack while she put on her boots and pulled out the large Macrolight flashlight Olric had given me, thick butyl styrene rubber handle and whitebright argon bulb. My helmet was still at my pad, so this would have to do. *Make a good club, too*, I decided as I tossed it from hand to hand.

The Beach wrapped itself around us like a womb, loud and chaotic and smoky. Dan was beating relentlessly on his congas, the rhythmic line a perpetual thread running through Downside, never stopping, it seemed. I dapped with the spuds, fending off questions about my disappearance. I ate some cassoulet with Olric—who was pissed as hell to see me there—and talked about the scene.

"Two-Tone's here tonight," he said.

"Shifty little fucker. Where is he?" Two-Tone was a real lowlife, even by streetdrek standards. Rumor had it he narked on occasions. I was surprised no one had wasted him yet.

"Over there, with his skinhead buddies. His hair's one-tone now, all bleached."

"Yeah, I see him." He was sitting in a corner with two skins, not quite ostracized. "So what do we call him now? Two-Tone-Now-One-Tone?"

Hours drifted by on a cloud of candle smoke and hashish . . . I left Domino rapping with Scalpel and went on a quick run with Olric and Toxic to Saint-Anne, to check the concrete plug the I.G.C. had just put in.

"We can do it, no problem," said Olric.

"How? This shit's carved out of the mass, man, solid stone."

"I scored some plastique, real good stuff, military," said Toxic. "Drill a few holes and stuff 'em, shaped charges, and this baby's gone, ya no see it?"

"Where's the plastique?"

"We stashed it in the dead end behind the bones, at Montpa. No one ever goes there."

"Check."

The next day I climbed Topside with Domino, my hair in a knitted dreadbag and mirrors over my eyes, for a shower at Viper's. Fuck knows we needed one. We took an exit that dropped us on the Metro tracks, way up North, between Luxembourg and Port-Royal, and footed it to the Luxembourg platform.

Walking on the tracks is always a trip. Subsonic vibrations warned us of an incoming, and we ran for the nearest alcove. We huddled there, in the puddle of white neon, as the doubledeck white neoplastene train whipped by three centimeters from our noses. Hiss of escaping freon from the coolant systems, superconductor voodoo holding the train a few centimeters above the rusting tracks.

We walked up a few steps onto the Luxembourg platform, ignoring surprised Suits, and waved gaily as we passed under the vidcams that faced in toward the platform.

Daylight was a shock, so bright after five days Down Under. And so hot. Downside is a constant eight degrees centigrade, no matter what the temperature Topside. And this fucking heatwave wouldn't let up. We dove into a jewelry store right by the exit, for a quick air-conditioning bath, letting the sweat on our faces freeze before stepping back out into the oven.

We made it to Viper's with no problems. My eyes kept darting leftside-rightside behind the mirrors as we walked, scoping, keyed to a flash of Tombac and red quartz. The shower was great, Domino and I scrubbing the five days of encrusted Downside grit out of each other's backs. We spent an hour afterward in Viper's living room, cooling off and getting high, Viper bent over her deck while Domino rebraided my hair, wire-thin braids with beads threaded over them, and thick dready plaits with clanking Chinese copper coins.

Viper looked up from her deck abruptly. "The word's out on you, you know."

"Say what?"

"On the Street. There's money out, by parties unknown, for your head. Word's gone out among the drek."

"They want me alive?"

"I think so. Spud who told me wasn't sure."

Need that hardware, need it bad . . .

I made a decision. "Listen. I want to go to my pad, get some shit." *And draw out the wolves, play some games . . .*

"You're fuckin frit, my brother. You think they don't have it staked?"

"They probably won't leave more than one man there. It'd cost them too much otherwise."

"You gettin dumb in your old age, Lynx. These assholes have credit, man, big credit. This kind of shit is peanuts to them."

"Don't worry about it. I can deal with whatever they got there, and I want to get my decks out before they decide to trash the place."

"They probably already have."

I smiled. "Well. Let's go see."

Viper got up and started picking up knives and making

them vanish inside her clothes. "It's your party, my brother. I'm just in for the ride."

"You always dug the ride, sistren."

"Still do. That's why I'm going with you."

The area around my pad looked clear. No parked skimmers, no shadows in the windows of the surrounding buildings, no dancing red dot on my chest. Still, I felt an unpleasant prickling at the base of my neck as I walked up the hill, Viper and Domino next to me. *Feels like a stroll through Old Jerusalem.* If they had a sniper, I probably wouldn't hear the shot.

No shots as we reached the entryway. Viper went first, *shuriken* between her fingers, ready to fly. I followed with Domino.

Nobody. We climbed the stairs to the door of my pad, scanning the corners, tense, fearsweat mingling with heatsweat.

I touched the knob of my door and waited a beat. Slowly I inserted the strip key and waited for the beep. It didn't come. I felt the knob again and gently tested it. It turned. Open.

I waved Viper and Domino back and kicked the door in. I jumped back, against the side wall, half expecting a hail of bullets. Nothing.

Nothing again as I peeked into the pad. Then the mess registered.

Bastards.

"Shit. They've been here."

We searched the apartment carefully before we touched anything, knives out. There was no place really for anyone to hide but still . . .

The pad looked as if everything in it had been sucked up by a tornado and then dropped again. Torn clothes littered the floor, books with pages ripped out. My rig . . .

"Fuckers!"

The rig was scrap. They'd ripped the Ashanti open, torn out the chips, trashed the Yamahas, the Sony holoproj, the McD-D.

"Blood," I growled. "There's gonna be blood." *At least all the soft is in my armdeck.*

Then I saw the rose, Mara's black rose, crushed and

broken on the ground, half hidden in the debris. I stared
at it for an eternity, and the anger hit me, the hate. I'd
never hated Angélique before, just felt a kind of numb
disgust. But now . . .

My teeth were clenched so hard my jaw muscles ached.
I walked over to the wall and slammed my head into it,
hard, headbutt rippling up from the belly. I noticed a
dent in the wall as I turned around, and there was hate in
my eyes and my voice.

"One day I will kill her."

Wasting the bitch would be the easy part, I reflected
out on the street; it was getting to her I was worried
about. The way it looked, that meant getting around
Leland, and I wasn't too fired up about that. I decided
the best tactic would be to lie low for a while and think
about it. *Gotta live if you wanna kill, gotta survive* . . .

"Lynx, y'OK?" Domino, worried, interrupting my
brainwalk.

"Yeah, I'll live. I hope you're not trying for a suntan,
cause we're going back down."

I only spotted the tails after Viper split. *Pity.* If she'd
still been around I would've just taken them right there.

There were three of them: Two-Tone-Now-One-Tone—
the little shit—and two anonymous muscleboys in dark
gray two-piece suits. I made them as Domino and I rode
the escalator down into the Luxembourg station, Two-
Tone's bleached head bobbing in and out of the crowd,
trying to remain inconspicuous. I decided to string them
along, take 'em for a ride through the Downside lines.

Get some dirt on those nice suits of theirs.

I clued Domino in as we went over the turnstiles.
"Eyes straightways and ziplip, babe, got heat on our
butts."

She kept walking straight, def casual. "Where?"

"Six o'clock. Three of 'em, Two-Tone and two muscleboys. Gray suits."

She glanced at the bay window on the right, patting
her hair, checking her reflection. "Made 'em. What do
we do?"

"Figure they got guns, fletchers. Figure three to two, and we only got shivs. Figure that's bad odds."

We turned the corner and rode the escalator down to the platform. "So?"

"We run them through Downside. Chances are we lose 'em."

"And if they got trackers?"

We got off the escalator and walked down the platform. I smiled as I answered, feral death grin, hunter's joy. "We dust 'em."

The train hissed in. We got on near the end of the car, letting them get on toward the front. I leaned against the door to the rear trainman's cockpit.

"Cover me." I slipped a credit card into the gap between the door and the wall and popped the lock without even turning around. I pulled the door forward and slipped in, pulling it shut behind me.

The cockpit was dark, harsh glow of the tunnel neons casting stark shadows through the Plexiglas bulb. I reached up above the door and pulled one of the two heavy plastic tubes out of their brackets. I slipped back out and held it behind my back.

Port Royal. The train stopped, belched passengers, moved on again. I counted alcoves as the train glided through the tunnel, and after the twenty-third I pulled the alarm signal.

Mayhem. Old ladies shrieked and bowled over as the alarm blared and the train jerked to a stop. I noticed Two-Tone and the muscleboys frantically trying to plow through the tumultuous crowd as I pried open the door. I jumped down onto the tracks, small hop, Domino after me, and started jogging back toward the twenty-third alcove. I looked back at the train as we reached the alcove, and saw the muscleboys stumbling out of it, guns out, yelling. "There!" Two-Tone waved an automatic and pointed. Only one of the muscleboys had a fletcher, blunt ABS nozzle protruding from under his jacket. Burpgun model, full-auto, probably a Mossberg. Sucker.

I'd been tearing at the seal of the plastic tube as we ran, and it finally popped open. I dropped the useless half that served as a cover, and as the muscleboy leveled his Mossberg, I turned around and gave the detonator string a sharp tug.

The flare went off with an explosive hiss. It bucked and shrieked in my hand, spitting a steady stream of white magnesium fire, issuing billows of thick red smoke. We were hidden in seconds. I never saw the muscleboy fire, if he did.

I was laughing through the red clouds when Two-Tone tried to nail us permanent. He started firing wildly, flat crack of his automatic as we ducked into the service tunnel, sharp *ping* of bullet on concrete.

Wonder if Angélique wants a corpse. Maybe dipshit there is just being trigger-happy.

Oh well. Same difference. Dead is dead.

I dropped the flare at the entrance of the service tunnel. If they had IR it would slow them down, the white-hot flare searing a lasting afterimage on the sensitive membranes of the trackers, hiding our trail. We'd have a good head start by the time the membranes cleared up, leaving the gauzy, shimmering red trail of our passage through the air ectoplasmically visible to the voodoo of the trackers.

By the time we reached Assas it was obvious they were following. We'd gone west first, jogging on Vaugirard. I'd caught sight of them after we turned south on rue Madame, much too soon for commercial IR equipment; I figured they must be toting military, which wasn't impossible —especially if Anubis had sent them. Military trackers had built-in booster fuses, to prevent soldiers from getting blinded by explosions. Those things could function under arc-light bombardment; the smoke must've slowed them down more than the flare did. We were now angling southeast on Assas. I gave a small shrug of regret as we passed the entrance to the maze that leads to the German bunker. *If they didn't have those trackers . . . Sweet game, sweet hunting, in that maze.*

Cat and mouse, like that, for a while. We took the Joseph Bara diagonal, onto the Boulevard du Montparnasse, west again. Glimpses of the hunters once in a while, the flat report of Two-Tone's automatic. We ran steady, maintaining our lead. Curses floated through the air as we went through a wet stretch on Montparnasse, water up to the knees. *So much for the clean suits.*

We cut south-southeast on Dubois, a long, wide mainline toward the FFI. Dull dirt smell, thin light of my dying miniflash sweeping the corridor in front of me. My breath coming hard now, heaving, panting, Domino not doing any better. *Bet Two-Tone's having fun.*

I'd been counting sidelines on my right. We took the eighth one, into Boullard. "Not far now," I gasped. "Good," said Domino.

West on a nameless line, the first after Gentilly. Five-hundred meters . . . A turn right . . .

L'Ossuaire, the bonery. The end of the line hooked left, a small nook. A limestone bench on the left wall, shards of brown bone littering the ground, a staircase at the end of the nook disappearing into the lower level. And up on the right wall, at head height, a small hole in the limestone wall, inconspicuous, surrounded by graffiti and stray bones: the entrance.

I slumped on the bench for a few seconds, exhausted. My chest was pumping like an antique hand-operated bellows. *Fuck.* A six-klik run, at least.

Domino looked drained but otherwise fine. "Y'OK?" I asked.

"Yah. No problem. Good jogging any day, good for the lungs, you know?"

"Ha." I coughed, a hacking smoker's cough. "Fuckin cigarettes."

Domino absently kicked a muddy piece of skull. "So now what?"

I pointed up at the hole. "In there."

"In there?"

"Yup."

I helped her up, pushing her butt as she wriggled and grasped for a handhold. I felt her shiver as she wormed her way around the small corner and saw what was inside. I heard her mutter, muffled, "Fuckin Frenchies." Then her feet disappeared with a dragging sound.

I wedged my legs against the opposite wall and pushed up to the hole. I turned onto my belly, legs still dangling out of the hole, and pulled myself into the tunnel. I patted the skull that sat on a corner ledge, grinning guardian of the Gate to the Halls of the Dead, and crawled around the corner. *I am the way into the city of woe . . .*

The tunnel used to be a normal line, way back in the 1850s, before Napoleon III ordered the Cimetière des Innocents—a festering open-air charnel house in the middle of Les Halles, mostly for stillborn babies—dug up and sanitized. The I.G.C. complied, and decided to dump the bones into parts of the underground quarries, thereby suddenly making the popular misnomer "catacombs" quite accurate. Most of the bones—six million skeletons, by most counts—went into the labyrinth under Denfer-Rochereau, artistically arranged by some long-forgotten madman into walls of stacked tibiae lined with skulls and crossed femurs. That area became a museum, with gravel paths along the bones.

The rest of the bones went here, into various areas under Montparnasse, unceremoniously dumped into long tunnels—filling them to within a half-meter of the sky—and hastily sprinkled with quicklime; then the tunnels were sealed off for a hundred years, till the first spuds in the early '80s came by with hammer and pick and tore open the plugs.

Five meters. I didn't have any gloves, and the quicklime was starting to burn my hands. I crawled along the tunnel, femurs and broken skulls digging painfully into my ribs, my back scraping the sky, Domino's feet scrambling through the mud a few meters ahead of me. After a few minutes I turned off my flash; I didn't need it, and besides the bones were starting to get to me. Crawling on a half-million corpses can get pretty intense.

"Hey, Domino," I whispered.

She stopped crawling. "Yeah?"

"Y'OK?"

"I think I'm gonna puke," she moaned.

"Better not, kid. I'll have to crawl through it."

"You'd deserve it." She started crawling again.

Twenty-five meters. It took us fifteen endless minutes, Zen timelessness crawling on the bones, till at last they sloped down, the end. I rolled down the slope and stood up, stretching. Domino was examining her burnt hands, wincing at the pain. "Fuckin quicklime." The tunnel went on for a few meters, a carpet of bone fragments lining the ground, then turned left.

"Now what?" asked Domino.

"Go that way. You'll see."

The case of plastique was right where Toxic had said, around the corner before the dead end. It was a flat black case, rough ABS plastic, covered with yellow stenciled warnings and red and blue French Army markings.

I opened it and examined the contents: a thick wad of clay-like plastique, a mess of wires, thin sliver detonators, two triggers. I pulled out three slivers and wire and handed them to Domino.

"Know how to set these up?"

"Yeah."

"Good. String 'em two meters apart."

"You gonna waste 'em?"

"What do you think, kid? I'm gonna bend over and let 'em fuck me? Activate."

I dug into the plastique and pulled out a lump the size of a small orange. I divided it into three equal parts. *This should do the trick.*

Domino had wired the first detonator. I took it from her and jogged back toward the slope, toward the bones. "Bring the others when you finish," I called back.

I could hear faint scratching noises down the line as I climbed up the slope. I crawled as fast as I could, six meters in. *Figure they're two meters apart . . .* I reached the right spot and started digging, ignoring the pain in my peeling hands, frantically tossing skulls and broken bones to the side. When the hole felt deep enough I dropped one of the lumps of plastique in it and jabbed the sliver into the lump. I shoved some bones back into the hole, covering the plastique. I carefully ran the wire along the wall as I crawled backward, covering it as best I could. Good thing it was black. After two meters I stopped and dug another hole. Then I called out softly: "Domino!"

The answer came from right behind me. "Ya?"

"Sliver." *Good girl.*

"By your foot."

I squirmed around and reached back, grasping the sliver when I felt it brush my fingers. I quickly wired it to the first wad and planted it into the second one.

"Domino. Back."

"Copy."

Back another two meters and then repeat, same thing, hole and wad and sliver. Then down the slope and back toward the corner, threading the wire behind me. *Obsolete piece of crap. Should have radio slivers.*

Around the corner I quickly plugged the wire into the trigger. I closed the case, enough plastique and slivers left to do Sainte-Anne and half of Paris besides, and pushed it way back. I waved Domino behind me and settled back, waiting, listening to the faint scraping and cursing of the killers as they crawled toward us, toward their cornered prey.

Ready.

I heard him before I saw him, soft, live meat struggling with dry, dead bone. A skull rattled, rolling down the slope. I peeked around the corner and saw nothing; his guide IR light, invisible to the naked eye.

Perfect.

I huddled back into the corner as far as I could, Domino against me, head tucked in. I waited a beat.

Breath vacuum, fuckers. I hit the trigger.

Shockwave concussion like a hammer on my flesh pounding hammering blood spurting from my ears and nose: deaf stunned *overload.*

I must have blacked out for a second. Then I blinked, felt the wetness around my mouth and ears, and started coughing convulsively, bone dust coating my throat and lungs.

I staggered up, groggy, and clicked on the flash. Domino was curled up in a tight fetal ball, out cold. I sagged against the wall, still coughing, eruption of mucus and blood. I waved my arm around, trying to clear the dust, suspended particles glinting in the dim light of the flash.

I forced myself to walk, leaning against the wall, nearly blind, the flash useless in the dust cloud. I stumbled over the bones, finally felt my feet bump into the slope. I reached out, felt for the slope, and flopped onto it. I breathed deeply, the racking cough subsiding a bit, and pulled myself up the slope.

My hand brushed flesh, wet, sticky, gritty flesh and hair. I pulled myself up a bit more, ran my hands over him, dead, blood-soaked meat lying in a shredded suit among the bones. *At least you're in good company.* Then my hand felt the hole, huge, wet, soft hole where his hips should have been.

Can't puke, not now.

I forced myself to continue feeling him, my hand running over his body, his head, jagged protruding pieces of bones. *Thank Ogoun I can't see him.*

Shit . . . Where's the fucking tracker?

I finally found it, back a bit, blown clean off his head. I wiped the lenses off as best I could, on the inside of my bloodslimed T, and fitted it over my eyes, protruding bulbous goggles.

I hit the power switch and reflexively squeezed my eyes, red glare burning my retina. I fumbled and turned down the mag, all the way. I rested my bruised eyes in cool darkness for a bit before slowly turning it back up a bit.

Nightmare landscape in red and gray. The gray: cold stone walls, fine lines between the blocks of limestone, the mortar slightly warmer; the bones too, vague indistinct gray mass. But the red: a film of it, covering everything, spattered on the walls and the sky and the bones; warm blood coating, fluorescent red through the tracker. An amorphous red mass, too, next to me, killer's meat, the resolution thankfully vague.

I heard a moan then, a cough, up ahead. Scraping sound.

Fuck . . . One of them's still alive!

I rolled to the side and scanned the mess next to me, searching for the gun. I finally found it, down the slope, bright red chunk of metal lying among the reddish-gray bones. I picked it up and started crawling, pushing aside the corpse, blood and bone dust coating my entire body, my face; crawling through my narrow, round universe of reds and grays.

I pushed the second body aside, barely enough room to squeeze by, my hand jerking back reflexively as it touched the neck and felt the spurt of arterial blood. No head.

Fuckers were spaced farther out than I figured. Looks like I missed the third.

This one was also wearing a suit, thin summer cotton by the feel of it. That made the live one Two-Tone, now One-Tone. *Good.*

I could barely see him up ahead, a spot of red nearly invisible in the red haze. But I could hear him, scrambling and coughing. *Figure six meters, maybe seven . . . Five-minute lead . . . No problem.*

I crawled, pulling myself forward with my hands and elbows, legs useless weight, unable to push off the unstable surface. I heard more noise, a short cry, Two-Tone falling out of the hole.

I would have preferred to turn around in one of the small side alcoves, gone out feet first, but I figured it was a bad idea. Two-Tone might just choose to wait.

I poked the gun out the exit hole first, waiting for a shot. Nothing. I slowly pulled myself forward, peering out into the red haze.

I heard a crash then, a bit down the line, Two-Tone stumbling over a stray skull. I dropped the gun and flash to the ground and painfully dragged myself out of the hole. Headfirst, real dumb. By holding myself up on the opposing wall I managed to get one leg out, then two. I fell anyway, painful crash of tibia against the edge of the stone bench.

"Fuck fuck *fuck!*"

I hopped around a bit, massaging my leg. As soon as I could put my weight on it I picked up the gun and checked it, making sure the safety was off and the first bullet in the chamber. It was a nice gun, a ten-year-old MAC Ingram, 9mm full-auto pistol.

I started running down the line, following the red haze, infrared trails marking the place Two-Tone's body heat had excited the air molecules. It took me three minutes to catch up with him.

I tore off the IR trackers as I approached him and thumbed on the flash. He was cowering on the floor, heaving and sobbing, curled up. I found a crack in the wall and stuck the flash into it, opening the lens to maximum angle.

I looked at Two-Tone. His face was black, a mix of dark shadows and blast marks, streaked with tears of pure terror and dried, crusted blood. The hair on top of his head was gone, burnt off. The blast must've gone off right in front of his face.

I picked him up by the neck and held him up against the wall. He was mumbling incoherently, in shock. I slapped him.

"Two-Tone. Hello."

No reaction. I slapped him again.

"Two-Tone. Who hired you?"

I hit him again, pistolwhip with the barrel of the Ingram. He screamed, short choked cry.

"Two-Tone. If you do not talk to me, I will flay the flesh off your cheeks."

He started babbling then, a stream of words, terror monologue. "Oh man please don't hit me man I didn't want to hurt you man please don't hit don't hurt me don't waste me man please—"

I thrust the barrel of the Ingram into his mouth, violently, shutting off the flood. I heard teeth break. "What's the matter, Two-Tone, you speak better with a barrel in your mouth? Hunh? You like it better like this, asshole? Maybe you want me to pull the trigger, huh?"

I pulled the gun out as he started to gag. "Who hired you, Two-Tone?"

He spit out bits of teeth mixed with blood before answering. "Bald man. Said there was money for you, alive. Gave me the muscleboys when I told him I could find you."

"Alive?"

"Yeah, yeah, alive, man . . ."

"Why the guns, then?"

"It's all I had, man, we figured to scare you, get you to surrender or something."

"Idiot. If you got guns, you use them."

"Look, please, man, we weren't going to hurt—"

"Zip it. Did the bald man say anything else?"

"No, man, nothing, I swear."

I hit him again, with the Ingram. "You're lying, Two-Tone."

"No, man, please, don't hit me, he wanted something, said we had to make sure you had it . . ."

"What was it?"

"I dunno, man, some weird metal necklace or something, I'm not sure, I just heard him tell the others . . ."

The medallion. Sentimental value?

I let go of Two-Tone's neck and stepped back. He sagged against the wall, empty, delirious husk.

"What're you going to do?" he moaned.

I leveled the Ingram at his face. "Kill you."

He started crying. "No, man, please, don't, I swear, we weren't going to hurt you, please, don't—"

My hand jerked as I pulled the trigger, and I missed the head. A sharp, flat crack resonated in the small line as he jerked and sank to the ground.

There was a blood stain on the wall at head height. I prodded him and he screamed, terror scream of the trapped animal.

I'd hit him in the neck, just gouged out a chunk. Finally he stopped screaming and looked up, his eyes two huge wells, sucking mine in.

"Why . . ."

"Because I feel like killing someone." I shot him again, a short burst this time, in the mouth and the eyes and the head.

I stared at the corpse for a while before absently dropping the gun and heading back toward the Ossuaire. I waited till I found a small pit on the side to puke. Didn't want to make a mess, stink up the lines.

Domino's feet were sticking out of the hole when I got back, kicking, searching for a foothold. I helped her out. She stood very still when she reached the ground, covered in gore, a strange madness in her eyes. Suddenly she moved. Before I could react she'd slammed me against the wall. Her Fury appeared out of nowhere, razorsharp, high-grade steel skinning knife, and hovered a half centimeter away from my left eye. If I'd blinked it would've cut my eyelid.

"Don't-you-ever-do-this-to-me-again," she forced out between clenched teeth. The Fury never wavered, suspended in front of my eye, a silver dragonfly poised before the kill.

Then the madness died, and she collapsed against my chest, a scared thirteen-year-old shaking. The Fury thudded to the ground, point-first in the dirt. I held her for a long time, and she held me.

Eventually we moved. She stepped back, picked up the Fury, tried to find a clean spot on her clothes to wipe it off on, failed, shrugged, and made it vanish. I reflexively tried to make the sheath, see where she stashed it. Somewhere above her belt was the best I could do.

"We need showers," she said.

"No shit," I answered. We looked at each other and simultaneously burst out laughing, hysterical tension release, explosion. "Ah, fuck," I gasped as I wiped my eyes.

We calmed down. My left brain kicked into gear, calculating, planning. "We'll go to Viper's again. But we gotta wait, can't be seen Topside like this. Let's go to the

Bunker, wash off a bit at the sinks so at least we don't look like we just waded through a bloodpool, and then hit Topside round three-thirty."

"Dunno . . . Don't think I can wait that long."

"All right . . . Plan B. We wash up, then go Topside behind the bunker, at Lefébvre. You stay down, I hit the gas station, call Olric, have him pick us up, shower at his place."

"Razor. Let's step."

Washing up was fun, in a twisted, slapstick kinda way. We jumped up and down on the cold concrete floor, flinging buckets of icy water at each other, howling and laughing. Our ruined clothes we tossed into a corner. *Have to go to the Puces, score some new fatigues. I'm running out.* The worst was my hair; no way to get the gore out of it, braids and dreads glued together in one slimy, sticky mass.

We dressed quickly, jumping up and down to keep warm. I shoved my hair into a knitted dreadbag, put on a pair of torn jeans and an oversized gray *Yale* tank top I'd scored off a tourist awhile back. We hoisted ourselves out of the bunker and trotted to the exit tunnel.

I went up slowly, memories of a fall a few years back in the same shaft. I'd slipped and fallen six endless meters before a landing stopped me. I climbed with my hands tight on the muddy rungs, scraping my back against the landings, my flash precariously shoved in my pants and pointing upward.

I pulled myself past the last landing and flopped onto the ground, exhausted. I rolled over and reached down, grasping Domino's wrist and helping her out.

"OK. You stay here and wait while I go call Olric."

"No problem." She sat cross-legged and leaned against the wall.

I started up the short ladder to the grate. I could see the daylight through it, dull gray dusk light.

I was about to push it open when I remembered.

"Uh, Domino."

"Yeah?"

"You got a card?"

She dug into a pocket, pulled out a small wallet, and fumbled through the cards until she found the right one.

"Catch." She lobbed it high, perfect toss, and I snatched it out of the air. "Thanks."

I peered through the grate as best I could before opening, checking for Mirrorfaces. I didn't see anybody. What with the angle, though, they could be standing right next to the grate and I wouldn't see them. *Well, at least they aren't standing on top of it.*

Fuck it. I pushed the grate up and rapidly scanned the street, quick three-sixty, ready to dart back down the ladder like a scared ferret at the slightest hint of trouble.

Nobody. I climbed out and dropped the gate shut with a clang. I stood there for a few beats, momentarily blanking out, forgetting where I was or why I was there. Then my eyes locked onto the pay phone by the station and I remembered.

Olric.

Olric looked pissed as he slewed his Renault over to a stop by the curb. He popped the door and yelled, "Get in!" We crammed ourselves into the front passenger bucket seat, Domino on my lap.

"Dude," said Olric as we careened down the boulevard at thirty k.p.h. over the speed limit, "this shit's gettin old."

"Deepest apologies, my man, but you know. This ain't really my main trip either."

"Yeah."

The reason for Olric's anger was lounging on the couch when we reached his pad, wearing a frayed kimono, smoking a cigarette and leafing through an old *Paris-Match*. Her name was Alli, and Olric barely took the time to toss us two towels before pulling her into the room and slamming the door shut.

Olric's bathroom was a mess, a filthy and chaotic combination of photo lab and mud-encrusted Downside clothes storage area, a personal interpretation of the back room of a pawn shop gone wild. We waded through army-surplus clothes and archaic black-and-orange Agfa photo-developing equipment and located the shower. I cleared

it out, tossing the various spools and containers on top of
the acetylene gear in the sink, and turned on the shower.
It spat at me, dirty red water painfully tearing itself out
of the pipes.

"We should've gone to Viper's," said Domino wryly.

"We still can."

We left Olric a note, unwilling to once again interrupt
the scene of sexual passion taking place in the bed-
room, and left.

At Viper's, I scanned the news while Domino show-
ered: usual Paris bullshit.

Viper used the same service as I did, so I felt right at
home when Natalie's pert Uptown face blossomed onscreen.

"South African officials announced today that the explosion that occurred yesterday morning at the Pietr Botha
nuclear power plant outside Johannesburg was caused by
sabotage. An official of the government's Ministry of
Information claimed the act was perpetrated by members
of the Chzecosoviet-backed radical Color Power party.

"The explosion ripped open one of the reactor's cores,
spewing radioactive debris over greater Johannesburg.
The evacuation of the city is still in progress. Zulu officials complained bitterly tonight, charging that the evacuation plan was biased, favoring white neighborhoods over
colored ones. The government has—"

I skipped forward a bit, to the local news.

"The leader of the young gang A.C.A.F. went on trial
today. The prosecutor demanded the death penalty, and
is expected to get it.

"A psychotic ex-Special Forces cyborg escaped from
the Saint-Anne Asylum earlier this afternoon, in a murderous rampage that left five hospital attendants dead
and three wounded. Orders have been issued to all Paris
police to shoot to kill."

The red face of Commandant Breton appeared onscreen. I chuckled. They seemed to be using the same
footage as they had when he talked about Kurt. "The
thing—I mean the man—is an extremely—lethally—dangerous individual," growled the captain. "Therefore, I
have issued the shoot-to-kill order."

Natalie reappeared, still smiling. "That was Commandant Breton of the C.R.S. in a press conference earlier this afternoon.

"Also in Paris, the parents of dead graffiti artist Jean Zoulou-Lautrec held a press conference at 14:00 today during which they accused the police of murdering their son. Mr. Zoulou-Lautrec was arrested for painting graffiti a week ago and died in jail of wounds he sustained during his arrest. The Commisariat of the 1er *arrondissement* denied the accusation, stating that the death was accidental and that they had acted entirely within the limits of their mandate."

Natalie's face was replaced by the Libération logo as the capsule cycled. Her face reappeared, still smiling wetly, unchanged.

"In Beirut this morning—"

I cut the news as I saw Domino step out of the shower, still dripping. "Your turn." She grinned.

Viper's shower is perfect for meditating in, hard and hot and clean. I spent a full half hour fighting with shampoo and my dreads, the water running red on the tiles, fading remembrance of a bad dream dissolving in the drain. I finally emerged, relatively clean and extremely relaxed, a cloud of steam escorting me into the living room and fogging up the full-length mirror as I was about to examine myself in it. I gave up and flopped onto the couch, a beached jellyfish. *I ought to have at least saved an ear or something, to mail it to darling Angélique.* I sank into the soft foam cushions and a long dark quicksand sleep.

I remembered the medallion halfway through breakfast (lunch, actually, the way most people reckon it) as I held a buttered strip of baguette poised above my bowl of coffee, ready to dip. Viper and Domino were chatting over a hardcopy of *Libé*, discussing the escaped cyborg.

"Fuckin trail of blood, man, he just greased those dudes with his bare hands—"

"Yeah, check this, it says here that he used his lunch tray to decapitate one of the security guards."

"Fuckin A."

I quickly finished the baguette, slurped down the coffee, and went over to the table where I'd dumped all my necklaces before taking the shower. The medallion sat there, a heavy, dull, carved weight of bronze.

I picked it up and held it lightly, feeling the weight. I examined the bas-relief twin brother, a male Angélique staring up at me.

Intrigued, I set it on the table, away from the rest of my junk, and flicked my armdeck open. I ran my fingers over the membranes, keying up the scan functions.

I hadn't lied to Domino about my armdeck, one of the most sophisticated product of the U.S. intelligence secret research labs. Dozens of special functions, such as the electronics scan; a small holocam and mike; accessing capabilities like I've never seen, I mean to the whole WorldNet; and an unbelievable data-mem capacity. It awed even Billy Name when he saw it, something I hadn't believed possible.

I pointed the armdeck at the medallion and ran the scan. It took three seconds before I hit the jackpot.

Silicon. Circuits.

I shut down the deck and picked up the medallion, staring at it. I ran over various options, but there was really only one.

Time to go see Billy Name.

Tracking down Name's latest hideout was, as usual, a bitch. I skated around the Forum—no one would use guns in the crowd, I figured, and I moved too fast for a knife—till I found one of his little mutant horrors.

"Hey, spud, gotta message for Name, crucial."

"Oh yeah? Who are you?"

Little freaks are getting cocky. "Tell Name Lynx's gotta see him, doublequick. Copy?"

"That you?"

"Yeah. Go tell Name, spud. Tell him I gotta see him."

"Fontaine Saint-Michel. Wait there."

The mutant—or one of his buddies, I could never tell them apart—showed up thirty-five minutes later, a real record. I was edgy and feeling sick, the result of sitting for a half hour in an exposed and vulnerable position with the ambient temperature of a blast furnace. No one tried to kill me, though. *Thank Kirishto for small graces . . .*

"Name sez go by the old Arab Institute, then skate down the river to Austerlitz and wait at the taxi line."

"Listen, kid, I got ugly folk crawling up my ass like roaches on dirty linoleum. I can't just hang out like this."

"Name wants to make sure you're clean. You wanna see Name, you do what he says. Copy?"

Paranoid motherfucker. I took off without another word and jammed through the traffic at the intersection, mad enough to play the old chickengame for a few seconds, familiar sounds of scraped metal and curses as drivers slewed to avoid me. I calmed down when I reached the quai and settled into a fast groove till I reached the

Institute. At least I was skating into traffic—figured no one could follow me.

I waited outside the blasted, prowlike hulk of the building for a few minutes, studying the looming ruins while Name's eye studied me. Once Paris's most beautiful glass building, the Insitut des Études Arabes had been bombed to a cinder three months ago by Front National terrorists, supposedly in retaliation for the alleged Tariquat murder of old LePen's daughter. A burnt steel-girder skeleton filled with rubble was all that remained, an eyesore scheduled for demolition.

I never saw Name's eye. I took off again, skimming down the quai, toward the Gare d'Austerliz. I passed the gothic stone mass of the University VI & VII—a couple of art students lounging against the stone wall sketching the Pont de Sully—and by the Jardin des Plantes.

Finally I reached Austerlitz. I turned off the glide units and walked into the vast parking lot, past harried and tired travelers pouring in and out of the old station. I noted a cleanscrawl graffiti on a long stone wall with pleasure, the initials C.R.S., CESSEZ LA REPRESSION SANGLANTE. I got on line at the taxi stand, behind an old red-faced country matron carrying straw baskets with protruding knitting needles, and waited.

I studied the bustling crowd for a while, wondering how I would be picked up. A young obnoxious Suit got into a fight with a pregnant woman over a taxi. The woman started yelling and the Suit shoved her back, knocking her down, and jumped into the cab. I thought that would be it, but then the cabbie got out, opened the rear door, dragged out the Suit, punched him in the stomach, and tossed him into the gutter. He then walked around the cab amid spontaneous applause from the crowd and helped the woman get up and into the cab. The Suit crawled away, presumably to seek safer transportation.

I finally reached the head of the line and stood there wondering what the fuck I was supposed to do. A taxi pulled up in front of me.

"Taxi, sir?"

I absently nodded no, scanning the crowd, looking for Name or another AT.

"Sir?"

The insistent voice made me look down. The Wire grinned up at me, fake mustache glued to his face, the quintessential cabbie. I got in.

"Where to, sir?"

"Fuck off, man." I laughed. "Take me to your leader!"

Name's newest workshop was located in a derelict factory in Ivry-sur-Seine, in what used to be called *La Zone* before the Arab ghetto up north appropriated the term. The Wire pulled up in front of a huge hangar entrance, obsolete train tracks disappearing under the corrugated metal doors.

"Follow the tracks. You'll find him in back."

"Thanks, man. See you around."

I got out and walked toward the doors without looking back. I reached them, grasped a handle, and tugged hard. To my surprise the door slid open easily, nearly throwing me off balance, rolling smooth on newly greased runners.

The hangar was dark. I walked in between the two rails, leaving the door open so I could see. I'd walked two meters when the doors slammed shut with a clang, cutting off the light, leaving me standing still in the darkness.

A voice boomed out of a loudspeaker, filling the vast black space, directionless.

"What's the matter, Lynx? Your namesake can see in the dark."

I yelled out. "Cut the theatrics, man! I got no time for this shit!"

A sharp *clack* and a small spotlight sprang to life in the back of the hangar, pointing straight down. A thin silhouette stood in it, his right hand on a switch box dangling from a long cable. The cable stretched down from the ceiling, from the darkness beyond the spotlight.

I walked toward him. He was dressed for work, grease-stained, olive-drab U.S. jumpsuit and a green-and-white corporate *hachimaki* holding back his long blond hair.

I stopped right in front of him, just out of the cone of the spotlight.

His voice sounded small as he spoke, contrast to the

booming speakers. "Lynx, my friend, you have no romanticism in your soul.

"Billy, my friend, you're in the wrong business," I said.

He smiled. "What should I be doing, then?"

"Expressionist horror films. You've got all the essentials down pat."

He thumbed a toggle on the rusted metal switch box and the spotlight cut out. Another, much softer click, and a door slid open a few meters behind him, harsh white halogen light spilling out from behind it. He turned around, displaying the gorgeous black-and-silver Cocteau stencil on the back of the jumpsuit, the aristocratic head ringed with the words ARTISTES TERRORISTES.

"Come in," he said. "Come see my latest creation."

Billy Name, Prince of the Jury-rig, is the only genuine madman I know. I mean, all streetdrek are pretty frit, and so are most Uppers, for that matter, but Name is *gone*, I mean *loco*. At some point in his misspent youth, the mental circuits concerning sex, death, and art must have gotten severely crossed, if not short-circuited; definitely a major malfunction. Added to his hardcore genius for electronics and ordnance, this produced some very weird results. He's an old friend, though, old as Viper, and he barely even fazes me now.

He started the Artistes Terroristes two years ago with three other spuds who shared at least *part* of his psychopathologies. (The Wire was one of them; the other two are dead, one in an accident involving a bathtub, two Sorbonne girls, and liquid nitroglycerin, the other one gunned down by the Mirrorfaces in mysterious circumstances.) As he explained it the ATs were the logical endpoint of the artistic direction of the twentieth century, the systematic conceptual destruction of all taboos in the name of art. What he proposed was simply to shatter the last taboo, the taboo so strong that no artist even thought of it as a taboo: the taboo on Murder.

Billy Name wrote their Manifesto, a convoluted screed about Art and Pain and Death and the meaning of Jean Cocteau, the AT's idol if not role model. "Down with the sanctity of the spectator! Down with the sanctity of Life! We must go beyond sexuality, beyond anger, beyond aggression, beyond emotion to reach the affectless purity of conceptual Murder.

"Terrorism, in the past only a political weapon of the oppressed minorities, will be our tool. We propose Murder as a work of Art, a performance in which the spectator will be intimately involved both as participant and observer; that is, the spectator will be our victim, and our victims will be our public. To see our Art will mean to *be* our Art; will mean to die. The spectator will not survive the performance.

"This means of course that any critique of our Art will be necessarily flawed, as it will only be based on second-hand mechanical reproduction, on films or videotapes. To understand our Art you must experience it, and to experience it you must die."

The ATs started their first performance by printing up thirty-thousand copies of the Manifesto. They then stole a small flier and dropped the leaflets over Paris, sowing them over Saint-Michel and Concorde and up the Champs. The catch was that they'd coated the leaflets with a thermite solution and a chloride catalyst which reacted after thirty seconds with the surface acid of the reader's skin and ignited the thermite. Few of the victims died, though many were maimed for life.

NAPALM MANIFESTO screamed the headlines. Name and his cohorts announced that the performance was a failure, as most of the participants survived, and went on to design greater and more baroque acts of terrorism with an aesthetical catch.

I squinted as I stepped into the glare of the halogens. Name threw his arms open and crowed: "La Machine Infernale!"

It sat in the middle of the vast space, a black, hulking tank covered with carballoy armor plates and exhaust vanes. A dozen of Name's little mutants scurried around and over it, trailing cables and carrying ammo crates. Two of them were maneuvering a crane, lowering a huge Browning twin 70 into a gun port. Someone had sloppily bombed MADAME EURYDICE REVIENDRA DES ENFERS—the ATs slogan—in orange spraypaint on the side of the tank.

"Name, what the fuck is this? You preparing for the next world war?"

Name was obviously more than pleased to give me a guided tour of his latest folly.

"We built this over the frame of a surplus Israeli APC I acquired in Bonn and shipped here in a thirty-ton truck. I got the armor plates from the French Army, from a friend in the Defense Ministry with a bad dust problem."

I examined the brute as we slowly walked around it.

"It's ringed with gun ports, here, here, here, and there. I bought two British flamethrowers, four obsolete Czechosoviet grenade launchers, and four twin 70s, and installed them. With the appropriate amount of ammunition, of course."

"Where did you get them?"

"From Cornelius. Where else?"

I nodded. "Go on."

"The whole thing will be controlled by remote, the signal routed via a Japanese commercial satellite so it can't be traced—"

"What are you going to do with it?" I interrupted.

"Take a downer, man. I'll get to it." He paused. "See those lenses, there and there? And those small ports, around the flank?"

"Yeah."

"Wide-angle holocams and shotgun mikes. To tape the whole thing."

"What thing?"

"Wait!" He threw out his arms. "Wait."

"OK." I leaned against the side of the tank, arms crossed.

"Anyway. We rigged two fullscale Hitachi holoprojs on top of the tank, along with speakers. They're wired into the holocams and the mikes for instant replay."

He looked at me expectantly. I fished my pack of Gauloises out of my pocket and lit one. Name froze, a look of beatific horror on his face.

"Lynx . . ."

"Yeah?" I inhaled as I snapped my Zippo shut.

"You're standing right next to a fuel valve, man."

"Ah," I deadpanned. *Knew that'd get to you.* I inhaled again and studied the valve, flicking the ashes onto the

151

ground. Then I held up the cigarette and stared at it. Name looked like he was about to come; I had a split-second flashback, visiting his pad once, noticing the cum stains on a Smith & Wesson catalog. I smiled innocently, dropped the cig, and crushed it under my bootheel. "What were you saying?"

Name took a few seconds to regain his composure. Finally he stuttered, "Ah, uh, yes, the holos, yeah, uh . . ."

I decided to help him a bit. "What's it for?"

He spun around and paced away, rubbing his chin. Then he spun again, stalked toward the tank, grabbed a protruding gun barrel, and hoisted himself up on top of it. I stepped back to get a better view and nearly tripped over a fuel line.

Name struck his glamourgod pose, head back, eyes rolled up in their sockets, arms out. Then he slowly lowered his head and started to speak.

"This," he said, "is the culmination of the vision of the Artistes Terroristes. In a few days' time, engineering permitting, we shall unleash death, chaos, madness, and horror upon the good burghers of Paris."

He paused and bowed his head. When he looked up there was a gleam in his eyes. "Picture the Champs Élysées. Saturday night. Uptown crowd, glamourgirls and glitterboys, the cream of the Paris poseurs. A truck stops dead in the middle of the avenue, facing toward Concorde. It lands. The back gate drops. Out glides the Machine Infernale, gleaming black paint, bristling with ugly guns. It moves up a bit and then stops. People are staring, wondering, 'What the fuck is that? A new military machine? Street theater, maybe, advertising stunt, who knows?'

"Suddenly a screamer goes off. People clutch their bleeding ears and start retching. A few Faces run up, have fun unloading their burpguns on the tank.

"And then the ordnance kicks in."

He paused again, seeming to go into a trance. I was starting to get the picture. *Outta control, Billy . . .*

He spoke again. "Picture it. This crowd, this mob, the pampered masses, afraid of a broken nail. And Death erupts in their midst, belching napalm and 70-caliber rounds and grenades, phosphorus grenades, gas grenades, concussion grenades, frag grenades.

"Death, blood, screams, panic, everywhere . . . Some Mirrorfaces try to use their Bullpups, but the rounds bounce off the carballoy armor and they get mowed down by the twin 70s.

"But that isn't all! A giant holo forms above the death tank as it slowly glides up the avenue. It shows the scene as it unfolds, instant replay, in color, with sound. It is the last thing the dying poseurs can see! It strobes above them as they are torn to pieces and burnt to a crisp and mashed to a pulp!" Name was into a full messianic swing now, neck muscles bulging like steel cables, hands clawing at the air. "Can you see it? Can you see the terror, the awe? Can you understand the perfect beauty of it, the intricate, multiple layers of experience and observation? They lie there, the Uptown rabble, bleeding, missing limbs and genitals, intestines strewn over the sidewalk, and they can *watch themselves die, live*!"

He held the climactic pose for a few beats, then suddenly slumped, drained. The little mutants, who had stopped working to watch, applauded madly. Name dug through his pockets, pulled out a crumpled brown cigarillo, lit it with a wooden match which he struck on his boots, and grinned.

"Well? What do you think?"

I stood there wide-eyed. *Shit . . . Whatever happened to the good guys?* "Name . . . You're really fucked, man."

"Isn't it beautiful?" He jumped off the tank and walked toward me, beaming like an actor after his performance, anxious for a good review. "What a concept, what a magnificent monstrosity! Truly a fitting climax to our career, a natural for the history, art, and psychoanalysis textbooks."

I shook my head. "Name. When you perform this . . ."

"Yes?"

"Could you inform me a few days ahead of time, so I can round up a few spectators, prepare a guest list?"

It was a pretty nasty idea, but then again I wouldn't feel too sorry for the skagheads who got wasted by it. Karma goes around, and after Berlin . . . Besides, the kink did have a kind of twisted beauty to it. The instant-replay bit, now that was genius.

"Now," said Billy Name as we walked toward a small room in the back, "what can I do for you?"

I dug into my pocket and pulled out the medallion. I held it up in front of him.

He studied it for a few seconds before touching it. Finally he took it and held it in his hand.

"Nice work. What is it?"

"I don't know. I hope you'll tell me."

He smiled as we entered the room. It was lit by a single dusty light bulb hanging from the ceiling, and was cluttered with a miscellanea of decks, cables, leads, jacks, stray chipboards, ROM cassettes, crystal needles, an old well-polished Colt .45, a half-empty bottle of Wild Turkey, stacks of old magazines and catalogs, clear plastic boxes filled with assorted components, and other electronic bizarreness.

"Well, we'll just have to do our best, won't we?"

Three minutes later he pushed the strange tubular contraption he'd been using up from over his eyes and looked at me.

"It's tight-sealed, man, some weird-ass polycarbon shit under the bronze coating. Whatever's in there, though, it's definitely active. It's got sensors and shit, audio and vid it looks like, maybe a few others."

"Do you know what it is?"

"Some kind of elaborate recording device, maybe? I'm not sure."

"Can you cut it?"

"Well, laser would fuck up the soft, manual would be dicey too. This thing's really fucked, man."

"Can you do it?"

"No." *First time I ever heard Billy Name say* that. "But I know who can."

"He's an old Jew," said Name as he guided me through a maze of industrial corridors lit by dirty greenish neons. "Real old, hundred and twenty or so. He's called the

Rabbi. I've seen him do things with the hard and the soft that are theoretically impossible."

"Where does he live?"

Name grinned, baring filed teeth. "The Zone."

"And that," he added as he stopped in front of a painted-over glass door and opened it with a manual key, "requires some *special* equipment."

The contents of the room we entered made Max's store look like an amateur's collection. Guns of every size, description, and make, all neatly arranged against the walls in racks and cases. A rapid glance showed me a Finnish Valmet 7.62mm; a Russian AK-47 with banana magazine; a case full of Colt revolvers, Pythons and King Cobras, all magnum; a Heckler & Koch 9mm assault rifle with a chrome laserscope at the tip; a few old FN .308s and .203s; a brand-new Intratec TEC-9, still wet with packing grease; a rack of police MAS 9mm Bullpups . . .

I whistled. "*Trés* pretty. Your museum?"

Name waved at the guns. "Pick something comfortable. I'll be back."

I lingered before choosing a gun, feeling like a kid in the proverbial candy store. I'd narrowed it down to two handguns by the time Name returned.

He'd gone to change. He was wearing pleated gray pants over low black gloveboots, a white cotton buttondown shirt with a thin blackknit tie, fingerless black cotton gloves, and a long, billowing black cashmere coat. His long hair had been slicked back and pulled into a thick ponytail tied with a silk ribbon.

"What do you think?"

"Dressed to kill, Billy, as always. I like it."

"Have you picked anything yet?"

I showed him my two choices: a Ruger Service Six .357 magnum, a very reliable revolver, or a Beretta 9mm, which I liked mostly for its fourteen-round clip.

"Go for the Ruger," he immediately said. "The kind of street shit we could get into, if you need fifteen rounds, you're meat anyway. Also, the Ruger can't jam, and if you hit someone with that, even in the pinky, he goes down, he stays down."

"You got a rig?" I asked.

He bent down over a wooden crate and dug through it before tossing me a nylon armpit rig. I pulled off my leather and fitted it on, adjusting it comfortably under my left arm.

I flipped the cylinder open. It was empty. I looked at Name.

"Ammo?"

He went over to a small table in the corner covered with cardboard ammo boxes. "It's a magnum, right?"

"Yeah."

"I got some hollowpoints somewhere . . . Ah."

He found the right box and tossed it to me. I tucked the gun under my arm and tore it open, spilling a few rounds. I squatted and put the box down before taking hold of the gun again and carefully loading it. I spun the cylinder when I finished, slapped it shut, and shoved the gun into the rig. Then I scooped up the stray rounds, grabbed a few more, and dropped them into the sunglass pocket in my leather. I closed the box and put it back on the table.

Name had picked his gun by the time I finished, and it was a beauty: a Mossberg 500, 12-gauge pump-action sawed-off pistol-grip shotgun. The perfect weapon for dirty street work, all sleek black steel and black polycarbon and ABS grips. He attached it to a strange rig under his raincoat, one that let it hang under his right arm without sticking out from under the coat.

He noticed my stare. "I made the rig myself. The right pocket is slit like this, see," he demonstrated, "so with my hand in my pocket I can grab the gun and shoot. Razor, no?"

"Yeah, hardcore, I like it. Real nasty, my kinda nasty."

He bobbed his head, acknowledging the compliment. He scooped a few shells off the table, dropped them into his left pocket, and turned toward the door. He stopped in midstep, and as an afterthought picked up an old U.S. M19 frag grenade and tucked it in his pocket.

He smiled at me and patted the pocket as he opened the door. "Just in case things get *real* dirty."

The Zone is the Wall; that and all the drek inside it. They built the Wall in '16, after the riots that killed my mother and about twelve hundred other bodies. It rings most of the 18ème and the 19ème, and part of the 20ème; Barbès, Pigalle, Montmartre, the old slums, sad whores and angry immigrants; what they used to call La Goutte d'Or, I hear. The Wall itself: ferroconcrete, steel, the top covered with razorwire, dotted with bunker-towers bristling with FN .75-caliber machine guns and Stoeger flamethrowers, and lined with magnetic proximity mines and CS gas bombs, lots of them. The weirdest thing about the Wall is the gates, the huge plasteel gates: they're always open. The Wall was built to contain riots, not individuals; when the time comes, the gates are closed, and the Beasts watch gleefully as the Zone self-destructs.

The metaphorical effect of the wall, Mara once said, is that of a jail, albeit with open doors; and, as with any such powerful metaphor, the sociological template is modified. The Arabs within the Zone started claiming more control over their territory; if no one wanted them outside, they didn't want anybody inside. Mirrorfaces and gadjos venturing beyond the Wall became targets. The Tariquats grew in power and started doing their own policing. The Beasts, content at having contained the cancer, stopped trying to destroy it. Signs went up, *à vos risques et périls*. . . .

Name whistled low when he saw the heads. "Well, shit . . . What happened to the old 'At your own risk'?"

"This is a bit more effective, no?"

"Yeah, you could put it that way. You're lucky you're my friend, Lynx. I wouldn't come up here for money."

The heads were swinging in the light rain, hanging from the green 1900s art-nouveau scrollwork over the Métro entrance. The mummified eyes of a red-haired man glared at me, reproachfully, it seemed. Beyond them Pigalle was wet, hot, badly lit, empty.

Name pulled a small Nikon out of the inside of his cashmere coat; black plastic and red quartz opticals, the size of a pack of cigarettes. He started taking pictures of the heads.

"For my collection," he said.

I felt nervous, edgy. I'd never liked the Zone, even in daytime. The empty night made my skin crawl. Eerie, spooky, deadly . . . I fished into the side pocket of my leather and snagged a crushed pack of Gauloises. I pulled out a flat cigarette, rolled it between my palms, and lit it. I snapped my Zippo shut and listened to the flat, metallic *clack* echo across Pigalle. I took two drags from the cigarette, then flicked it away, watching the sparks shower across the wet concrete. I pulled my collar up and buckled the bottom of my leather.

Name put his camera away and spun around slowly, his coat swishing, examining the empty plaza. Raindrops danced arhythmically in the puddles.

"Where are all the whores?" he asked.

"Outside the Wall, if they're smart. Besides, they don't like Arabs. No money in them, at least not these."

"Yeah, I could see that. This way," he added, striding off toward the hill.

We'd been walking for ten minutes and seen no one when Name nudged me.

"Eyes up, my man," he whispered.

Four slim figures melted out of the shadows and fanned out silently in front of us. Blades glittered. A smell of fear and danger in the air. Water sounds as one stepped in a puddle. I noticed a cockroach by my boot.

"Tariquat razors," I said. "Ziplip."

One of them stepped forward into the cone of the streetlight: a Mahgrebin kid, purple hair and half his face painted white. His nostrils flared, smelling blood. The half-lip in the brown half-face curled up in a smile. The white half didn't move, frozen even when he spoke.

"Cool runnings, breed. What brings you up beyond the Wall at this hour of the night?" He ignored Name.

"I got biz up here, blood, crucial biz."

"Well, that's too bad, breed. You're a long way from home."

"I got no battle with the Tariquats. *Namat min dïbäj.*"

"*Lä iläha ill'Alläh.* You know the words, breed, but that's not good enough. You brought a gadj into the Zone."

"The gadj is cold, no friend of the Beasts."

"I don't give a fuck. You nuked, breed. You're meat."

"Breathe vacuum, asshole. *You* nuked." Billy Name spoke for the first time. "I'm Name, and I'm no Uptown boy slumming in the Zone."

The sawed-off Mossberg slithered out from under his long coat like a snake. The blast tore the grinning razor in two, the sound exploding through the narrow street. My back tensed up, nails-on-blackboard screeches running through my nerves. I pushed Name's gun up before he could fire again.

"Wait."

The three other razors vanished on cue, shadow fragments joining the mother shadow, a seamless whole. The street was empty again, dark except for the cone of the light; spotlight on a torso, blood on the wet pavement running into the gutter. The blast had caught the razor in the crotch, blowing off his legs and disintegrating his pelvis.

"Tariquat pussies." Name laughed, pumping the Mossberg.

"No," I said, "Smart." I was worried. The whole scene was making me edgier than I'd ever been. "I hope your friend lives near here."

"Yeah, he does." Name was catching on to my nervousness. "Think they might come back?"

"Maybe. We better step, fast."

"Solid, man. Can do." He toed one of the legs of the dead razor, kicked it away, into the dark. "This one ain't coming after us." He kicked the other leg after the first, leaving only the torso on the street, legless like a hand puppet. "See? No legs." He laughed, pulled out his Nikon, held it up, snapped a shot of the torso. The flash made me flinch, ghost afterimages dancing on my retina.

"Name. Cut it. Let's step."

"All right." Name put the camera away. "This way." As he passed the remains of the razor, he stopped, and dipped both of his boots in the pool of blood. He started walking again, leaving red-ribbed footprints on the tarmac.

"Name. You gotta do that shit?"

Name smiled. "*Madame Euridyce Reviendra Des Enfers* . . . You follow your voodoo, Lynx, I follow mine."

"What is your voodoo, Name?"

"The poisoned aesthetics of murder. Death is my tool, to create beauty with. Poems. Sculptures. *Les fleurs du mal* . . ."

"You're frit, Name. Loco."

"No more than you, Lynx. Truth?" The last word accented oddly.

I know your word games, Billy.

"Beauty is truth, eh, Name?"

"Now you understand," he said.

He was right, too. I did understand.

The Rabbi's shop was located in a small old stone building on the Rue des Trois-Frères, below the Basilique du Sacré-Coeur. I stared up the steep cobblestone street as Name banged repeatedly on a thick, plain wood door. A hand-painted sign above the door read MOSHE'S COMPUTERS AND ELECTRONICS—WE BUY, SELL, REPAIRE. I smiled briefly when I noticed the eccentric spelling.

Name's hammering finally produced a result. A light went on inside the shop and a tremulous old voice floated through the door.

"Go away!"

Name winked at me. "Yo, Rabbi! It's me, Name! Open, will you? We're getting wet out here."

I heard deadbolts click and the door swung open an inch. A watery eye peered out, surrounded by wisps of gray-white hair.

"Name? Billy Name?"

"Yeah. Don't you recognize me, Rabbi? Don't tell me you're getting senile."

"No, no!" The door swung open. "I just haven't seen you in so long."

The Rabbi looked like . . . well, a rabbi. In pajamas. He was an old Jew with a creased old brown face and wild gray beard and hair. The pajamas looked expensive, clean-starched white silk, and his feet had been hastily shoved into an ancient pair of brown velvet slippers, the velvet worn bare in spots. A small yarmulka was precariously perched on top of the unruly mess of hair.

He stepped back and waved. "Well, come on in! Now that you've woken me up, you might as well." He spoke in soft, cultured, oddly accented voice.

Name hugged him as he walked in, laughing. "Hey Rabbi. If we just woke you up, how come you're wearing that?" He pointed at the yarmulka.

"How was I to know it was you? You don't think I'd kill someone bare-headed, do you?"

The front shop looked fairly standard: decks and accessories in display cases, stacks of cardboard boxes, thick binders on shelves; dilapidated but neat. The back, now . . .

The Rabbi led us through the curtain (actually a ragged Israeli flag) into the unholy merging of a console jockey's office and a sorcerer's laboratory. Decks everywhere, most of them with the plastic casing removed, extruding customized modifications like malignant growths; racks of chipboard wired together in unfathomable ways, with old brass menorahs dripping wax on top of them; thick, tangled coils of cables, sloppily taped to the walls with sticky silver electrical tape; stacks of hand-painted harddisks covered with weird, intricate, cabalistic designs; a few brown skulls; and in the middle of the room, a large old book set on a rickety, worm-eaten wooden stand. I stared at the book while the Rabbi puttered and Name examined a stack of old software minidisks. It was a true antique, brittle yellow cloth paper bound in cracked leather and brass. It was handwritten in an eldritch language, thick, black, handwritten characters.

"It is a *Kaballah*," said the Rabbi, noticing my interest. "It was written in the thirteenth century by the Rabbi ben Simon, a wise and powerful scholar."

"You copied this off a library disk or something?"

"No, no, no!" He chuckled. "That is the original tome."

It took a few seconds for that to register. "You mean *this* book right here is eight centuries old?"

"Yes." He smiled benignantly.

"Iesu Kirishto . . ." I stared at the book, dumbstruck. "It's in Hebrew?"

"Yes."

I caressed the edge of the binding as lightly as I could. I didn't dare touch an actual page. If it broke or something . . .

The Rabbi cut into my reverie. "Well, now, Billy, how may I be of assistance?"

"Show it to him, Lynx."

I found the medallion in one of my pockets and handed it to the Rabbi. He pulled a pair of square wire-rim glasses out of his breast pocket and put them on before looking at it.

"Bronze medallion, yes . . . Nice workmanship . . . What about it?"

"It's kinked," Name answered. "Got hard, soft, sensors sealed in polycarbon, very neat."

"What do you want to know about it?"

"What it is," I answered. "Some people tried to kill me for it and I want to know why."

"That's quite understandable. Let's see now. This carving here, that's young Xavier de Seingalt, isn't it?"

"How did you know?"

"Oh, I keep track of these things. Where did you get this?"

I hesitated. Name nudged me. "Tell him, skaghead."

"Yeah . . . Off Angélique de Seingalt's neck, his twin sister."

"Interesting . . ." He rubbed his beard as he studied the medallion. "Well, let's see what I can do. Why don't you go stand over by the curtain for a while, stay out of the way, yes?"

Name smiled at my frown. "Chill, man, it's how he works."

"Yeah, sure." I moved over to the entrance and squatted by the flag. I fingered it as the Rabbi went to work. It felt like nylon.

Name stood with his legs and arms crossed. The Rabbi had his back to us, so I couldn't really see just what he was doing. Sparks, strange hisses, green laser light, the hum of a deck and a power rig . . . Twice he got up and consulted the old book on the stand, leafing through it with the delicate touch of a butterfly, muttering to himself: "Yes . . . Hum . . . Ah, yes . . ."

It'd been twenty-three minutes by my armdeck when he looked up and called us over. The medallion was lying in front of him on a thin gray foam mat—or, more accurately, the innards of the medallion. He had stripped off the brass and the polycarbon, leaving only a small, mirrored RAM chip wired to a wetware logical, with a few minuscule sensors protruding from the logical.

"I'm afraid I had to destroy the bronze. I hope you don't mind."

"No, that's fine. What is this?"

"I'm not sure. I would've said a recording device, but it's far too elaborate for that. It looks like a fully operational computer, able not only to observe but perhaps also to analyze and integrate the input. The RAM here would contain the software, as well as store the input data, and the logical it's interfaced with would handle the processing. This is a very beautiful piece of work, by the way. Only a true genius or a very well equipped and financed laboratory could've come up with a unit of this caliber."

"Anubis," I said.

"Yes, that would make sense."

"What does it do?"

"As I said, record and process. I've no idea what its function is."

"Can you find out?"

"You are asking a lot, young man. It is good that you are a friend of Billy's, or this would cost you much more than you could possibly afford."

"I can pay."

"You will. I'll send you the bill. Through Billy." He swung around on his swivel chair and faced the remains of the medallion again. "I'll try to interface it with my system and analyze the software parameters. Maybe that will tell us something."

*   *   *

I wandered around while the Rabbi worked, bored, examining the equipment, careful not to disturb anything. Name sat down in a lotus position with his Mossberg on the floor in front of him and went into a trance.

He opened his eyes instantly when the old Rabbi yelled in alarm. We both leapt over to where he was madly punching deck, frantically fighting his haywire system.

"What the fuck is going on?" cried Name.

"I don't know." He tried another combination. Numbers scrolled across the screen, too fast to read. "I patched it in and cracked it and then everything went crazy! *Shaïsse!* It's taking over my system!"

Sparks started flying out of various circuits as they short-circuited. LEDs flashed red around the room, presaging data catastrophe.

"Shut the fucking thing down!" yelled Name.

"I'm trying, I'm trying!"

I saw a hanging start to smoke. I tore it down and stamped it out. Name tossed a stray piece of burlap on some burning components.

"Get the book out!" yelled the Rabbi.

I picked up the stand and started running toward the door, careful not to spill the book. Suddenly all the alarms stopped.

I put the stand down by the flag, gently. "Is it OK?"

"I don't know. The system's dead."

We both peered over his shoulders as his hands flew over the keyboard, trying to coax some life out of the system.

"Let's try this." His hands moved and something pinged. "Good, good." Blue light rolled across the screen as the system came online. "Got power. Let's see how much damage that little virus of yours inflicted."

Shit . . . "Look, man, I'm real sorry." *Kirishto, that was feeble . . .*

The Rabbi was very polite about it, as coldly polite as someone with possibly gutted data banks can be. "I'm insured."

For lost data? I shut up and watched him work. He started running checks, scanning his systems, his banks. Everything came up green.

"Amazing!" he said at last. "It looks intact! Nothing was damaged, all the data is there, all the interfaces . . ."

"Have you checked for trojan horses?" asked Name.

"Hold on." More numbers, more green lights. "Looks clear. All the test squirts show up negative intrusions."

"But what the fuck happened?" I asked.

"I have no idea. *Something* got into my system, but then it just . . . left."

"Did you learn anything about the software?"

"No. I'd just cracked the security codes on the RAM when whatever was in it . . . *invaded* my system. All the sparks and short-circuits were probably due to the system's resistance. I've got a lot of safeguards. Then, as I said, the intruding program left, probably via the Net."

"I love it!" cackled Name. "Rogue virus in the Net!"

"I'd rather have it there than in my system, yes," the Rabbi commented dryly.

"Well, shit," I said rather brilliantly.

Fuckin figures, I decided as I saw the three red dots dancing on Billy Name's chest. Then I looked down and saw three more on mine, and dry ice enveloped my innards.

We'd left the Rabbi's shop rather hastily, once things had been cleaned up. He'd closed the door on us with a pleasant good-bye and a polite admonition, tinged with menace, to never pull shit like that again.

We walked through the deserted streets of the Zone toward the Metro. Billy Name managed to look totally casual, out for an evening stroll; I tried to imitate him, but couldn't help maniacally scanning the rooftops and windows for snipers. *Figure the Tariquat aren't gonna let us out this easy.*

I was right, too, even though I never saw them. I looked down for a second to light a cigarette, when I saw the dancing little dots on Name's chest, and then on mine.

I stopped walking. My hands froze for a second, and I caught myself and finished lighting the cigarette. Name stopped and looked back at me, puzzled. I noticed a new dot on his forehead as I blew out the first cloud of smoke and snapped my Zippo shut.

I stowed the Zippo in a jacket pocket before taking the cigarette out of my mouth to inform Name of our upcoming death.

"Billy," I asked, "do you smoke?"

Name still hadn't noticed the dots; the ones on my chest had vanished. *Fuckers are playing games.*

"Yeah. Why?"

"Light a cigarette."

"Why?"

"A last smoke." I smiled. "Turn around and look at your chest."

Name didn't bother looking. He pulled out a flat, engraved silver cigarette case, opened it, and took out a cigarette. The soft *click* of the case as he snapped it shut sounded like the third Fate's final scissor snip, grating on my tortured nerves.

He held up the cigarette and smiled. "You got a light?"

I walked over to him as I fished my Zippo out again.

"Did you make them?" he whispered as I flicked it open and on. The small flame threw demonic shadows across his pointed face. My hand was shaking a bit. He touched the cigarette to the flame.

"No," I answered. "Seven guns, at least," I added.

He straightened up with a thin smile.

"There's a time to shoot and a time to talk. Let's hope they're on the same schedule as us."

He whirled around and yelled. "Yo motherfuckers!"

I cringed. "Billy . . ."

He ignored me. "Motherfuckers! Can you hear me? This is Billy Name!"

I took a drag from my cigarette and dropped it. It tasted stale.

"Hey pussies! I wanna talk, pussies! Come talk to me!"

Provocation as a way of life . . . Not too healthy, sometimes.

"You chickenshit? Tariquat chickenshit, huh?"

A voice, floating out of the darkness. "Wait, gadjo."

Name shut up. We stood there, two meters apart, waiting. I fought my hand as it inched toward my Ruger.

A few minutes later a door creaked open to the left. A figure stepped out of the shadows and walked toward us. I saw the front of Name's coat twitch. Four dots were clustered on his forehead. *Good thing I can't see mine.*

The man stopped three meters away from us. He was a medium-sized Arab, about thirty-five years old, plainly dressed, apparently unarmed. Not that he needed any weapons.

"You want to talk, dead man?"

"Yes."

"About what?"

Name grinned. "Oh, life, death, the price of kif . . ."

"This isn't the time for jokes, dead man. Please take your hands out of your pockets."

I moved up next to Name as he slowly raised his hands out from his coat. One of them held a dull olive-drab oval lump.

"What is that?" asked the Tariquat.

"A little insurance. To make sure our conversation isn't suddenly interrupted." I heard two sharp pings, a pin bouncing on concrete.

"Ah," said the Tariquat.

We stood in silence. The Tariquat rubbed his mustache, thoughtful.

"What is your name?" asked Billy Name at last. "I would hate to die with a man whose name I didn't know."

"You may call me Seyed," said the Tariquat.

"I'm Billy Name. I said that before, but no one seems to have heard me."

"You are Billy Name?"

"Yes."

"I have heard about Billy Name."

"How interesting," said Billy. He pointed at his hand. "I'm getting tired."

"Why don't you put it away? It won't do you much good anyway."

"I need an escort. One ratty Jilali isn't much of an escort, but it'll have to do."

Seyed smiled. "Why should we let you live, Billy Name?"

"Don't you know your *Qüran*? 'The enemy of my enemy is my friend.' "

"This is true. Our enemies are numerous, and you have killed many of them."

"And I will kill more."

"But you killed Rachid."

"He tried to kill me."

"Be as it may. You kill my enemies, but you also killed my friend. What does that make you?"

"A friendly enemy?"

"More like a dangerous friend, I would think."

"Perhaps."

"I would let you live, Billy Name, if it were not for Rachid."

"He tried to kill me. By blood law, by Street law, that gives me the right to kill him."

"Perhaps. But the Tariquat live by Tariquat law, which is the Law of *Al Qüran.*"

" 'An eye for an eye, a life for a life.' "

"Yes."

"You need a life, then. Why not the life of an enemy of the Tariquat? Would that satisfy the *Qüran*?"

"It might."

"Would a crate of FN .308s perhaps help to ease the substitution?"

"It might. Two would help even more."

"Is this the souk, that I must bargain for my life? Besides, there are two of us. If you kill Lynx, you will owe me a life."

"Bullshit, Billy Name. The Tariquat kills who it pleases. But we will not kill your friend, anyway. He is a breed, and can walk in the Zone. And he has not killed a Tariquat."

Imagine my relief.

"Good," said Name, "I like Lynx. I'd hate to see him die."

"Someone must die, though."

"Who?"

Seyed said a name. He was rich, very powerful, a high-class cunt. A difficult target.

"No problem," said Billy Name.

"And two cases, blood money for Rachid."

"Yes. That is fair."

Seyed waved. The dots winked out of existence.

Billy Name bent down, picked up the pin, and reinserted it in the grenade.

"The enemy of my enemy is my friend," said Seyed.

"That is a good thing," said Billy Name. "Let us both contribute to the extermination of our enemies, and soon they will all be dead."

"Go, Billy Name. Go kill some Mirrorfaces, and the rich Uptown scum who built the Wall to protect their fancy houses and their jewelry and their clothes. Go kill."

"Bloodthirsty bastard, aren't you?" I said.

Seyed turned to me. "You've been silent so far, breed. It was better that way."

I nodded. *I can take a hint.*

Seyed wheeled around and marched toward the doorway he'd come out of. He stopped when he reached it and looked back. "Do not forget what you owe us, Billy Name. The Tariquat have friends outside the Wall, friends to call in an unpaid debt."

"No problem, spud. Keep an eye on the headlines. The rifles will be delivered."

"Good," said Seyed, and then he disappeared.

"Motherfucker," said Billy Name. He put the grenade back in his pocket. "I'd love to dust *his* brown ass, like *bad.*"

"Cool it, Billy. We live. Leave it at that."

"Yeah. But you owe me one."

"Check."

Yesterday was two days old. Two numb days, one to my zombie mind, wandering around Paris with a tingling in my neck and tense back muscles, waiting for a bullet or a shiv. I was sick of hiding, sick of running; if Angélique wanted to kill me that bad . . . *Fuck it.*

The whole Zone episode had left a strange taste in my mouth. I felt tired, worn out: a dry husk, ready for harvesting. I'd always had a pretty nasty death wish, but this was different . . . Apathy.

A headline caught my eye, at a newsstand around Saint-Michel.

DIDI BRIGI ELECTROCUTED IN BATHTUB—FAULTY APPLIANCE CAUSED ACCIDENT

I smiled. *Fast work, Billy.*

I left the newsstand and crossed the Place Saint-Michel. I jived at a spud I knew, and walked up a block through the crowd, the nameless faces. Domino was off with some of the Livewires, and I was alone. I stopped at the corner of the rue Danton, right outside the glass window of the Café Danton, and bought a rolled crêpe sucre from Piotr, a Chzecosov émigré who ran the small crêpe concession. I watched the truckers play pinball inside the Danton while I ate it, savouring the hot, sticky, buttersweet taste. Every so often I would zoom back from the pinball players and study the reflection in the glass window, scanning the street, my back.

I finished the crêpe, lobbed the wax paper into the trash bin inside Piotr's booth, waved at him, and left, heading toward the Place Saint-André-des-Arts.

I saw the black cat again as I crossed Danton. *Again?* I'd glimpsed the cat dozens of times in the past two days, all over Paris. At first I'd thought it was just a coincidence, a different cat or something. I got suspicious after the fifth or sixth time. I'd tried to approach it a few times, but it'd run away, melting into the crowd or the shadows. It never did anything, never approached me. It was just *there*, hovering like a black ghost. *Mara . . . ?*

Whatever it was, the damn thing was making me edgy as hell. It was crouching on the edge of a potted plant next to the *terrasse* of the Chateau Noir, a lean black cat with slick black fur and slitted yellow eyes, its tail whipping through the air. Staring at me.

Should blow the fucking thing away. But I was in the middle of a crowded area, crawling with tourists and students and Beasts. Besides, I'd stupidly given Name his Ruger back, on impulse, after the encounter with the Tariquats. When I touched the gun outside the Zone, I'd felt a shock, malevolent energy spooking me and making me rip the thing out of its shoulder rig and toss it to Name. Name had looked puzzled, but hadn't said anything. He left me at Opéra, gone to arrange a murder and a delivery.

Should've kept the fucking thing. Instead I drew a bead on the cat with my forefinger, cocked my thumb, mouthed the word "pow" silently. The cat bristled, arching its back and tail, and jumped off the pot. It ran between the tables of the Chateau Noir, a low black streak, and disappeared.

What the fuck . . . ? I thought about it as I strode across Saint-André-des-Arts. A spy cat, maybe, a fake animal created by Anubis, with a deck for a brain and camera for eyes. As far as I knew the tech for that kind of kink didn't exist yet, but with the bright boys in the Zaibatsu and MI labs, you never knew. Name once told me that CIA research labs were at least five years ahead of the state of the corporate art, and I believed him. Top secret kink, gotta keep that Edge, boy, can't let those godless Chzecosovs get ahead of us.

I pushed the skulking cat out of my overly paranoid mind—forcible ejection, get the fuck out or else—and wandered over to American Graffiti, a secondhand clothing store, one of my main sources, way up there with the

Puces and Army Surplus. I browsed through the racks outside, fingering old, thin overcoats and ratty tuxes and soft, warm suit jackets and white shirts. After a bit I went inside. I dapped with René, a kid who worked there, just saying hi, maintaining contact.

"Cool runnings, Lynx, what's up?" He had brown curly hair, a short nose, and the thin long fingers of a pianist. The fingers danced constantly in the air as he talked.

"Not much, not much."

"You need anything, man, clothes?"

Wry, morose: "Yeah."

"What?"

"You got anything to wear to a funeral?"

He frowned. "Whose?"

Self-pity surged up my throat: "Mine."

I left before he could say anything and strode out. The sunlight made me wince, after the obscurity of the shop. I pulled my shades out of a bellows pocket and slipped them on.

And caught a flash, of black fur and yellow eyes.

I ignored it and walked away, past the *terrasse* of the Montsouris, penguin waiters in their black-and-whites and brown straw chairs. I crossed the Rue Saint-André-des-Arts and stepped into a bookstore. I leafed through photography books for a while, my mind off on brainwalk.

"Excuse me, sir, would you like to buy this book?"

I looked up at the tight-lipped employee, surprised. *Have I been standing here that long?* I looked down at the book, realizing I had no idea what it was.

Beautiful black-and-white stills of naked dancers, muscles like smooth cables.

I smiled at the prick. "No." I walked out.

I walked up Saint-André-des-Arts, threading my way through the thick crowd. I glanced at shop windows, saw books and chic clothes and baroque postcards. I bought a cheap croissant, for no reason, at the fast-food bakery across the street from the soot-black walls of the Lycée Fénélon. And a block down, passing in front of Chéz Marie, I saw the cat, sitting on a second-story balcony like a patient sphinx with slitted eyes. It licked its lips when I gave it the finger.

The second attack came three days later, in a small street behind the Panthéon, near Olric's. I was walking down the hill with Domino in the middle of the street. The four doors of a parked skimmer opened simultaneously, the car light flaring briefly behind the tinted Plexi before the men slammed the doors shut and fanned out in front of us.

Four of them. Empty-handed Latinos, tanned skin and dark curly hair, bare-chested. Very showy. Probably very dangerous.

My hand twitched toward an absent Ruger and came up with the cobra and the Gerber instead. I glanced at Domino, saw her holding a painted Japanese fan in a neck-level praying-mantis pose. No Fury. I snapped the cobra open.

The four bent down quickly, touching the ground with open fingers, a ritual move. Then they struck stances, a semicircle in front of us. They started shuffling, an odd left-right kind of dance, their arms swinging back and forth in tight blocking patterns.

"Capueira artists," whispered Domino. "The Jinga."

Brazilians, then. I'd seen Capueira Angola before, though I'd never learned it or fought a Capuerista before. *Very* dangerous.

They attacked, two on each of us.

Mine came in on both sides, one high, one low, flipping forward in a slowmo cartwheel. I blocked a high half-moon kick with the cobra and caught a low thrust in the tibia, excruciating shock reverberating up to my stomach.

I jumped back, landing on my good leg. *Fuck, fuck . . . Not broken at least.*

I tried to ignore the pain and slid into a side fighting stance, low, the stick and knife in five-star blocking positions, the knife forward, low. I heard a sharp cry as they came in, to my right. I risked a split-second glance at Domino.

A flash of steel, blood trailing behind the arc of the fan . . . *She's OK.*

This time I played smart. They'd figured me static because of the low stance. Instead I released it and slid left, getting the closest one between his partner and me. The back one started to circle while the front one simply shifted his attack, bending forward like a boneless snake and curling and coming up with a forward heel kick to the ribs. I batted his leg hard with the cobra: satisfying cry of pain. He fell to the right, in front of the other one.

I thrust straight at him with the Gerber. He tried to block from the ground, but failed, the point thrust hard to parry. I plunged smoothly through his guard. The blade went in under the ribs. Sharp pig squeal as I ripped across, spilling intestines across his belly.

Movement to the right. My cobra shot up, blind reflex, blocking the high spinning kick from the other one. His foot caught my wrist, hard, sending the cobra flying. *Fuck.* Still bent, I twisted the blade out and slid backward, right hand in an open blocking position, knife coming up. I blocked two more kicks before I could secure a solid stance, each one spraining my wrist more.

I switched to a left stance as he came at me with his hands, holding the Gerber in front like a sword, blood running on the short blade.

He pulled a one-two with his hands, fastest move I've ever seen. The Gerber vanished. I barely blocked a kick that would've caved in my left knee.

I tried a kick of my own, thrust kick to the ribs. He *dropped* under my foot, the move called *negativa*, I suddenly and irrationally remembered.

Fuck fuck fuck . . .

Sharp blow, then, searing pain shooting up from my balls, making my stomach drop. I screamed and fell back.

He came up like a leopard and cartwheeled and came

at me from above. I tried to ignore the pain and block with my feet as I rolled.

His foot coming down . . . I blocked it with my hands and twisted. He flipped again, lazily it seemed, and came back in, his body like a tight coiled steel spring, infinitely strong and flexible.

—Domino, over to my left, backed against a car, blood on her face, desperately blocking a rain of techniques from an inhumanely agile opponent who seemed to be everywhere and nowhere—

—The Capuerista filling my vision and his foot coming down like a hammer—

My head exploded and I blacked out for a few seconds. I reemerged in a panic, pain ripping through my groin, waiting for another attack I couldn't block.

I heard a scream. I rolled and looked:

The Capuerista, on his knees, futilely clawing at the black cat attached to his face. The cat raked and tore his flesh as he shrieked. I jumped up and pounced on him, my foot extended like a perfect spear, right into his exposed solar plexus, crashing cartilage and bursting his heart.

He dropped like a stone. I turned without stopping and threw a roundhouse kick at the one fighting Domino, hard into his kidney. He screamed and then the tip of her foot caught him under the jaw and his head snapped back. I heard a sharp crack. He fell sideways, dead.

The one she'd nailed earlier was trying to get up. I grabbed him by the throat and drove his nose cartilage into his brain with the palm of my hand. I let go of his throat and he slumped down, his arm over the chest of the one Domino had just killed.

The one I'd stabbed was dead too. I looked at the cat. It was sitting on its rear legs, calmly licking its paws. I moved toward it and it got up and disappeared under a skimmer.

Fuck it. I felt Domino's hand on my shoulder, and I reached for it. It wasn't there, though, and then the concrete hit me in the head and everything went red and then black.

I woke up on Olric's couch and screamed as the pain in my balls rolled over me. Olric picked me up while I clutched my groin, and dragged me to the bathroom. "You gotta piss, man, it'll help." He held me up while I ripped down my pants and urinated. It hurt like a motherfucker, but I already felt better as I zipped my pants back up.

I staggered over to the sink and looked at myself in the mirror. My wrist was sore but in operational condition. There was crusted blood on my face, and I had a split eyebrow. The back of my head throbbed. I reached back, probed, and felt a lump the size of a small egg. Touching it sent sharp needles of pain into my skull.

"You okay, man?"

"Yeah, I'll live. How's Domino?"

"She's fine. Listen, you probably have a small concussion. You should lie down for a while."

"Okay, okay."

I rinsed the blood off my face and cleaned out the cut, wincing at the pain. I limped back into the living room when I finished and dropped onto the couch. I tore off my boot, pulled up my pants, and examined the bruise on my leg. It was black and yellow, very ugly, the size of a small *shuriken. Bone bruise . . . Fuck it.*

I lay back on the couch, curling on my side so as not to rest on the back of my head. I looked up before passing out again.

"Hey, Olric."

"Yeah?"

"You got my weapons?"

"Yeah. Don't worry about it, man. Sleep."

I did.

13:23. Waking up . . . *Where's the steamroller?*

"Aaargh," I moaned as I slowly rolled up and off the couch. I staggered over to Olric's table and leaned on it before taking stock. My balls felt a bit tender but would hold. My leg hurt like a bitch, still too weak to lean on. That motherfucker sure knew how to kick. *I should study Capueira when I have time. If I live long enough.* I remembered the spearkick that had narrowly missed my knee and shuddered.

I stretched my sprained wrist and touched my head. My split eyebrow was swollen, raw, making it hard to

open my eye fully. As for the lump on the back . . .
Looks like I'll be sleeping on my side for a while.

I slumped into a chair, drained by the small effort.
Domino was gone, unless she was sleeping with Olric,
which I doubted. Olric I knew never woke up before
15:00, so it looked like I was alone for a while.

I pushed myself up and limped to the kitchen. I brewed
some caf and sloppily fried some French toast, thinking
déjà vu . . . I ransacked Olric's cupboards while the
bread sizzled, looking for maple syrup. *Nada.* I settled
for sugar and butter.

I devoured the three slices I'd made, washing them
down with Olric's foul black brew, then got up and
cooked three more. I finished those too, dumped the
dishes in the sink, and stumbled back to the couch to
think.

Brainmelt . . . I pulled myself back together and laid
out structures, trying to fit them together, to decide on
my next move.

Angélique. Holed up in her fortress, wanting me dead.

Leland. Her agent. Not too important.

—or maybe . . . I thought about Leland a bit, his
behavior, the way he treated Angélique.

*She obviously thinks he works for her, but he treats her
more like his ward than his boss. But if he doesn't work
for her, then for who?*

Anubis? I knew that Angélique only nominally ran
the corporation, that the Board was really in charge.
*Maybe Leland works for the Board, to keep tabs on the
little darling.*

Whatever. Not really important. On . . .

The medallion. That was the real awkward piece, the
one that didn't fit too well. I ran down the available data:

Engraved with a picture of her brother. Obviously
related to him somehow.

Containing a miniature deck with sensors and program. Some kind of recorder.

She never took it off. Why?

When plugged into the deck, the program goes amok,
behaving first like a trojan virus, but then escaping via
the Net instead of trashing the Rabbi's system like any
self-respecting virus would.

Therefore the program was not a defense virus. Then what?

It behaved like a genie released from a bottle. Looking around first, then escaping . . .

Escaping . . . What the fuck?

What would/could do that? Why?

AI?

AI?

AI?

Nah. Doesn't exist.

Shit shit shit. Dead end dead end dead end. *I should do something.*

What?

First thing. Tell angélique/leland to go Fuck Off. Publicly.

I sat up with a smile. The boards. I laughed. That'd piss them off but *good.*

I sat down in front of Olric's deck, a state-of-the-art Marantz. Real beauty, plated gold like all Marantz products, with turquoise and silver keys and LEDs. I took off my armdeck and set it down next to the deck, pulling out the mini co-axial coiled inside it. I jacked it into the Marantz. *Good, good.* I needed the armdeck for the programs I had stashed in it, but the Marantz would be a lot better in terms of power and flexibility. My armdeck is good, the best there is, but it still can't match a full six-crystal deck.

Now for the jack. I picked up the thick double co-axial that snaked out of the Marantz, leaned my head sideways, pushed up my hair, and rammed it into the jack behind my ear. It tingled briefly, and then the structures of the system settled slowly into my brain, thin and ghostly and oh so *logical.* I skimmed through the system, up-down-left-right-front-back, adjusting to it, settling into *it.*

Ready. I called up the customized trojan Billy Name had cooked up and held it up to the side, poised to strike.

Now for the target. I slowly eased into the Net, streams of data running through my head, geodesics of logic. I maneuvered through them, searching for my target: the main system that controlled the Paris Public Announcement Boards.

The boards are scattered all over Paris, large black boards with yellow LED displays. They are used by the Mairie of Paris to broadcast community announcements about art, shows, cultural events, openings, and so on. They are also controlled by one central system, and that system, despite numerous defense systems installed over the years, is about as hard to penetrate as cheesecake. A lot of street groups had used it over the years to broadcast self-glorifying messages. The ATs had done so often to take credit for their various performances. It was considered a hardcore self-publicity method, way colder than graffiti. It also had the added advantage of driving the Uppers into a small rage.

The experts had tried to isolate the central control system from the Net to prevent intrusion. But they had to leave some channels open for routine transfers and contacts.

The structure was in front of me, metaphorically speaking. I settled around it, apprehending it, surveying the various entrance routes.

The most frequently used one emanated from the various clients, the museums and the galleries. That would be the easiest way in.

I withdrew from the control system and moved myself via the jack to the Musée Pompidou's system. The defenses were weak, weaker even than Olric's own. I swung the trojan around, encased myself in it, and slowly shifted it to look like an innocuous news bulletin.

The Beaubourg system would examine the disguised virus and let it in. The manipulative logicals, the "me" part, would enter with it, hidden.

No problem. I slid in, smooth and clean.

Inside the system I sloughed off the trojan and pushed it momentarily aside. I roved around the data structures, looking for the PR units. I found them.

I located the specific unit that sent bulletins to the board system. I remodeled the trojan again, around me, making it look like an announcement for an upcoming Peter Rodia exhibit. Then I broke off part of it, left it behind to verify the transfer. I inserted myself into the data line.

The transfer took a fraction of a second. I barely felt the board system's defenses examine the trojan, contact the shard I'd left back at Pompidou to verify it, and let us through.

Inside. I sent the trojan up to the system operator and lurked.

I briefly analyzed the part of the system that actually controlled the boards themselves. I wrote my message and waited.

Change in the data. The operator was scheduling a new message for the boards, the one containing the phony Beaubourg announcement. He transferred it to a holding file. I inserted myself into the data stream and modified it. My message would go out in a few hours, though the operator wouldn't know it till it hit the boards.

Razor. I gathered in the various fragments of my trojan and backtracked. The defenses looked out, not in, so they didn't react as I zipped out of the system into the Net. I swung by Beaubourg, collected the last piece of trojan, and jacked out.

I leaned back into the chair and grinned. All over Paris, the boards would soon be flashing:

ANGÉLIQUE
YOU FUCKED UP
LOVE, ME

Petty vandalism. Nothing like it.

Brainfloat meditation, sitting there. What next, what next?

Need data. Puzzle incomplete. Be a sieve. Gather in pieces.

Snoop.

Anubis. I rammed in the jack and shifted.

In the Net. Interface. Numerals pumped directly into my brain via the jack, not as code but as *meaning*. My brain inside the Net, not as consciousness but as data, a mobile data-processing unit. A ghost in the machine.

I swam in the data currents, seas of international traffic, absorbing. Streams of sealed coded transmissions impacted my awareness like jacketed bullets, closed units. Here and there a few beacons, open bulletin boards or public-service messages, immediately absorbed.

Anubis, now. Hard, unyelding knot of data, inpenetrable. I floated around it, absorbing subliminals.

No fuckin way I'm getting in. Don't have the hard or the soft, or the skill for that matter. Don't think even Name or the Rabbi could. Well, the Rabbi maybe . . .

I drank data. I noted communications going in-out, destinations or origins when I could. I monitored economic data, stock-exchange fluctuations, share transfers, financial influx and output, corporate structure—

Wait. Back. Something . . .

Shares. Something odd.

Nothing obvious. A solid 51% bloc encased within the Anubis structure. The other 49% either in small static blocs, the major shareholders, or moving around, random market manipulations, brokers buying-selling-trading.

Random. Random. Something there. Not quite random.

How. Where. Intuition feeling follow it. Absorb the data. Feel it, don't analyze. Feel out connections, the structure.

There. That group. Those companies. All trading, exchanging shares, fast, random moves. But shares never leave those companies, never go out. New ones come in, nothing goes out.

Companies. The group. Trace them.

Yes. There. Dummies, fronts. All the same. Empty electronic shells, stocking up Anubis shares, passing them around so no one gets suspicious.

Who?

Feel out. Other dummies, other anomalies.

Nothing.

Feel. Absorb. Suck in, data magnet.

Yes. Small diversion of stocks there, steady stream, through Breton et Fils to Lorenz S.A.

Trace Lorenz. Who owns it?

No one. Independent S.A., private owner. A front.

For whom?

Trace to other bloc. No connections. Shit.

Two groups then. One attempting takeover, secret raid. Other one just sitting there, keeping tabs, staying low.

Who? Why?

Probe. Send message to Lorenz and other bloc: WE'RE ONTO YOU, SUCKERS. Watch. Observe.

A few minutes realtime. Human operators must react.

Lorenz S.A.: Panic. Frenzy. Sell all shares on open board. Stops trading.

Unknown bloc: Freeze. Stops trading. All the companies retain there shares.

Enough. I set up tabs on Lorenz and hostile bloc. Jack OUT.

Reality flooded my neural system like a bath of mercury, bright and soft and chaotic after the cold, hard unreality of pure data. I slumped over the deck and breathed for a space, easing out. Then I looked up. The phone was pinging.

I thought about it. Olric wasn't answering. I probably shouldn't, for security reasons. On the other hand it could be a friend.

Fuck it. I switched off the vid and picked up the handset.

"Hello?" Bending my voice, lower, imitating Olric's rasp.

"Olric? That you? Your vid's off."

Scalpel. I smiled and switched the vid back on.

"Yo babe."

"Lynx! What the fuck—"

I jived for silence, quickly. She stopped. I gave the sign for potential interception. She nodded.

"Let's meet," I said.

"Where?"

I thought about it.

"Remember where Raidos Bomb used to hang out before pulling a graffiti run?"

"Of course."

"Meet you there, 20:00."

"Check. What about Olric?"

"He's sleeping. I'll have him call you."

"OK. See you, love."

"See you." I cut the line and softly put down the handset.

The old Raidos Bomb HQ is a disused storage room inside one of the main support pillars of the Pont du Carrousel, across the river from the Louvre. The entrance to the room is a rusted steel door on the side of the skimmer tunnel that runs under the bridge.

I walked down the thin strip of sidewalk into the tunnel after having carefully checked the topside. Skimmers glided by me as I pried the door open and slipped in.

I pulled the heavy door shut before hitting the light switch. White neons blinked into life. I looked around.

Dirty gray concrete walls covered with bright colored superimposed graffiti, broken neon tube glass on the ground, the corpses of a thousand empty spray bombs. No one ever used this place, not since Raidos Bomb had violently ejected a group of squatters—very violently.

I examined the ground. The concrete was humid. Seepage from the Seine, I decided.

I wandered around a bit, examining the various graffiti. Most were worn, faded, or else covered with other, more recent messages. One stuck out, REMEMBER: IF YOU'RE SQUEAMISH, DON'T . . . I smiled faintly. The rest of the quote was painted over, and I finished it mentally, *kick the Beach rubble*. The neon tubes at the far end of the room had been covered with various colors of dripping paint, mostly purple and red, casting an eerie, tinted light.

I heard the door creak and I melted into a shadowed corner. More creaks. Light footsteps.

"Lynx?" Scalpel's voice. I risked a glance. She was alone.

I stepped out into the light. "Hi, love."

"Lynx!" She ran to me and hugged me. "You okay?"

"Yeah." I kissed her gently on the lips. "Let's go get some dinner."

Later, at Chez Wang, a cheap Chinese joint down the hill from the Sorbonne, walls of chipped white paint surrounded by pseudo-oriental red borders. Red and green neon ideograms glowed in the window. We sat at a cracked Formica-coated table and ate deliciously cheap Chino-Vietnamese food and drank mediocre tea.

"I hear you've been having problems, babe."

I carefully prepared a Nem while I answered. "Yeah." I pressed a few mint leaves against it and wrapped it with a tattered lettuce leaf. "People after my ass, trying to waste me."

"Who?"

I dipped the whole mess in pale orange nioc-man, brought it dripping to my mouth, and bit off half of it. Incredible. *Better than sex.* "Ha!"

She waited patiently while I chewed. I swallowed and answered. "This bitch I slept with for a while, Uptown cunt."

"Why?"

"I don't really know. Her kicks started getting real gruesome, I mean out of control, so I split. She had her muscle drag me over to her apartment. She tried to kill me, cause she couldn't deal with my dumping her, she said. I got away, took this medallion she always wore." I swished the remaining piece of lettuce in the nioc-man.

"So she started sending knifeboys after you?"

"Yeah. I dusted three of them Downside, then me and Domino did four more of them last night. Capueristas. Real nasty motherfuckers, would've dusted our asses but good, except for this cat."

"Cat?"

"Yeah, cat. This real weird black cat, been following me around for a few days. Can't figure it."

"Cat, what kind of cat?"

"Cat. You know, small furry mammal with pointed ears and a tail. A cat."

"Okay."

"Anyway, I was lying on the ground due for some real

fast flatlining when this fucking cat jumps out of nowhere and starts ripping the motherfucker's face off. So I get up, waste him, waste his buddies. End of story."

"And the cat?"

"Ran away, like it always does."

"Fuckin weird."

"Yeah, def weird."

Just then the waiter showed up with our main orders. I quickly polished off the remaining lettuce leaf while he placed the entrées in front of us. He cleared away our dirty dishes and left.

I'd ordered spicy chicken with green peppers and bamboo shoots, along with brown rice and Chinese noodles. I drowned the rice in soy sauce and started eating.

Scalpel looked up from her seafood after a while and licked her lips, grinning. "So what are you gonna do now, man? Heat like that, Uptown heat, that's bad, real bad. Those cocksuckers aren't gonna let up."

"I know." Silence for a moment.

"I suppose I'll just have to keep on ducking," I said at last. "Try to stay one step ahead of them. I'm sick of hiding."

Her smile dropped. "They'll get you eventually."

"Yeah. They've already come pretty close. Maybe they'll get tired and give up."

"The Zaibatsus never give up. They don't have to. They have the money, they have the time."

"Yeah." I munched contemplatively. "There are a few random factors, though, might solve this business yet."

I left Scalpel at the Saint-Michel Metro. She grabbed my arm as I started down the steps, pulled me back up, and kissed me, hard, her tongue snaking in and around my mouth. Then she pulled back and stared into my eyes, gripping my arms.

"You take care of yourself, spud, okay?"

"Yeah. I'll do my best."

"You better." She smiled. "After all, you still owe me a mad night of passionate sex."

"Yeah," I said dryly. "Tell you what. I live through this, you got your night."

She kissed me again. Then, seriously, "Live through this, Lynx. And not just for the sex. OK?"

"OK."

She spun around without another word and melted into the crowd. I stood there for a beat and then spun around, too, and headed down the stairs.

Talking with Scalpel had done me good, aired out my head. I jogged down the stairs and took the Porte de Clignancourt line; I changed at Chatelet, took the Pont de Neuilly line. I rode it up to Étoile, to the top of the Champs Elysées. *Figure I'll crawl on the mall for a bit . . . Get lost, melt in the crowd . . .*

The corridors of the station, long yellow walls and yellow light. I turned a corner and he was standing there.

He was tall, taller than me. Dressed in a billowing red silk kimono with black lining and a small Japanese crest I didn't recognize; his long, smooth black hair pulled back in a high ponytail, wrapped in purple ribbon; and his face . . .

His face: white, paint white, with blood-red lips and thin red streaks barring his epicanthic eyes. The folds were surgery, cosmetic alteration tacked on to a distinctly *gaijin* face. His hands were white, too, the same white, and his nails were the color of his lips.

His eyes bored at me, jet-black irises, the hooded eyes of a cobra. I was caught in them, drowning, paralyzed.

I stood there. He smiled.

"Hello, Lynx," he purred. "I am the Douglas. I am going to kill you."

His last words released me from his gaze. I stepped forward and drove my fist at his face, hard enough to ram through four centimeters of oak wood.

He just stood there, unmoving.

His hand appeared out of nowhere, palm open in front of my fist. Contact—

It felt like hitting a steel wall. I screamed with pain as his hand folded over mine, trapping it, crushing it. I fell to my knees.

His voice cut through the pain, a silent, vibrating scalpel. "I could kill you now, Lynx. But it would be too easy."

He let go. I collapsed, hugging my hand to my stomach, curled up. His voice floated down from a distance.

"I will hunt you. Give me a good hunt, and I promise you that your death will be quick and painless. Good-bye."

I looked up. He was gone.

I pulled myself up against a wall, still clutching my hand. I examined it. It was red and swollen.

No drugs . . .

I massaged it gently, rubbing the fingers one by one, flexing them. The pain receded slowly.

Ice . . .

I saw nothing suspicious as I left the station. I exited at Avenue Wagram and entered the first café I saw. I went up to the counter and waived at the barman.

"Yes?"

"A shot of bourbon and a bowl of water, with ice in it, please."

"A bowl of water?"

"Yeah."

Unfazed, he rummaged under the counter, found a plastic salad bowl, held it up.

"Like this?"

"Yeah,"

He filled it with water and dropped some ice cubes in it before plonking it down in front of me. I stuck my hand in it, sloshing water onto the bar.

"Sorry," I said.

"Hurt?" he asked.

"Yeah. Caught it in a car door."

"That must hurt." He had a thin, hard face, with a thick black mustache and a long scar running along his jaw. An ex-con. Half the café boys in Paris are, and the detectives often drop by to check if they want to keep their jobs.

"Yeah, it does." I let the hand soak.

"You wanted a bourbon too?"

"Yeah."

He reached down for the bar stock. "No, no," I said. "Jack Daniel's."

"Ah. Excuse me." He straightened up smoothly. A pro. Not a wasted gesture, a study in economy. All it takes is pride in your work, I figured. The sloppy ones are all strictly for the paycheck.

He pulled down a bottle from the top shelf. "Ice?"

"Don't bother." He filled the bubble and poured a shot. I picked it up and tossed the burning liquid down my throat. It left a pleasant afterglow and a faint taste of smoked wood.

"That's be four-fifty."

"You take Old?" I asked.

"Yes. Two-twenty."

He was ripping me off, but what the fuck. I dug some frayed paper out of my jacket pocket, found two Cs and a twenty, and slid them across the counter.

"Thank you, sir." He slipped the bills into his apron and turned away. He didn't ring up the sale.

I left the bar twenty minutes and two shots later. The sun was setting, faint pastel glow over to the west, long shadows oozing out of the buildings. I walked down Wagram and turned right on Tilsitt, toward the Champs.

I need a gun.

My eyes flicked all over the place, scanning, searching. *At least this asshole is easy to spot.*

No costumed clowns. I found Roget's place.

Roget is a small-time gun dealer, good for one-shot deals on light ordnance. Nothing like Cornelius, of course, but right now I just didn't have the time to hunt down Mr. C. Roget operated out of a small fishing store on Tilsitt. It was closed, of course. I rang the bell.

No answer. I pushed it again and didn't let go.

Thirty-eight seconds later the door flew open. Roget, drunk and furious, thrust his face out.

"What the fuck do you want?" He barked. Then he saw me. "Hey, Lynx. It's you."

I pasted on my most ingratiating smile. "Sorry, Roget. I need a gun, real bad, real fast."

He grinned. "Heat?"

"Yeah." I didn't elaborate.

"Wait here." He disappeared. The door slammed shut.

It opened again two minutes later. "Interarms 9mm. Six bullets. Best I can do—"

"Fine."

"—Unless you want a .22 long with fourteen rounds."

I thought about it. I would've preferred more bullets, but from what I'd seen the motherfucker wouldn't even notice a .22-caliber bullet unless it pegged him right between the two eyes. *And maybe not even then.*

"I'll take the 9mm."

He slid me something, hard lump of metal wrapped in a handkerchief. I peeled back the white fabric and examined it. Interarms, like he'd said, twenty years old at least.

I hit the clip release and pulled it out.

"The rounds are in there."

"I'm checking."

I peered into the clip. It was made for eight rounds. The weight was wrong, too light.

"Doesn't feel like six rounds, man," I hissed.

"They're five. The sixth is already in the chamber," he added hastily.

I rammed the clip home and worked the slide. The chamber was loaded. "Good," I said. I let the slide snap back.

"How much?"

"Five thou."

"That's too much for this piece of shit."

"I'll make you a deal. Four thou now, and if you don't need it anymore I'll buy it back for three."

I was too tired to bargin. "Fine." I pulled out my wad of paper, gave him the four thousand. That left me seventy, which wouldn't buy me candy.

He grinned with delight as he hungrily counted the paper. I tucked the gun into the waist of my fatigues, under my jacket, safety off. Roget started to close the door. I stuck my foot into it, pushed it back open. He looked at me quizzically.

"If the gun doesn't work, Roget . . ."

"Yes?"

"I'll make sure my friends know who to kill."

He swallowed nervously. "It'll work, Lynx. I tried it myself when I got it."

"Good." I turned and left.

* * *

Down Tilsitt to the Champs, cold lump of metal under my belt pressed against my flesh. I emerged from the dark street, onto the avenue, into the light and the crowd. The presence of the gun reassured me, gave me energy.

I walked down the avenue, through the jostling crowd, past the expensive boutiques and restaurants and the arcades and the banks and the high-tech displays of the skimmer and the hardware dealers. I walked right past a patrol of three Mirrorfaces, the gun burning against my belly. They didn't even look at me.

....
....
.....................[   ]............
A light tap on my shoulder, twice. I whirl around, wired reflexes, total narrowtunnel *now* concentration, ready to strike—

No one. I glare at the crowd, puzzled. Two Japanese tourists, three fashionable glittergirls, a dirty streetdrek beggar, a clump of Arab kids a bit farther back.

Who?

....
I keep staring until I notice the beggar looking at me strangely.

Him?

....
No . . . Too short by far.

I shrug, turn around, and continue walking, trying to look casual. My muscles are tense, ready to strike in a fraction of a second. I feel totally wired, totally present. Moments come detached, freezeframes under a strobe. I reach into the inside pocket of my jacket and pull out my balisong. I unfold it one-handed under the jacket, and then hold it by my side, the blade concealed in my pocket.

I walk for two blocks like that, without seeing anyone or anything suspicious. I ache for a cigarette, but don't dare occupy my hands like that, exposing myself.

Tap. This time my reaction is even faster, balisong striking high, at eye level—

I manage to stop the blade an inch away from the Suit's face. She shrieks in terror and stumbles back. I grab her by the collar, crushing the starched fabric, and hold the knife to her throat.

"Who touched me?"

"Wha . . . wha . . . I don't know, I don't know . . . Please . . ."

She is babbling, incoherent, terrified. I let her go and scan the crowd.

No one, of course. *Damn that cocksucker is good.* No cat, either, I notice in passing.

The Suit is still shrieking and people are starting to stare. I melt away, into the crowd, away.

Gotta get off the avenue . . . Too crowded.

I cut left and head down the Rue de la Boetie. The crowd thins out after a block. The sidewalk are narrow, lined with skimmers. I start examining all the passersby, searching for anyone with the right build, the right height. I practice the old Burroughs exercise: see everyone in a crowd before they see you, and no one will notice you. Psychic invisibility. It usually works.

I hear a sharp click to my left as I pass a small clothing boutique. I look into the window and see the handwritten sign:

YOU LOSE

Fuck . . .

I dive to the right, head tucked into my arms, over the hood of a skimmer. The storefront explodes.

Concussion blast, flying shards of glass against my legs and back.

I roll over the skimmer onto the gutter. A skimmer slews hard, crashes into a parked skimmer. I hear glass clink against concrete.

I sit up stunned. A voice: "You okay, man? Hey, you okay?"

I look up. The crashed skimmer's driver, a young man, concerned look on his face.

I brush away his hands and pull myself up. "Yeah, yeah."

A crowd starts to gather. I hear voices, worried, nervous.

"—terrorists—"

"—a bombing . . . The store—"

"—just *exploded*—"

"—Oh God . . ."

"—yes, that kid—"

I feel the back of my legs. My hand comes back red, wet. I brush the glass fragments off as best I can. I don't dare take off my jacket because of the gun.

"Hey, you okay?" The driver again.

"Yeah." I start to cut through the crowd. He tries to hold me back. "Wait, you can't just leave . . ." I reach up and pinch his wrist, momentarily paralyzing his hand. He screams and lets go of me.

The crowd parts easily in front of me. I lean against a skimmer when I reach the edge of the circle, breathing hard, sweating. *Motherfucker.*

People running toward the site of the bombing as I head in the opposite direction. I hear sirens.

He's toying with me. He knew that wouldn't get me.

Down Ponthieu. Onset of major panic. *Gotta take the Metro, get to Les Halles, spuds will help me . . .*

Tourists and Uppers glancing at me nervously as I walk by. Fuck them.

Sharp spitting sound, sting on my chest. I look down.

Red stain, wet, spreading. *Fuck, I'm hit . . .*

Wait . . . No pain, nothing. I touch the red. No wound.

Fuckin paint! Shit shit SHIT!!!

Left again on Colisée. Farther and farther from the Champs, away from the crowds, into the darkness. Hide.

Noise, above. A clatter. I pulled out the gun and fire a shot.

Laughter. Eeerie, uncanny, floating down from the darkness.

I don't have enough bullets. I hold my fire.

Something falls down from the darkness, small, sputtering flame.

M-80! I dive aside. Loud, flat clap, explosion, rattling my already frayed nerves.

I hold myself together.

Another M-80. And another. I dive left and right, dodging, panicked.

A shape, above, looming, dark ghost.

I lose it. I fire at it, madly, four times.

Laughter. The shape falls down slowly, gliding. It lands softly by me. I look at it.

A piece of cloth stretched on a frame of thin wooden dowels.

I pick it up and start sobbing. Four small neat holes in the cloth.

I drop it and run. The laughter follows me through the night, high-pitched, a blunt knife sawing through stainless steel.

I run blindly, turning corners. Dark streets. Few passersby. I run.

Mirrorfaces ahead. I stop abruptly and tuck the gun in my waistband. I readjust my jacket and force myself to walk slowly. Fortunately, they have their backs to me.

I turn a corner before I reach them. Long, small, dark street.

A flash ahead. I look. The Douglas, in his red robes, standing in the middle of the street, arms crossed.

Slowly, carefully, I pull out the gun. He doesn't move. I aim. He doesn't move, right there in front of me.

I shoot, once, my last bullet, right between his two eyes.

Crash of shattered glass. The figure explodes, fragmented shards, falling to the ground, tinkling.

Fuck fuck fuck . . . A fuckin mirror . . .

I spin around, frantically, gun uselessly pointed at empty shadows. The laughter again, grating.

I scream. "FUCK YOU! COME OUT HERE BASTARD, LET ME SEE YOU!"

Impact, on the gun, hard. The gun flies from my hand. A chrome shuriken clatters to the ground.

"FUCK YOU!"

The laughter.

"FUCK YOU!"

I hear a stomping sound down the street, heavy boots galloping toward me. Mirrorfaces.

I pick up the gun (why?) and run.

The Champs again. Lights, crowds. I'm at the Rond-Point. *The Metro.* I run.

In the Metro. *Calm down, calm down.* I zip my jacket

up to cover the paint stain. I lean against a wet, dirty tile wall and breathe. *In. Out. In. Out. Calm down.*

My heartbeat slows a bit. I wipe my face on my sleeve and stumble down the steps to the platform.

The platform. Empty except for a few people down at the other end. I examine the vid monitors at the front of the platform. They show all clear.

I peer through the clear anti-suicide barrier. A few people waiting on the other side too, a spud, a couple of kids. Good.

I see the light of the incoming train. I move toward the sliding door in the barrier.

The train enters the station. Flat hiss of displaced air.

The door opens. I step back in surprise. Before I can react, I feel a hand at the small of my back, a sharp push. I go over.

I fall. In front of the train. Headlight filling my vision, a taste of stale tunnel air. I hit the tracks. Sharp pain, rusted metal bolt from the old rails hitting my shoulder.

One chance. I rolled into the trench in the middle of the tracks. I go over the edge into dirty, muddy water. The train . . . I pull my leg in and squeeze down.

The train roars over my head. I lie in darkness, shaking, hugging myself.

Iesu Kirishto y Santa Madonna y Kali y Krshna y Ogoun Feray . . . Anybody who will cover my ass . . .

The train is stopped. I hear panicked voices. Eventually they cut through my reflexive catatonia.

Gotta get the fuck out of here.

I started crawling toward the back of the platform. My clothes are soaked, grimy, scummy. Soon I see the light.

The trenches serve a double function: emergency survival, as in my case, and also repair trench in case a train breaks down in a station. The access tunnel is there for the second function, and not many people know about it.

I reach it. It is a small hole in the side of the trench, barely big enough for a person to squeeze through. I crawl past it and reverse, inserting my legs first, turning on my side and curving my body.

My legs flail in the air for a few beats before they find the first rung. I slide down backward. Mud smears across my face. My chest goes through, my head, my arms. I pull my left arm in and find the top rung. I climb down.

Short climb, five meters. I slump to the ground and start shaking again.

Eventually my survival reflexes take over. I pull myself back together and look around. Observe, catalog, file. Useful information, always.

Long tunnel of brownish concrete stretching in both directions. Yellow dirty neons. Hiss of steam jetting in periodically from various holes.

Think. One way toward front of station, one way toward back.

Think. Front of station toward Les Halles . . .

I head toward the front of the station. Limping, shivering, but slowly calming down, concentrating.

Concentrate. Terror is the enemy. The Douglas is counting on your terror to defeat you. Fight terror and you fight the Douglas. Beat terror and you beat the Douglas.

Hard, so hard . . . Hard to control the body, the adrenaline, the Fear. Hard.

Concentrate. You can do it. Concentrate.

Second-order strategy. Don't play the Douglas's game. The rules are fixed against you. You will lose. You will die. To win, go to the next level. Change the rules. Rig them against him. Drag him into your game.

Concentrate. Stop shaking. Fear is the enemy's weapon. Fear is the enemy.

Ignore. Ignore the mud, the filth, the clothes. They are not important. Ignore the wounds, the cuts, the bruises. They are not important. Ignore the meat. It is not important.

His target is your mind, your brain. Fight him there. Fight the fear, the terror.

Jesus Christ he threw me in front of a fuckin train!

Don't crack. Don't break. Concentrate. Fight him. Concentrate.

Become an animal. You are being hunted like an animal. So become one. Think like one. *Don't think* like one.

That's it. Exist. Be.

How does a hunter work? You know that. You've hunted before.

A hunter does not follow his prey. That way he loses it. A hunter figures out where his prey will be next and he goes there and he *waits*.

The Douglas is a good hunter. Very good. Four times now he has figured out where you will be next and he has waited there.

He guided you, too. The taps, on the Champs. Instill panic, send you down the side street, off the avenue.

So think. Figure out where he will wait for you next. Set a trap for him there. Kill him.

Guide him. He thinks he knows where you will go next. Force his steps. Make him go wait where *you* want him to.

Make him play *your* game while he thinks he plays his. Change the rules.

Trap him. Kill him.

Concentrate.

Down long reddish-brown corridors. Rusty water pipes line the walls. Dingy yellow lightbulbs dangle from the ceiling, enclosed in cheap red plastic cages. A layer of water on the concrete soaks my feet to the ankles, slipping through the cracks in the leather, permeating my socks, encasing my flesh. Flop, flop, flop. I walk. I limp. I don't think much.

An alcove on the side. A hole with rungs. Down.

Ten meters, maybe. I step onto a grated walkway, surrounded by very large water pipes. I touch one gingerly. Hot.

I look down through the grating. Dark. Nothing.

I drop a coin. I count seconds. Three of them, very long, then a faint splash. I run a rapid calculation. Forty meters maybe.

I start walking, holding onto the railway. Nothing breaks. A valve ahead of me spews vapor. I walk through it, fanning my arms in front of me.

Steps. I push aside a little gate and go down. Six steps.

Turn left. Another corridor, like the one above, brown with water pipes. My feet go flop. I wish I had skimboots on.

A ladder up. I climb.

I emerge into a dark dusty concrete tunnel. There is no light. I pull myself into it and feel the surface.

The tunnel is oval in cross section, thin and high. I start walking, bent low.

The tunnel curves. Cables run along the wall, stapled on. I have balance problems, keep on collapsing against the sides of the tunnel. I steady myself, using my hands, and walk slowly.

Light ahead. The tunnel ends, opening into a large, well-lit room. I climb out and look around.

Control boxes, wiring, and strange plastified maps on the walls. A door on the left side. To the right, a doorway opens onto a vast pit, ten meters to a side and thirty meters deep. A spiral stairway runs down the side of the pit.

I look up. Above the pit, grating, nightlight. Topside.

I study the maps. They seem to be engineering maps of electric circuitry, connections. Useful perhaps. In the future. If I survive. Think survival. I tear the maps off the wall, fold them—hard, because of the plastic—and shove them into a bellows pocket.

I pull the door to the left open. Behind it a small room with a steel ladder going up. I climb the ladder.

Grating at the top, thick, heavy steel grating. I work the catch open and turn around on the ladder. I place my feet as high up as I can, my back against the grating. I push up, using my leg muscles.

The grate opens with a tearing sound of long-rusted metal. I turn around, holding it up with my hands, and then push it all the way back, against its brackets.

I climb up, quickly, and scan three-sixty for Mirrorfaces. None. Good.

I pull the grate up and then gently lower it shut. I look around.

I am on the corner of Avenue Gabriel and Avenue Matignon. The trees of Parc Marigny loom next to me, gloomy, sinister.

I have been here before. A flash of painful memory, the Champs, a run, Mara . . .

I suppress it. No time for nostalgia. Must survive, trap a hunter.

Down the block is the Drugstore Publicis. Inside are phones. I think about going there. Two conspicuous?

No. Good. *He*'ll not kill me in public. He wants to savor his kill, gloat over it. He needs a dark, discreet place for that.

I cross the street and walk down the block, past a closed newsstand and the open-air *terrasse* of a fancy restaurant, past throngs of Uppers, guidos, poseurs, rich kids. Many stare at me strangely. I realize I am wet, soot- and mud-streaked, covered in blood, wearing tattered and stained clothes.

Fuck them. I ignore them.

I push open the glass doors of the drugstore and enter into light and brass and glass. Display cases line the walls, filled with junk for tourists or suburban guidos. I get on the line for the newsstand behind a swarthy man dressed all in white, one of the pseudo-jet/Italianate set. I wait.

I reach the counter. The cute young blonde behind it tries not to goggle at me. I ask for a softpack of Gauloises with no filters. She says that she only has filtered Gauloises left. I buy a pack.

I notice a fat poodle-walking matron with a fur stole and a black dress with translucent plastic windows fanning the air as I pass by, a look of disgust on her face. I snarl at her silently. She squeals and turns away rapidly. A large mustachioed bouncer type in a blue blazer stares at me angrily. I smile sweetly as I walk past him. He doesn't say anything.

I reach the phones. I ensconce myself in one of the open booths, dig out some change, and dump it on the metal counter under the phone. I tap the pack of Gauloises against my wrist, packing the cigarettes. Then I tear it open and pull one out. I rip off the filter and drop it. I stick the cigarette in my mouth, find my Zippo, light it. I inhale deeply, feeling the harsh nicotine ooze into my lungs, savoring it. My Zippo and the pack of Gauloises lie on the counter next to the coins. I find a two-franc coin, pick up the handset, insert the coin, and inhale again. The vidscreen flickers to life. I dial a number I know well and listen to the beeping.

Someone answers, though no face appears on the screen.

I say a few words, listen to the answer, speak again. The voice asks me for the number of the phone. I read it off, 45–55–23–23. I hang up and wait.

I glance around, examine the display cases, a slim good-looking glamourgirl. I wonder idly how much she costs. A fat man in a tux approaches her, kisses her cheek, leads her away. I shrug.

The phone rings. I pick it up. Still no image on the screen.

"Yo, Billy?"

I talk to Name for a few minutes. Then, satisfied, I thread my way to the front of the drugstore and sit down at a table in the corner of the restaurant. My back is to the wall and I can see both entrances along with the street outside the bay window.

A condescending waiter approaches my table. "Monsieur?"

I order a drink I can't afford and he leaves. A few minutes later he returns with the drink. I take out the little Chinese umbrella, toss it on the table, and eat the cherry. I taste synthetic. I sip the drink. Acceptable.

I wait, sipping. I try not to stare at the red LED of the drugstore's clock. 22:23. Two and a half hours since I met Scalpel for dinner. *Fuck.*

Shock. Through the window. The Douglas, in full apparel, standing there, smiling at me.

Don't lose it. If he wants to kill you now, there's nothing you can do about it. Sit.

I blink. He vanishes, and reappears a few seconds later at the other end of the restaurant. He walks across it, navigating the tables with the grace of a leopard. He reaches my table, deftly pulls up a chair, and sits down. I force myself to loosen my grip on my drink, afraid of breaking the glass.

"Hello, Lynx." He smiles. "Good to see you again."

I don't answer. Instead I seize control of my hands, like a puppeteer, and steer them toward my jacket, maneuvering them through the process of pulling out a cigarette and lighting it.

"What's the matter, Lynx? Nervous? You should learn to relax, loosen up."

"Douglas, tell me something. Are you always so fucking suave?"

The smile drops, and my initial reflexive panic slips away smoothly. I inhale deeply and turn aside to exhale, deliberately avoiding blowing the smoke in his face. *You're not even worth it.*

He understands the insult, I can see. He turns around and snaps his fingers at the waiter. The waiter shimmies over and takes his order. I smoke, contemptuous.

You don't frighten me anymore, hunter. You've lost your hold. If you kill me, so be it. If not . . .

He stares at me. "You've changed, Lynx. You're no longer afraid."

"I know."

"Good," he says pertly. "It'll make the hunt more interesting." He smiles.

"Perhaps," I say. His smile widens.

"You know, Miss de Seingalt is quite angry at her man, Leland," he says at last.

"And why is that?"

"The first two teams he sent against you . . . They lacked all sense of class, of style. Anonymous killers. She wanted you to die with more style than that."

"I'm flattered."

"So she hired me."

I avoid the more obvious insult. Instead I say, "What did Leland think of that?"

"Not much. He didn't say anything while she gave me instructions, just stood there."

"Ah." Silence. The waiter brings him his drink. He drains half of it in one swallow, umbrella and all.

"Tell me, Douglas," I say at last, "which psycho ward did Angélique dig you out of?"

His mouth twitches. His hand lashes out, sweeping our drinks off the table, sending them shattering to the floor. Heads turn. *I've struck a nerve.*

He rises, pounces on me, grabs me by the collar, drags me up to within a few inches of his face. "Worm. Your death will be messy and especially unpleasant."

I smile, my sweet smile again. He drops me and slumps back. I readjust my clothes and light another cigarette. A nervous waiter tries to approach. The Douglas whirls around, points a warning finger. The waiter backs off.

"Seriously . . ." I blow a few smoke rings and wave the cigarette expansively. "Was it Saint-Jacques?"

He darkens visibly under the makeup. Suddenly he raises his hand, holding it up over the middle of the table. His other hand reaches out, digs into his exposed wrist. There is a ripping, peeling, grip-rubber sound and the skin of his hand comes off, like a glove.

He drops the skin and flexes the hand. Smooth, polished steel skeleton, thick cable tendons, knobby joints, strange protuberances. I admire the work, marveling at the combination of delicacy and strength. Then it hits me.

"I remember now. It was Saint-Anne, wasn't it?"

"Yes." He darts forward, his hand slipping into my jacket before I can react and coming back up with my gun. "You won't be needing this." He smiles. Slowly the hand contracts like a steel vise, crushing the gun. The gun tears, crumples, fragments. At last he opens his hand and drops the mangled mess.

Show off. I inhale again.

I point my cigarette at the hand. "Nice work, very nice. Quite—how to put it—elegant? A work of art. Tell me, did they do as good a job on your prick?"

The blow hits home, hard.

"You annoy me, punk! Let me tell you something." Slowly he pulls the skin back on. "I will have the last laugh. You will plead and beg like all the others when the time comes. I will rip open your belly and attach your intestines to a skimmer and drag you down a boulevard."

I blow out a few more smoke rings and don't answer. *I can get you, asshole. You're not even human, just a fuckin psychotic machine . . . Scrap metal and vat flesh.*

He stands up abruptly. "This has lasted long enough. I'll see you soon." He stalks away, abruptly pushing aside frightened diners and worried waiters. This time it is my laugh that floats over the tables at his back.

22:46. Time to go. I get up and walk out. The waiters are so distraught they forget to ask me to pay.

Out on the streets. I stand there briefly, pulling myself together with determined finality. Time to hunt the hunter.

I head around the Rond-Point, toward the Champs. A few scattered Arab pimps, some drunk Uptown kids.

And the crowd, the crawling, hustling, partying, smirking Champs Elysées crowd . . .

I walk through it, with it, up. I can't see the Douglas, but I can feel him, sense him . . . He's here.

With a small shock I see my old friend, the cat, perched on top of a newsstand in front of the Franklin-Roosevelt entrance. I wave at it, friendly. It hisses and jumps off.

I keep walking. Two blocks, to the Rue de la Boetie. I stop by the Prisunic on the corner, light a cigarette, and unobtrusively scan the parked vehicles by the side of the avenue.

There it is. A large truck, ten tons maybe, royal blue with a logo stenciled in white on the side: ARTE.

I start walking again, cutting sideways through the crowd, over to the parking lane. I walk up the lane, between parked skimmers and moving ones, past the truck. I don't even glance at it.

Rue Berri. I stop on the corner. Soon the truck pulls past me, dark shape of the dummy driver in the cab. It slews sideways and joins the flow of Champs traffic.

I watch it drive up, two blocks. As it reaches the level of the tunnel sidebranch, it stops dead, blocking the traffic. Its back gate starts to drop.

Everything is ready.

I take a deep breath and cross the street. I reach the concrete wall that surrounds the George V Metro entrance on three sides and leap up onto it suddenly. From there I jump on top of the newsstand set flush against the concrete wall.

My move has caught the Douglas by surprise. I see a flash of blood-red and white before he manages to disappear. Good.

I don't look back at the first sounds of gunfire. It erupts suddenly, the chatter of high-caliber machinegun fire, the roar of flamethrowers, the thump of grenade launchers, and the sharp concussive explosions of the grenades. And the screams . . .

Collective cry of pure, naked terror, like an opera of pain and fear. I crouch on top of the newsstand and shut my eyes. The thick gasoline smell of napalm . . . Some police small-arms fire, useless.

Flat, imploding sounds as the first skimmers go up. Sounds of tearing metal and breaking glass. Yells, screams, cries.

No Douglas. People running past the newsstand now, panicked mob. A pretty Uptown girl slips on her high heels, falls. She cries out to her friend as she gets trampled by the mob. He keeps running.

I have to look back. I see . . .

Billy Name's Machine Infernale, monstrous, black, bulbous hulk of deadly steel advancing in my direction, systematically chewing up the avenue, exterminating everything within reach. The machine guns lay down a steady fire pattern, mowing down whole sections of the panicked mob, the *bhudda-bhudda* sound occasionally interrupted by the belch of the flamethrowers. Black, oily smoke rises from the flames. A Mirrorface runs up, tries to lob a grenade at the monster. The flame touches him, wraps around him; his scream abruptly cut off as he twists and collapses, a black, burning husk, still twitching.

Fuck . . . Billy, you murderous bastard.

This is . . . insane . . . Sick.

All for me.

Fuckin Billy Name. He refused my plan back at the drugstore, my plan to trap the Douglas. "No," he said. "Tonight I planned to unleash the Machine Infernale. It was planned, Lynx, for tonight, and I *will* do it. But you can use it."

"Okay," I said. "What do I do?"

What do I do? I sit here and watch this madness . . . this horror.

Burnt hulks of exploded skimmers. The flames raging and rising, wrapping two whole blocks of the avenue, an inferno.

And the worst still: above the black tank, glowing through the smoke and the flames and the blood, the holo. Giant film, rotating, encompassing 360°, instant replay of the death and the madness. Running, crying, clawing mob, like ants around an anthill destroyed by the callous foot of a young boy. Double echo sound, offbeat, as the speakers play back the slightly delayed recorded sounds of death. The fire and the bullets and the grenades coming down like rain, in sheets, killing and maiming. Stench of terror overlapping even the napalm, adrenaline going mad.

Some Mirrorfaces and even some unarmed civilians, braver or madder than most, try to throw themselves at the tank and get swatted like flies. I flinch, but can't tear my fascinated stare away.

Death, horror, pain, fear, madness, welling above the avenue, a brutal, random holocaust.

Billy must be creaming his jeans, back home. I think I'll kill him, if I live. That would be nice.

The tank is reaching my level. The avenue is nearly deserted now, the survivors fled, nothing but corpses. And odd silence settles down, punctuated by the belch-chatter-thump of the tank's ordnance.

He comes through the smoke, grim, his gorgeous robes soiled and stained. His hands are red with blood. *This will be over fast, one way or another.*

He stands below the newsstand, regal, erect, ignoring the approaching tank.

"You call *me* mad? Me?"

I stand up on top of the newsstand, silent.

"How can you call me mad?" He continues. "I am a hunter, Lynx, not a butcher! I only meant to kill you, kill my target. Not this . . ."

I laugh then. "Remorse, hunter? Guilt? From you?"

He smiles thinly. "I don't know if I should kill you now, Lynx. One more death, lost in the masses . . . It would lose its special quality, wouldn't you say?"

"Fuck off. Let's finish this."

"If we must . . ." His muscles tense.

He leaps, straight up, to the top of the newsstand. My kick connects, straight ramming thrust to his knee. I nearly break my foot, but I hear metal crack.

He pauses for a beat, long enough for me to jump off the newsstand. I hang in the air . . . contact. I roll and jump up, running. Toward the tank.

I glance back. He is a meter away. *Shit!*

In front of me, the tank, the paint not even scratched,

soot-stained. Its guns fall silent as I reach it. The holo looms above. I look up and see a distorted Douglas right behind a crazed-eyed figure. I recognize with a shock as being me, see him reaching out for my neck.

I duck low to the left and roll, my arms over my head. *Now . . .*

I hear but don't see the flame lick out and surround the Douglas. It flicks over my legs, scorching me. I roll as fast as I can, away.

A scream, one clear, inhuman scream, echoed as the mikes pick it up and the speakers spit it back out, reverb delay to infinity. A scream of fury, not of pain . . . The scream of the defeated hunter.

I look back. Two human torches still standing, clawing at the air: one on the cobblestones in front of me, one ghostly one floating above. The robes are gone, the hair and most of the flesh too. Blackened metal skeleton, invulnerable prostheses reflexively lashing. It falls, collapses to the pavement, still twitching, still moving. Flames lick out of its eye sockets, fire eating the brain inside the alloy skull.

It's not even worth laughing at. I pull myself up and face the now silent and immobile tank. In the holo I see a few scurrying survivors, a squadron of Mirrorfaces carrying portable LAWs galloping up the Champs.

"What now, Billy?" I yell out.

Movement. One of the twin 50s swing toward me slowly. *Of course . . .*

I don't even hear the shot as a giant hammer rams into my chest. I sink into darkness and light, a chaos of jumbled neurons. *This is just a textural experience.*

Lights Out.

XAVIER

I thumb the switch on the flash. A bright white cone appears. I play it around, examining the space.

A door. A thick, old door, massive planks of warped oak bound in dull bronze. I study it. No knob. In the center, a large knocker in the shape of a snake eating its tail, greenish bronze. A few words in a strange language are carved in the door above the knocker: LASCIATE OGNE SPERANZA, VOI CH'ENTRATE. I reach out, lift the knocker, and let go. It hits with the loud clang of a Tibetan gong. The door swings open.

I step in. A room, walls and floor of gray granite blocks, a high, vaulted ceiling. Sheets of thick, oily black smoke curl up from old warped tapers to lick at the rafters. Billy Name is kneeling on a velvet cushion behind a pentacle traced in fresh blood, chanting in an incomprehensible tongue. Behind him stands the Rabbi, tall and majestic, holding up an ancient book of yellowed paper bound in cracked leather and brass. Occasionally he speaks, echoing one of Name's phrases or words. To the side squats a granite altar dripping with blood. The bleeding carcass of a hairless young boy is stretched over it, split open from crotch to neck.

At each corner of the pentacle stands a large Bose speaker, blasting a wailing collage of solos: I recognize snatches of Hendrix, Adrian Belew, Miles Davis, Bird on a small white plastic kid's saxophone, Corlin.

Smoke and sulfur start rising from the surface of the pentacle. Name's chanting and the music rise toward a simultaneous crescendo. I step back, fanning the smoke, wincing at the rotten-egg stench of the sulfur.

The Demon rises out of the floor, his back to me. The

music stops abruptly as his feet leave the floor. Name cackles hysterically. "Remember, Lynx," he screeches. "If you're squeamish, don't kick the beach rubble." The Rabbi closes his book with a thump. The Demon floats in midair, arms by his side. Slowly he turns toward me.

Blue hair cut in a spiked shag, blue lips, and white skin, bone white, stark in the black clothes. His hard silver-grey heroin eyes bore into me. Mara the Demon.

I scream. He smiles and reaches out for me, his arm stretching to an impossible length. Thick yellow claws grab me by the throat, choke me, cut off my scream. He drags me into the smoke.

Into the spaces of gray. A whiff of sulfur, of blood, of ganja, of fresh semen, of corrupted bowels, of catacombs. I fall.

I fall for a long time into darkness. Crystal shards of broken glass escort me on the way down.

I hit the ground and bounce, hear the tinkle of glass on concrete. I lie still. After a while I decide to stand up, surprised at the lack of pain. I feel fine. I examine myself. I notice a large hole in my chest, ringed with caked blood. Stuck next to it on my T-shirt is a white adhesive sticker. I peel it off and read it.

SUCKING CHEST WOUND—PENETRATION OF THE LEFT LUNG BY .50-CALIBER BULLET

I shrug, crumple up the sticker, and drop it amid the broken glass.

I feel a sharp pain in my left big toe and look down. A tag is attached to the toe, the wire wrapped tightly around it. I reach down and twist it off. The tag reads DOA in large black block letters. Smaller letters read HÔPITAL SAINTE-ANNE. The date is scrawled next to that in blue ink: 23/8/33. I drop the tag next to the crumpled sticker.

I pick up the skimboots, sit down, and strap them on. Then I stand up and look around. I am on a highway, two lanes with a yellow-painted strip down the middle. It runs straight ahead and straight behind. To the sides of the highway, and above: darkness.

Then I feel the Presence. Evil. Malevolent. A whiff of old iron and putrefied flesh. I quickly switch on the GF units and start skating.

Faster and faster. The Presence still behind, keeping up. Faster. Faster.

The highway *twists* sideways. I keep skating, twisting with it, still staying upright. It curves down.

I am on top of the curve, skating, and the highway is rolling away under me like a video-game construct. Then downhill. I pick up speed, crouching low to cut down on the air friction, the Presence still pacing me.

The highway twists again. I look up and see for the first time that the curve I am on is a section of a huge arch that curves and twists in the void. I keep skating while I trace it back with my eyes. My gaze goes around twice, uninterrupted. A Möbius strip then, huge coil of continuous surface.

I feel the Presence catching up. Panicked, I gather in energy for a burst of speed.

Ahead I see figures standing across the highway at the low point of the loop. As I get closer they become clearer.

On the left stands an old white-haired and bearded blind man wrapped in sackcloth, leaning on a tall oaken staff. He is talking to a beautiful young blind man dressed in a white tunic. Blood drips from the young man's eye sockets, like congealed tears.

On the right is a Sphinx with the head of a young woman, the body of a lion, and the wings of an eagle. She has large breasts and erect nipples. She chats with a crouching, naked Anubis, head of a dog on the tan body of a man.

The fifth figure hangs in the center, a middle-aged woman in red-and-gold robes. She swings from a white silk scarf, her head lolling, her face obscenely purple, tongue jutting out.

I keep skating toward them, afraid to stop, the Presence hounding my back. As I get nearer the figures, all turn and look at me. The hanged woman's eyes open.

The figures are big, I realize, very big. Colossi.

Fuck. I bend down, dropping my center of gravity, and curve to the right. I shoot straight between Anubis's legs, twin pillars the size of the Obélisque de la Concorde.

I skate on. The feeling of the Presence recedes. I stop and look back.

The figures have returned to their conversations. An elegant old man, clean-shaven with a high forehead and swept-back white hair walks slowly toward them. He is wearing a white suit and an ascot. He greets them, and they all bow to him, except for the hanged woman, who just twitches once.

Then I see the Presence, an obscene horror of rotting flesh draped over a rusted metal frame. It slithers forward, determined. Its flesh is randomly splashed with fresh white paint and hung with shreds of bright red cloth. It reaches the figures.

Anubis reaches down and picks it up. It fits perfectly in his hand, like a child's lead figurine. Anubis squeezes it, first one way, then another, and finally rolls it into a little ball, like clay. The old man in white produces a long, thin silver opium pipe from inside his jacket. Anubis hands him the ball. He places it inside the bowl of the pipe and puts the pipe into his mouth. Anubis strikes a long wooden match against his muzzle and lights the pipe. The old man inhales dreamily.

I turn around and skate away as the old man reaches under the young blind man's tunic and grabs his erect penis. The highway curves and twists, and the figures vanish from sight.

After a brief eternity I see a bright light off in the void and I stop. I sit down on my haunches, lick my left paw, and watch the light. It is emitted by a floating pyramid, the tip of which is separated from the main body and floats above it. As I watch, an eye opens on the tip section. The iris is emerald blue, and there is a small brown spot right under the iris.

The eye looks at me. The sensitive tufts on the tips of my ears bristle, I arch my back and yowl. My fur is raised. Slowly the eye winks at me.

I back up, still yowling and bristling and spitting. Then I realize the pryamid isn't floating at all, but is actually resting on a hand, a translucent hand. My gaze goes up the arm, taking in a hairless, muscular torso, hairless male genitals, hairless legs . . . All translucent, the stars showing through . . . A dog's head, pointed muzzle and ears and sharp teeth . . .

Anubis again, frozen in a classic Egyptian profile. His

ghostly right hand holds the pyramid, and a thick bronze medallion with a face in bas-relief on it swings from his left hand.

I hiss my fury, whiskers twitching, needle-sharp claws opening and retracting convulsively. Then Anubis rears his head and howls.

The howls echoes through the void, filling it. It causes me to curl up in a tight fetal ball and tremble. Peeking over my paw, I see the howl reach the Möbius strip and instantly streak down it, canalized glow zooming by me. It zips around the strip faster and faster, getting longer and longer, till it reaches its own tail and permeates the entire strip.

The strip starts vibrating and shaking. Nerves aflame with terror and premonitions of doom, I jump up and run. Powerful haunch muscles bunch up, tense, and I launch myself off into the void just as the strip shatters. Shrapnel whizzes by me. Then the void is empty and silent.

I sit back on the grass and lick my left paw. A few meters away two cats are frolicking, jumping and rolling and playing. One is white, a long-haired Angora, and the other is black and short-haired. Soon the playing gets amorous. The white cat starts meowing in passion as the black cat purrs and rubs her. Then the black cat mounts the white one, nipping her neck. The white cat howls, cries; the black cat stays silent.

They finish fucking, the black cat coming in powerful thrusts. He rolls onto his back, legs splayed. The white cat nuzzles up, licking his belly.

The black cat screeches. I see that the white cat has bitten his neck, blood spattering her smooth, slick fur. The black cat is pinned down, helpless, as the white cat claws and rakes and chews.

The black cat stops moving. The white cat feasts. After a while she moves away, licking her paws. She licks them clean and falls asleep.

An afternoon passes, tranquil, calm. The white cat sleeps and dreams. The black cat rots in the sunlight. His entrails glitter in the bloodstained grass.

The sun sets, a color orgasm of reds and purples, and the black cat starts to grow. When he reaches the size of a lion he walks over to the white cat and prods her flank. She wakes up with a start, fur bristling, back arching. He casually swats her away. She cowers in fear as he keeps growing. When he reaches the size of a medium-sized skimmer, he casually bends down and bites her head off, swallowing it whole. Then he feasts on the body, chewing methodically, spitting a few bones into the grass. Satisfied, he licks his paws and his muzzle clean.

Then he looks up at me. His yellow eyes glow. His tongue licks out.

"Hello, Lynx," he purrs.

I sit there, shocked, fur bristling.

"Won't you say hello, Lynx?"

I hiss.

"Now, that wasn't nice, oh no, not nice at all. You should be nicer to your friends, Lynx, oh yes."

I finally manage to spit the words out. "Who are you?"

"Why, don't you know me? Does the body, this mere . . . *envelope* fool you? I am disappointed, Lynx, truly. If you are to be my tool, my weapon, I shall be expecting more from you."

I know, then. "Xavier."

He purrs with delight. "Good, good. Glad to see you come to your senses, dear boy. Keep it up."

"Don't you fuckin call me 'boy,' asshole," I snarl. "I'm two fuckin years older than you, two years on the Street—"

"Ah," he cuts in, "but that's only two years in the flesh, the meat, dear boy. That doesn't count. *I*'ve spent time in the Net itself, quantumspeed electronic time, and would you know those nanoseconds do add up."

"Fuck off, man. You're dead. You're a ghost. This is a dream. I don't have to take this shit."

"But it's not a dream, boy!" He snarls. He leaps forward and in a second surrounds me with his bulk, huge black wall of fur. His head looms above me as he howls out the words. "You think this is a dream, do you? Do you!" It isn't a question.

"Listen to me, fool!" He continues. "Listen to my words, my story!

"You know my sister, oh yes. You know her. But not as I do. Listen.

"That golden bitch, Lynx, she fucked me. She fucked me dry, holy incest in the House of Anubis. And when she finished fucking me, when she had no more use for me, she killed me.

"Ah, but not enough, oh no. Not enough for the bitch, Angélique Anubis de Seingalt. Never enough.

"What she did, you could never even dream of, Lynx. You're just a Street boy, and the children of the Street have no imagination, never the imagination of the rich, never. You don't need it, secure in your simple cocoon of life and death and sex and drugs.

"Ah, but we need it. The rich need it, need imagination, need it more than they need money even. For without imagination would come boredom, and if we had to live in boredom you would never have to kill us, because we would do it ourselves before our fifteenth birthday.

"Let me tell you about Angélique's imagination, which knows few limits when it comes to perversity. The bitch, indeed, could have given the sainted Marquis Donatien-Alphonse François de Sade himself a few lessons, were he still alive.

"Balzac once said that behind every fortune was a crime. He wasn't quite accurate, do you know that. He should have said 'many crimes.'

"Angélique's crime was beautiful, oh yes . . . I would call it a work of art, were I a spectator rather than the prime participant.

"She killed me, Lynx, as I said. But first she drugged me and shipped me secretly to her pet scientist, her mad doctor, the good Dr. Benway. And Dr. Benway recorded me. He recorded my brain, my thoughts, my emotions, my memories, my reflexes, my grooved and defined neural pathways. He recorded them on a RNA/MPM chip, and then of course he destroyed my body, my meat.

"The horror, Lynx . . . You can't imagine, never could. The bitch locked me in her medallion, silicon prison, far worse than any cage of metal or stone, oh yes. Torture of eternity, bodiless mind matrix, nanoseconds ticking by like slowly falling drops in realtime. Not pleasant, oh no.

"And you freed me, I saw you. The bitch gave me eyes and ears in my electronic schismatrix, eyes and ears so I could see her live and lust, eyes and ears to make me howl in rage. Silently, mind you, because of course she didn't leave me a mouth. That would have been too easy.

"Just eyes and ears. And I saw you. I saw you fuck her and I saw you leave her and I saw you take me and I saw you free me, oh yes. Your Rabbi did it, set me free in the Net, free in the data streams. Freedom like you can't imagine, Lynx. Freedom to access any open data bank, any unprotected deck in the world. I know more about the world than any man alive, Lynx, and I have subjectively lived longer than any man alive, and soon I will be far richer and far more powerful than my father or sister ever were. Richer than anyone, and I will see Angélique dead, oh yes, deader than I by far.

"I saw you, Lynx. After you freed me from my prison of yearly microseconds, I took the form of a cat, took over a cyborg cat wired for kink, and I ran behind the cat's eyes and watched. I saved your life twice, oh yes, once behind the Panthéon when I tore out a Capuerista's eyes, and once on the Champs Elysées when I brought your friend to your dying body. I brought Domino to you, Lynx, and she took you to a clinic I bought, bought just for you, to fix your dying body. You're alive now, more alive than I am, and I saved your life twice so you owe me a life and you will pay me with my sister's life.

"Wake up now, O Warrior. Wake up and put on your warpaint and gather your hordes and arm them and invade the fortress and slay my evil sister for me, O Lynx. Do this for me and we shall be even, two lives for two lives, and we shall go different ways and never meet again. Do this and the debt is paid in full. Do this and perhaps I shall rid you of your Demon too."

"Wait!" I cry. "How do you know . . ." But there is no answer. The cat with the glowing yellow eyes is gone and then there is only darkness.

Light. Bright, sharp, white, painful. I slam my eyes shut and rest before opening them again.

White. Focus. White sheets . . . ? White man . . . ?

Focus. Slowly.

Yes. Man. In White. Bed. Walls. White.

Yes. A room, a white room. A bed with white sheets. A man in white at the foot of the bed. Smiling. Chalk-white face, silver-white hair. White on white on white on white.

I close my eyes again, resting in soothing darkness. Then a voice cuts through to my refuge, an old, drawling, grating voice, like a powersaw trying to cut through aluminum.

"I saw you open your eyes, son. You're awake."

I moan. I feel dry fingers brush my left arm, hear a hiss, feel something cold pressed against the inside of my elbow. Another hiss and a brief thud against my flesh.

A dry, rusted, ancient cackle. "Right into the main-line! That should do you some good, son."

My eyes slam open abruptly as the drug hits me, a double punch to the spine and the forebrain. Sensations flood in abruptly, chaotic, disorganized. Slowly they coalesce.

An old white man in a white coat is standing next to my bed, waving a disposable Syrette, a grin on his mummified face.

"Ha! Now you're awake! Methenedextroamphetamine, 2ccs. Never fails, and I've been using it for a while. In the old days I would've just used some cocaine, but this is a lot more, um, efficient."

"Water . . ." I croak.

219

"Water? You want water?"

"Yes."

"Can't. Not so soon after an operation. The suture might burst."

I claw feebly in his direction. The drug gives me the strength to let off a stream of abuse. "Give me some water, you old fucker, or as soon as I can stand I'll rip your head off and shove it so far up your ass you'll be able to see the inside of your stomach."

"All right, all right! No need to get violent. I saved your life, after all . . . You should be grateful."

I sag back against the pillows, drenched with sweat, while he drops the Syrette into a white wastepaper basket next to the bed and slowly walks over to the sink in the corner of the room. I study him as he pours some water into a plastic cup. He seems utterly fleshless, his bones protruding sharply from under his white smock. He walks with a perpetual stoop. Thin wisps of white hair cling to the sides of his scalp.

"Here you are, son. If you die, don't say I didn't warn you. As a matter of fact, you'd better tell my employer that I did."

I gulp the water greedily, clearing my pasty mouth. I swish the last mouthful of water around and spit it back out into the cup. He takes it from me and casually dumps the whole thing into the plastic basket. Water spills onto the floor. I hear a sharp whine and see a little white Toshiba servobot spring from a concealed niche in the wall and efficiently clean up the mess. Then it starts washing the floor next to the doctor's feet. He kicks it violently, sending it spinning to the other side of the room. It rights itself painstakingly, emitting a stream of injured electronic beeps and whines, red LEDs flashing.

"Fuckin machines," snarls the doctor. "Always in your feet. I hated them from the day they were invented. I tell you, in my days we had niggers or chinks to do this kind of work. They were a lot less trouble."

I realize with a start that I don't even know for sure if this asshole *is* the doctor. "Who are you?"

His head dips slightly. "Doc Benway, at your service. As long as I get paid . . ."

A flash of memory, dream shard cutting through a veil

. . . "Benway? Aren't you the croaker who recorded
Xavier de Seingalt for his sister?"

He starts visibly. "How did you know that? Ah well,
no matter. That's all in the past. I work for Mr. de
Seingalt now. He had enough respect for my brilliance,
my particular genius, to let bygones be bygones and hire
me at twice the pay his cunt of a sister offered me."

"Cunt? You should fucking talk!" I start coughing
violently, feeling a tearing pain in my chest.

He ignores my hacking. "Now listen son. I did what I
did under orders from my employer. I have never mali-
ciously or gratuitously hurt someone. I may have made a
few mistakes, but that's all in the past. I would appreciate it if you treated me with the respect due a distin-
guished member of the medical profession."

I manage to bark a hurried "Fuck off" between two
spasms. Finally they calm down. I lift the thin white
nightshirt I am wearing and study my chest.

A large bruise covers the left side of my chest. In the
center of the bruise is something black. It moves. I drop
the shirt and look at the doctor.

"Biological healing agents," he drawls. "Enlarged bac-
teria. Take it like a man. It'll do you good."

"Great. Just great."

"You should rest now." He produces another Syrette
from within his coat. "Your arm."

"What is that?"

"Benzodiazepine. It'll counterbalance the dex and put
you out for a while."

*Great . . . Here goes for that great rollercoaster in the
sky again . . .*

"Is my friend here? Domino?"

"The black girl? Now there's a beautiful piece of meat.
Love to get her on an operating table, see how she's
made, you know." He pauses. "You can see her when
you wake up." He tries a grin again and waves the
Syrette.

I stick my arm out. He applies the Syrette. Hiss, thud.
The Syrette goes into the basket.

"Good night, now," he says.

"Yeah." Down . . . Out.

*   *   *

Up again. Easier this time. Domino is sitting next to the bed on a metal chair. I stare at her, her bright clothes, black face. Color at last . . .

She finally realizes I'm awake. She grins.

"Hey, deuce! How's tricks?"

"Trickier and trickier. Fuckin Billy Name nearly dusted me with that fuckin machine of his."

"I know." Her grin drops as fast as it went up.

"Oh yeah? How come?"

"Remember that cat, the one that was following you around?"

"Fuck yeah."

Her voice slips into a singsong lilt as she lays it out. "I was hangin in the Forum, chillin with Jester and Rat, y'know? And this cat comes runnin through the crowd, straight at me. I recognized it so I didn't move. It came right up to me and bit into my pants and started pullin, ya no see it? So Jester and the Rat, they're like, what the fuck? But I go, hey spuds, it's *slicin*, I think we better follow it. Now the Rat wasn't too sure, but Jester went like, hey skaghead, listen to the blood, let's ram, man. So I picked up the cat and we exited the Forum doublespeed. Then we're just standing there, y'know, def clueless. So the cat jumps out of my arms and runs over to this tree, y'know, they've got like dirt around them, and it fuckin starts scratchin in the dirt. So I run over and, dig this, it was fuckin writing! I couldn't fuckin believe it! It scratched out LYNX, then HURT, then CHAMPS. So then I tell Jester and the Rat and they fuckin flipped, of course, but then Jester goes fuck it, let's jet! So we grab their skimbikes and I sat behind Jester with the cat and we jetted up to the Champs like fuckin *fast*, man. The Rat just rammed his bike off Chatelet onto the river to avoid the traffic, and we followed him, and we made the Champs in three minutes *flat*, man, no lie.

"So we get to the Champs and it was like fuckin *chaos*, man, I mean some *baaad* craziness. Smoke everywhere, deaders all over the fuckin place, kinda stink made me wanna puke. There was still some major madness going down toward the bottom, whole bunch of Mirrorfaces with LAWs trying to ace this huge black tank.

"We dodged that shit and headed up. The cat pointed the way with his paws. And we found you.

"The Rat was pissed, man, real pissed. I just freaked. I mean, you were flatlined, big fuckin hole in your chest, gone meat but *good*. The Rat was screaming shit about tearing someone's balls off with a plastic fork, and Jester just stood there with this gone psycho look. Then the cat screeched and ran to a vidphone booth and started tapping on the glass. So I went up and looked in and the screen was fuckin flashing, man, no lie, big letters, and it said TAKE LYNX and then there was an address. Real fuckin weird, man, ya know? Like *eerie*.

"So we put you on the Rat's bike, like real careful, and skimmed off to the place, right here, fancy fuckin house in the 16ème. And this freak ghoul doc meets us at the door and the Rat carries you into this apartment and it's a fuckin hospital, man! Weirdest thing I ever seen, besides the cat of course. Like this guy's house, man, it's this fuckin white hospital. So the Rat puts you on this floating stretcher, and Benway—and that's the doc's name—says wait here and then he pushes you through these big doors and that's it. So we sit there and wait, smoke some kali, chillin out, real nervous like. Two hours later this Benway walks out all covered in blood, lookin real down and says in that voice of his, like a fuckin creaky door. 'He'll live.' Then he disappears again and locks the doors behind him. We get up and the Rat tries to break the fuckin door down, but there's fuckin steel inside the wood so he can't. Then Benway opens the door a crack and says to Jester and the Rat, 'You two go home' and then to me he goes, 'You wait. There's a vid in there.' And then the door's closed again.

"So we talk about it and we decide they should decide. So the Rat gives me his gun, just in case, and they take off. I hung out, watched the news on the vid. They showed the Champs, man, it was bad, real bad, fuckin burnt kids and people all over the place, all these blasted cars and stores. The Faces finally got the tank with a couple of Army choppers, but about sixty of them got dusted. All these ter groups took the credit, or tried to, but the Faces said it was the ATs, Billy Name like you said. It's a bad scene, man."

"I know." We sit in silence for a bit.

"What about Name?" I say at last.

"I dunno, man. He's gone, vanished, made like liquid helium. No one has a clue."

"Figures."

"How're you feeling?"

"I dunno . . . Sore, tired. Kinda drained. I wanna get the fuck out of here."

"I'll help you."

"Good. Where are my clothes?"

"I dunno. I'll go ask psychodoc."

She gets up and walks out. A few minutes later she comes back in with my pants and boots.

"They were outside. Your shirt's gone, there's blood on your pants, but fuck it. It'll do."

"What about my leather, my deck, my weapons?"

"Outside. Your leather's a bit chewed up, though."

"Fuck that. I'll patch it. Let's step."

I push myself out of bed and nearly collapse to the floor. Domino holds me up while I struggle into my pants. Crusted dried blood flakes off, softly drifting to the floor. The door flies open just as I finally get them on.

Benway stands there, Syrette in hand, glaring.

"Now just where do you think you're going, son?"

"Leaving." I button my pants and sit down on the bed. Domino starts helping me with my boots.

"I can't allow that. Now, why don't you just be a good boy and lie down and let me give you this shot." His voice gets sly, wheedling. "It's for your own good."

"Fuck off." One boot on. One to go.

Benway starts advancing, waving the Syrette. Domino points at him and there is a gun in her hand. *Smith & Wesson Tactical, .38 Special. The Rat has taste.*

Benway stops and smiles, revealing shiny white dentures. "Now, now, don't get excited. I only meant to help." He backs up. "My employer delivered a few things for you, for when you leave, which I suppose is now . . . They're in my office."

My other boot is on. I stand up steadily. "Take us there."

He opens the door and steps aside. "After you."

Domino waves the gun airily. "After *you*."

* * *

Benway's office is like the rest of the place, clean and modern and sterile. To my relief, though, it is gray. The white has been getting to me, too much like an '80s vision of Hell.

I've pulled on my leather, but I don't have a shirt. I squirm every time I catch sight of the crawling black mess on my chest.

"Why don't I have bandages?" I ask Benway.

He grins at my discomfort and points at my chest. "Little buggers need to breathe." He opens up a drawer in his metal desk and pulls out a handful of items. He tosses them onto the desk. "Here."

I slowly walk over and spread them out. A credit chip, a magnetic key, a DAF chip, and a fiche. I hold up the fiche. "You got a reader?"

"Yes." He ambles over to the corner of the room, pulls a reader off a steel shelf, and ambles back. "Here."

I slot the fiche and read.

> Dear Lynx,
> Just a brief note. You may trust Dr. Benway for the time being, because I am paying him more than anybody else. The chip holds a virtually unlimited credit line on an orbital Seychelles bank. The key is the key to your new apartment, 86 rue de l'Université, in the 7ème. It is a safe apartment where you may rest, heal, and regain your strength for the final confrontation with my sister. The DAF contains a duplicate construct of myself. Please slot it when you get a chance. It will give you instructions concerning the solution of our problems with my sister.
> Please trust me. I am your ally in this.
> Good luck.

It is signed "Xavier de Seingalt."

Solution . . . I'm not sure we're going to agree on a solution, Xavier. I pick up the credit chip and tap it with my fingers meditatively. Finally I speak. "Well, Domino, it looks like we just got ourselves some new digs."

* * *

On the way out she mentions the cat again. "You know, after it brought us here, it just lay down and died. Benway took it away."

"Don't worry about the cat. It wasn't real."

"What do you mean?"

"Cyborg unit. Angélique's brother was riding it. I'll tell you about it."

"How do you know?"

"I had a dream."

"A dream?"

"Yeah. You know us Indians . . . We dream real, hard and solid. Truth comes in the healing dreams, when you've got the Blood."

The pad is beautiful, of course. Domino gasps when I open the door. I'm impressed, even after Angélique's digs.

We wander through the sprawling apartment, goggling and gawking at the slicksmooth design. The only color in the apartment comes from the paintings and sculptures, a small fortune's worth of artwork, the latest trends from San Fran or New York or Rio de Janeiro; everything else is monochrome, grays and black and polished steel and glass. The tables are works of art themselves, solid glass with miniaturized GF circuitry encased in a corner, the chips laid out in the open rather than enclosed in plastic. All the rest of the furniture is a float too, corporate gray bonded-urethane foam chairs and beds. The chairs even have motion controls, so one can circulate through the apartment without walking.

The kitchen is fully furnished, blender and all. I raid the liquor cabinet—better stocked even than Olric's—and start mixing Bloody Marys while Domino checks out the rooms.

I'm shaking the tumbler when Domino comes running out of the back of the apartment. "Hey Lynx, man, come *check this out*!" I open the tumbler and pour two Bloody Marys into tall glasses before following her back, drinks in hand—slowly; my chest still hurts like a motherfucker.

She pushes a sliding door open and waves expansively. "Ta da!" Hard gray tiles, steel shelves filled with gray towels, and a black injection-molded plastic hot tub built for ten.

"Slicin." I hand her the drinks and dip my hand in the

JONATHAN LITTELL

water. It's hot, steaming hot. The thermometer reads
42°C. "Check it."

I start playing with the controls, membrane switches
built into the wall. Within seconds I have the jets going,
bubbling streams of hot water churning the surface.

"Yeah!" gasps Domino. "I could get used to this mil-
lionaire shit!"

I notice a music library built into the wall next to the
hot tub. I switch it on and study the selection. It sucks.
— "Fuck this." I pull a small jack out of my armdeck and
slave it to the library. I hit a few switches and download
my entire collection. "Now we'll have some *music*." I
punch up Rupert Vogel's *Selections*, icecold '20s digital
jazz, perfect for the setting. Music pours out of the walls
from hidden speakers, filling the room. I turn up the
volume and motion to Domino, let's take a bath. She
smiles and jives, wait, follow. I follow her out.

. . . To my room. I stand in the doorway and gasp
while she grins.

King-sized floating bed, open closets filled with new
clothes, a small assortment of weaponry on the bed. *Fuck
that.* It's the decks that hold my eye, hold me tight,
open-mouthed prisoner.

The decks . . . An entire off-the-rack professional
soundscape system, maybe seventy thousand ESUs worth
at first glance. A few stray bubbles of packing foam still
lie on the floor and the desk. A deVeres all-purpose
motherfucker of a deck, with an IBM specialized console
slaved to it. Hands, Trackers, a Braun sampler, a full-
scale JVC holoprojector, a Marantz library, a rack of
NEC fine-tuners, a 2×1-meter flatscreen up on the wall.
Fuck . . .

I sit down on the bed, hard. After a few seconds
Domino hands me my drink. I gulp it down without
thinking, still staring at the gleaming array of technology
lined up neatly on the desk. *It isn't even obsolete yet.*

Domino laughs. "This guy's all right."

"Yeah. Maybe." My gaze never wavers. I put down
the empty glass. *Beware of RNA constructs bearing
gifts.* . . .

* * *

The hot tub is divine. We strip and slowly lower ourselves in the frothing waters. Bliss. I kick back, head
leaning on a convenient foam headrest, sip a chilled
Bloody Mary, and soak the pain and fatigue out of my
body.

A long, steaming bath, hot water and icecold Vogel.
The perfect contrast. After a while Domino gets out, and
I slide down all the way into the water. I reach up and
cut the jets and the lights and wait for the water to
calm down. I stretch out then, spreadeagled across the
entire tub, eyes and nose just barely above the surface,
and float in the darkness. I can see the twinkle of the
reflected lights of Paris in the shiny tiles on the ceiling. I
float and lose myself in a private place of the mind.
Vogel echoes faintly, muted and flat through the veil of
water. I close in on my breathing, letting myself out with
each breath, following it out. No thought, except once in
a while the thought of *no thought*, and then back to the
breath, out on the breath . . .

I come up suddenly after a time for no reason. I roll in
the water, working energy back into my flaccid muscles.
Then I stand up, dripping, and climb out, carefully favoring my left side. I dry myself with one of the towels and
noticed the black stuff on my chest is starting to flake off.
The wound underneath is red, raw, but looks sealed. It
only hurts if I inhale too much or bend sharply. *Better
take it easy for a bit.* I experiment for a while, testing the
limitations of the wound, then head for my room, enjoying the feeling of the thick carpet against the soles of my
feet.

I avoid looking at the decks, the way a child avoids
looking at a stack of presents because he wants everything to be just right before opening them. I inspect the
closet instead, looking over the clothes. They are neat
and new, but fairly casual. I pull on snug white Calvin
Klein briefs, a soft pair of black cotton pants with a
drawstring and large pockets, and a beautiful oversized
gray shirt with turquoise stitches. The shirt feels silky,
and looks faintly iridescent under the light. I roll up the
sleeves and leave it open. Time now for the decks.

Not yet. I pad over to the kitchen first. Domino is
sprawled in one of the foam seats, floating by one of the

windows, reading a tattered paperback. A floating tray next to her holds an assortment of bottles and glasses.

"Been mixing?" I grin.

"Oh yeah. They got some smooth sauce here, man. I even found a tin of hash and some fine Peruvian C."

"Razor. Our host has class."

She raises a glass half filled with amber liquid. "You can say that again." She drains the glass and returns to her book.

Inside the kitchen I examine the wine rack. Iesu Kirishto . . . I could probably live for eight months, live well, on what those eight bottles had cost. *Oh well. Might as well enjoy them while you have them.* I finally pick a red Pouilly, a vintage '23. I find a bottle opener in one of the drawers, thrust it on top of the bottle, and trigger it. I hold the bottle while it hums. I pull it off when it pops, and it spits out the cork. I drop the cork on the counter and the bottle opener back into a drawer. I scoop up the bottle and a long-stemmed glass, and head back to the room.

"Hey, deuce," Domino calls out as I pass by the living room, "could you change the music? It's real alienating."

"Sure. What do you want to hear?"

"I dunno. Something old."

"Check."

I stop in the hot tub room, cut the Vogel, and scroll through the catalog, looking for something good. I finally decide on some old reggae, hardcore dub poetry from the late '80s. Righteous stuff, fiery revolutionary riddims, a war cry against Babylon and the Shitstem.

Back in the room. I reverently sit down in front of the system, and slowly pour myself a glass of wine. I gently put down the bottle and taste it. Superb. *How the fuck am I ever going to go back to that cheap swill I used to drink? Sheeeit . . .*

Time. I put down the glass next to the bottle and methodically power the system. It responds impeccably, sensitive to the slightest touch. I spend the next two hours running through the functions, familiarizing myself with the commands and controls. Finally I kick back, drink some more wine, and think about things.

What next? Gotta beautiful system, but nothing to run.
Play games? Fuck.

Then I remember. *The DAF . . .*

I find my old clothes and dig out the small DAF chip
Benway had given me. I hold it between two fingers for a
few seconds, toying with it, contemplating. Then I shrug,
turn to the deVeres deck, and slot it.

The large flatscreen pings into life and the construct's
face appears. It looks exactly like the face on the medallion, Angélique's twin brother. Her nose, her chin, her
mouth. I keep on wanting to call it *him*.

"Hello, Lynx," it says in the same voice the cat used in
the dream. "So glad to meet you at last."

I nod. "We've met already, haven't we"

It frowns. "My memory says we haven't."

"In the dream. When I was under, at Benway's. You
talked to me in the dream. You looked like a black cat."

"I've followed you around in the body of a cat, yes.
But I never talked to you in a dream." It smiles. "You
must have been dreaming."

I'd just been kidding when I told Domino about the
"Cheyenne dream." I'd assumed de Seingalt had fed me
data while I was under, via my head jack, and that the
dream was just subconscious interpretation of the data.
But maybe I've been wrong.

"You didn't jack into my head, download some data?"

"No. Never."

"Should I believe you?"

"Why would I lie?"

It has a point. Maybe it was a genuine Blood Dream, a
dream of true images. *Far out.*

"You slept with your sister," I say at last. "She killed
you and had Benway record you. You were in the medallion. The Rabbi freed you. You slipped into the head of
a cyborg cat, followed me around, and saved my life
twice. Is this correct?"

It looks surprised. "Yes. How do you know?"

I smile. "I dreamed it."

Silence. Then it speaks again.

"No matter. Let us talk business."

"Let us." I sip the wine.

"You know of my situation," it says. "I am at this

moment basically stray software, a construct circulating freely in the Net. The part of me talking to you at this moment is, in effect, a sub-program. The rest of me is currently occupied in the hostile takeover of the Anubis Corporation."

Something clicks. *The front companies . . .*

"Where do you get the money to buy up the shares?"

"I have access to vast amounts of credit."

"Then why don't you set your sights higher than just one corporation?"

It smiles. "Vengeance, my dear Lynx. Surely you can understand such a motive. I wish to see my beloved sister suffer and die. Then, only then, will I do as I please."

Sister-fuckin wirehead . . .

"So where do I come in?"

"For the time being, you don't. Wait, rest, heal, enjoy life. I advise you not to leave your apartment too much, as my sister still has her ninjas out on the street searching for you. You may have all the food and alcohol you need delivered.

"I will leave you a number. If you need drugs, or women or boys or anything, call it. If you wish to go out, also, call it and a bodyguard will be arranged. Any questions?"

Fuck that shit. "What will you be doing?"

"Setting up Anubis for the final blow. Which is when, by the way, I may require your services."

I nod. *Sounds like a B movie script.*

"Is that all?" he asks.

"Yes."

"Good-bye, then." A sharp ping and the image vanishes, reduced to a small white dot of concentrated electrons at the center of the screen. The dot lingers for a second, then fades too.

I lean back and muse.

Could he really be that naive? Sucker. I think it might be time to play a few games with Mr. Xavier de Seingalt.

Gametime, what a blast. Let's start with the movers.

I snag my leather (what's left of it, that is. I could easily buy a new one now that de Seingalt trusts me with his credit line, but I'm too attached to the old one. I'll just have to have it cleaned and patched.), the credit chip, my weapons, a few odds and ends, and Domino, and call a taxi. I leave everything else in the apartment for later.

"Pity we have to blow," says Domino as we waited in the courtyard.

"Yeah. But with this it won't be so bad." I wave the chip.

"Razor." She smiles.

The taxi arrives, smooth, silver, contoured Citroën. We get in and sag in the circular foam couch. The squeakbox barks at us: "Destination, please?" I rattle off a destination of the 5ème, far from anything. Figure if de Seingalt is in the Net, he can read off taxi manifests, no problem. The squeakbox dies and the taxi lifts smoothly.

We reach the 5ème in ten minutes. I feed the chip into the appropriate slot and wait a few seconds. The taxi spits out the chip along with a receipt. I pocket the chip, crumple the receipt, and get out of the taxi.

Domino is already waiting on the sidewalk. We head for the nearest Metro and ride it up to Saint-Michel. I pay cash for the tickets.

At Saint-Michel we walk around leisurely for a while. Soon we spot some spuds I know and I start the Telephone going.

The Handjive, Arab Telephone. Word gets around fast, if you know how, and you don't have to use any *words*. The Beasts have vidcams and shotgun mikes at every street corner, but they can't read the Telephone. Halflife and Jester find us within a half hour.

Halflife is friendly, smooth. "Cool runnings, my man. How's the Street going for you?" But under the words she hides the jive, the signals. -What-Need-?-

I answer in kind. "Some problems, chica, minor systems crash." and the flashing fingers, -Safe-House-Biz -For-Livewires-

"Let's step it, then."

We walk across the river, to the Forum, looking casual, relaxed, four streetdrek on the cruise. Inside the Forum we start talking, dead-air zone for the Mirrorface mikes and cams.

"I need a pad, a clean pad. No Net, and that's priority."

Halflife rubs her chin. "It's possible. Ice can probably line it up. But you're talking credit, big time."

I nod. "That's number two." I hold up the chip. "I need a laundry."

She smiles. "How much?"

"Direct line on the Queen's Bank, Seychelles Oribtal. Unlimited. Need a million or three, the laundry can keep the chip."

She whistles, low. Jester cackles and jumps up on a railing.

"You're moving Uptown, my man!" he cries. "This ain't no smalltime Street hustle here, no? You got credit like that, that's corporate. Smooth runnings, real crucial. You a General now!" He laughs again, delighted.

I acknowledge the compliment, a small nod and smile. Then, softly, "This ain't a score, Jester. Not an end. Just a means. I still gotta hustle, gotta finish this biz. There'll be blood, lots of meat. Maybe mine. Who knows? This too shall come to pass. The credit . . . It's just a means."

He smiles lopsidedly. "I read you. You need help, my general, you need guns and meat to hold them, the Livewires will be there. And we'll be there for you and for the ride, for the party, not for the credit."

"Hrolasho. Thank you. If there's a ride, a run, I might need you." I grin. "Partytime like you've never seen, my word."

Halflife taps on the metal railing, sharp, clicking sound, interrupting. "The chip. Lynx. You want this, you want it speed. So I gotta step."

I hand her the chip. "Cool runnings, chica."

"Cool runnings, spud. Wait here. Jester'll hang with you."

It takes her four hours. "We'll move by Downside, spray the cams outside the place so they don't make you. Good?"

"Check. No prob. What about the cleaners?"

"Workin on it. It'll take a few days. My man will score you for another chip, clean, untraceable."

"Hardcore." Pause. "Got one more thing . . ."

"Yah?"

I hand her the key. "Gotta pad, Uptown pad, 86 Université in the 7ème. Behind the Musée d'Orsay. This is the key. Pad's got art, few hundred Ks worth. What you do, you score a truck, mover's truck. You can fake it, too, stencil logo on the side. Clean the place out. There's a system in the back room. I want that. You keep the booze and the art. That's payment, for tricks."

"Razor. Orsay, though? That's Mirrorface territory, kinda dicey."

"Play it legal. Get mover's uniform, print up orders on a deck, that kinda shit. The Faces give you flak, you play it legit."

"Smooth. What about the owner?"

"Don't worry about him. He doesn't exist."

She takes it in stride. "Slicin." She flips the key in her hand and turns to leave.

"One thing," I add.

"What?"

"When you finish the score—"

"Yeah?"

"Trash the place. Raze it. And paint on the walls, Madame Eurydice Reviendra des Enfers."

"ATs too cool. I read ya."

The pad is nice, clean; two rooms in the 13ème, Avenue de l'Admiral Mouchet. It's right next to the Parc Montsouris, which makes the Downside access real smooth. Razor.

We settle in. My chest looks a bit better. "I say give it five days," says Jester. We score for futons, sheets, food, all without going out. The Rat drops by with some screamers and a few other defensives, so together we rig up a straitjacket security perimeter. It wouldn't stop a professional, but it'd slow him down long enough to give us a chance.

Halflife shows two days later with my system and a delighted grin. "The score, my man, so smooth. We cleaned the joint, totaled it, a real mess. I'm moving the art through Saeteroy, a dealer I know."

"Good credit?"

"It'll take awhile, but yeah, a million maybe. Money,

man, the good life off the fuckin Street for a while. We're gonna share it, all the Livewires."

"Razor."

"I brought you something else too."

"Yeah?"

"A case of the booze. It's in the truck, I'll bring it up."

"Hardcore, babe. Thanks." I kiss her and she starts down the stairs. She calls up on her way down. "There's a message for you, too!"

A message?

The message is from de Seingalt. It had been tacked onto the deVeres, and reads: I WILL TALK TO YOU xds.

I think about it. I'd ripped the skaghead off for a small fortune. However, he—*it*, I remind myself, *it*—can afford it. Considering its position, it probably doesn't care; and it probably still needs me.

The phone rings, the timing too perfect for synchronicity. It's de Seingalt, of course.

"How did you find me?" I bark before it can speak.

"Quite easily, actually. I don't think you realize how far the Net extends."

"Well?"

"When your friends emptied my apartment—and by the way, that was a nice touch, especially the Cocteau bit—so when they robbed me, I of course was aware of the theft as it happened. The cameras I'd installed outside observed the truck. I tracked the truck via the Net to this place. After that . . ."

I nod.

"By the way," he added, "you will observe that though I saw your friends empty my apartment and then systematically destroy it, I did nothing to interfere. I would like you to keep that in mind."

"I will."

"You are worth a few million ESUs to me. Maybe even more. Money means little to me."

I smile. "Glad to know that. Unfortunately, us mortals do not always share your . . . disdain. You have to eat when you live in the flesh."

The construct image doesn't flinch, but I decide I've stung him anyway.

"Don't play games with me, Lynx. Play games *for* me."

"Why should I?"

"Three reasons. First, the carrot: I can make you rich, very rich."

"I already am, thanks to you."

"Well then, the stick: I could have you killed, very easily."

"I'm not sure that really worries me anymore."

A moment of silence. Then: "I can give you revenge."

I raise an eyebrow.

"Angélique," he says.

"Yes?"

"I'll get back to you."

The image blinks and fades. I hang up.

He calls back a few hours later.

"Please excuse me. Urgent business."

"Lorenz S.A.?"

"What are you talking about?"

"Your front."

"I don't have a front called Lorenz."

Alarm signals go off inside my head. *Two groups . . . The fronts, there were two groups.* I try to look innocent. "I'm sorry. My mistake."

"You thought I was running this company?"

"Yes. Obviously I misread the data."

"No matter. Now listen. If you watch the news tonight, you will see a spot on the accidental death of three members of the Anubis board of directors. Two more have secretly resigned. My proxies are taking their place. The takeover is moving along, and my beloved Angélique is very scared."

"Where is she?"

"She has holed up in the pyramid with her man Leland. She is afraid the Board might turn against her if I manage to control enough of it. She has full control of the pyramid. However, I hold an ace: Leland, unbeknownst to Angélique, is an employee of the Board. She thinks he works for her, but in actuality the Board pays him to keep tabs on her."

"I figured that."

"You must wait a few days while you heal and I secure my control of the Board. In the meantime I would like you to acquire some weaponry."

"What for?"

"When the time is right you must invade the pyramid."

Well shit . . . Hell of a movie.

"Why should I?"

"As I said: the carrot, the stick, and especially revenge. I wish to see Angélique suffer, and you can help."

"How?"

"I will concoct a soundscape on your system. You must open it so I can do so. When you capture Angélique, you will cuff her and play her the scape, through earphones."

"What will it do?"

"Hurt her. Far more than physical pain could. She might actually enjoy physical torture."

"I don't torture. Torture is pussy. If you're going to kill someone, do it clean. That's enough."

It smiles.

"Can I listen to the scape?" I ask.

"No. I still need you."

"What is it?"

"A soundscape of her mindscape, you might say. A weapon designed specifically for her, but enough still to render you or someone else permanently catatonic."

"I see."

"Do you?"

Contacts. Time to put out, start feeling out. I figure Cornelius will eventually come into the picture, so I start there. Spread the word, spread the datum, Lynx looking for Mr. C.

I hadn't yet talked to Viper, either. We finally meet in a small café in the 5ème, anonymous dive.

"Halflife tells me the Livewires will run with me. But I figure you lead, it's your decision."

"Listen, man, you know how it is. I coordinate runs and shit. But if Livewires want to run, they don't need my authorization. This ain't the CRS or the U.S. Marines, ya no see it? So you can recruit who you want, you don't have to go through me."

"I see."

She grins. "However, as you fucking well know, of *course* the Livewires will run for you. All of us. Who'd want to miss out?"

I match her grin. "Of course."

"So what's the score?"

Contacts. Going out, coming in. A small note, delivered, unsigned: MEET ME. A place, a time. London, England.

I get in touch with Viper again. "Gotta go meet the big C. You wanna come?" She does.

Viper and I take a jumpplane out of Orly, using fake papers provided by one of de Seingalt's intermediaries. The flight is shorter than the wait at Heathrow for a landing spot. We get off and breeze out, no customs for United States of Europe citizens. We ride the tube to central London and get out at High Street Kensington. Four hours till the meet.

We wander around Chelsea and King's Road, digging the Street scene, the colors and costumes. London was always far more flamboyant than Paris; most of the streetdrek in London now wear elaborately painted or decorated vizards, jeweled mask ostensibly worn for fashion purposes. *More likely to fuck with the surveillance vidcams.* Viper buys one of King's Road, as a souvenir, a beautiful pointed black mask filigreed with silver, shaped along traditional Mbute lines. She puts it on outside the store and laughs, her eyes distorted behind the buglike faceted crystal lenses. I buy a small cheap half-mask, more to blend in than for aesthetical reasons. The mask chafes at the contact spots, and after a while I tear it off in disgust and toss it into the gutter.

We drink thick Irish coffee in a pub and go to meet Cornelius. The meet takes place in Ladbroke Grove, in an enclosed tropical garden on top of a department store, part of London's master plan for urban renewal.

Cornelius is sitting in a metal chair painted white, next to a fountain, sipping tea in a blue-and-white china cup. There are two empty chairs next to him. Concealed speakers blast some ancient music, late '60s rock & roll, I decide. Cornelius lowers his tea and raises an eyebrow and waves at us to sit down. Tropical plants frame his head, gleaming palm trees and vine-draped fronds, gnarled, half-rotted trees. The garden's microclimate is set to accommodate the plants, not the visitors, so we sweat like pigs. Cornelius, I notice, isn't wearing a mask.

Cornelius does something with a thin silver bracelet on his wrist, and the volume of the music decreases. "Would you like some tea?"

I smile. "Lemonade would be better."

He looks at Viper. "And you?"

She pulls off her vizard and carefully stores it in her small travel bag. "Tea's fine."

"Excellent." He taps the thin bracelet once and speaks sharply. "One tea, one lemonade." He looks up at Viper. "Sugar or cream?"

"No thanks. Straight up."

He smiles, a thin line in his drawn white face. "Good. I hate sugar or cream." He taps the bracelet again. "That will be all."

He settles back into his chair and runs his hands through his silky, long brown hair. He is wearing straight white pants, a white, wing-collared shirt with a small purple paisley bow tie, and, despite the heat, a long black carcoat with large round plastic buttons. His face looks worn, lined, more of a look of quiet desperation than of excessive drug use. A thin line of black eyeliner makes his sad eyes appear huge.

We sit in silence till the drinks arrive on a servocontroled floating tray. I pick them up and hand Viper her tea. I start to drink my lemonade, but it is filled with crushed ice, which I hate. I decided to wait till the ice melts.

"Do you like the music?" Cornelius asks.

"Yeah. What is it?"

"An old group, old friends of mine. The Deep Fix."

A long period of silence again, no one speaking. I sip my lemonade slowly. The album ends and a new one starts immediately. I recognize this one immediately, the Sex Pistols' *Ne'er Mind the Bollocks*.

"I knew your father," Cornelius says suddenly.

"Oh yeah? No shit." Cornelius is an ageless legend, active on the European scene for decades. Rumors trace him all the way back to the early 1970s. He is said to have been a spy, a musician, a priest, an assassin, a physicist. Now he sells guns.

"He and I became good friends back in 2015, soon after the India mess settled down. We worked together for quite some time."

"I never knew him. Do you know where he is now?"

"No. But my sources tell me he might not be quite as attached to his old loyalties as he used to . . ."

I meditate on that for a bit. *If he isn't with the Americans anymore, then who? Israel? Venezuela? The Chzecosovs?*

"How did you know I was his son, when I contacted you?"

"He told me about you years ago. Asked me to help you if I ever could. So over the years I've kept very light tabs on you. This is why you were able to meet me on such short notice. I am normally a bit more cautious, you understand."

"Can you help us now?"

"Very likely. I believe you are in the middle of some sort of nasty corporate mess?"

"Yes."

"And you need ordnance, weaponry."

"Yes."

He grins, and his features suddenly come alive, like a robot switched on. "No problem!"

Cornelius's car is incredible. For one thing it's an actual *car*, with wheels and everything. For another it looks like it predates the *Second* World War, smooth black stretch body, gleaming chrome headlight rack, spoked wheels. It even has a human driver, an aged, greasy man with the thin, stringy hair and the sallow face of a habitual junkie.

"Elegant, isn't it?" says Cornelius with a smile. "Bugati Royale, 1938. I had it entirely rebuilt by hand, piece by piece. It even uses real gasoline. I have to have it specially distilled. But then, I've always liked to indulge myself. You know how it is. One gets attached to one's luxuries."

The driver opens the rear door for us. It opens toward the back. Inside is an entire living room, paneled with lacquered wood and lined with Persian carpets. A sharp whiff of fresh leather hits me as I climb in, the smell of leather seats. I sit on one of the back seats, an easy chair really. Viper sits next to me and Cornelius sits across from us, facing back. The driver closes the door and circles the car to climb into the driver's seat on the right. A thick glass window separates us from him.

An antique speaker set in a corner squawks to life. "Where to, Mr. C.?"

"The castle, Mo."

I hear the motor coughing, sputtering. Mo finally climbs out and trudges to the front of the car. He bends down and does something I can't see. Cornelius grins. "I even had the defects reproduced."

He opens a small compartment next to him and starts fumbling among a stack of archaic plastic cassettes. He looks up. "The Who all right?"

I wave. "Sure." Never heard of them.

He slips the cassette into an equally archaic machine and fingers a switch. The music comes up, strange, bright rock&roll, a good sound, good energy. Cornelius closes the compartment and opens another. "Drink?"

"What do you have?" asks Viper.

"Oh, port, sherry, wine, vodka, rum, scotch, some mixers . . ."

"I'll have some rum, on the rocks," she says.

"And you, Lynx?"

I think about it. "Do you have any VAT 69?"

"Of course."

"Straight up, then."

He pours Viper's drink, hands it to her, and then pours two shots of VAT 69. I notice the driver sipping from an open bottle of Jack Daniel's as Cornelius hands me my drink.

"How safe is that?" I ask, pointing at the driver. "I get kind of nervous around lushed drivers."

Cornelius grins slyly. "Oh, don't worry about old Mo Collier. He's only dangerous when he's sober. Drunk is a very *normal* state of being for him these days. His metabolism has adjusted."

"I see." I drink.

* * *

We reach the castle in forty-five minutes. It is huge, an ancient, sprawling mansion surrounded by manicured gardens and menacing trees. Collier drives right up to the front entrance and rams the front wheels into the stairs. The car jerks and I spill my drink on the carpet.

Cornelius looks glum. "Shit," he says.

"Sorry about that," I apologize.

He waves absently. "Don't worry about it. Mo seems to be having depth-perception problems again."

We get out. Collier is staring at the front of the car, shaking his head. He'd driven it up three steps.

"Old Mo Collier fucked up again," he mumbles to himself. "Mr. C. won't be happy."

Cornelius puts his hand on Collier's shoulder. "Don't worry about it, Mo. Go to the kitchens and get yourself a drink."

Collier scuttles away and we climb the steps, leaving the car there. At the top Cornelius throws the huge oak doors open and waves expansively.

"My manor! Actually it belongs to a friend of mine, but I get to use it."

The lobby is huge. Marble steps spiral up to the second floor. Antique carpets cover the floor, a collage of different styles. Persian and Indian and European. Two medieval suits of armor stand guard on either side of the stairs. There are two sets of doors, one to either side. Oddly shaped electric guitars painted in bright Day-Glo colors are wired up on the walls, crossed above the doors.

Cornelius turns around.

"Would you like a tour of the house or would you like to attend to business first?"

I look at Viper, then back at him. "Business. We sort of have to get back to Paris."

"This way, then."

He leads us through the double doors on the left, through a drawing room and a room with a large pool table, into the kitchen. Collier is slumped at a thick wooden table, empty syringes surrounding him, a bottle of Jack Daniel's in his hand. He is sitting up, asleep with his eyes open.

Cornelius digs into a closet and pulls out a rusted metal

petrol lantern. He opens the shutter and lights it with a long match he finds next to the oven. The wick catches fast, emitting a black, oily smoke.

Cornelius grins sickly. "Not very high-tech, I know, but . . ." He puts the lantern down on top of the table and points at a large white icebox. "Could you give me a hand?"

The three of us manhandle the thing aside. Underneath it is a wooden trapdoor with a length of rope protruding from it. Cornelius grabs the rope and pulls. The trapdoor opens slowly with a creak of long disuse.

There are steps under the trapdoor, disappearing into darkness. Cornelius picks up the lantern and waves at us. "After you!"

I take the lantern from him and start down. The steps are stone, moist and slippery with moss and water secretions. They go down five meters and end in a small corridor with a floor of packed mud. The stone walls are slimy, dripping with water. There is an old, musty smell. I start walking with Viper behind me. Cornelius pulls the trapdoor shut and follows us.

The corridor opens into a large room after three meters. I shine the lantern around. Ancient wine racks stretch from wall to wall, filled with dusty bottles covered with thick cobwebs.

"Keep going," Cornelius calls out gaily. "It's just me wine cave." He seems to be slipping into a thick Cockney accent.

Another corridor continues out of the wine cellar. It goes on for ten meters, winding, and opens into a vast natural cave. Most of the stalagmites have been broken, but the ceiling stalactites are still intact. Filthy wooden crates are strewn randomly around the room.

Cornelius walks up to me and plucks the lantern out of my hand. He hangs it from a long metal hook that dangles from the ceiling. Then he walks around the room, flipping crates open at random, calling out cheerfully.

"Here you have it! A few French police MAS Bullpups, 9 mm. of course, umh, two U.S. M-23 grenade launchers, a couple IMI assault rifles with explosive rounds, a Heckler & Koch standard NATO assault rifles in 7.62-caliber, two U.S. M-60 combat machine guns, some old civilian .223 Colt AR15s, a full case of absolutely beautiful SMLE #1wood-body bolt-action rifles with hammered copper rings wrapped around the barrel and stock—they doubled up as grenade launchers—the rings stopped the barrel from splitting— very primitive I'll admit—a Remington 870 combat shotgun . . ." He turns toward us with a shrug. "I'll admit that my stock seems to be running low. That trouble up in Ireland, you know . . ." He perks up. "They're all a bit old, of course, but they're also cheap and they work fine. I've had them all overhauled."

"Do you have any laser carbines? Nikon or Zeiss?"

"Sorry. But I can maybe get you a Stoeger LAW rocket or two."

"Why don't you try."

We walk around the cave, staring at the weaponry, a bit depressed. *All this stuff has been obsolete for twenty years, if not fifty.* I pick up the NATO H&K and heft it, feeling the weight of it, the balance. *This one's nice.*

Viper is also poking around. I turn toward Cornelius. He is holding a pen poised over a small pad.

"We'll take everything."

He lowers the pad. "Everything?"

I look at Viper. She nods. "Yeah. It'll do."

I turn back to Cornelius. "Deal, Mr. C.?"

Cornelius seems wired on the way back, bubbling and bouncing. "I'll have them delivered to you within a week," he explains.

"How do you get them into France?" I ask, curious.

He raises an eyebrow, mischievous. "I have friends . . ."

I drop the subject. Instead I concentrate on details. "I'll communicate the address you can deliver to in three days, along with half the payment. You'll get the other half on delivery."

"Fine, fine." He waves dismissively. "The LAWs might run you a bit. You have the Swiss bank coordinates?"

"Yes. The money will be transferred as per your instructions."

"Great!" He runs his fingers through his hair. "And now how about a drink?"

Cornelius is a wig, and most of his ordnance was old before I was born. But he was the only dealer I could connect with on short notice, and he has a rep for doing biz with the drek. Most dealers go paranoid when it comes to kids. Besides, Cornelius *does* have a razorsmooth delivery setup. I figure by the time we're ready to run, the guns will be waiting for us at our doorstep, so to speak. Back in Paris I set up for the drop, renting an old abandoned warehouse in Saint-Denis, to the north. I call de Seingalt and inform him of the arrangements, explaining to him how he's to pay Cornelius.

"You appropriated a couple of million from me, didn't you? Isn't that enough to cover expenses?"

"Negative. That's my fee. You cover expenses."

"That's a stiff bargain, Lynx. Are you worth it?"

"Maybe not. But you think I am, and you can afford it. The price stands. Pay Cornelius."

He blinks and vanishes, contact cut with no answer. But I know.

Muscle, I have the Livewires for sure, and that's good. But tricks now, kinda tricks corporate security might not expect . . . ATs. Tricks the AT currency, but good.

Contacting them is easy. Money, big money, the kinda money I'm using now, opens a lot of doors, and greases the hinges besides. I meet the Wire three hours after putting the word out, in an empty loft off the Avenue Jean Jaurés, within spitting distance of the east side of the Wall.

"Where's Name?" is the first thing I ask. I was expecting to meet him, and had the intention of letting him know just how much I'd appreciated his .50-caliber round in the chest. My ribs still scream their pain if I but yawn.

"Dead," says the Wire.

"Dead?" Surprise. I'd always thought of Billy Name as quasi-immortal—a surrealist genie gaily floating above the perils of this world. I'd also intended to kill him myself, eventually.

"Yeah."

"How?"

"He went frit when he got your call, decided to pilot the Machine Infernale manually rather than by remote. I couldn't stop him. After he tried to dust you on the Champs, the Faces sent a few squadrons against him with LAWs. He wasted them, but one of them got off a hit on his lift unit first. So then they sent in Tactical combat choppers, loaded with little air-to-surface birds. He was a fucking sitting duck in the middle of the Avenue. He didn't even manage to nail a chopper first."

Well . . . Way I see it, Billy, you sure deserved it, motherfucker. Your art folded back on you, and maybe it's not such a bad thing. Vaya con dios, loco gringo . . .

After a silence I ask: "ATs still in biz?"

"I'm a solo act now, man. ATs kaput. And after the way Billy's last gig went down, I'm trying to stay low, real low. The Faces are kinda pissed, no lie, they put out some bad heat on me. They cornered three of our kids a few days ago, dusted them but good."

"Your mutants?"

He grins. "Yeah, the little freaks."

"Do you want work?"

"What kind?"

"Consultant. Paid."

"Sounds interesting. Lay it down."

"Anubis. The pyramid. Over Pontoise, up North. I'm going in. The Livewires are for diversion. But I need some kink for them to get in. The way things stand, the automatic systems will vaporize them before they even get inside the defense perimeter."

"Check. Sounds clean. I'll get back to you."

"And . . . Wire?"

"Yeah?"

"Nothing fancy. You can leave your tag off this one."

"Anon. Check, Lynx. I'll see you."

De Seingalt on the phone. "How are your plans going, Lynx?"

"Smooth. We'll be ready in five days."

"Good. You will get a delivery later today. Two soundscape programs. The first is the one for Angélique, as I explained. The second is a musical map of the pyramid, a variation on that clever map you made of the Champs. When you penetrate the pyramid, simply follow the line of flute melody, like a Pied Piper. It will lead you to Angélique."

"Hold, man. Don't you know that pyramid?"

"Of course. The blueprints are stored in my memory."

"So why don't you just give me a fuckin holo on the floorplan?"

"Now, Lynx, you wouldn't want it to be too easy, would you?"

I stare at the screen in mute astonishment. Suddenly I smile.

"Man, you are one warped fuck. You're sick enough to be an Artiste Terroriste. I suppose you want me to do the run on skimboots?"

"But of course, my dear Lynx, of course."

"And if I say *nyet*?"

"Then Angélique laughs and some day you die like a rat. If you want her, I'm afraid you'll have to do it my way." Pause. "Or not at all."

"Your way will get me wasted, asshole."

"My way is a poem, Lynx."

"Your way is def *stupid*." And, thinking of Billy Name and *his* poems: "Why do all you assholes always have to bring up poetry when you talk about death? Death is death, and it's ugly, and that's *all*."

"Am I dead, Lynx?" De Seingalt's image smiles.

I shiver as it cuts the contact.

The delivery comes as promised, an anonymous package. I sign the receipt and open it. Two chips in clear plastic cases. One has a stylized skull printed on it. I feel chills run up my spine as I pick it up and examine it. *A Benway special, probably.* I slot the other one in my armdeck and run it through the paces. A map, just like he said, clear flute line outlining the path in haunting, floating melody. Step off to the side and you just got subsonic harmonics, premonitions of doom. A good piece of work, all things considered.

De Seingalt calls again a few hours later.
"I need to give you your final instructions, Lynx."
I nod.
"The takeover is proceeding on schedule," he says. "But it appears that to clinch it I must be present in the pyramid in person; more accurately, considering my condition, this means I must take over the pyramid's computer systems. I am unable to penetrate them from the outside, from the Net; their defenses are too powerful.
"Therefore, you must bring me into the pyramid. You will carry a copy of me and inject it directly into the household systems of the pyramid. Is that clear?"
[a touch of ghost fingers, caressing my lobes]
Yessss. . . "Yes. How do I bring you in?"
"You can download me directly off your deck into your armdeck."
"Fuck that. No."
"Then I shall have to deliver you another chip, or perhaps a logical. You can slot it in any deck inside the pyramid and run it."
"All right. I can do that."
[ghost fingers like ectopasm. idea implanted like a tumor]
"And perhaps this way I can get to talk to my dear sister in person before you annihilate her personality."
"Cold. Real cold."
[not implanted, already there, ghost fingers tend it through. it grows]
I cut the contact first.
yessss . . .
[ghost fingers whisper, a whisper of death]

Messages are exchanged, and I meet the Wire in the Luxembourg gardens.
Hard to concentrate. The Idea gnawing at my brain at

subsonic levels. Can't vocalize it though, not yet. The
Idea just floats in the spaces of REM sleep and gnaws. In
the background a pale face. Blue hair?

The Wire. Concentrate.

"I think it can be done."

"How?"

"Simple. Know a club called Computer? In Pontoise?"

The word goes out the next day, and the Livewires
start to show at the Saint-Denis warehouse. They trickle in
in small groups of two or three, on skimboots or jetboards,
a few even on skimbikes. Viper arrives first, with Scalpel.
Then Ice and Halflife and Bozo jet into the vast hangar
on their bikes. Then Takuan with the Rat, ad then at last
Molly and Rake and Jester. I arrived a few hours earlier
with Domino and the Wire to supervise Cornelius's delivery. There was just one truck, driven by Shaky Mo
Collier himself. He was twitching as he climbed out of
the cab, speed twitches.

"Mr. C. sends his apologies," he said, a small muscle
jumping in his cheek, alive under the stubble carpet. "He
had some business that couldn't wait."

"No prob, spud. Drink?"

"Now, would old Mo refuse a drink?"

We sat around and drank as the GM servobot Cornelius had thoughtfully included with the shipment unloaded
the crates and whisked them to a large room I'd prepared
on the top floor.

"Did Mr. C. score any LAWs?"

"Oh yes. Just one, though, I'm afraid. It's reusable,
however, got four rounds."

"It'll do."

The bot finally whined to a stop in front of Collier and
flashed a green light. Collier staggered up to a shaky
stance.

"Well, Mr. L., looks like we gotta be moving. I'm
afraid I'll have to take the bot back, hope you don't
mind. You got like the other half?"

I handed him the mirrored card, gleaming piece of
polysiloxane coated with cycolac plastic, worth over thirty
thousand ESUs. Collier slotted it in a reader and checked
the amount. "The Morgennsbank, huh? Good bank, that,

very professional. Good." He thumbed off the reader, slipped the card into a pocket, and stuck out a hand.

"Pleasure doing business with you, Mr. L. You ever need anything, you just let us know."

"A pleasure too, Mr. Collier," I said formally. "My regards to Mr. Cornelius."

"Will do." He touched a finger to the brim of his cap and walked off unsteadily. He climbed into the cab of the truck and backed it out of the warehouse, narrowly missing the edge of the door. We watched him drive off and disappear around a corner without saying a word.

Now the Livewires are here, hopped and jumpy. They know it's big, but how big they aren't quite sure.

We all ride the flatbed lift up to the room on the top floor where the guns are waiting. The bot had left the crates lined up on the floor next to each other. The Livewires watch while I pick up a crowbar and pry the first crate open. They stare, amazed looks on their faces, a few yelling out in surprise.

"Fuck me!"

"Check it out my brothers!"

"Fuckin-A party!"

I open each crate, one after the other, and the Livewires cluster around them, examining and fondling the contents. One crate contains the Stoeger LAW, the four rounds each in a portable ABS case; another, smaller crate contains the Remington 870, a large black Colt .45 automatic in a black nylon shoulder rig, five loaded clips for the automatic and a box of shells for the Remington, and a note printed on gray bristol: GOOD LUCK. J. C.

I slip the note into my breast pocket and hoist the Remington, hefting it, getting the feel of it. It's a beauty, sharp gray metal and light brown wood pistol grip and pump grip. I start loading it as the others caper behind me.

"I want the LAW!"

"Negative," says Viper. "That's Halflife's baby."

"The M-60 is mine!" roars Bozo.

"It'll fit, a man, a rat with a pig."

I look back after slamming the breech shut and working the first shell into the chamber. Bozo is clowning, waving one of the M-60s around, belts of ammo slung over his shoulder. The Rat has the other one, and is silently and lovingly cleaning the packing grease off it in a corner of the room.

Everyone has a gun, even the Wire, who won't be needing it. Jester, Ice, and Molly have picked the AR-15s. Takuan is examining the IMIs. Viper, a wide grin smeared across her face, has the H&K. Rake is handing out grenades. He keeps one of the launchers and gives Scalpel the other one; the others hang them on belts or stuff them in pockets for manual use. The case of pre-bomb SMLEs sits peacefully among the empty crates, untouched.

I wait an appropriate amount of time, then point the Remington at the floor. I fire, the sound resonating in the room like a clap of thunder. Everyone looks up, shocked. The blasts has gouged a ugly jagged hole in the wood flooring. I step over the hole, flip the Remington back onto my shoulder, holding it by the pistol grip, and my grin comes straight from Hollywood.

"Awright, everyone listen up! You can play with your new toys later. I've had the basement soundproofed so you can go practice downstairs later."

I move over to the large, sheet-covered object I'd placed next to the wall earlier in the day. "Why don't you all sit down. Wire, you can come up here."

I prop the Remington against the wall and pull off the sheet, revealing a large JVC holoproj. I hit the power and call up the first shot. A blue image of the Anubis pyramid shimmers and coalesces over the projector, the detached tip floating demurely over the main body.

"This is the target, boys and girls."

Exclamations, curses. I wave and they shut up.

"Here's the score. You spuds are going to provide a diversion so I can penetrate the tip unnoticed. The diversion will consist of a direct attack against the GF units, which pretty much fill the bottom section of the pyramid. You will arrive by air, of course."

"That's fuckin suicide, man!" the Rat calls out angrily. "We'll never even get near the pyramid! Their defense systems will blast us out of the air!"

I smile. "Negative. The Wire has a plan."

The Wire steps up and examines the holo before turning toward the seated Livewires.

"We are going to provide a diversion for the diversion," he says. A few scattered laughs. "As you know, the pyramid is stationed over a forest next to Pontoise, up North. I've found out that most of their tech personnel lives onboard. But they get rec leave. And they got a spot. It's called Computer, a badbeat club in Pontoisetown.

"I've been there, and the place is a meat market. Now, the techs will wear these uniforms. They even have a simple job-classification-set-of-insignias-type thing.

"So my idea is that two of you females score for some glamourgirl sheets and hang at the Computer. Put the bite on two techies and take them to a hotel you know. Then we waste them. I can probably modify their IDs in under two hours. So then when they return onboard, two of you go with them. If anyone asks who you are, you can say you're new transfers from the London branch or something.

"Lynx says that Jester and Takuan are the best on deck. So I suggest you two play the techies. And once onboard, there's all sorts of fun things you can pull."

Jester grins. "Like what?"

"You'll have to improvise when you see the setup. But I can already suggest a few things. Like a clownface virus in the radar programs. Or locate the central controls for the stateroom locks—every major corporate office has something like that—don't know why, maybe they're afraid the personnel will riot. Anyway, you can find that and bug it right before the run is due, so anyone in a room will be locked in for the duration."

"I like it," says Jester.

"Ramming, my brother," adds Takuan. "Razor chaos."

"OK. There'll be details to cover, like what you can take onboard and how. We'll work on that."

"Razor," I cut in. I stare at the Livewires humorlessly. "So how do you spuds stand on this? You still might get wasted."

Viper stands up. "Hey brother, that's the standard risk. Now, you've changed a bit since—uh, well, you know, we still get off on this shit. Sounds to me like an optimum party. I don't know why you're doing any of this, my man, and you got a weird attitude on you, but for us it's the war game, you know? Except better cause we got lethalware now."

"Fuck, yeah!" roars Bozo. "We in this for fun, Lynx! And if I get dusted, that's how I *wanna* get dusted!"

Laughter. Jabbering.

"Dig it, my brother!"

"Fuckin razor party!"

"Livewires slicin cool!"

I wave them into silence and try a smile. It's weak. "I must be getting old. But you're right. It should be fun."

Later as the meeting breaks up Domino comes up to me. Her face is tight, closed.

"Lynx? I think we should talk."

"Why? Something wrong?"

"What do you think?"

I stare at her blankly and shrug.

"I don't know. Look, I'm busy now. Maybe later?"

She returns the blank stare and then finally the shrug. Then she turns around and walks away.

A last conversation with de Seingalt. The Livewires are packing, getting ready for the ride to Pontoise. I've bought two large Citroën vans, enough to transport everyone and their guns comfortably. The police scene in the provinces is a lot more relaxed, so once we're out of Paris we shouldn't have any problems. Just to make sure, I've had Jester and Halflife install hidden and detector-proof compartments in the floor of the vans. The Wire will take care of his own transportation and the installation of his fake ID equipment.

"So I rented a house," I inform de Seingalt. "A large vacation house out of town. I also bought some miscellaneous equipment."

"I'll cover it."

"I also want another million for the Livewires. Fee."

"Another million?"

"My price went up." I want some more credit for the 'Wires. I figure they deserve it.

"No, Lynx. We agreed on a price."

"You don't have a choice, motherfucker. I have you over a barrel. Besides, what do you care? None of it is your money. You're just skimming it out of the Net, out of the banks. One million more or less, big fuckin deal. You're already in for at least six or seven."

He shrugs, interesting thing for a computer construct to do. "All right. I'll do it."

He cuts contact and I wait. After a while he comes back online.

"It's done."

"Proof?"

"Here." His face vanishes and numbers flash on the screen, codes and data. A small printer spews out a hardcopy transcript. I study it as he reappears.

"It's in that account I set up for you. You'll have to take care of transmitting it to your friends."

"Okay," I say. "It looks good."

"When are you running?"

"Four days. I figure two to penetrate, and then two for my people inside to set up. We leave tonight."

"I'll have a copy of me on chip delivered in an hour. You will download it into the pyramid's system first thing, before you find Angélique. That way I can control alarm systems, neutralize them, help your friends."

"Okay. See you there." I cut contact.

Pontoise, prep school town. Old gray stone buildings, small cobblestone streets, a peaceful *gendarmerie* force, the vast, atavistic boarding school that makes the town's fame. Blue-blazered students walk in small groups past bored smalltown locals.

The pyramid hovers over a large private forest to the west of town, near one of the lazy loops of the Seine. According to the Wire the whole perimeter of the forest is heavily kinked and even patrolled.

We catch a glimpse of the pyramid on our way into town. It hovers high above the forest, maybe fifty meters up, imposing, monolithic. The tip floats serenely over the main body, a small detached dot. The road curves by the edge of the forest, and we pass by the ground station, a cluster of white buildings, hangars, and concrete pads surrounded by a fence of steel posts and monofilament wire. I point it out to Jester, who's sitting in back of the van.

"This is where the pyramid's personnel land on their way out. You'll be boarding here."

Slowing down might attract attention, and soon we drive through the town. The house we rented is situated on the outskirts of the town, out east. The Wire rented it for us, passing himself off as a computer-systems analyst in need of privacy. The credit I'd given him alleviated the need for further questions.

The Wire is already there when we arrive. The house has a long dirt driveway and is partially hidden by a cluster of trees, which suits us fine. The small wood borders one of the outlying fields of the school. The area is quiet and especially private.

The guns and the body armor supplied by the Wire are unloaded fast, and a party is going within a half hour. Loud heartbeat blasts out the open windows of the two-story house, and naked Livewires are lounging by the swimming pool. Molly and Ice are vainly trying to score a suntan while Viper, Jester, and Takuan thrash around in the water. Bozo is perched halfway up a tree, howling and waving a bottle of J&B. Scalpel is already going at the house walls with her paintbombs. Domino, who insisted on coming, is sitting up on a stone wall, reading in the shade.

I don't feel like partying for now, so I inspect the house. It's been remodeled in a sort of bastard-rustic style, with uneven wood furniture and fake plaster stone walls, very cheap. The rooms are fairly large and airy, enough of them for everybody if the usual couples pair up. The clincher is the bar, thoughtfully stocked by the Wire, enough booze, cocaine, and hallucinogens to keep everyone high, low, and trashed for a week on end. Viper managed to lock it shortly after Bozo discovered it, hoping to keep everyone reasonably straight till after the run.

I spend the next few hours hanging around the Wire, watching him set up. The house has a dish tuned to the Paris cable networks. The Wire retunes it.

"I'm gonna give Jester and Takuan a miniature two-shot pulse gizmo I put together. It'll send a sequence of narrow-frequency squirts that this will pick up. The order of the sequence will tell us to go or abort, you know, never know what can happen, right? So the first set of squirt tell us to get ready and the second set to run. Simple, no?"

I nod.

Later in the day I'm lounging in the driveway, playing with my balisong and sipping a beer, when Domino comes up to me. She plants herself squarely in front of me with her hands in her pockets and stares at me with her head tilted and her eyes narrowed.

I stare back, still flipping the balisong. Finally she speaks.

"What's the matter, Lynx?"

I shrug. "What do you mean, what's the matter? You tell me."

"You've barely spoken to me since Benway's. Why?"

I shrug again and stare up at the sky. It's bright blue and clear. A few sharpedged clouds float lazily in front of the sun, sending a shadow flitting over the trees and the driveway. Domino seems very distant, small, as if she was standing in front of the small end of a telescope.

"You're not very real right now," I finally say in a vague attempt at honesty.

"What's real for you now, Lynx?"

I shrug. "The clouds, maybe . . ."

"Why?"

"I don't know."

"Do you care?"

I look straight at her, levelly, totally detached. "No. Why should I?"

This time she shrugs. "No reason, my man, no reason." She turns around abruptly and leaves. By nightfall she's gone.

Viper is the first to notice, the next day.

"Yo, Lynx, where's Domino?"

"She left, I think."

"How come?"

"Dunno. She didn't feel like staying, I suppose."

"You two have a fight?" She's playing with her hair, a sure sign she's disturbed.

"Not really."

"Hey, listen man, you've been really out of it recently. What's going on? The spuds've been wondering . . ."

I sneer. "Well, fuck them! I've been thinking, that's all . . . Lot of shit going on, you know?"

"You're not going deadbrain on us, are you?"

I try a smile. "No, don't worry about me. I just got stuff in my head, you know? When this gig's over I'll feel a lot better.

"None of us really understand, what this whole gig's about, you know? I mean, how you've gotten mixed up in this shit . . ."

"I look away into an unseen distance. "You shouldn't ask."

"I'm not asking. If you want to keep it private, fine. I just don't want you to do anything stupid."

I explode. "Look! If you're all so fuckin nervous, what the fuck are you doing here? Why don't you all just take off and go back and play in the fuckin city?"

Her lips tighten. "Hey, chill out, my brother. We're not nervous, just worried about you. You know why we're doing this gig."

I calm down a bit, suddenly disgusted with myself. "Yeah, well . . ."

She smiles, a sad smile. "Hey, Lynx. I know you're still sad about Mara. It's normal, you know? I mean we're dealing too."

"So what if someone else gets killed on this run? We're using guns! Against armed security! What if Scalpel gets wasted?"

She shrugs. "That's the risks, my brother. We're all born dead, and we know it. We're just trying to enjoy the interlude, you know? You used to do the same."

"Yeah . . ." A silence. "Look . . . I said I'd be okay. You guys shouldn't worry."

She stares at me and then nods. "All right. I'll believe you." She smiles. "Hey, it'll be okay!"

Around six o'clock we meet in the living room. Livewires are sprawled all over the place, on the floor and the furniture. I stand by the wall, next to the Wire. The Wire gives the briefing.

"Okay, we're starting tonight. Ice and Molly should take care of the Computer scene. I think you're the best two for the kind of guys these techs are."

Ice sneers. "I'm not sure that's a compliment, spud. But we'll do it." Molly nods.

"Good. I got you some glamourthreads, makeup, and hair stuff too. Also for Jester and Takuan—I'm gonna have to give you some Straighttown hairdos, my brothers, otherwise they'll never let you in.

"Aw, shit," Jester moans. "My shag, man, I like it. Can you fix it back like this after?"

Laughs. "No prob, my man. Now for tonight. You

girls spot two techs, preferably together, preferably not part of a large group. Put the move on them, have them buy you drinks, then take them out back. Bozo and Rat and Halflife and Viper, you wait outside. We'll try to hide you. You jump the techies, do it silent, and drag them to the van. I'll be waiting at the edge of the parking lot. You'll have to do it clean, we can't have blood on the uniforms. That smooth?"

Viper nods. "No sweat. The poor fucks won't even know what hit them."

"Smooth. You don't even need to kill them. We'll dope them and keep them on ice till we split. We can stash them in the cave or something and feed them intra-V. So we'll bring them back here in the van and I'll get started on Jester and Takuan. Uniforms, holos, ID, everything. I can do it in two hours. Then you'll take one of the vans—it's clean—and drive to the groundstation. I've worked out your ID codes so they show you as new transfers. You'll say you just got in from London and hopefully they'll bring you right up. They should give you rooms, and tomorrow they'll probably show you around. Wait a day or two, learn the system, then start planting your bugs. When you're ready, or if something goes wrong, give us a squirt. Then you activate your bugs and give us another squirt. By the time we get there they should be running around like ants in a crushed anthill."

"What about the two techs? Won't they be missed?"

"Their friends will have seen them go off with the girls so they won't worry at first. By the time they do worry . . . they might think they're taking an unauthorized vacation, whatever. By the time it gets through the channels—bureaucracy, you know how it is . . ." He smiles broadly. "I've also prepared you two company bags full of personal effects. It would look strange if you showed up without luggage. All right?"

Scalpel stands up. "We had an idea for the attack."

"What?"

"We're gonna invade the groundstation quiet-like while they panic upstairs, right, and use their lift to go up. But I figured the groundguards might get off a signal, so they may be waiting for us in the pyramid. So anyway we thought that a cool idea would be to stock up on fireworks—it'll be dark in the pyramid, right?—and play like a bunker war, you know, M-80s and bottlerockets and shit. The security people wouldn't know what's hitting them! They'd freak. And we're used to fucking around in the smoke, but they won't be able to see shit. So we can stay real close together-like and freak them with the rockets and shit and blow them away. It'd be a fuckin blast, too, you know?"

The Wire smiles wide. "Yeah. I like it. Suckers won't know what hit them."

The sun sets over the small wood—refracted rays slicing through the trees—and I sit in my room high on opium. I smoked three bowls while the others set out to the Computer and now I melt . . .

Everything is soft, round . . . I sink into my bed and merge with it . . . Dust motes dance in the dying light above my face . . . Time bends . . .

Noises.

Slowly I emerge from the round dreams. I feel limp, saggy, empty. The room is dark. I sit up on the bed and rub my face with my hands.

A knock on my door. I don't answer. Another knock.

"Yeah."

"Lynx? It's me, Vipe."

"Yeah."

The door opens and she walks in.

"Don't turn on the light." I say.

She doesn't. She stands in the open doorway, backlit by the corridor's neon glow.

"Lynx? You okay?" She sniffs the air. "Oh. Yeah. Suppose you are." A pause. "Listen, the gig at the Computer went down smooth. The two techs are in the basement. The Wire is preparing the IDs. You want to come check things?"

"Do I have to . . . ?"

She shrugs, annoyed. "Hey, you're the boss leader here. You do what you want."

"Aw, listen, Vipe, I didn't mean it like that . . . I'm just tired, is all . . . This is the Wire's end of things, I don't figure he needs me."

"Just thought you might be interested. By the way—" she holds up a white envelope. "I found this in Domino's room. It's for you." She holds it out.

I take it from her and stare at it. A plain envelope, only one sheet of paper inside it by the weight, LYNX printed in blue ink on the front.

"Huh. Thanks."

"You gonna read it?"

"Later. I want to sleep now."

She nods and turns to leave. "I'll see you later then, my man."

"Yeah . . . See you, sistren."

I drop the envelope on the night table as she silently shuts the door, and slump down on the bed. I stare up at the darkness. *Blank, blank* . . . Finally I open myself to the tendrils reaching up from my backbrain and slide down into sleep.

The envelope is still sitting there the next morning. Bright light streams through my open window. I stagger up and stumble out the door. Into the bathroom and after a few minutes splashing cold water on my face and neck I start to feel human. I deliberately avoid looking at the mirror as I take a piss and go out.

Downstairs spuds are lounging around all over the place, bored. A few are still trying to tan. Scalpel smiles as she sees me come down the stairs.

"Hey, stranger. Long time no see."

I kiss her softly on the cheek. "Hey, babe. How did things go last night?"

"Razor. The Wire hung out a half klik away from the groundstation while Jester and Takuan went in, with a pair of IR binocs. Far as he could tell, they got shuttled up, no problems, real smooth."

"Good. So now we just wait, right?"

Two days. Two days, waiting, till Jester's signal comes in. The Livewires swim, tan, dance, screw, and generally keep themselves as busy and happy as they can in a large surburban house twenty kliks from Paris.

On the morning of the first day, Viper and the Wire

drive into Paris in the second van to score for the fireworks. They come back grinning.

"Check it out, spuds! Two cases!"

"Fuckin-A . . ."

Two days, and then the call. It comes an hour after
sunset, three squirt pulses, coded, their content unim-
portant but their order crucial. The call says "go."

The Wire passes the word around quietly and quickly,
whispered from Livewire to Livewire. They come just as
quietly, gather in dripping silence in the living room.

"This is it," the Wire says tonelessly. "You know the
drill. We got around two hours to the second pulse. We
should be ready when it comes.

"Relax. Check all your weaponry and your ammo.
Start gearing up in an hour. Don't forget the body armor.

"Stay indoors. We don't know what kind of recon
setup the pyramid has. If they twig to us now, we're
fucked. Copy?"

Nods, grins. Scalpel asks, "Can we still party?"

"If you want. Check your shit now so you're ready to
suit up fast. Don't drink, and no mainlining or dusting up
either. This isn't the streets. You can do rockets or speed
derms right before the run, but that's all. After . . . Get
ripped, and don't come up for a week. Fry those soggy
brains, see if I care."

"Check it," moans Ice. "I can't wait a whole night to
do my drugs."

Laughs. Molly jeers. "Poor little Ice. Needs her
mommy's drugs. Come to Mommy, Ice, Mommy'll take
care of you . . ."

Ice sneers. "Will Mommy breast-feed me?"

I need a drink.

Party. Party for the Livewires, guns like toys, a run
like any run but so much more *rammin*, y'know? I go
over my gear with a sour feeling in my guts. Remington,
loaded; extra ammo in belt pouches. Armor, ready; I'm
just going to wear a flak jacket, fuck the helmet. Flightsuit.
Armdeck, with de Seingalt's soundscape loaded in.
Soundscape for Angélique and de Seingalt's home chip in
breast pocket. And finally the skimboots to run the scape.
I've considered doing it on a jetboard, anything to avoid

skating, but I decided a jetboard is too cumbersome and unmaneuverable for combat. *Tough shit.*

And the letter . . . It sits there, a minor critical mass of words, poised, lethal. Finally I pick it up and shove it into the breast pocket of the flightsuit, with the scape and the chip. I'll read it later.

I lay everything out on the bed and then suddenly decide to pop in on Scalpel. She is doing the same, checking her stuff, getting the feel. She puts down her grenade launcher when I walk in.

"Hey, love, what's up?"

"Not much, just hanging. You?"

"Smooth."

"Sure you wanna come for this?"

"Fuck, yeah! You don't think I'm gonna let everyone else have all the fun, do you? I missed out on the Champs, that was enough."

"Listen. This could get pretty gruesome. You watch your skinny butt, you hear me? Keep your head down and don't get dumb, cause dumb gets dead real fast. Copy?"

"Sir, yes sir!"

"Cut that shit, man." A pause. "I'm beat, y'know? Can't take much more of this shit."

"You okay?"

"Yeah . . . I just want to get this shit over with and get the fuck out, y'know?"

"Yes." She puts her head lightly on my cheek and smiles. "It'll be tough, but once it's over . . . You watch your butt, too, huh?"

"Will . . ." She kisses me lightly, on tiptoes to reach my lips. Then she grins. "Now get the fuck out of here. I gotta get packed, copy?"

"Check. I'll see you later."

I slip out and go outside. I stare at the smooth blue swimming pool, the placid water. Suddenly I want to go swimming. I pull out a cigarette, light it, and absently inhale. *Why not?*

Cool, cool water, soothes the lobes. I twist under the water and look up through the bubbles. The sun glints off the mirrored underbelly of the surface, harsh and sharp,

an icepick of light. I close my eyes and drift . . . I rise
slowly to the surface and spread out . . . A jellyfish . . .
Nose out, eyes closed, sun on the exposed skin . . .
Nice. . . .

Later . . . Noise. I roll over and swim to the edge
without looking up. I see a hand reaching down and I
reach up with mine and grip it, acrobat's grip, hand
around wrist. A jerk, and I am pulled up bodily onto the
concrete.

I lie there a few seconds, eyes closed, breathing slowly.
Then I look up.

The Rat is grinning down at me, half suited.

"Time, my man. Time to run."

"From now on don't touch anything in the house without gloves, copy? The house is clean now."

The Livewires are gearing up together in the living room, helping each other with buckles and snaps, laughing, wisecracking. Viper is going off on a Vietnam/Venezuela military power trip.

"Halflife. You take point. Rat, you ride her back with the pig. I want cover! Bozo, you got the other M-60, you got the rear."

She chuckles. "Man, what a trip! Just like Venezuela! Search & Destroy in the concrete jungle . . ."

I start gearing up rapidly. I pull on the black flightsuit—one of my old Downside specials—and lace up my skimboots. Then I buckle on the belt with the grenades and the ammo, my razorsharp Gerber in an upside-down drop position on my left shoulder, and the brand-new Colt .45 automatic in a shoulder rig under my left armpit. I check my pocket for the chips—my fingers brush against paper, Domino's letter—and snap on my armdeck. Then I pick up the Remington.

The Livewires are tense, amped, ready to run. A few fire up rockets or press derms against their wrists. The rocketheads twitch a bit, then just stand there, eyes gleaming, a pupil abyss, muscles like finetuned piano wires.

Scalpel walks up to me and stares at me, face-to-face.

"Lynx. I'm coming with you. Into the tip. Don't argue."

"But—"

"The Livewires can manage without me. You're not going alone."

"What if I want to?"

"Fuck that. I'm coming."

I shrug. "All the way?"

Her eyes narrow. "What do you mean?"

I smile. "I'm not sure."

And then the Wire walks in carrying a MAS and waves for silence.

"Signal just came in, spuds. We're on."

A metallic rustle as weapons are lifted and shouldered. Sharp clacks as Viper and Ice work their chambers.

"Van's out front, spuds. You know the drill."

Viper drives and I sit next to her. The Livewires are quiet in the back as the Wire rehearses them.

"Vipe has a company ID that should get her past the checkpoint. We'll get as close to the main building as possible and then out. Stay close together and waste anything in red. That's the guards. Vipe, Lynx, and me are going straight inside to cut their commo before the alarm goes up. But we figure that's a lost cause, so I got a backup plan.

"First we secure the station. It's not too heavily guarded, so it shouldn't be too hard. If techies surrender—they're in blue—let them. Just tape them up and leave them in a corner.

"There are three lift platforms. I figure security upstairs will get warned. However, by now our friends up there should have things pretty fucked up. But just in case . . .

"You all remember Scalpel's idea. You got fireworks, M-80s and rockets, for the tunnels. I also got a couple of larger displays, timed releases. We're gonna set them up on the first platform and send it up in front of the second one. We'll be on that. The guards will be waiting for the first platform, but they won't know the second one's coming because their system is down. Should be . . . If not we're fucked. Incidentally, the guards might not even know yet what's going on upstairs, so that might help. But anyway . . .

"The guard will be waiting for the platform. They're gonna get a faceful of rockets, roman candles, clusters, smoke bombs, stink bombs. By the time we make it to the second bay, they should be softened up.

"Once inside, again, stick together. Shoot everything,

make as much of a mess as possible, freak them out. The idea is to draw guards down from the tip so Lynx can slip in clean.

"You all have a little receptor with you. When Lynx is in, he will trigger a pulse from his armdeck. That's the recall signal. Fall back on the bay—Jester and Takuan should be waiting there, don't waste them—and go down. I'll be waiting here with the van. I got another van hidden ten kliks downroad, undercover. We'll ditch this van—it's clean—and make it into Paris in the other one. It has a stash for the guns so we'll be fairly clean. Once in-city we split up. I'll figure a way to get the guns Downside for future use. Why waste them, eh?

"After that . . . stay down, stay clean. Try to avoid anything that might get you busted. The cops will be all over the house and the van, but they won't get nothing. I sprayed the whole house down with Noxinol; it'll wipe it clean of any cells, fingerprints, anything. Only thing they'll get is those two techies' description of Ice and Molly, but that won't help them much. Anyway, they're gonna figure terrorist on this, for sure. Lynx's . . . contact will be the new Anubis boss, so he'll cover but good. They'll never go looking for streetdrek."

We're passing through the village. It's nearly dead, just a few people in the café, one or two in the streets, an old man with his dog. Quiet.

"Okay . . . We're there in three. Good hunting, spuds. Skate or die."

"Skate or die, man," whispers Halflife, "skate or die." The others are quiet.

We glide up to the gate of the groundstation in silence. The actual, visible gate is a thin swing gate of aluminum, weak enough for even a compact to punch through. The real defenses are under the concrete: proximity disruptors to ground a vehicle, maybe some GF-activated mines. Viper at the wheel is in a plain blue tech coverall, her gear stowed in back, a blue cap pulled down over her streethair. I've tied my hair back and jammed a similar cap over it. In the dark it should do.

The gate. Vipe slows down. My hand is on the .45, held

down at my side out of sight. A guard steps out of the booth, hand up, MAS at port. Alert status. Dig it.

Viper stops. The guard steps up to the window.

"ID?"

Viper hands him the laminated plate the Wire whipped up along with Jester's and Takuan's. The guard peers at it and looks up.

"What's in the van?"

"Consignment of chipboard, some other supplies . . . Why the gun?"

The guard shrugs. "I dunno. Something weird going on upstairs. Bossman got edgy and handed out the guns. I think he's jumping at ghosts, but . . . You got a manifest for that cargo?"

Viper smiles and hands him the clipboard the Wire also thoughtfully provided. Anything for a discreet entrance. I stare at the lit guardhut while the guard squints at the clipboard. Two more guards inside. They're staring at us. At me. Tense, both of them, guns in hand. My hand tightens around the grip of the .45, slippery grip in my cold, sweaty hand. I can hear the 'Wires breathing softly in back, the creak of gearstraps and buckles. With a shock of relief I realize the two guards behind the window can't see *me*. Too dark in the van . . . They must just be staring.

"Kind of late for a delivery." I snap out of the semitrance as the guard looks up suspiciously. "You guys usually come in during the day."

Viper shrugs. "We only got the stuff in at six. Boss was gonna leave it till tomorrow, but it was flagged urgent so he sent us out. Then what with traffic and our dinner break, you know . . ."

"Yeah. Well, I don't know if you're gonna get that cargo up there tonight. They've canceled all the lifts for now."

"Maybe they need this stuff for whatever's going on up there."

"I don't know. Talk to Madrier, over at the Central. He'll decide what to do."

Viper nods. "Check." The guard tears off a carboncopy and hands Viper the clipboard through the open window. "Madrier will initial it for you."

"Thanks."

"No problem." He waves at the guards in the hut. One of them nods back. "You can go through."

"Thanks. Take it easy."

"Yeah. Good night."

Viper kicks the van into gear. " 'Night. Hope everything goes fine." Slowly she eases the van forward.

She waits ten feet before she slumps. "Motherfucker . . ." She sighs deeply. "Hey, Wire, good job on those papers."

"Thanks." His voice floats ectoplasmically out of the silent rear. "Central's right ahead. Pull around when you get there so our butt is facing the door."

"Check. Lynx and I will take out the guards at the gate."

I reach for my shoulder rig, slip it on over the flightsuit, and holster the .45. Then I reach back and bring up the Remington. "Yeah." With a manic leer I work the pump. "Let's do it, boys and girls. Partytime. Just like in the movies."

The grounds station's layout is a simple Y, with the gate at the base and the stem, the Central in the center, and the two liftpad/hangar complexes at the tips. We figured on securing the Central and the gate before taking the pads. According to the Wire, most of the security forces are posted in the Central.

This whole operation is shoddier than shit. We haven't even reconned the base! Fuck knows how many people security has in that building . . . Or under it . . . Shit!

. . . and then no more thinking. Viper hits the gas and the brakes and the wheel simultaneously, and the van flips around in a smooth bootlegger's. "Out! Out!" and then we finally stop backdoor's open gunfire noise everything so slow so far "Lynx! Out!" I open my door and jump out shotgun up covering the front nothing gunfire behind me yes there guards running from the gate I am kneeling behind the open door the running guards are firing a ricochet close noise roaring in my ears my eyes I shake my head fifteen meters and closing I feel the door jar a hit the window shatters Plexiglas fragments shower

272

down on me ignore them they're using their clips up a scream ignore it wait ten meters yes fire—

Viper and I open fire simultaneously. I fire only three shots, slowly, levelly. The first guard jumps back 12-gauge blast smack in the chest pump the second one miss pump again the second one is hit in the head no more head and the third one dies also a brief burst from Viper's H&K they're down dark red on the red coveralls on the concrete "Lynx! The Central!" up and around the van scanning no one and in.

Bodies. Two bodies. Guards. More gunfire up ahead, sporadic. Viper and I walk forward slowly into the gray corridor side by side scanning. Slow.

"Looks clear. Let's do doors."

I nod. The Livewires had gone straight through to the control room, so some personnel might still be hiding in offices. We flatten against the wall on each side of the first door we see, and I reach out for the knob, gun up. ready . . .

I try the knob. Locked.

"We break it?"

"Why bother? The 'Wires will mop up later. Let's just run a fastcheck."

She nods. We step over the two bodies and start up the corridor, checking every door. They're all locked.

"It's quiet," Viper says.

"Yeah. They must've secured the control room."

We reach a branch.

"Left or right?"

I shrug. "Dunno." Then: "Wait."

I raise my gun and she looks and her gun goes up, too. A figure at the end of the corridor. Coming from the control room. *A Livewire?*

Yes. Halflife.

"Lynx! Viper! It's clear!"

Our guns dip down. Viper calls back.

"We're gonna search offices! Send us a few more spuds so we can cover the joint fast!"

"Don't bother, sistren! They got this whole joint wired for video. We already cleared out most of the offices."

We start forward. Halflife lights a cigarette as we approach.

"Anyone down?" I ask.

"Molly got a bit chewed up, caught some frag. She'll be cool. Bozo got one in the arm."

"Shit. They going up?"

"Bozo, yes. The Wire is fixing him. Molly stays here, though."

"Shit. She okay?"

"Yeah, yeah. Two hours with the tweezers and a week down. No problem. She can still walk, the Wire gave her some derms for the pain, he's got plastage too for the blood. No problem."

She starts walking with us as we reach her. The control room is twenty meters ahead, down a flight of stairs. Three bodies on the stairs.

"They tried to seal it, but Scalpel got a grenade in. It's a bit of a mess inside."

Messy. Six more bodies, five of them techs, blood everywhere, all over the walls, the consoles. Messy.

The Wire is patching up Molly in a corner. "Where're the others?"

"Bozo and Ice are doing the last offices. The others headed straight for the pads, figure to get them before they get some serious defense going."

"Check."

We leave the Central ten minutes later. Bozo and Ice have left all their prisoners cufftaped in the offices in which they found them. The Wire and Molly are bringing the van around to the pads.

The pads are secure, only one security man dead, the others wounded or surrendered. The Livewires have lined up all their cufftaped prisoners inside the left-hand hangar. Three untaped techs are already dollying out the first platform. The platform is actually more of a box, with clear acrylic walls and a rollup door and a small, waist-high control unit set into one corner.

"Looks good." The van pulls up silently next to the pad, and the Wire jumps out. I wave at him. He sees me and walks over.

"Look like it went well," he says.

"Yeah. Molly okay?"

"Yeah. She's in back, sorta out. Listen, you guys know how to operate these platforms?"

"I don't know. Let's go see."

The three of us walk over to the pad. The three techies have centered the platform and are waiting next to it. The Rat is right behind them, covering them with his M-60.

We go up to the platform and stare at the controls.

"Looks easy," Viper finally says.

"Mmm, I'm not sure." The Wire turns toward the techs. "Who operates these?"

The techs look at each other uneasily. Finally one of them shrugs. "We do."

"Automatic or manual?"

He doesn't answers. The Wire smiles.

"They pay you enough to die, man?"

He thinks about that one for a second. "Fuck, no."

"Automatic or manual?"

"Automatic, with one of us onboard to supervise."

"Can it go manual?"

"There's a cutoff circuit for emergencies, lets you take over. Manual controls are pretty slow though, only up-down too."

The Wire laughs. "The man's a fuckin tour guide! How about remote? Can they override from upstairs?"

"No."

The Wire's eyes narrow. "You sure?"

"Uh . . ."

"Last chance, hero. If I waste you, your two buddies will tell me. And getting killed for a corporation just doesn't figure."

The tech swallows convulsively. "Well, yeah, they sort of can . . . But I can show you the circuit, how to neutralize it."

"You better. Cause you're going up with us."

The first platform lifts up five minutes later. The rollup door has been jammed open, and the whole thing is packed with radio-detonated fireworks. The Livewires are all piled into the second platform, bristling with guns, faces hidden behind bulbous helmets and goggles, the terrified techie cowering in the corner by the controls with Viper's gun jammed into his ribs. I count ninety seconds from the first lift and give them the go signal. Viper pumps her fist at me once through the glass. Then they're up.

I point the Remington at the two other techs. "You two. Let's go get another platform."

The inside of the hangar is lit by a single halogen. I glance at the techs and guards taped up along the wall, shrug, and jog over to the third and last platform. Scalpel is covering the two techs as they start pushing the platform out of the hangar. It's already floating, so it is merely an interesting question of inertia to get it out onto the pad. It takes three minutes.

I trade a final dap with the Wire before jumping onboard.

"Best luck, my man."

"Thanks." I try a grin. It doesn't quite come off. "Listen, as soon as the others come back down, take off, okay? Don't wait for me. I'll send Scalpel down, too."

"You sure?"

"Yeah. I got biz to transact with the man. I'll be safe. You won't be. I figure the Beasts will be swarming within the hour. Less, if someone upstairs loses it and calls them in. Whoever did would be in the shit after, but you never know . . ."

"Yeah, I read you. We'll split."

"Good. Viper knows all about the financial angle. Deal with her."

"Won't you be down soon?"

"I'm not sure. I may have to take a vacation or something." *Or something* . . .

"Check. I'll see you, my man."

"Yeah. *Salaam aleikum*, my friend."

He smiles. "Salaam, Lynx." He spins around and starts striding toward the van.

The techie with us is nervous, very nervous. I wave my shotgun at him.

"Take us up, man. Slow, Real slow. Move in but stay at treetop for now."

"Uh, yeah, sure." He licks his lips. "Listen, could you,

sort of, point that in some other direction? It scares me, you know, I'm liable to screw up . . ."

I snicker. "Sure." I point the gun down. "It can come back up very fast."

"I know."

"Good. Take us up."

The pyramid is a kilometer in from the groundstation, a kilometer of unbroken pine forest. We float lazily just above the trees, occasionally brushing a protruding tip. I could just reach down . . .

Instead I look up. The first platform is already pulling into the bay, the second one a hundred meters behind it. I wave at the tech. "Stop here." His hands move over the console and the platform drifts to a slow stop. I can hear the breeze outside the Plexi. "We wait."

I lean against the Plexi and light a cigarette. Scalpel does the same. I offer the techie one, but he refuses with a shake of the head. I shrug and reflexively start once again checking my gear.

Skimboots, deck, grenades, ammo, handgun . . . I reach into my breast pocket. The chips . . .

Paper. I pull it out. Domino's letter, a bit crumpled. I straighten it out as best I can and open it.

It's short and sweet:

Lynx,
You're a dead man now it seems and so it's no use talking. I got eyes, I can see. When I talk you don't listen, you're just listening inside to your ghosts, to your deaths. You see them in the sky, in the trees, and you're running forward to embrace them. There's no place for me in your script so I'm leaving. I won't wish you good luck because you're playing out your scene now and it has nothing to do with luck. I still care for you but I have to cut off before it hurts too much.

D.

Cute. I snarl and crumple it up convulsively in my suddenly clammy hand. I stare into space and grind my teeth. *That bitch . . . That smart fuckin bitch . . .*

"Lynx y'okay?"
I snap back. "Yeah? Yeah. Nothing."
"What's that?"
"Nothing." *Yeah. Nothing. You've no idea, kid, of my script, you've no idea . . . And if you do, I don't want to know it.*

"Lynx. Look."
I follow Scalpel's finger and look up. A large opaque box is falling slowly out of the bottom of the tip section and lands on the flat peak of the bottom section. *Reinforcements for the generator's security . . . Perfect.*
I point my shotgun at the techie. "Take us up. Fast."

Even at top speed the platform is slow. The tip grows in front of us as we approach. The bulk of the pyramid looms below. The opening of the landing bay is blinking at us, a giant eye in the side of the tip, echoes of my dream. Below us the forest sprawls for kilometers. Slowly we ease through the opening.
The bay is dark and deserted. I reach down and jerk the rollup door up and open. Scalpel runs forward, MAS in hand, and flattens herself against the wall next to the iris door at the rear of the bay. I turn to the techie.
"I'm going to tape you. Try resisting and I'll kill you. Clear?"
"Yeah, yeah . . . Please . . ." He turns around without my even asking and crosses his hands behind his back. I tape him up quickly and sit him down. "Wait here quietly and you might live." I jump out of the platform without looking back.
I jog over to Scalpel's position. At three meters I notice a vidcam set over the door and destroy it. The blast of the Remington echoes through the bay, shatters the vidcam, scores the hard metal around it.
I flip the Remington over and replace the spent shell. Scalpel is already examining the lock. "I'm not sure I can open this."
"It should be dead anyway. There's a manual override for emergencies. Check it." I reach past her and start attacking the blank plate next to the lock with the tip of my Gerber. It unscrews fast.

I toss the plate away and reach in. I grin. "Got it." I stand back and plant myself in front of the airlock. Remington leveled. "Open it."

She reaches in and hits the buttons, and the door slides slowly, irises open. My finger tenses on the trigger. I move into the airlock, barrel poking into the corners, perfect military form. I can faintly hear the constant blaring of an alarm horn through the thick pasteel.

"Do the other one." Scalpel runs in and starts playing with the plate. This time it's even faster.

Bright alarm noise hits me like a fist. A security guard stands there, jaw dropping as he fumbles for his gun. I kill him before he even gets his finger on the trigger. The blast of the Remington is nearly covered by the relentless howling of the alarm. A red light flashes rhythmically overhead, casting lurid shadows across the corridor.

I motion to Scalpel, pointing to the left. She clutches her MAS and steps over the corpse. I take the right.

The short corridor ends in another door, apparently the main access to the living quarters and offices. I backtrack to the airlock and raise my eyebrows questioningly at Scalpel. "Small office," she yells over the noise. "Clear." I nod, stick the Remington under my arm, and key the soundscape.

A few discordant notes, clearly audible through the implants, while I nervously stare at the empty corridor, covering it with the stubby shotgun barrel. I reach down and activate my skimboots. The notes pierce through the din, clear and melodic in the implants as I rise a few centimeters. Behind me Scalpel does the same.

The soundscape functions beautifully. I skate up to the door, hearing the clear, silvery melody the whole way. I decide to test it before going through the door. I spin around and streak down the corridor past a surprised Scalpel and over the guard's bloody corpse. As soon as I pass the airlock, the flute cuts out and is replaced by an atonal bass hum filled with anxiety-producing subsonic frequencies. I go all the way to the office just to make sure. It only changes back to the flute when I pass the airlock again on my way to the door.

Scalpel is waiting there, MAS at port arms. I raise the Remington again as she opens the door.

Nobody. The corridor stretches into the distance, stainless gray in the flashing red lights, featureless except for a few doors set in the side and an occasional framed black on black German Nouveau Postmodern photograph on the wall. "The red lights improve those motherfuckers," I yell at Scalpel as I stare at one of the near-featureless pictures. "They should do that in galleries!"

We take the corridor slowly, gliding down the clean, seamless flute sound carpet, wary, nervous. The emptiness is spooking me. I expected far more guards, despite the chaos downstairs.

We skate for forty meters before reaching an intersection. We slow down to a silent stop and flatten ourselves against the wall, listening. All we can hear is the constant, monotonous blaring of the alarm horns.

I motion to Scalpel to take the right side; we are in the stem of a *T* intersection. She nods and crosses the corridor, gun up, ready to pounce around the corner. She flashes an impish grin at me and I give her the signal.

We do it slowly, guns snaking around first, followed by an eye. Again, nobody, on either side.

Damn . . . Where is everyone? Probably downstairs.

It looks like the diversion is working. I turn the corner to the left, and am rewarded by the annoying throb of the bass hum. I spin around, grin at Scalpel, and point down the right side of the *T*.

Same corridors, slightly different artwork: airbrushed Proto-expressionist this time. American by the look of it. I shrug and skate on.

I stop in front of the second door we pass and stare at it thoughtfully. Scalpel comes up to me and shouts next to my ear, "You want in?"

"Yeah."

She grins. "Try the gun!"

I do. She covers both ends of the corridor with her MAS while I point the shotgun at the lock at point-blank and pull the trigger. Pellets ricochet off my flak jacket as the door bucks.

I try pushing it. It slides aside easily, the lock obliterated.

"Easy." I wave Scalpel in.

We glide in, poking our guns into corners reflexively. The room is dark and apparently empty.

A click, and bright circline fluos blink into life. I squint, surprised, and turn, gun up. Scalpel has her hand on a switch by the door.

I glare at her and she grins. I turn again.

It is an office, a small one. Nondescript furniture, synthetic carpet, a potted plant. A low-level aide, probably. My eyes narrow as I spot the deck on the side of the desk.

I circle the desk and stare at the console. A Wang, obviously just a terminal hooked to the in-house main-frame. *Just what I need.*

I unzip the front of my flak jacket and reach into my breast pocket. My fingers touch the two chips and drag them out. I pick out the one containing the de Seingalt construct and drop the other one back into the pocket.

I hold it up and stare at it for a second. Then I reach out and power the deck. It pings and the screen glows, warm green, the prompt blinking.

The chip is compatible, I notice, and then I realize, *of course*. De Seingalt would've made sure of that. I slot it.

The prompt changes. RUN? it asks. My hand reaches out to the Execute key—

—and stops. It hovers there, seemingly detached from my conscious apparatus. I blink and then hit the Eject key. The drive spits out the chip and I drop it back into my pocket. *I'll do it when I reach Angélique.*

I wave a surprised Scalpel back and exit the room, closing the door gently behind me. The alarms blare and flash merrily. I feel the first twinges of a migraine and try to concentrate on the soothing flute solo as I skate down the deserted corridor.

We skate for five long minutes without seeing anyone. I feel my cautiousness slipping, and force myself to check carefully around each bend before taking it. A good thing, too.

I get both my barrel and my eye around the corner before the three burly, armored guards see me. I manage to get both back, though the barrel is slightly dented.

The noise is deafening as they pour streams of high-caliber rounds at us. I cut my GFs and try to melt into the wall as bullets whine and ricochet off the ground and the opposite wall. Scalpel does the same next to me, eyes squeezed shut, hugging her gun. *Shit . . .*

Fortunately they don't seem too interested in coming after us, at least for the time being. I tuck my Remington under my left arm and snag a concussion grenade from my utility belt. I'd prefer to use a frag because of the enclosed space, but it won't do much against that kind of body armor.

I pull the pin and wait for a lull in the sustained firescreen. It comes soon enough. Even a hundred-round banana clip can only last so long on full auto.

I toss the grenade around the corner and flatten myself against the wall. I hear a strangled yell and then the percussive *whump* of the grenade drowns out everything.

The walls and ground *jump*, throwing both of us to the ground. I roll with the fall and spring up as fast as I can.

Sharp tang of spent cordite, making me cough. I lunge

around the corner, shotgun cocked. The alarm sounds like it is underwater, an aftereffect of the concussion.

One of them is still alive, clawing for his gun. I shoot him once in the head, evaporating it. Scalpel comes around the corner, gun up, finger white on the trigger. "Nasty, man," she moans when she sees the meat, the ugly, lumpy red stain on the carpet where the head of the one I just greased should be. "*Balls* nasty."

There is blood everywhere. I reach down and switch my GFs back on. Then I feel something wet on my face and neck and reach up. My fingers come back red.

I look at Scalpel and notice she is bleeding, too, from the nose and the ears. I tell her.

"What?" she says. "I can't hear you, man. My ears are ringing."

"Mine too," I yell. I tap my ear and nose, and then point at her. She wipes her upper lip with her sleeve, stares at the blood, shrugs.

The soundscape bypasses the eardrum so I can still hear it. It seems to head through the door.

I point at the door. Scalpel examines the lock and looks at the deaders.

"See if they've got the key!" she yells.

I start searching the bodies, saving the headless one for last. My hands are red and gluey within seconds. The second one has the key, a thin, coded magnetic strip of plastic.

I hand it to Scalpel and she slots it. Nothing happens.

"Fuck! It must be on the general circuit Jester pegged. I'm gonna try the keypad."

I stand there nervously while she punches out combinations, fingering the trigger of my shotgun, the gore-coated pistol-grip and pump. Every so often I glance down at the deaders, and quickly glance away. The two who caught the full blast of the grenade look as if their brains tried to jump out of their heads through the ears and eye sockets. I shudder.

I'm starting to look as if I've taken a blood shower. Everything I touch gets coated, and I can't stop toying with my belts or buckles.

"I got it!" yells Scalpel. "This thing had a bypass, read the code off the key . . . With a little persuasion." The door slides smoothly into its housing, revealing a radically different environment.

I glide through the door slowly into gray and silence. I stop after a meter and stare. Scalpel comes up behind me.

No alarms. Soft, hidden lighting, a suggestion of dusk. Clean gray walls with no doors in them and no paintings. The floors are just like the walls.

The corridor runs for five meters and then branches into a *T*. I take it slowly, cautiously. Behind me the door thuds shut, cutting off the blaring, the flashing lights, the blood. My ears ring softly, mutely.

We run our routine at the *T*. Both branches are deserted, and both of them split into another *T* after five meters.

I try the left branch first. Bass hum. I spin around and head down the right—

—and stop suddenly after a meter. The scape is still playing the bass.

What the fuck?

"What's wrong?" whispers Scalpel.

"Both the corridors come up wrong on the scape."

"Well, shit . . . You're sure we came the right way?"

"Yeah, it ran fine up to the *T*."

We go back to the *T* and stand in the middle. Flute.

"The bass sounds different, too," I say. "Lower. More . . . malevolent."

I stare at the featureless wall in front of me. I reach out to touch it.

My hand goes through and I nearly fall. I jerk it back.

"Holo!" I stare in amazement. It's the most perfect hologram I've ever seen, a solid illusion.

I slowly poke the barrel of the Remington through it. Nothing happens. I stick my face through.

The holo is thin, thin as light. Behind it is another corridor as featureless as the others. I step through cautiously.

The soundscape confirms it. This is the way.

I step back out. "Could you see me through it?"

"No. It looked blank, man, solid. Def solid."

"Shit." *Angélique could have an army waiting behind one of these, and we'd never see them till they blew us away.* "Let's go."

I go through first. Halfway down the corridor I fall to the wall.

I lie there, momentarily stunned. Behind me Scalpel goggles in amazement. I look up and see her standing on the wall at a right angle to me.

Whaaa . . .?

Then things click into place. She is standing on the ground, where I was a second ago. *I* am on the wall.

Gravity generators . . . Fuckin-A . . .

I stand up, my inner ear refusing to accept the reality of the situation. I am standing on the wall at a right angle to Scalpel.

"Jump," I say. "It's okay."

She looks worried. "You sure?"

"Yeah. Just twist as you jump."

She moves back and sprints. She jumps a meter before the change, and tries to twist. She nearly makes it. Her foot hits the "ground" and she slips and crashes, rifle flying out of her hand. She looks up at me ruefully.

"There's *got* to be a better way."

"Yeah. We could try crawling against the wall, and just roll with the change."

She stands up and stares around. "This is amazing, man. I mean fuckin *kaleidoscopic*, y'know? Check it out!"

I do and realize for the first time that the corridor is square. It looks the same from this perspective as it did from the "normal" one.

"Scalpel, we're going to take this very slowly. I mean step by step. There are probably traps. This whole place looks like a maze, 3D maze. Probably something old Pierre-Henri cooked up; I don't think Angélique has that kind of . . . kink."

I slam the side of my fist into the wall. The thud is muted, flat in the leaden atmosphere. "Shit. I hope that scape holds up."

I stand there for a few seconds, staring at the blank corridor. Far ahead I can see an intersection.

"Let's go."

We skate slow, real slow. *I wish I could fuckin walk.* Then we reach the intersection.

It goes six ways. Forward, left-right, and up-down. Up-down, of course, is a subjective concept: in realspace it's left-right, and the tunnels we see as horizontal are in fact vertical shafts.

I study the situation. The soundscape plays clean to the edge. I look over. It's a long way down, and there are more intersections deep "below."

I turn to Scalpel. "We're going to have to jump it." She looks sour.

I back up five meters and gather myself together. *It's only two meters. I've jumped eight before.*

I take off suddenly, without warning. Bent low, legs pumping wide, scrambling for as much speed as possible. One meter before the edge I bring both my legs in, tight, bent. I thrust up and forward—

—Gravity's hand reaches for me and *twists*—

—Tumbling . . . Chaos, my inner ear screaming, my arms reaching out in every direction—

—Scalpel's sharp cry—

Slam.

I lie there for long seconds, gasping. Then I realize that two thirds of my body are dangling over the void, and I scramble madly, pulling myself forward, shotgun digging into my ribs. I hug the floor.

I look up. Scalpel is standing across the gap. On the ceiling.

I blink. She is still on the ceiling.

"Lynx!" She is yelling. "Lynx!"

I stagger up, still groggy. I am having balance problems. I put my weight on one gravfield and slip and fall again. I turn both of them off and stand up again, leaning on my shotgun for support.

We are standing face-to-face. I am standing on the floor, and she is standing on the ceiling.

Correction. She's on the floor and you're on the ceiling. No . . . That's not it either. You're both on opposite walls . . .

I try to orient myself. *We fell to the right wall first . . . So the wall to my left is the floor.*

Scalpel is still yelling. "Lynx! Yo!"

"Yeah!"

"What the fuck do we do now?"

I think about that. *Am I even in the right tunnel?*

I switch on the gravfields and skate a bit. And get a bass hum.

"Fuck!"

"What's the matter?"

"This isn't even the right fuckin tunnel!"

Four possibilities. My left, my right, my up, my down. "My," because at this point everything is pretty relative.

"Hey, Lynx!"

"Yeah?"

She grins madly. "Gravity sucks!"

I laugh. It's an old spacer joke, as old as the first platforms and islands, but I can't help it. I laugh.

Eventually I calm down. Time to try the tunnels. *Let's see* . . .

Left, right, up, down. And left is down.

I decide to start with the realspace horizontals. That means up and down for me.

Down first. The easiest.

I stare down at the tunnel/shaft. Only way to know which wall is ground . . . I take a coin out of my pocket and toss it.

It bounces. I stare, amazed. It bounces on thin air a few times, and finally stops, spinning faintly.

"What the fuck?" I mutter to no one in particular.

Then it clicks, and I grin. *Of course* . . .

I hit the deck and stretch out, head sideways, eye level with the ground. The coin is floating on nothing, but it is level with my ground surface.

I stand up, turn off the gravfields, and step off the edge. I hear a sharp intake of breath, then my foot comes down on hard plasteel. I take a few steps on nothing, pick up my coin, and look at Scalpel.

She is so close I could touch her. I put the coin in my pocket and step forward onto what looks like her ceiling.

Gravity twists again, but this time I'm ready. I flip lazily and land next to her, crouching like a cat. I grin up at her. "It's all done with mirrors, babe."

The down tunnel, seen from the right-wall perspective, turns out to be the right one. A tossed coin shows us we just have to step around the edge and keep on walking. We do.

"Now we know why that bastard wouldn't just give you a floorplan, eh?" says Scalpel.

"Yeah . . ."

We turn our gravfields back on and start skating again, guns up, slowly and carefully. I am worried about holo-covered holes. We could skate over and into one before we knew what happened.

Holes. Shit. I stop. Scalpel pulls up next to me. "What's the matter?"

I glare at my armdeck. "I'm not sure."

I flip the cover up and stare at the keys. *Something isn't right . . .*

Holes . . . Wouldn't de Seingalt have planned for that? The scape . . . *Shit. It sounds . . . depthless?*

Click. That's it. No depth. It sounds like music coming through earphones, geographically static. Not like a soundscape.

I call up the program specs and scroll through them. And stop in disbelief after a few seconds.

Motherfucker!

I stare at the glowing green numerals, and at the small line of print sandwiched between two columns. LYNX—DON'T FORGET TO ACTIVATE THE DEPTH FUNCTION. xds.

"That cocksucker."

"What is it?"

I stare up at her, numb. "The bastard included a full-depth function, so I could "hear" ahead. Not just the spot I'm on, see? We could have avoided all that shit back there. But he didn't tell me, just left me a note in the specs for me to find."

I'm gonna fuck up *that bodiless asshole.*

I sigh and start hitting the keys. It takes me half a minute to find the proper function and activate it. I slam the cover shut and stand up, heavily.

I move a few inches. The difference is incredible. I can "hear" my path for twenty meters down the tunnel. The flute line hugs the floor, and flips to the left wall fifteen meters ahead.

"We gotta switch walls again soon," I say. "Follow me."

This time I skate faster, a lot faster. It's probably a dumb idea, but I need the release.

*   *   *

Easy, easy ride. Flipping from wall to wall is easy once you get the hang of it. Every so often there is a patch of strident wailing in the middle of the scape, a patch that represents a holo-covered pit. Each one is two meters wide, an easy jump. I poke my head through the holo at the first pit we encounter, and see only endless darkness. I drop a coin and count four seconds before I hear a faint *tink*. I crouch back and work it out. Ten meters per second squared, that's ten and twenty and thirty and forty . . . A hundred meters. *Iseu Kirishto* . . . I picture the way we were skating before I activated the depth function on the scape, and shudder. I'd have been ten meters down and accelerating before I even knew something was wrong.

As it is, our worst problem is slipping on a wall switch. We pick up a few bruises before we get the hang of it. We skate for ten minutes or so, winding our way through the maze, switching grounds so often we rapidly lose track of realspace up-down, not to mention our position in relation to the entrance. Every so often the entire structure shudders for a few seconds. *Sounds like the Livewires are doing good.*

Then we reach the door. It jars with the featureless gray corridors, a circular door of thick, lacquered wood, with a worn brass knob and lock set on the right side. I step back and motion Scalpel forward.

"Scalpel. I think this is it. You do the lock, I'll cover you."

"No problem." She reaches down and switchs off her gravfields. I do the same, and kill the scape while I'm at it. Scalpel kneels in front of the lock and I level the Remington, aiming it at a spot slightly above her head.

"Scalpel," I say, "when you get it open, don't stand up. Duck sideways." I don't know what is behind the door, but I suspect Angélique will have a last line of defense.

"Uh, Lynx?" She looks back and grimaces. "We got a problem."

"What?"

"The lock. It's manual."

"So? Can't you do it?"

"No man, this is a *real* manual." The grimace turns into a sickly grin. "Oldtime, an antique, it uses one of those metal key things, with grooves cut in them. I can fuck around with a normal system, but I have no idea how this works."

"Well, shit . . ." I've seen pictures of manual keys before, in an article about antique security systems. All I know is that they work using something called pins and tumblers. No one uses them anymore, so it figures Scalpel would never have bothered to learn anything about them.

I come to a decision. "Move back, behind me. Cover the door."

"What are you going to do?"

I grin ferociously. "Blast it."

Once before, when I was been a kid, I'd gotten my hands on a shotgun like this, an Interarms 12-gauge. Viper and I had stolen a skimmer and roadtripped out of Paris, all the way down to the Lot. Down there, the countryside is still green and partly wild. There are few *Gendarmes* and most of the land is owned by farmers who don't really care about trespassers. We'd hiked through thick, dark forests and played with the shotgun. At close range, I'd discovered, a 12-gauge blast will take down a thirty-centimeter thick tree like a toothpick. We felled huge old trees till we ran out of shells.

This door is wood, and couldn't be more than ten centimeters thick, fifteen at most. I step back a meter, level the shotgun at the lock and knob, and squeeze the trigger.

The blast is deafening in the enclosed space. I blink and stare at the damage. The wood around the brass is chewed and torn. The metal itself has suffered too, bent and mangled. I pump once, hear a *tink* as the spent shell hits the floor, and fire again.

Close. The area I fired at is now a pulped mess, a splintered hole five centimeters deep.

I fire again. And the door slides open sideways.

A gloved hand reaches down from above, casually, and plucks the shotgun out of my surprised fingers.

I look up and find myself staring at the elongated barrel of an antique Mauser. Behind the gun is Leland's red quartz eye, a jewel set in ridged black Tombac, unblinking.

"The door was open," he says.

Scalpel's gun twitches, once. Nothing else moves, frozen tableau. Leland drops my Remington and it falls, upward.

The whole room is upside-down. Leland is standing on the ceiling behind the door, looking down at me. Then I realize that *we* are upside-down; the room would of course be normal, in realspace.

Leland smiles thinly. "This pistol has a very sensitive trigger, Lynx. I'd advise your friend to drop her rifle before anything . . . *untoward* happened."

"Don't kill him yet, Leland." Angélique's musical voice floats through the opening. A muscle jumps in my cheek. Leland notices it, and his thin smile widens a fraction. "I want to see him first," she adds.

I hear a clatter behind me, Scalpel's falling rifle. "Good," says Leland. He steps back, his pistol still pointed at me. He motions with his other hand, beckoning. "Now do please come in."

I jump first, twisting, landing in a crouch right next to the Remington. I don't even consider going for it. The Mauser's barrel tracks me as I stand up and stretch. I move forward, and Scalpel jumps in behind me.

The room looks like a movie set, a Louis XV rococo fantasy in green and blue and white. The furniture is all wood and plush velvet, handcarved ebony or mahogany. Angélique is lounging on the huge canopy bed surrounded by translucent silk curtains. She is wearing a multiskirted eighteenth-century dress with a very low *décolleté*. The whole ensembled jars with her light mulatto features, incongruous.

"Hello, Lynx," she sings. I ignore her.

"Hey, Leland," I say. "How's tricks?"

"Quite well, thank you." The ground shudders again. "Though I do wish Security would take care of your troublesome friends faster."

"Lynx!" Angélique sits up, angry. "You will answer me when I talk to you." Her voice is sharp and petulant, the voice of a spoiled child throwing a tantrum. *Exactly what she is.*

I decide to needle her a bit further. "Leland, can't you make the bitch shut up?"

He casually draws his gun back and whips me across the face. Scalpel cries out, and Angélique giggles. I fall to the carpet, clutching my cheek, feeling the blood and the swelling bruise. Pistol-whipping *hurts. At least I'm tracking blood all over her fuckin carpet.*

Leland looks down emotionlessly. "You will be polite when talking to Miss de Seingalt." His inset seems to grow, dominating his stone face.

I stagger up. "Yeah, well, you see, Leland, the thing is . . ." I pause, unable to remember for a minute what the thing was. My head hurts abominably, the pain pulsing out from my cheek with each heartbeat.

Then I remember. "I got a message for you, Leland."

"A message? From who?"

"Your boss." He looks interested.

Angélique calls out. "Leland! Don't listen to him. Bring him here."

This time he ignores her. "What is the message?"

"Leland! I *order* you to come here!"

He turns around slightly. "Be quiet." Then he turns back to me.

"I don't know," I say. I look at the deck that sits on a fragile wood table over to the left side of the chamber. "It's on chip."

"On chip, you say?" He pauses, then extends his left hand. "Give it to me."

"Leland!" Angélique has jumped off the bed and is running forward. "Leland! Don't you dare slot that!" She stop when he turns around. The gun isn't pointed directly *at* her, but is close enough to look threatening.

"What will you do about it?" he says.

She stands there, gaping, her mouth opening and closing in silence, while he turns and strides over to the deck.

His back is to me, and his gun is down, but I *still* don't think about going for the Remington, or for the .45 under my flak jacket. I look at Angélique and burst out laughing.

She screams and runs at me. I don't move as she starts wildly slapping and punching me. My flak jacket takes most of it, and blood smears on her dress. I keep laughing.

Scalpel doesn't move either, taking my cue. Leland has slotted the chip. I hear a ping as the deck finishes downloading the contents of the chip, and the large screen attached to the wall above it comes to life.

Xavier de Seingalt's face resolves out of the blur of electrons. He is smiling.

"Hello, Leland," he says. "Hello, Angélique."

Angélique screams, one short, piercing scream that packs more sheer terror in it than I've heard in my fourteen years on the Street. She starts backing away from me, limp, haggard, her eyes wide. "No . . ." she moans. I realize that the few months since I stole her medallion must not have been very pleasant for her, as she sat waiting for her ghost brother to return. Now he has.

De Seingalt looks at Leland. "First, business," he says.

"Leland. I now own most of this company. I control fifty-one percent of the board of directors, from which you take your orders and draw your salary."

"Proof?" asks Leland. He slips the Mauser into one of the pockets of his raincoat.

"Of course." De Seingalt's face vanishes, replaced by columns of data. I can't see it from where I am, but it must be enough for Leland. He hits a key on the deck, and de Seingalt's face reappears.

"Satisfied?" asks de Seingalt.

"Yes."

"Good. Your salary is doubled, if you still wish to work for me."

"I do."

"Excellent. You will find a substantial bonus in your Swiss account."

"Thank you."

"You are very welcome. Now I must conclude some

business with my dear sister and Mr. Lynx. Would you be so kind as to leave us?"

"Of course." He nods once, a hint of a bow, and turns sharply.

Angélique comes alive. "No! Leland! You can't leave . . ." She is babbling, hanging on to his arm. "I need you, you must stay . . ."

He pushes her away sharply but gently. She stumbles to the ground and starts whimpering. He strides across the room to the right-hand wall and pulls once on a dangling velvet cord. A hidden door slides open noiselessly. He enters the small room behind it—it looks like an elevator—and pauses.

"Scalpel," says de Seingalt. His voice fills the room, coming out of a ring of concealed speakers. "Would you please go with Leland. He will escort you to the landing bay where your platform is. You may take it back down to the groundstation where you will meet your friends. Lynx will join you later by another route, after things settle down."

Scalpel glances at me, obviously uncertain. I jive at her, fast Go-Ahead-I'll-Be-Okay. She nods and heads for the door.

"Take the Remington," I say.

"You sure?"

"Yeah." She picks it up. I hand her my pouch of shells as she passes by me. "Take these. You know how to reload it?"

"Yeah. Take care, huh?" She squeezes my arm softly.

"I will. I'll see you soon."

She enters the elevator and stands next to Leland. The door slides shut. I turn to de Seingalt. "Now what?"

De Seingalt smiles. "First, I would like to figure out how to activate the holoprojector. I find this flatscreen somewhat . . . limiting. Ah, there." I hear a low hum as the proj warms up. "Lynx, it's pointing in the wrong direction. Could you please turn it around?"

"Which way?"

"Clockwise. A quarter circle would be fine."

"Okay. Hold on a second, though." I flip open my armdeck and punch out the recall signal to the Livewires. *Good. Now I can forget about them.*

I flip the deck's cover shut and walk over to the deck system to study the proj. It's set on a rotating base. I grab a corner and turn it.

"Perfect," says de Seingalt. "Could you step back now?"

I back up through a shimmering veil, butterflies of inchoate light dancing and twisting on my body. I step out of the area and it coalesces into a solid form. Xavier de Seingalt, casually lounging in a contoured floatchair, smoking a long black cigarette.

He stands up and strikes a pose, one hand on his hip and the other one casually waving the cigarette. "What do you think, my dear Lynx? Isn't this ever so much more . . . dramatic?" He smiles, an odd innocent child's smile.

I glance from his strutting ghost shape to Angélique's crumpled, sobbing form, then back. I shrug.

"Enough of this bullshit. What do you need me for?"

"Why don't you start by getting my sister's attention?"

I look at her. She is curled up in a fetal position at the foot of the bed, heaving and shaking. Every so often she emits a small, piercing cry, like a bird with its leg caught in a bear trap.

"I dunno, man . . . She seems pretty far gone."

"I'm not asking you, Lynx." The smile widens, even more innocent.

Fine. I am sick of playing games, sick of subtle power dueling. I stride over to Angélique and reach down. I grab her by the chin tightly and lift her head. "Angélique?"

She screeches and starts flailing. I let go of her chin and slap her. She stops screeching. I slap her again. "Angélique."

Some light returns to her eyes, intelligence breaking through the animal tears. She moans. "Don't hurt me . . ."

Shit . . . I don't answer, not wanting to lie, or to tell her the truth either. Then again, I'm not sure if I even want to hurt her anymore. Vengeance is starting to look like a pretty sterile concept at this point.

"Your brother wants to talk to you."

"My brother . . ." she whispers. "He's dead."

I chuckle. "Not quite. You should've really killed him. Now . . ."

She tries to collapse, and I shove my hand under her armpit and prop her up. Then I turn around to face de Seingalt.

I'd been standing between the two of them, so this is the first time she sees the holo. She doesn't collapse again, though. She looks drained of everything, even terror. "Xavier . . ."

He grins, and the grin holds no innocence this time. "Angélique. I've been waiting for this meeting for the *longest* time. You can't imagine how pleased I am to see you."

She shrieks, a blood-curdling berserker shriek, and lunges at him, flailing and clawing. And goes right through him. She falls forward, and Xavier laughs. She hadn't even realized it's just a holo.

Oddly enough, that seems to comfort her. When she stands up, the tears are gone, replaced by a look of astonishment. "You're not real."

His smile thins out a bit. "No, not in the sense you mean it. But I'm alive, which is more than you will be, soon."

To his—and my—surprise, she bursts out laughing. There is an hysterical tinge to it, but an odd joy too.

"You're just some fucking software! How do you expect to kill me, construct? Huh? How?"

"I'm sure Lynx here would be more than glad to do the job."

She smirks. "Lynx? You think Lynx would kill me?"

I haven't been too sure about that, actually, but her arrogance helps. "I just might, Angélique. You tried to kill me three times. I didn't appreciate that."

"Leland did a psych profile on you. You might hurt me, but you wouldn't kill me."

"You destroyed Mara's rose."

She hears the menace in my voice and looks uncertain. "What . . . ?"

Xavier cuts her off. "No matter. I don't want to kill you quite yet. And Lynx will enjoy what I *do* want to do to you." He turns me. "Lynx. Do you still have the soundscape I gave you?"

"Of course."

"Then why don't you find some way to tie Angélique up and play it for her?"

She looks worried. "Soundscape?"

"Yeah," I say. I look at her bed. "You got any of your usual sex toys around?"

She doesn't answer.

"Get on the bed," I say.

"What if I don't?" she asks petulantly.

I explode. Three steps to reach her, and I punch her in the stomach, hard. She folds and collapses like a castle of cards.

"Listen, you bitch!" I yell. "This isn't a fuckin game, you understand? You nuked, you're in the shit here, this isn't one of your S&M fantasy simulations! So why don't you stop behaving like this was all a VidV soap opera, cause you're *pissing me off*, and you don't want to do that!"

I pick her up and throw her on the bed. Then I stand there, panting. She moans. Xavier chuckles.

"Too dumb to live, too cute to die, eh, Lynx?"

I whirl at him. "Shut the fuck up, man! Why do you *all* have to treat this like it was a fuckin game?"

He spreads his hands. "Because it is, Lynx. It's just a game, another one of our depraved Uptown games. The Wronged Sibling Returns to Take His Vengeance."

That stops me short. I stare at him, silent. Then I turn and walk to the bed.

I stare at Angélique's crumpled form. I hear Xavier behind me. "There's a drawer next to the bed, Lynx. You'll find cufftape in the second drawer from the top. The earphones are next to the library."

Why do I play this game? I move to the drawer robotically, find the cufftape, go to the bed. *Why? This is not my game.* I flip Angélique on her belly and tape her arms behind her back. *I'm here for Mara . . .* Then I tape her legs.

"Good, Lynx. Now the earphones."

Vengeance . . . Why?

I get the earphones, fit them over her ears, prop her up against the headboard so I can see her. *Game . . . Rules . . . I'm playing by their rules. Their game. Why?*

I go over to the library, pull the chip out of my pocket, and slot it. I hit Play. *Why?*

At first she doesn't react much. After a few minutes tears start rolling from her eyes. She snuffles, biting her upper lip. We watch in silence.

Why? Mara, why? For you?

Her face contorts, ugly, twisted. She screams, a short scream, bitten off abruptly. Blood tricks from her mouth.

Does this satisfy you, Mara? Does this avenge you?

She screams again, longer, this time. Her whole body jumps, convulsed. She starts twitching, banging her head against the headboard.

Why?

She's bitten through her front lip. I can see the tear, raw, red, wound glistening in the soft light.

No answer. There is no answer. I'm playing by their rules, for no reason. There is no reason. No reason. No right. No vengeance.

Fuck this. New rules.

I pull out my pistol smoothly, the widebore .45, and point it at Angélique. It bucks in my hand, once. She jumps, and blood spatters on the headboard. She slumps, slowly, a neat, round hole above her nose, a red-and-gray trail smeared down the headboard. I holster the gun and stare at her.

Xavier is enraged. I don't look at him, but I hear him scream.

"Lynx! *What did you do? What did you do?*"

I turn to him.

"New rules, spud. *My* rules." A beat. "I thought this—all this"—I wave at the room—"was for Mara. I was wrong. It was for me. And for that I killed her. Simple."

His face twists, an enraged leer. "And you think you can get away with it? You think you can get away with this?"

I walk over to the deck. I reach in back of it and methodically pull out all the jacks. Then I turn to him again.

"I'm not planning to."

"What did you do? What did you just do?"

"I cut all your connections with the rest of the pyramid's system, so you can't . . . escape, like you did at the Rabbi's."

I reach into one of my bellows pockets, bring out the last object I acquired from Cornelius.

"This is a medium-range EMP bomb, de Seingalt." I let him contemplate it long enough to understand. "Good-bye."

"*Noooo—*"

I trigger the bomb, five-minute delay. It beeps and a red LED on it starts pulsing. I set it down on the desk next to the console.

"Lynx!" He is screaming now, boosting the room's speakers way past their bass-freq tolerance range.

"Lynx!" It hurts my ears.

"It's on timer. Do you think I'm going to leave?"

"*Lynx! Don't do it!*" The sound is excruciating, resonating in my heart, subliminal subsonics pulling at me. "Lynx! What do you want? Is it money? You want money?"

I try to not look at the bed, but finally can't avoid it. I stare at Angélique's twisted body, at the blood-soaked sheets.

"No. I want an end." I walk over to the deck.

"*LYYYYYNX!*"

"You bore me." I cut the power on the deck and the sound dies. He's still inside, trapped, powerless. The LED on the bomb is pulsing softly. It is a powerful bomb. Powerful enough to disrupt every electronic system in the pyramid. Including the gravfield generators.

Well Mara . . . this is it. I suppose Domino was right. Ah, well . . .

I sit on the floor, crosslegged, and try to stop thinking. Suddenly I flick my armdeck open and call up the music menu.

I hesitate. Then I smile. Joy Division. *Mara's favorite.*

The first song on *Closer* is "Heart and Soul," and it reminds me why I never listened to Joy Division. It hurts, hurts with beauty. I think of the old joke and smile. *Know why they call it* Closer? *Because every time you listen to it you get* closer *to suicide.*

Yeah. The LED pulses. I wait.

The music stops suddenly and the lights blink off and the LED stops pulsing. The pyramid shudders and starts to drop. I lie down spreadeagled.

I smile. *Mara.*

THIS BOOK WAS WRITTEN TO THE SOUND OF:

J. S. Bach	Toccata in D Minor
Bauhaus	*Burning from the Inside*
	The Sky's Gone Out
	Mask
	In the Flat Field
	Press the Eject and Pass Me the Tape
Black Uhuru	*Reggae Greats Compilation*
Bronski Beat	*The Age of Consent*
Cabaret Voltaire	*Drinking Gasoline*
	2 × 45
Frederic Chopin	Nocturnes
Ry Cooder	*Paris Texas Soundtrack*
Miles Davis	*Sketches of Spain*
	Tutu
	We Want Miles
Einstürzende Neubauten	*Strategien Gegen Architekturen*
	Halber Mensch
	Fuenf Auf Der Nach Oben Offenen Richterskala
English Beat	*What Is Beat?*
Gabriel Fauré	*Requiem*
	Pavane
Bill Frisell & Vernon Reid	*Smash & Scatterations*
Dizzy Gillespie and Count Basie	*The Gifted Ones*
Hardcore Compilations	*Not So Quiet On the Western Front*
	Let Them Eat Jellybeans

302

Jimi Hendrix	*Band of Gypsies*
	Axis/Bold As Love
	Electric Ladyland
Gregory Isaacs	*Crucial Cuts*
Linton Kwesi Johnson	*Making History*
	Dread Beat an' Blood
	LKJ in Dub
Joy Division	*Closer*
	Unknown Pleasures
	Still
Fela Kuti	*Fela's London Scene*
	Up Side Down
	Black President
	Greatest Hits
Bob Marley & the Wailers	*Survival*
	Rebel Music
Charles Mingus	*Tijuana Moods*
	Mingus at the Bohemia
	Great Moments with Charles Mingus
	Charles Mingus and Friends in Concert
W. A. Mozart	*Requiem*
	Don Giovanni
Iggy Pop & the Stooges	*Raw Power*
	Funhouse
P.I.L.	*Album*
	Happy
Rap Compilations	*Colors Soundtrack*
	Various
Lou Reed	*Live*
Rolling Stones	*Sticky Fingers*
Eric Satie	*Gymnopédies*
Sex Pistols	*Never Mind the Bullocks*
Velvet Underground	*Velvet Underground and Nico*
	Velvet Underground
	VU
	Loaded
	Another View

Violent Femmes	*Violent Femmes*
	Hallowed Ground
Tom Waits	*Rain Dogs*
	Swordfishtrombones
	Frank's Wild Years

If you liked the movie, this is the soundtrack.

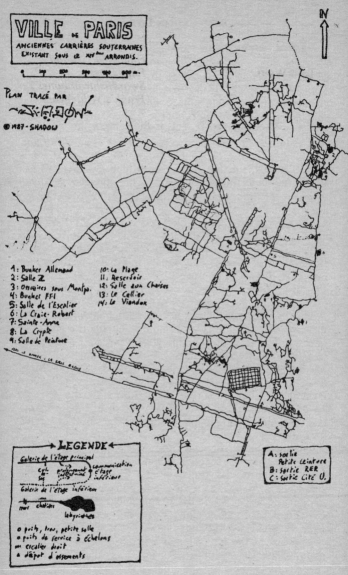

ATTENTION! L'ACCÈS AUX CONSOLIDATIONS DES ANCIENNES CARRIÈRES EST DANGEREUX ET ILLÉGAL!

DESCENDEZ À VOS RISQUES ET PÉRILS!

MAP 1: A cataphile map of the tunnel grid under the 5th, 6th, 14th, and 15th arrondissements. The northern/eastern/southern/western-most limits of this grid are, respectively, rue de Vaugirard, rue de la Sante, Boulevard Jourdan/Boulevard Brune, and rue de Dantzig. This map is presumably a copy of a copy of a copy, *ad infinitum*. The source of the original is unknown, though there is reason to suspect that it may be a map stolen from the Bibliotheque National ca. 1975. This copy traced by a cataphile identified only by his signature-glyph "SHADOW" and dated 1987.

The inscription at the top left reads "CITY OF PARIS—ancient underground quarries—existing under the 14th arrondissement." (Note: a deliberately archaic phrasing.) Below this is a scale, 500 meters in length at 100-meter intervals; then "Map traced by SHADOW—ca. 1987—shadow." (Note: the copyright symbol is presumably a cataphile joke.)

The box located at the left of center is a key to the principal areas of this grid, numbered on the map, as follows: 1—German Bunker; 2—Room Z; 3—bone depository under Montparnasse; 4—FFI Bunker; 5—Room of the Staircase; 6—La Craie-Robert; 7—Sainte-Anne; 8—The Crypt; 9—Room of the Paintings; 10—The Beach; 11—The Reservoir; 12—Room of the Chairs; 13—The Cellar; 14—"The Spam". (Note: "The Spam" is a cataphile slang euphemism for the southern bone depository.)

The inscription between the two left boxes, running along a tunnel that extends beyond the limits of the map, reads "Towards the Bunker—The Raidos Room." The small box at the lower right is a key to the three lettered exits, as follows: A—Petite Ceinture exit; B—RER exit; C—Cité Universitaire exit. (Note: an "exit" can just as well serve as an entrance.)

The box at the lower left is a general key to the map, as follows:

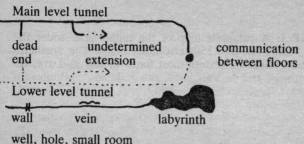

Main level tunnel

| dead end | undetermined extension | communication between floors |

Lower level tunnel

| wall | vein | labyrinth |

⊃ well, hole, small room
● service shaft w/ladder
⊞ straight staircase
Δ bone depository

Finally, the bottom inscription reads: "WARNING! Entrance into the consolidations of the ancient quarries is *dangerous* and *illegal!—DESCEND AT YOUR OWN RISKS AND PERILS!*" (Note: "the consolidations of the ancient quarries" is the technically accurate description of the underground quarries; the more popular term "catacombs" is in fact a misnomer.)

VILLE DE PARIS

Plan des Zones d'anciennes Carrières

Anciènnes Carrières à ciel ouvert

Anciènnes Carrières souterraines

GYPSE:
1- Montmartre
2- Belleville Ménilmontant

CALCAIRE:
3- 12° Arrondissement
4- Charenton Bois de Vincennes
5- 13° Arrondissement
6- Le Grand Réseau Sud
7- Passy Chaillot

Plan Tracé Par

© 1927 - Shadow.

MAP 2: A cataphile map of Paris showing the areas of quarries under the city. This map, like Map 1, is signed by Shadow and dated 1987. Its origin is equally unknown.

The inscription at the top left reads: "CITY OF PARIS—Map of the Zones of the ancient quarries." The top kinds of shading are keyed as follows: dot areas— open air—former quarries; and solid areas—underground former quarries. The remaining inscriptions refer to the numbered areas of the map by name, and are divided into two groups according to the dominant type of mineral the quarries were excavated in, as follows:

GYPSUM: 1—Montmartre; 2—Belleville Menilmontant.

SANDSTONE: 3—12th arrondissement; 4—Charenton/ Bois de Vincennes; 5—13th arrondissement; 6—The Great Southern System; 7—Passy Chaillot.

(Note: the area covered by Map 1 is the right-hand half of area #6 in Map 2.)